Praise for D

"Tara's sharp ... brought to life under the topnotch writing of Diane Kelly." —*Romance Reviews Today* (Perfect 10)

"Readers will find themselves laughing out loud."
—*Romance Reviews Today* on
DEATH, TAXES, AND SILVER SPURS

"[A] sure-shot success!" —*Fresh Fiction*

"Witty, remarkable, and ever so entertaining."
—*Affaire de Coeur* on DEATH,
TAXES, AND GREEN TEA ICE CREAM

"Be prepared for periodic unpredictable, uncontrollable laughing fits. Wonderful scenarios abound when it comes to Tara going undercover in this novel about tax evasion, drugs and (of course) guns. Good depth of characters and well-developed chapters are essential when casting a humorous series, and Ms. Kelly excels in both departments."
—*Night Owl Reviews* on DEATH, TAXES,
AND HOT PINK LEG WARMERS

"Plenty ... round out this laugh-... ch's Stephanie Plum s... er series will enjoy th... ktails of Tara Hollowa... *RT Book Reviews*

Death, Taxes,
and a Satin Garter

DIANE KELLY

St. Martin's Paperbacks

This is a work of fiction. All of the characters, organizations, and events portrayed in this novel are either products of the author's imagination or are used fictitiously.

DEATH, TAXES, AND A SATIN GARTER

Copyright © 2016 by Diane Kelly.

All rights reserved.

For information address St. Martin's Press, 175 Fifth Avenue, New York, NY 10010.

ISBN: 978-1-250-09482-7

Our books may be purchased in bulk for promotional, educational, or business use. Please contact your local bookseller or the Macmillan Corporate and Premium Sales Department at 1-800-221-7945, extension 5442, or by e-mail at MacmillanSpecialMarkets@macmillan.com.

Printed in the United States of America

St. Martin's Paperbacks edition / August 2016

St. Martin's Paperbacks are published by St. Martin's Press, 175 Fifth Avenue, New York, NY 10010.

10 9 8 7 6 5 4 3 2 1

$\mathcal{A}$cknowledgments

It takes a team of people to get a book into readers' hands, and I'm grateful to have such a fantastic force working on my books!

Thanks to my editor, Holly Ingraham, for being so smart and insightful and a joy to work with! Many thanks also to Sarah Melnyck, Paul Hochman, and the rest of the team at St. Martin's who played a role in getting this book out into the world!

Thanks to Danielle Christopher and Monika Roe for creating such perfect and attention-grabbing book covers!

Thanks to my agent, Helen Breitwieser, for all of your work in furthering my writing career!

Thanks to Liz Bemis and the staff of Bemis Promotions for my great Web site and newsletters!

Thanks to my fellow members of Romance Writers of America, its volunteers, and the incredibly savvy national office staff!

Thanks to my super-smart son, Ross, for answering all of my technical questions and not making me feel as clueless as I surely am. You're the best son a mother could ever hope for!

Finally, thanks to my fabulous readers! I love connecting with you through the stories, and I know you'll be rooting for Tara as she pursues the ever-evasive Flo Cash and a catfishing Casanova. Enjoy!

chapter one

*T*uned Out

"Figured you might need some extra caffeine this morning." Nick shot me a wink as he raised a steaming white take-out cup and stepped into my office.

"Because it's Monday?" I asked coyly as I took the cup from him. The fact that it was Monday had nothing to do with my need for a jump start this morning. Nick, on the other hand, had everything to do with it. We'd stayed up quite late last night. I'm not one to kiss and tell, so let's just say that Nick and I were playing Uno, if *Uno* what I mean.

I took a sip of the life-giving latte and sighed in bliss, casting a smile at my coworker/boyfriend/Uno partner. Nick was tall and muscular, with dark hair and eyes the color of Kentucky bourbon. Nick had a thick, short scar on his left cheekbone and a slightly chipped tooth, but these minor imperfections only made him seem more manly. But his good looks were simply a bonus. What mattered much more to me was that he was hardworking, honest, and loyal, not to mention an expert at Uno. His sweet romantic gestures, like bringing me my favorite latte this morning, didn't hurt none, either. I wasn't sure what I'd done to deserve him, but I sure was glad he was mine.

His shiny gold belt buckle gave off a glint as he plopped down into one of my wing chairs and propped his cowboy boots on the corner of my desk, making himself at home. He gestured to the huge stack of files on my desk. Seemed there was *always* a huge stack of files on my desk. "Whatcha working on today?"

"The Flo Cash case."

Nick and I were both special agents for IRS Criminal Investigations, tax cops who pursued those who willingly evaded their obligations to Uncle Sam. Some people considered themselves above the law and left law-abiding citizens to foot the bill for roads and military defense and Social Security and national parks. That's where we special agents came in. We worked to make sure everyone paid their fair share. It might sound like a mundane job, but, trust me, it was anything but. During my fourteen-month tenure with Criminal Investigations, I'd gone undercover in offices, an Italian restaurant, and a strip club. On several occasions, pissed-off tax evaders had fired on me. One tried to blow me up with an improvised explosive. Hell, I'd even been tackled by security at the airport and attacked by a weaponized rooster. What other job would offer this kind of action and excitement? Certainly not my former job as a CPA.

Given the potential dangers, working as a special agent required good weapons skills. It also required excellent financial skills. We IRS investigators were the cream of the crop when it came to federal financial detectives. We were experts at ferreting out funds, hunting down hidden accounts, and seeking out secret stashes of cash. Not that our jobs were easy. We just made it look that way.

My largest current case was against Florence "Flo" Cash, a popular local radio personality who hosted a morning talk show from 7:00 to 11:00 AM on weekdays, broadcasting to listeners during their morning commutes.

In her daily *Cash Flow Show* on KCSH, Flo offered stock tips and investment advice. She also answered financial questions from callers, offering her opinions along with clever, sometimes-cutting commentary, and a healthy dose of sound effects.

Problem was, neither Flo nor the radio station she owned had paid a penny in taxes in years. With so little reported income, it was highly questionable how Flo could pay her personal bills and the station could continue to operate. The person responsible for asking the questions and getting answers was me, IRS Special Agent Tara Holloway, five feet, two inches of chestnut-haired kick-ass in cherry-red steel-toed Doc Martens and an end-of-season-sale suit.

Nick cocked his head. "Find anything good in Flo's file?"

The file contained a meager stack of financial reports collected by the auditor who'd visited Flo Cash months before. He'd had no luck wheedling information out of the woman, and the accounting records she'd provided showed a surprising dearth of activity, to which she'd responded, according to his report, "with only a shrug." No doubt she'd be a pain in the ass. Fortunately, I was used to dealing with pains in the ass. Sons of bitches, too, as well as the occasional rat bastard and sociopath. By the time a case got kicked up to Criminal Investigations, the target had been given plenty of opportunities to come clean and pay up but had steadfastly and repeatedly refused. A stupid move on their part. Because now they had to deal with *me*.

I pulled Flo's W-2 from the file and held it out to Nick. "This is interesting."

He took the paper from me and looked down at it. "Twenty-one thousand dollars? That's all the radio station paid her last year?"

The station was owned and operated by the KCSH Radio Corporation, which, in turn, was wholly owned by Flo herself. She served as both the host of the *Cash Flow Show* and the corporation's Chief Executive Officer, Chief Financial Officer, and Chief Operations Officer.

"Yep," I replied. "She paid herself only a few cents more than minimum wage." She'd claimed a bunch of personal exemptions, too, enough to ensure that no federal income tax was withheld. Of course she didn't have to worry about state income taxes. Texas was one of a small handful of states that imposed no state tax on personal income.

"Minimum wage?" Nick's brows drew in to form a V. "How can she live on that?"

"Good question. She inherited her house in Lakewood Heights from her father when he passed away eight years ago, so she doesn't have a mortgage to pay. But there's still annual property taxes of twelve grand, not to mention homeowner's insurance, car insurance, food, utilities, gas, and all the other normal bills people have." My own bills included my Netflix account, an inordinate amount for cat treats, and my Neiman Marcus credit card, which seemed to be perpetually maxed out. Also my recurring payment to the salsa-of-the-month club. This month's flavor had been Black Bean Mango, a surprisingly tasty combination.

"Did she inherit money, too?"

"Not much," I replied. "Her father lived to ninety-eight. Her mother had died the year before at ninety-six. They'd used up most of their funds by then for their own living expenses and care. According to the probate records, there was only a little over seven thousand dollars left in Flo's father's bank account when he passed."

"Does Flo have other income?" Nick asked. "Interest or dividends or proceeds from stock sales?"

"Only in nominal amounts. She doesn't seem to have much in the way of investments."

In other words, things didn't add up. And when things didn't add up, it was usually because someone had been playing hide-and-seek with their cash.

I pulled Flo's previous three years' tax returns from the file and showed them to Nick. "Take a look for yourself. Every year she ends up with no taxable income once her itemized deductions and personal exemption are applied."

Nick flipped through the returns, his eyes scanning the pages. "She's filed single status every year, so she doesn't have a husband footing the bills." His eyes went from the page to me. "Does she have a roommate or live-in boyfriend? Maybe a rich aunt or sugar daddy helping her out?"

Cash gifts from a family member, friend, or significant other could explain how Flo managed to stay afloat on such a small salary, yet she'd offered no such explanation to the auditor. Most people didn't like the IRS poking around in their business any more than absolutely necessary. If she'd received gifts, why hadn't she provided evidence of the gifts to the auditor and nipped this investigation in the bud?

I raised a shoulder. "Rich relative, sugar daddy, buried treasure, who knows?" Hell, maybe she'd sold her plasma or a kidney. Of course I wouldn't rest until, one way or another, I had the answer. Nick knew it, too. I was nothing if not tenacious. In most cases, the answer to how people could live beyond their apparent means was that they had a source of unreported income. People seemed to think Uncle Sam wouldn't catch up with them. *They better think again.*

A head topped with a strawberry-blond beehive poked itself through the doorway. The head belonged to our boss, Luella "Lu" Lobozinski, also known as "the Lobo." Lu had come of age in the sixties and had maintained her towering hairstyle ever since. Same went for her go-go boots, blue eye shadow, and false eyelashes, which, ironically, had now come back in style. Rihanna and Kim Kardashian had seen to that, no pun intended.

Lu narrowed her eyes at me and Nick. "You two better be working. I don't pay my agents to just sit around and flirt with each other, you know."

As if Nick and I didn't put in dozens of hours of overtime every year. I rolled my eyes and held up the file. "We're discussing the Flo Cash case."

"Oh. All right, then." She turned to Nick. "Any chance you can help Carl move this weekend?"

It was the curse of owning a pickup truck. Someone was always asking for help with a move. Of course Nick wouldn't mind in this instance given that it was Lu who was asking. She might be tough on us, but that's because she had high expectations and only hired agents she knew could meet her rigorous standards. She encouraged us to be our best, and she had our backs with those up the chain of command when, despite our best efforts, things went awry. We couldn't ask for a better boss. She couldn't ask for a better boyfriend, either. With his crisscrossing comb-over hair, polyester leisure suits, and shiny white buck shoes, Carl wasn't much to look at. But he more than made up for it with his personality. He was a doting, affectionate, generous man, and he treated Lu like a queen. Both of them had lost their spouses and were getting a second chance at love. It was sweet.

"Anything for you, Lu," Nick said. "You know that."

Lu had maintained Nick's office for three years, keeping it waiting for him while he'd been stuck in Mexico after a violent target identified him in an undercover investigation and Nick had been forced to play along with the guy or risk a horrific death. Yours truly smuggled Nick back across the border and helped him nail the bastard. Not to brag on myself, but I kick ass.

"How about Sunday afternoon?" Nick suggested. "I'm tied up Saturday. Tara's dragging me to her best friend's fancy wedding and I've got to be fitted for a tuxedo." He cut a wink my way. We both knew I wasn't dragging him anywhere. With many of our friends planning to attend and Alicia's parents springing for an open bar, the wedding was sure to be a lot of fun. "Besides, Tara's parents are coming in for an overnight visit."

Nick had invited my father out on his bass boat. Dad never passed up a chance to go fishing, and my mother never passed up a chance to visit her only daughter. Besides, she needed a new pair of shoes to wear to Alicia's wedding and Dallas offered far more shopping options than my small hometown of Nacogdoches in East Texas.

"Where's Carl moving to?" I asked.

"My place," the Lobo replied.

I sat bolt upright. "Did you finally accept his marriage proposal?" Carl had been hounding her for weeks, proposing time and time again. His persistence had even scared her off for a bit, though she'd missed him horribly and the two had eventually reconciled.

"No," she said. "We realized that at this age getting married would complicate things legally and financially for ourselves and our children. We'd have to redo our wills and the deeds to our houses. That would take a lot of time and cost us a small fortune." She threw up her hands. "And don't even get me started on benefits and beneficiaries and all of that mumbo jumbo."

"So you two are going to shack up?" I teased. "Live in sin?"

She snorted. "Not much sinning going on at our ages. Not that it's any of your business."

Nick chuckled and asked, "How much stuff does Carl have to move?"

"Not much," Lu said. "I've got a full house already and

no need for most of it. He's just bringing his favorite chair and a desk."

"That'll work," Nick said.

"All right, then. Carry on." With that, she turned on her shiny white patent-leather heel, the fringe on the bottom of her dress swinging as she headed back to her office.

Nick retrieved his cell phone from the breast pocket of his shirt and checked the time before returning it. Pulling his feet off my desk, he stood. "I've got a conference call in fifteen minutes. I better git."

Though Nick was a senior special agent and I was still a relative rookie, our offices sat directly across the hall from each other. He had nice, sturdy furniture, though, while I had to put up with a wobbly chair and a file cabinet with sticky drawers.

I took the tax returns from Nick and gave him a two-fingered salute. "Later, gator."

While Nick returned to his office, I took a more thorough look at the KCSH corporate records. The expenses were first on my list. Only three people other than Flo had been issued W-2s by the corporation, the small staff including two young men who handled the radio station's technical tasks and an equally young woman who took care of administrative matters. Given the limited staff, the salaries account was minimal, right at $150,000 including Flo's paltry pay.

The biggest expense was for syndication fees. Flo Cash's *Cash Flow Show* was the only original, local show offered by the station. The remaining content included syndicated financial programs, such as the popular *Dave Ramsey Show* and *Bull Versus Bear,* a show that went into extensive up-to- the-minute detail on the stock market.

Like the house Flo had inherited, the building that housed the radio station had long since been paid off, with taxes, insurance, utilities, maintenance, and repairs being the only current costs. No mortgage meant no mortgage interest deduction. A minor amount of equipment was still being depreciated, and there was around five hundred dollars in office supplies expense and eighty-nine dollars in postage, but that was pretty much it as far as expenses went.

I took a look at the income next. The primary source of revenue for most TV and radio stations was advertising fees. When Flo's father had owned and managed the station, Flo had been in charge of selling ads. She'd been damn good at it, too. Back in those years the station had brought in hundreds of thousands of dollars in ad revenue. In the years since Flo had owned the station, however, the advertising income reported by KCSH hadn't even been enough to cover the expenses, leaving the corporation with a net loss each year, the most recent being over three grand.

Of course, it wasn't necessarily unusual for a business to have a bad year or two and to even run in the red. Airlines and carmakers seemed to do it for years at a time, bank loans keeping them afloat. But such was not the case where KCSH was concerned. There was no interest expense deduction, indicating there were no outstanding loans. The accounts payable, which indicated the debts the station owed to others, had not increased appreciably, so the station didn't appear to be behind on its bills. Flo's equity account, which showed her investment in the corporation, had increased, meaning she'd put money back into the station. But given her paltry salary, where had that money come from? She appeared to have no investment accounts or other liquid assets like CDs, and the days of people hiding money in their mattresses were long gone.

Something wasn't right.

Hm-m . . .

I logged on to my laptop, brought up the KCSH Web site, and clicked on the live stream icon to listen in. Flo

took a call from a sixty-year-old man wondering whether
he'd saved up enough to take early retirement.

"That depends," Flo said. "How long are you planning
on living?"

"Well," the man said, "I don't drink or smoke—"

"So you haven't even *started* living," Flo shot back, following her retort with the standard drum and cymbal
sound effect. *Ba-da-dum.* She asked him a couple more
questions, finding out how much he'd saved and how much
he spent per month. "Sorry, buddy," she replied. "It's too
soon for you to be put out to pasture." An elongated cow
sound followed. *Moo-o-o-o.*

The next caller was a recently divorced woman who
wanted to know whether she should sell the house she'd
been awarded in the property settlement. "It's got more
yard than I can keep up on my own," the caller said, "but
we got a really good interest rate when we bought it a few
years ago, so the payments are low."

"Keep the house," Flo advised. "It's a good investment.
Hire yourself a young, hot gardener who works shirtless."
The advice was followed by a canned wolf whistle sound
effect. *Woo-wee!*

The *Cash Flow Show* lacked the reserve and sophisti-
cation of most financial programs, but I had to admit that
Flo Cash was entertaining and able to explain complicated
money matters in a way that non-financial folks could understand. It was no wonder she had a large and loyal following.

Flo ended her show with her standard signoff. "That's
all for today, folks. Now go out and make your money
make money for you!"

The *Bull Versus Bear* show came on next, the male announcer discussing which Big Pharma stocks were currently up and which were down. *Bo-ring!* As a financial
expert, I should probably have found the discussion to be

more interesting, but frankly, I didn't think the so-called experts could predict with any real certainty which stocks would be winners and which stocks would be losers. If so, they'd all be multimillionaires who'd no longer need to work on a talk radio show, right? Heck, in my opinion, playing the stock market was no different from playing blackjack or poker. A little skill was involved and some people had a knack for spotting trends, but mostly it was pure dumb luck.

By that point, I'd done all I could do until my in-person meeting with Flo scheduled for the following afternoon, but I kept the KCSH stream playing while I worked on some of my other cases. Every time the programs paused for a commercial break, I jotted a quick note identifying the advertiser. Most of the commercials were bare-bones ads in which Flo merely chattered on about the benefits this or that business offered to its customers, but a few of the commercials were more extensive, including music, jingles, and a professional voice actor reading the lines.

By the end of the day, I had a list of seventy-three businesses that had been advertised on KCSH, including multiple restaurants, an exterminator, a mattress store, and even a masseuse. *Wandering Hands—have table, will travel.* With so many commercials, KCSH should be raking in the advertising revenue.

I pulled out the list of advertising clients Flo had provided to the auditor and compared it to the list I'd jotted down. Sure enough, the vast majority of the businesses mentioned on the air were not included in the station's income records, their payments unaccounted for, a veritable smoking gun.

Flo Cash certainly had some explaining to do.

And I wasn't about to take a shrug for an answer.

chapter two

$\mathcal{A}$ Little Somethin'-Somethin'

After work, I headed over to the downtown Neiman Marcus store to meet my best friend and roommate, Alicia, in the bridal department for her final fitting.

I smiled at another woman in her late twenties who was looking over the dresses with her mother, my gut feeling a small twinge of envy. Shopping for a wedding dress must be so much fun. It was like getting to play Cinderella. Not that I'd ever been much of the Cinderella type. At just five feet, two inches tall, I was closer in size to one of Snow White's dwarves than a princess, and I would never put up with an evil stepmother bossing me around. *You want the floors washed? Do it yourself, you old ninny.* I also tended to frequent the clearance racks, which were generally devoid of fancy gowns and glass slippers. Still, what woman didn't like getting all gussied up on occasion and being the belle of the ball?

I found Alicia standing in front of the three-way mirror in an oversized dressing room, turning side to side to examine herself from every angle. It was the same routine she'd done back when we'd been roommates in college, dressing for weekend dates, though this time she didn't ask whether her outfit made her ass look big. These days, thanks to Kim Kardashian, having a big ass had become a good thing, rendering the question moot.

My eyes met Alicia's in the mirror, and my hand went involuntarily to my heart. "You look absolutely gorgeous!" I meant it, too. She practically glowed.

Alicia stopped moving and smiled at herself in the mirror. "I do, don't I?"

The seamstress smiled, too. "You're a beautiful young lady," she told Alicia.

Alicia's dress was a sleek, strapless dress fitted tight through the bodice and hips and erupting in sequins around the hem. The contemporary style went perfectly with her thin figure and the short, asymmetrical cut of her platinum-blond hair.

Alicia and her fiancé, Daniel Blowitz, had planned a formal black-tie wedding for a Sunday near the end of the month. The event would be held at one of the area's most beautiful wedding chapels, with dinner, dancing, drinks, and general revelry to follow in the ballroom. I could hardly wait. As hard as I worked, I could use some revelry.

I reached into my purse and pulled out the small box that held the pearl bracelet my favorite aunt had given me for my sixteenth birthday. I'd been thrilled! It had been my first piece of jewelry that hadn't come from a gumball machine or been made of plastic. I wore the heirloom only to special events, but I remembered Alicia remarking on its beauty when I'd worn it years ago at our graduation ceremony from the University of Texas in Austin. Ironic how pearls were considered objects of beauty when they were the result of an oyster coating a parasite or other irritant that had invaded its shell. Pearls, in essence, were nothing more than shiny, shimmery squatters.

I held the box out to my friend. "If you don't have a

'something borrowed' yet," I told her, "I thought you might want to try this."

Alicia took the box from me, opened it, and emitted a squeal of delight. "Oh, my gosh! This is the bracelet you wore to graduation!"

"You remember it?"

"Of course," she said. "How could I forget something so pretty?"

She undid the clasp and I helped her fasten it to her wrist. She took another look at herself in the mirror and began to tear up. "It's perfect, Tara. Thanks."

It was indeed perfect, a subtle touch of traditional style to complement her modern dress. Warm tears welled up in my eyes, too. Alicia and I had been through a lot together. Tough accounting courses. A stream of bad boyfriends. Study breaks and heartbreaks. Our first real jobs at the accounting firm of Martin & McGee. Four grueling tax seasons, putting in eighty-hour workweeks. Even a few flu seasons and hangovers. We were as close as most sisters. And now she was moving on to the next phase of her life. I knew we'd continue to be important to each other, continue to be a big part of each other's lives, but I also knew that things would change, too. As happy as I was for my friend, I couldn't help but feel a sense of melancholy and loss.

She gave me a gentle hug and stepped back, her gaze meeting mine. "You're the best, Tara."

"Don't you forget it," I barely managed to choke out.

Her tears threatening to spill over her lids, she waved a frantic hand in front of her eyes. "I can't cry! I can't risk getting mascara on the dress!"

"Uh-oh." The seamstress stepped forward, reaching for the zipper. "Let's get you out of it."

Twenty minutes later, Alicia was out of the dress, back into her everyday clothes, and walking beside me as we exited the store. "I've got my 'something borrowed' now," she said, "thanks to you. My 'something old' is a lace handkerchief that every woman in my family has carried at their weddings since the dawn of time. But I still need something new and something blue."

"Let's hit The Galleria." With nearly a hundred stores, surely the mall would offer many things new and blue to choose from.

"Good idea."

After a quick dinner of soup and sandwiches at a café overlooking the ice-skating rink, we made our way to the Victoria's Secret store.

I held up a pair of sheer red panties I found on a table near the entrance. "Here you go. Something new."

Alicia eyed the tiny swatch of fabric in my fingers. "Those might be new, but they barely qualify as 'something.' There's not enough material there to cover one butt cheek, let alone two."

"That's the idea. Duh."

She snatched the panties from my hand and returned them to the pile, turning her attention to a white lace pair with tiny bows on the adjacent display. "These are pretty," she said holding them up.

"Mm-hm," I murmured in agreement. "Fit for virgin angels."

I followed her to the checkout stand, sampling the colognes and lotions on the glass shelves near the counter as she purchased the pair to wear under her wedding dress. Reeking of fruit and flowers, I led the way back out into the mall.

She waved a hand to clear the air that trailed after me. "My God! How many different scents did you try?"

I raised a shoulder. "Seven? Eight?"

"You smell like a florist. But at least I can check 'something new' off my list now."

I stopped and glanced left and right. "Where to?"

"I have no idea," she said. "All I know is I need something blue."

We headed right, meandering along, glancing in windows until we reached the Dallas Cowboys Pro Shop. I gestured into the store, which was filled with blue pendants, blue jerseys, blue sweatshirts, blue socks, and blue hats in knit, ball cap, bucket, and beanie varieties. "There you go," I said. "It doesn't get any bluer than that."

"No way am I wearing fan gear to my wedding."

"On we go, then."

Despite wandering in and out of nearly every store in the mall, Alicia still hadn't decided on her something blue by the time we were forced to leave at closing time.

"I know," I said, "Let's look at garters on Etsy when we get home. Surely they'll have a blue one."

Alicia's face brightened. "Good idea, Tara."

We headed back to my town house, where Alicia was shacking up with me until the big day. After shedding our work clothes, changing into our pajamas, and pouring ourselves glasses of peach sangria—Nick's mother's recipe—we took seats at my kitchen table, logged on to the Etsy site, and ran a search for "blue garter." Dozens of options came up, the screen filled with photos of elastic, lace, sequins, beads, and ruffles.

My creamy cat, Anne, hopped up onto my lap, and I ran a hand over her back as I pointed to a polka-dot garter on the computer screen. "What about that one?"

Alicia crinkled her nose. "Too girlish. I'm getting married, not going to prom."

As Anne purred on my lap, I gestured to another garter that was royal blue with black lace. "How's that?"

Another nose crinkle. "Too sexy."

"It's a *garter*," I said. "It's supposed to be sexy."

"I know," she said, "but I don't want to look like a tramp on my wedding day."

"I bet Daniel will want you to *act* like a tramp on your wedding night."

"That's different," she said. "My grandmother won't be watching then."

"Lord, I hope not!"

I eyed the screen. The garters could make fun party favors for the bachelorette party I'd be hosting in a couple of weeks. I'd order a dozen later as a surprise.

My other cat, a fluffy and enormous Maine coon named Henry, padded purposefully into the kitchen, giving me his usual look of disdain and a short, scratchy *mrah*. Translation: *give me a treat or I'm pooping beside the box tonight.*

I scooped Anne up in my arms and scurried over to the pantry to round up their treats. *Do these cats have me wrapped around their furry little fingers or what?*

A minute later, I was back at the table with my roommate, resuming my review of the garter selections. Just as Goldilocks wouldn't settle for porridge that was too hot or too cold, Alicia declared another garter too itchy looking and a fourth too cheap looking before finding one she declared, "Just right."

I took a look. It was *just right*. Light-blue satin with ruffled white lace trim and a beaded heart appliqué. "It's perfect," I agreed.

Alicia whipped out her credit card, input the information, and placed the order. Once she received the confirmation, she crossed the words "garter" and "something blue" off her wedding to-do list. "Now I just need to finalize the music list for the DJ." She turned her attention back to her computer, clicked a few keys, and maneuvered the mouse before turning the laptop to face me. "What do you think?"

My eyes began to scan the list. " 'Unchained Melody'? Really?" I opened my mouth and stuck my index finger inside in a gagging motion.

Alicia narrowed her eyes. "It's a classic. Besides, I like it and it's *my* wedding."

"Point taken." My gaze continued down the screen. " 'Brick House.' Always a good one. Ditto for 'Play That Funky Music,' though I'm not sure it's politically correct to ask only a 'white boy' to play it and to do it till he dies."

She groaned. "You're overthinking it."

The list included many must-play songs like Gloria Gaynor's "I Will Survive" and AC/DC's "You Shook Me All Night Long," but it was woefully lacking in my favorite genre. Not a single Luke Bryan or Brad Paisley song caught my eye.

When I reached the end of the list, I raised my palms in question. "Where's Garth Brooks? Lady Antebellum? Willie, Waylon, and the boys?"

"Do I really have to go there?"

Unlike me, Alicia was not a big fan of country music, *God save her soul.*

"Yes," I insisted. "You have to go there. This is a Texas wedding and the state statutes require at least three songs that guests can two-step to."

She cut me a look. "I don't think that's true."

"Okay," I said. "Maybe it's an unwritten Texas wedding law. But it ranks right up there with doing the Chicken Dance and offering the guests a choice between champagne and beer."

"All right." She flailed her hand at the screen. "Add some country to the mix if you must."

"Mind if I add some swing for my parents?" Those two loved to "cut a rug." Their words, not mine. But I had to admit that they knew their stuff. With their moves and energy, they put dancers half their age to shame.

"Of course," Alicia said. "After everything your mother did for my bridal shower, I owe her."

So did I. While my mother was an excellent cook and could bake like nobody's business, I, on the other hand, had no business setting foot in a kitchen unless it was for a Pop-Tart. I'd served as the official hostess for Alicia's recent shower, but my mother deserved all the credit for the tasty treats we'd served. I was lucky to have such a devoted, doting mother who was so skilled in household matters. My future children, however, were screwed. I hoped they'd like Pop-Tarts.

I typed in several song suggestions, already looking forward to slow dancing in Nick's strong arms. As I perused the revised playlist, my mind wandered back to my first dance with Nick. We'd been working a case against a televangelist who'd been fleecing his flock, dipping his hand in the collection plate to pay for his fancy clothes, car, and house. After trailing the preacher to Louisiana, Nick and I had ended up at a roadside honky-tonk. One thing led to another and the next thing I knew Nick was twirling me around the dance floor. I'd been dating another guy at the time, but when my head kept spinning after the song ended I'd known it was over with Brett and that Nick was the one I belonged with.

When I turned the computer back to Alicia, she e-mailed the list to the DJ, sat back in her chair, and took a long swig of peach sangria. "That's the last thing I had to do. I'm finally done with all of the wedding details."

"I've got the plans made for the bachelorette party, too," I told her.

She clapped her hands in glee. "Where are we going?"

I wagged a finger. "Nuh-uh-uh. It's a surprise."

A surprise that would involve a limo, champagne, lots of singles, and a male exotic dancer named Fiero.

chapter three

Cashing In, Cashing Out

It was a few minutes before two o'clock on Tuesday when I arrived at the KCSH building in my plain sedan, otherwise known as my G-ride. The building was basic, small, and square, its orange brick exterior sporting irregular masonry where bricks had been patched and replaced over the years. The call letters "KCSH" were mounted on the roof, the metal rusting in spots. There was only one window in the building, a small one next to the glass front door. In the parking lot sat a small pickup, a VW Beetle, and a 2015 Cadillac ATS Coupe. The Cadillac belonged to Flo. Per my research, the ATS was one of Cadillac's least expensive models, starting just under forty grand, but still nothing to sneeze at. Her car was painted a shade called opulent blue metallic, ironic for someone who reported no taxable income, huh? The license plate frame bore the name and slogan of the dealership. *Ledbetter Cadillac—Better Cars for the Best People.*

I stepped up to the glass door, finding it locked. Putting a hand over my eyes to shield them from the sun, I peeked through the door. A young brown-skinned woman in a brightly striped knit dress sat at a desk inside. She looked up at me and called, "Are you the agent from the IRS?"

"Yes, that's me!" I called, noticing her eyes narrowed slightly at my reply. I wondered what Flo had told her about me. Probably that I was some pushy bureaucratic tyrant or some other such nonsense.

The young woman reached over to a device on her desk. A moment later there was a *click* as the lock released, followed by a *buzz* that ended once I pulled the door open. Inside, a live feed from KCSH played through speakers mounted on the walls, a familiar male voice expounding on the student loan crisis. One of the syndicated shows.

The young woman gestured to a duo of faux-leather chairs situated along the wall next to the door, a magazine rack containing the latest issues of financial magazines standing between them. She lifted the receiver for her desk phone. "I'll let Miss Cash know you've arrived."

"Thanks," I replied, taking a seat.

As she informed Flo of my arrival, I glanced around the tiny lobby. The walls were covered with photographs of famous people who'd been interviewed at the station, everyone from President Lyndon Baines Johnson to Alan Greenspan, former Chairman of the Federal Reserve. There were also several photos of men who'd played football for the Cowboys or basketball for the Mavericks. A snapshot of Mark Cuban, too. Flo Cash and her family had rubbed some pretty famous and influential elbows. The only elbows she'd be rubbing in the next few minutes would be mine, which were dry and in need of lotion.

A door opened in the back wall and there stood Florence Cash. She looked to be around fifty and sported dark curly hair and a turned-up nose. Her makeup was minimal, only a light coat of mascara and a soft sheen to her lips. ChapStick, if I had to hazard a guess. Though she wore stylish rectangular-framed glasses, her remaining attire could best be described as designed-for-comfort. A pair of stretchy leggings. An oversized T-shirt that hung to mid-thigh. A pair of those lightweight walking shoes that were half loafer, half sneaker. None of Suze Orman's stylish business jackets for Flo Cash. You'd never know from looking at the woman that she was a wealthy media magnate who came from a long line of successful radio broadcasters and station owners.

Still, I couldn't much fault Flo for her dress. I might watch an occasional episode of *Project Runway,* but I didn't always keep up with the latest fashion trends. Besides, Flo owned the place and didn't have to answer to anyone. And it's not like her audience could see her over the radio waves. This wasn't television, after all. Why not dress comfortably? Heck, if I were in her shoes they'd be slippers.

"Hello, Miss Cash." I extended my hand. "I'm Special Agent Tara Holloway."

"No need for introductions," she said, ignoring my hand. "You know who I am and you told me your name on the phone."

No pretense at politeness, huh? Flo might be an even bigger pain in the ass than I'd expected.

"Follow me." She turned and headed back down a short hall. On the immediate left was a door with a unisex bathroom sign affixed to it. A small supply closet sat on the opposite side of the hall. Beyond that the wall was divided, the lower half being solid and the upper half being glass. The room on the left contained an abundance of tech equipment being tended by a twentysomething bearded guy in jeans and a T-shirt, a Styrofoam cup with a red straw sitting on the console, a green drip running down its side. He was drinking either toxic waste or some sort of lime- or apple-flavored slush.

Flo turned into the room on the right. This room, too,

contained some technical equipment, though far less than the other room. A large console was situated on the wall that faced the glass, looking like the dashboard of the Starship *Enterprise*. What all those buttons and knobs and dials were for was a mystery to me, though I suspected one of them shot lasers and another could send us rocketing into space at warp speed.

Mounted on the wall over the console was a rectangular light with a white plastic cover that read: "ON AIR" in red lettering. Of course the light was off now that Flo wasn't broadcasting live. A large microphone sat on a stand at the front of the console. As least I knew the purpose of that piece of equipment. It was also clear what the long panel of buttons was for. Sound effects. Each was marked with a sticker identifying the sound it would make. *Moo. Slap. Crash. Game show buzzer. Bee. Old-timey car horn. Toilet flush. Applause. Crickets. Screeching tires. Ticking clock. Boing. Chickens clucking. Explosion.*

Alongside the microphone sat an oversized green ceramic coffee mug with the KCSH logo on one side and the words "TUNE IN TO THE FLO CASH CASH FLOW SHOW!" on the other. The handle was shaped like a dollar sign. Looked like some type of commemorative cup she gave away to the folks she hosted on her show. She'd kept this particular cup for herself, steam rising from the surface, a tea bag draped over the top. Lemon Zinger, if my nose wasn't mistaken. To the right of the console sat a coffeemaker. Though the red light was on, the liquid in the carafe was clear. Looked like Flo used the machine not to make coffee but rather to heat water for her tea.

A cushy rolling chair with an added lumbar support pillow sat in front of the microphone. Flo plopped herself down into the comfy seat, reaching behind her back to adjust the pillow. Once she was comfortable, she leaned back, intertwined her fingers across her abdomen, and stared at me, waiting for me to begin, not a bit of concern on her face or in her countenance. *Total Zen.*

Though she had yet to invite me to sit, I took a seat on the only other chair in the room, a small rolling stool, and placed my briefcase on my lap. I opened the clasps—*snap-snap*—and removed a copy of the auditor's report. "I trust you've read the auditor's findings?"

"That little piece of speculative science fiction?" she scoffed. "Sure, I read it."

"So you're aware that the IRS has some unanswered questions. Such as how you've managed to pay the station's bills and your own personal expenses given that KCSH has reported virtually no profits for several years and you've only paid yourself minimum wage."

She heaved a long-suffering sigh. "I'll tell you the same thing I told that squirrely auditor. The big days of radio are long gone. Everything's gone Internet now. With music downloads and podcasts, listenership is way down. Which means ad revenue is way down. The only reason I even keep this station up and running is because it's my family's legacy."

While her explanation might have made sense in a vacuum, it didn't jibe with the information contained in the KCSH tax returns for the time prior to her succession to ownership eight years ago. Up to that point, KCSH still showed healthy profits. In fact, Flo herself had enjoyed a six-digit salary as the advertising manager. And while it was true that people had more entertainment options these days, radio was still going strong. People listened to the radio in their cars, while working in their offices and garages. As for myself, I listened to a country station on my drive into work each day and tuned into *A Prairie Home Companion* on NPR every weekend for my fix of folk music and down-home humor. People even live-streamed radio broadcasts through their computers. Nope, radio wasn't going anywhere.

No point in debating the status of radio as an informational and entertainment medium, though. What this investigation came down to was numbers. I pulled out the ledger that detailed the ad revenue. "This is the detail on your advertising revenue. I counted seventy-three different advertisers when I listened to your station yesterday, but only a dozen or so clients are listed in your accounting records." I arched an accusing brow. "The businesses that aren't listed paid you in cash under the table, didn't they?"

She chuckled. "Sorry to burst your bubble, sweetheart, but they didn't pay me at all."

Sweetheart? I ignored her attempts to insult me, maintaining my focus on the case. *Why would she mention the businesses on her radio station if they weren't paying her to promote them?* "Care to explain?"

"It's easy." She gestured to the report. "The ones listed are the paying clients that we run professionally produced commercials for. The other businesses I mention are simply personal recommendations, not paid ads."

"What do you mean, 'personal recommendations'?"

"Just like it sounds. I'm giving my own opinion on businesses whose products or services I've used."

Huh. My smoking gun seemed to have cooled a bit. "Why would you mention the businesses for free on air?" After all, that airtime could be sold to a paying customer.

She gave me a patronizing smile. "Karma. If I put positive things out in the universe, give my listeners some good recommendations, maybe good things will come back to me."

I wasn't buying her karma crap for one second, and she still hadn't explained how she was keeping herself and the station afloat. "So how are you making ends meet?" *Receiving some other type of unreported income, perhaps?*

She offered the same shrug she'd offered the auditor.

I gave her a pointed look. "A shrug isn't an answer, Ms. Cash."

She scoffed once more. "Well, if you must know—"

"I must." *Unless you want to go to jail.*

"—I've been blowing through the money I earned when my father was still alive. When I was raking in the big bucks as the ad manager."

Hm-m. Savings could explain how she was able to pay the bills despite currently receiving only nominal income. Still, I'd seen no evidence of cash holdings or investments on her tax return. There'd been no interest, dividends, or stock sales reported. "Where is that money being held, exactly? A bank account? CDs? Stocks? Bonds?"

She snorted. "You know as well as I do that if my money was in a financial institution they would have reported the earnings to the IRS."

"Of course," I said. "So the fact that there's been no reports means you've put the funds in foreign institutions or offshore accounts, or in the name of a nominee." In other words, somewhere that the earnings could not be traced to her.

"I've done no such thing!" she snapped back.

"Then where's your money?"

She hesitated briefly before responding. "It's sitting in a safe."

Now it was my turn to scoff. "A *safe*? Are you kidding me?"

Did she seriously think I'd believe that the woman who constantly advised her listeners to *make your money make money for you* would keep her funds in a safe, where they'd earn nothing? Have no chance of going up in value? The mere idea was preposterous. Then again, perhaps it wasn't so much preposterous as purposeful. The IRS could levy a bank account, seize CDs and investments, put a lien on real estate. But cash? It could be hidden out of reach. And despite being made of paper, cash didn't leave a paper trail. Ironic, huh?

When Flo replied only with another shrug, I said, "Okay. I'll bite. Take me to this safe."

"Can't."

"Why not?"

"Because the safe is in my house and my house is being treated for termites as we speak. You go inside right now, it'll be the last thing you ever do."

No, the last thing I'd do was drag her ass into the house with me.

A smirk played about her lips. "Of course if you want to go inside on your own I'd be happy to give you the combination to the safe. Far be it from me to get in your way."

This woman was getting on my last nerve, but I fought the urge to slap the smirk off her face. "When will the treatment be completed?"

"Seventy-two hours."

How convenient that she'd scheduled the termite treatment for today of all days, knowing that I'd likely ask to see the cash. "Seems risky to leave a safe full of cash in the house. What if there's a fire? Or if someone breaks in while you're out?"

"I've got an alarm system. Besides, it's a big safe. Weighs a couple hundred pounds and it's bolted to the floor. It's not going anywhere. It's fireproof, too."

She'd certainly thought this through, hadn't she? "How much money is in the safe?"

She raised a palm. "Couldn't say. I don't keep count."

My gut clenched in exasperation. Why tax evaders thought we agents would be stupid enough to believe their ridiculous stories was beyond me. "You expect me to believe that a woman who hosts a financial talk show has no idea how much cash she has on hand?"

Another shrug, this one halfhearted and single shouldered. "You can believe what you want to believe, Miss Holliday. Makes no difference to me."

She'd likely misstated my name in an attempt to show further disdain and disrespect, so there was no point in rising to the bait and correcting her.

"I live by that Latin motto," she said. "*Carpe diem.* When the money's gone, it's gone."

That would be *carpe dime* rather than *diem,* wouldn't it? "And when it's gone, what will you do then?"

"I'll figure something out."

This woman would do well to learn two other Latin phrases, "mea culpa" and "habeas corpus." I was more determined than ever to prove her guilty of tax evasion and throw her lying ass in jail. If she'd thought being obstinate and difficult would discourage me, she was wrong. The bullshit she'd tried to feed me today only motivated me all the more to see justice done.

I shoved the paperwork back into my briefcase, closed it, and stood. "I expect you to meet me at your house on Friday to show me the safe."

"It'll have to be after six," she said. "I work until five and then I'll need time to drive home."

"Six it is." With that, I showed myself out.

Back in my car, I fumed. Flo was wasting my time. Hers, too. Of course she seemed to have much more time than I did, so wasting it must not be a big deal for her. I, on the other hand, never had enough of it and it chapped my ass to have to spend it chasing after uncooperative people like her. Why couldn't they just come clean and pay up? The few who did usually got little more than a slap on the wrist. Really, it was such a better way to go.

I cranked the engine and punched the button to turn on

the radio, which was still tuned to KCSH. Flo's voice came over the airwaves. As if I weren't sick of listening to that woman already.

"You listeners might be curious to know that Special Agent Tara Holloway from the Internal Revenue Service was just in my office here, making a bunch of wild accusations and demands."

Wild accusations and demands? All I'd done was try to get Flo to be honest with me. At least she'd gotten my name right this time. No more "Miss Holliday."

"But I'm not scared," she continued. "I'm not going to let some little power-hungry pipsqueak railroad me." The *toot-toot* of a train whistle followed her words.

Power-hungry pipsqueak?

Railroad?

Toot-toot?

Flo Cash better be careful who she messed with or she'd no longer have to worry about her cash flow. She'd have to worry about her *blood* flow.

chapter four

On the Hook

When I left the station, I aimed directly for Flo Cash's house to verify whether it was actually being treated for termites. As I drove, I continued to listen to KCSH. While one of the syndicated shows now played, Flo took advantage of the commercial break times not only to promote several local businesses but also to let callers berate the IRS on the air.

"The American tax rates are sky-high!" one man exclaimed. "Between income taxes and Social Security taxes, I'm lucky to get home with half of my paycheck."

Even though I knew the jackass couldn't see or hear me, I nonetheless glared at my radio and responded to the caller, "Feel free to move to Belgium, Germany, or Denmark."

All three of those countries had higher income tax rates than the United States, as did Hungary, Austria, Greece, and the United Kingdom. Those nations with the lowest tax rates tended to be oil-rich countries in the Middle East, such as Kuwait, Qatar, Bahrain, and Saudi Arabia. Macedonia also had a very low tax rate, though its public debt had more than doubled in the last decade. At some point, the system would have to be rethought or it would implode.

Another caller suggested that Flo "should've tossed that IRS agent out the door!"

I would've liked to see her try.

As I turned onto Flo's street, my eyes were nearly blinded by lights so bright there must've been a nuclear explosion. Blinking and squinting, I finally managed to make things out. A yellow van sat at the curb, a big plastic bug on top with disco balls for eyes. The mirrored eyes reflected the sun, which sat low on the western horizon, the rays refracting like laser beams. Seriously, those bug eyes were a public hazard.

I pulled to a stop in front of the house, which was fully enclosed in a blue nylon tent. Yep, Flo Cash was indeed getting a termite treatment. Or maybe she was hosting a circus or a tent revival instead. Both of the latter would require a tub of water, either for the animals to drink from or to perform impromptu baptisms.

The van at Flo's house featured the logo for Cowtown Critter Control. Cowtown was a nickname for Fort Worth, Dallas's country cousin that sat a half-hour drive to the west. Surely there were dozens of exterminators in the city of Dallas. Why would Flo have hired an outfit from the next town over?

Two technicians decked head to toe in hazmat gear came around the corner of the house, carrying tanks of chemicals. They headed to the van, opened the back, and stashed their gear inside.

I climbed out of my car and walked over the van. "Hello there," I said, raising a hand in greeting. "Just wondering what Cowtown Critter Control is doing all the way over here in Dallas."

One of the men glanced my way. "We go where the boss tells us to."

That was something we had in common. But I bet their boss didn't sport a beehive. A beehive on an exterminator would be ironic, huh? "Do you do many jobs in Dallas?"

"No," he said. "This is the first one I've ever done. Our usual territory is Fort Worth and the surrounding suburbs."

Hm-m . . . "So what's special about this particular job that you were sent all this way?"

"I didn't ask." His tone indicated he'd become impatient with my barrage of questions. "I just do what I'm told. If you need an exterminator out this way I'd suggest you look online."

With that, the man I'd been speaking with closed the back doors of the van—*Slam! Slam!*—and circled around to the driver's seat. The other tech climbed in on the passenger side.

If I wanted answers, looked like I was on my own.

Wednesday morning, I woke more determined than ever to see Flo Cash get her due. On the entire drive home from her office the day before I'd listened to caller after caller phone the station to make disparaging remarks about the IRS and the "unfair tax system."

What a big bunch of whiners.

The 1 percent thought the graduated tax rates were inequitable. Those who lived paycheck to paycheck resented the lower capital gains rates that benefited only those fortunate enough to have disposable income to invest. The middle class, who benefited little from tax programs designed to help the poor or to encourage the wealthy to invest their excess funds, believed they shouldered too much of the burden. Nobody on any point of the earnings spectrum thought the tax system was equitable.

Fortunately, though, I didn't have to deal with Flo Cash today. A good thing, too. I wasn't sure I had much restraint left. One more *toot-toot* or *pipsqueak* and I'd poke her in the eye with my mechanical pencil or drive my G-ride through the wall of her radio station and provide a real-life sound effect. *CRASH!*

This morning I was working on another case, one involving a catfishing Casanova who'd met several local women on a dating Web site known as the Big D Dating Service and duped them out of thousands of dollars. Many such victims felt horribly embarrassed that they'd been so naïve and went only so far as to notify the dating service and file a police report. But not so in this case. Three of this particular catfisher's victims had found one another online after each went public with their stories in the hopes of tracking down the man who'd ripped them off. They'd banded together and approached the Texas Attorney General's Office, the FBI, and the IRS, hoping one of the agencies would take on the case and help them nail the bastard.

With the limited resources available to the state and federal governments, priority normally went to scams perpetuated on a wider scale. But when Lu had received an urgent and impassioned letter from the women she'd empathized with their plight and decided to offer some help. Or, more precisely, she decided to offer them *my* help. After all, it was unlikely that the crook had paid taxes on the funds he'd weaseled out of his victims.

I'd just returned from filling my mug with coffee in the office kitchen when Viola, Lu's secretary, buzzed me on the intercom. "Your nine o'clocks are here."

I jabbed the button. "I'll be right down."

I left my coffee on my desk and headed down the hall, where I found three surprisingly attractive, nicely dressed women engaged in conversation at Viola's desk. Perhaps it was wrong of me, but I'd assumed women who'd fall victim to an online con artist would be older, lonely sad sacks. These women appeared to be anything but. In fact, they looked more like the types of women you'd see sipping chardonnay with their friends at a book club.

"Good morning," I told the ladies, holding out my hand. "I'm Special Agent Holloway."

"Leslie Gleason," said the first, giving my hand a firm shake. Leslie looked to be in her mid-forties, with cute blond ringlets framing her thin face. Her turquoise dress brought out the blue of her eyes and hugged her slim curves, stopping just below the knees to show off well-toned calves that told me Leslie was a runner.

The next woman was a petite Latina with skin the color of *cajeta*. She looked to be in her mid- to late thirties. She wore a silky blouse and jeans with a pair of cute wedges. My gaze stopped on her pendant, which featured the face of a friendly feline.

"Cute necklace," I said. "I love cats."

"Me, too," the woman said, taking my hand. "I'm a veterinarian. Dr. Julia Valenzuela."

The third woman appeared to be a mix of Asian and Caucasian, fortyish, and tall. Her sleek black hair hung in a face-framing bob. She wore a pale-blue blazer over an ivory blouse and navy dress pants. "Nataya Lawan," she said, introducing herself.

I gestured for them to follow me back to my office, stealing a wing chair from Nick's space so that I could accommodate all three.

Once they were seated, I slipped into my chair. "I've read over your letters and looked at the documentation you sent."

They'd submitted documentation including copies of the fronts and backs of the checks the catfisher had each of the women cash for him. All three were third-party business checks made payable to Jack Smirnoff and drawn on an account purportedly in the name of Wellsource Insurance. All three checks were the amount of two thousand dollars, all three were dated on the same day in late March, and all three had been returned when the account had been found to be false.

I pulled the copies from the file and held them up. "What can you tell me about these checks?" I asked. "And about the man who asked you to cash them?"

After exchanging glances with the other two women, Nataya spoke first. "The man I knew as Jack Smirnoff gave me the check at breakfast one morning. He'd asked me to meet him at a pancake house. We'd been out several times and had really hit it off. Or so I'd thought." She frowned in memory and continued. "Anyway, he'd told me that he was a psychologist and that he lived in Colorado—"

"Colorado?" I repeated. This was news to me. Their letter hadn't mentioned that he lived out of state.

"Right," Nataya replied. "Denver, to be exact." She looked at me expectantly, and I nodded for her to continue. "He said his wife had suddenly passed away last fall. He told me he was having a hard time dealing with all of the memories in Colorado and was ready to make a fresh start in Dallas. He was living in one of those extended-stay suites while looking for a place to buy here in town."

Leslie chimed in. "That was the same story he told me."

Julia let out a frustrated breath. "Me, too."

Nataya continued. "He said that his wife had a twenty-two-year-old son from her first marriage and that the son had lived with them. The son was supposedly a deadbeat who couldn't hold a job because he'd stay out all night partying with his friends and was too lazy to get up and go to work in the mornings."

Again, the other two women nodded in agreement.

"Jack claimed that his wife had provided well for her son in her will, though she'd directed that the funds be placed in a trust for his benefit so that he couldn't squander it all away. The terms of the will appointed Jack as the trustee of the trust. Jack had also said that his stepson received two thousand dollars a month from an annuity, payable directly to him, no strings attached."

Nataya went on to tell me that Jack's wife had left him only twenty grand in her will, but her son had nonetheless filed a lawsuit, claiming Jack had unduly influenced his mother to put the funds in a trust and that she'd always told the son that he would get all of her property outright on her demise. In other words, Jack's stepson was challenging both the trust and Jack's token inheritance.

Leslie continued the saga. "Jack's bank accounts and property were supposedly frozen by the court until the lawsuit could be tried or settled. Jack said the check was a payment from an insurance company for sessions with his clients, but that he couldn't deposit the check into the joint checking account he owned with his dead wife or her son might get his hands on the money and blow it going out to party with his friends."

Julia chimed in now. "That's what Jack told me, too. It all made sense to me."

"Me, too," said Leslie.

"It's certainly a plausible story," I said. It was all a lie, of course, but not so far out in left field as to be immediately recognizable as a fabrication.

Nataya crossed her ankles. "Jack asked if I would mind cashing one of the checks for him. He said it was no problem if I was uncomfortable doing it, that he could cash it at a check-cashing place, but he said that those places charge very high fees and it seemed ridiculous for him to pay the fee to them when he could give it to me instead."

The other women murmured in assent. Looked like he'd given them the same story.

"He was very nonchalant about it," Nataya said, heaving a sigh, "not pushy at all. So, I decided to go ahead. I figured if the check was bogus my bank would know right away and tell me on the spot. With as fast as everything gets processed these days I didn't think there was any risk."

Unfortunately, the idea that one bank could immediately verify the existence and balance of an account at another bank was a myth that led many an unwitting victim to their financial doom. The truth was that each bank's information was kept private from the others and that it still took a day or more for checks to be run through the systems and verified. Meanwhile, the victims' banks often gave their customers the benefit of the doubt, cashing the check immediately rather than making their customers wait for the funds to clear. It wasn't until later, when the check proved invalid, that the customers would suddenly find themselves holding the bag, the funds debited from their own account to repay the bank for the NSF check.

Nataya frowned. "He made me feel pretty damn stupid."

"Don't," I told her. "Con artists can be very crafty."

She wouldn't be the first person to be taken in by one of these scammers, and she wouldn't be the last. Even celebrities had fallen for catfishing scams, including Thomas Gibson, star of the TV shows *Criminal Minds* and *Dharma & Greg,* who'd sent a video of himself in a hot tub to the fictitious woman who'd lured him in online. Notre Dame football player Manti Te'o had also fallen for a young woman he'd met online. He'd mourned when the girl allegedly died, only to find out she'd never even existed in the first place. *What kind of sick person would play on someone else's emotions like that?*

Of course I had to admire the Chechen women who catfished some members of ISIS online and conned the jihadists into sending them thousands of roubles via QIWI Wallet, a Russian electronic cash transfer system. The women might be con artists, but it was hard to fault them when their victims were responsible for killing so many innocent people and instigating a heartbreaking refugee crisis. As far as I was concerned, the men got what they deserved. A little bitch slap from karma.

Nataya sighed. "I can't prove it, but I'm pretty sure Jack stole my credit card, too."

"What makes you think that?" I asked.

"During our second date," she said, "when we were in the middle of our dinner, I got a phone call from work. I didn't want to be rude, so I took my phone outside the restaurant. I left my purse behind. A few days later, I went to use my MasterCard and I couldn't find it. I called the credit card company and they told me there'd been all kinds of charges made at clothing and shoe stores in The Galleria the day after my date with Jack. Over four thousand dollars' worth."

Whoa. Not exactly chump change. "Did you report the fraud to the police?"

She nodded. "I know they can't do much, though. This kind of thing happens every day and they've got more important things to deal with."

It was true. The amount of credit card fraud was overwhelming. Most police departments merely took a report and filed it away, never to be looked at again. The perpetrators knew it, too. Few were caught and prosecuted. The risk was minimal.

"It didn't even cross my mind that Jack could have taken my card," Nataya said. "At least not until after the fiasco with the check. I just figured I'd accidentally left the card somewhere or dropped it or something. But when I found out the check I cashed for Jack was a fake I remembered that I'd left my purse at our table when I took the call. We were seated in a back corner, so it would have been easy for him to go through my purse without anyone noticing."

Even if someone had noticed, they might have assumed Nataya trusted her date or she wouldn't have left her purse in his care. Or they might have assumed Jack was her husband and that the situation was totally normal.

"Did you talk to security at the mall?" I asked. "Request to see videotapes?"

"No," Nataya said. "My bank agreed to reverse the charges, so there was no harm done. At least not to me. The stores suffered losses, of course."

"Can you send me a copy of the credit card bill?"

"Sure."

Leslie leaned forward. "I've done a lot of online dating and I've had catfishers hit on me before, but usually it's obvious. They'll claim to be a model or an aspiring actor or a sports figure, post a photo of a really good-looking guy with washboard abs, and go overboard with the flattery to try to draw you in. But Jack did none of those things. He brought me a small bouquet of flowers on our second date, but he didn't come on too strong."

"That's how he was with me, too," Julia agreed. "He seemed like a really nice, down-to-earth guy. Genuine, you know?"

"Exactly," Nataya said. "I mean, he was a cutie, don't get us wrong. In good shape, too. But what really made me fall for him was that he was such a good—"

Uh-oh—

"Listener?" Julia interjected.

"Exactly!" Nataya said.

Thank goodness. I'd been afraid she was going to say he was a good *lover.* My stomach had turned at the mere thought of a guy misleading all these women and sticking his you-know-what all over the place like some type of sexual switchboard operator.

"I felt the same way about Jack," Leslie replied, looking from the other two women to me. "He wasn't like other men. He'd actually look you in the eye when you were talking rather than stealing glances at your boobs."

Julia nodded. "He'd ask appropriate follow-up questions."

"Yeah," Nataya said. "He really paid attention and seemed to care. I assumed that's part of what made him so successful as a psychologist."

Call me a cynic, but maybe his attentiveness and concern should've been their first clue that Jack Smirnoff was too good to be true. In my experience, men would just as soon keep the conversation light and paid only enough attention to a woman to keep her on the hook. Even Nick, as wonderful as he could be, gave me only his partial attention if I tried to engage in any real conversation while a Cowboys or Mavericks game was on. I'd learned to approach him with significant topics at more opportune times and to keep my musings short and to the point. Of course, the reverse was true, too. Unless something was on fire, he knew better than to interrupt my bathtub reading time. These things didn't mean we didn't love each other or weren't fully committed to our relationship; they were just realities, the typical types of negotiations couples make.

I jotted down a note—*good listener*—and turned my attention back to the women. "Did any of you try to verify his identity or story in any way?"

The first thing I would do if approached by someone on a dating service site would be perform some cyber-sleuthing. I'd take a look at his Facebook page, Google his name and see what might pop up. Of course with me being an IRS agent, I had access to many more databases than the average person. I could take a look at the criminal records to see if the guy had a rap sheet, pull up his driver's license to verify his address, check the motor vehicle records to see what kind of car he owned. I could also quickly search the vital records and court filings to take a look at birth certificates, marriage licenses, and lawsuit information.

"I did a little bit of snooping before our first date," Leslie said. "I didn't find a personal Facebook page for him or anything about his practice online. When I asked him about it, he said that he worked as a subcontractor at a mental health facility and that everything was kept very private due to the health privacy laws. He also said that he dealt with some emotionally unstable people, so he didn't like his personal life and whereabouts to be easy to find."

"That's what he told me, too," Julia said. "It sounded reasonable."

Nataya cringed. "This might sound morbid, but I searched online for an obituary for his wife. I wanted to make sure she was really out of the picture."

"Did you find one?" I asked.

"I did," she replied. "It was printed in *The Denver Post*." She gestured to my computer. "You can find it. Just search for 'Christine Smirnoff.'"

I logged on to my computer, entered the name and the word "obituary" in my browser, and ran a quick search. Sure enough, an entry popped up on the *Denver Post* site, the black-and-white photo depicting a fortyish woman with a broad smile and dark, wavy hair. Per the listing, Christine E. Smirnoff, a local psychologist and avid hiker, had passed away from an undiagnosed heart condition late last October. She was survived by her son and husband. In lieu of flowers, the family requested donations to the Sierra Club.

Hm-m . . .

I pulled up the Colorado Department of Public Health information and searched for the name Christine Smirnoff among the death certificates. A few entries popped up. Some contained alternate spellings of the first name or similar names such as Christopher Smirnoff, but none of the deaths had occurred in the preceding year. I eyed the women over my screen. "There's no death certificate for his alleged wife."

Julia frowned. "So the obituary was a fake, too?"

"Looks that way." Whoever this Jack Smirnoff really was, he'd probably bought the obituary to make himself look legitimate, to create an air of verisimilitude. *Wow. Look at me using big words this morning. My high school English teachers would be so proud!* I asked the women a few more questions to ascertain more about Jack. "How many dates did each of you have with Jack? Where did you go? What did you do? What topics did you talk about?"

As I listened to their stories, I learned that Jack had a standard MO. Over the course of two weeks, he'd taken each of the women out to dinner twice, first at a chain restaurant, then to a more upscale place on their second date. On their third outing, he'd suggested doing something more personal to each of them. He'd jogged at White Rock Lake with Leslie. Taken Nataya to a traveling Broadway show. Went to a tasting at a local winery with Julia, even buying her a bottle to take home. It was after their third dates that, on the exact same day, he'd taken Nataya to breakfast, Leslie to an early lunch, and Julia to a late lunch, casually asking each of them whether they'd mind cashing the checks. He seemed to have found a tried-and-true formula and stuck with it.

By my estimate, he'd spent between two and five hundred dollars wooing each woman. Given that he'd taken each for two grand, he'd earned at worst a fifteen-hundred-dollar profit per victim, an immediate 300 percent return on his investment. He certainly wouldn't get that kind of earnings from trading on Wall Street or a certificate of deposit. And all he'd had to do was eat some good food, spend a little time with attractive women, and *listen*.

My gaze ran over the women. "Did he go into the bank with any of you when you cashed his checks?" If so, there'd be surveillance camera footage that could be used to convict him.

"Not me," Nataya said. "He received a phone call just after we arrived at the bank. He stayed outside to take the call while I went inside to cash the check."

"Same thing here," Julia said.

Leslie frowned. "Me, too."

The incoming calls surely weren't coincidence. Chances were the calls were as bogus as the checks he'd given them to cash. "Did any of you actually hear his phone ring?"

All three replied in the negative. "No." "Not me." "Didn't hear a thing."

Julia looked from Nataya to Leslie and back to me. "I'd just assumed his phone had vibrated in his pocket."

The other two nodded in agreement.

"What kind of car did he drive?" I asked the women.

"A Mercedes convertible," Julia said. "An SLK two-fifty model."

Leslie let out a huff. "The nice car was part of the reason I trusted him. He looked like he'd done well for himself and had plenty of money."

"Any chance you know the plate number?"

None of them had it, though all three had noted that the car bore Colorado license plates.

I jotted a note on my pad. *CO plates.* "I can check with the restaurants, see if they have outdoor video cameras that might have picked up his plate number." With any luck, they'd have exterior cameras to catch customers who attempted to dine and dash. "Where did he stay when he was in town?"

"The Omni," all three said in unison.

"Did he ever invite any of you back to his hotel room?"

They all answered in the negative this time, too.

"So you can't say for certain that he was actually staying at the Omni, right?"

Leslie said, "He had a key card from there. It fell out of his pocket on our second date."

Nataya rolled her eyes. "Same here."

Julia groaned. "Ditto."

The key card could, in fact, mean he'd stayed at the Omni. But the fact that he'd invited none of these women back to his hotel and made a show of dropping the key so that all three women would take note seemed like a ploy. More likely he'd swiped the key or perhaps spent a single night at the hotel and failed to turn the keys in on checkout.

"Besides his sob story," I said, "what else did he tell you about himself?"

Nataya looked up at the ceiling, Julia tapped her finger on her cheek, and Leslie chewed her lip, all in thought.

Leslie responded first. "He said precious little about himself, now that I think about it. Any time I asked him a question, he'd give me a short answer and find a way to turn the conversation back to me or my interests."

Julia chimed in next. "Same here. I hate to admit it, but after all the losers I've met through the dating site it was refreshing to meet a guy who didn't have a huge ego and expect me to fawn all over him."

Nataya concurred. "The only specific thing I can remember him saying is that he liked Elton John's music. 'Crocodile Rock' was playing over the speakers at one of the restaurants while we were waiting to be seated and he sang along with it. At the time I'd thought it was cute." She punctuated her words with a groan.

Not exactly the kind of information I needed. "What about photos of him?" I asked. "Do you have any?"

All three whipped out their cell phones and showed me pics they'd taken with Jack. In each of the photos, he sported short, dark-brown hair and eyeglasses with oval lenses and black frames. He had a lean but athletic build. He appeared to be Caucasian, though his skin tone was a little on the olive side.

Leslie had a photo of Jack leaning back against a tree on the shore of White Rock Lake. Julia and Jack had done a fun, up-close selfie of the two of them holding up glasses of chardonnay at the winery, smiling big smiles at the camera. Someone else had taken a photo of Nataya and Jack standing with one of the costumed actors from the Broadway show at a meet and greet in the theater lobby.

I mulled things over for a moment. "I'm surprised a con artist wouldn't balk at having his picture taken." Most preferred to hide under rocks, the same place they probably crawled out from.

Julia jabbed a button on her phone to close the picture. "The fact that he wasn't concerned about me taking his photo made him seem for real. If he hadn't wanted his picture taken I would've thought that maybe he was lying about himself and that he still married or something."

The other women murmured in agreement.

"I've also got the photo he used in his profile on the Big D site," Nataya said, holding up her phone to show me the head shot she'd downloaded. He wore the same eyeglasses in the profile pic as he did in the other photos.

"E-mail all of the pics to me," I instructed, giving them my IRS e-mail address. "I'm not sure if any information can be gleaned from the photos, but it can't hurt for me to take a closer look."

As they worked their phones to send the photos my way, I asked whether there was anything else they could tell me about him. "Anything that might provide a clue as to his real identity or help me track him down. Anything that caught your eye or ear. Even the smallest detail could help."

"There was one thing," Leslie said. "After we went jogging at the lake, he opened his trunk and got a towel out of a gym bag inside. When he pulled out the towel, something that looked like a black belt fell out and I asked him if he did martial arts. He said no, that the belt was some type of strap he used when he worked out. I didn't have any reason to doubt his explanation at the time. But now?"

Now? She had every reason to doubt anything the guy had ever told her.

Nataya sat up straighter in her seat and cut a glance at Leslie. "Now that you mention it, I remember seeing a martial arts medal in his glove compartment. You know, the kind that hangs around your neck?" She moved her hands as if to indicate a long ribbon draped over her shoulders. She went on to explain that when Jack stopped for gas on their way to the theater her allergies got the best of her. "I was having a major sneezing fit and had used up all the tissues in my purse, so I opened the glove box to look for a napkin while Jack was outside filling the tank. I spotted the medal inside. I asked him about it when he got back in the car, but he said it belonged to his stepson."

Hm-m. Had he been telling the truth about the strap and the medal? Or was Jack Smirnoff not only a con artist but also some type of ninja warrior?

"Could you tell what type of martial arts the medal was for?" I asked. "Karate? Tae kwon do, maybe?" I knew there were a few other forms as well.

"I have no idea," Nataya said, cringing apologetically. "All I remember is that the medal was gold and round and depicted two people throwing kicks at each other. The ribbon had red, white, and blue stripes."

I jotted down the description, though it sounded like a fairly typical type of award.

"Anything else?" I asked a final time, offering suggestions that might jog their memories. "Did he have a parking sticker on the back of his car that might indicate where he works or lives? Root for a particular college sports team? Take any prescription meds that you know of?"

Apparently he'd done none of the above. The women offered nothing further and I realized I was grasping at straws. Of course you never knew when one of those straws might pay off.

Having collected all of the information I could from the women, I typed up affidavits for them to sign. After printing them out, I led the trio to Viola's desk so that she could notarize the documents. When the affidavits were complete, I walked the women back to the elevators. As they waited for the car, I told them I'd do my best to try to track the man down and see that justice was done. Still, I had to be careful not to get their hopes up.

"The chances of me finding the guy are slim," I warned, "Even if I find him, there's a good chance he's already spent most, if not all, of your money." Which meant there might be no funds left for him to pay taxes on his ill-gotten income or restitution to these women.

"Frankly," Julia said, "I'm more interested in seeing him put behind bars than I am in getting my money back."

"Me, too!" Nataya snapped. "Losing a couple grand wasn't nearly as bad as the humiliation."

Leslie was a bit more pragmatic. "Me? I'd just love a chance to kick him where the sun doesn't shine."

With any luck, Leslie would get that kick in.

chapter five

*H*ooking Up

After the women left, I returned to my office. Unfortunately, as much as I wanted to help these women and see justice done, I also knew that if Jack Smirnoff were captured today he'd likely get a mere slap on the wrist. While six grand was nothing to sneeze at, it was a paltry sum compared to many theft by deception cases. Moreover, he'd hadn't preyed on anyone who couldn't withstand the loss. Judges tended to go harder on con artists who preyed on the elderly or poor. Leslie, Julia, and Nataya were all successful women on solid financial footing. In order to put this guy behind bars, I'd have to show that there were more victims and a significant sum of money involved.

I spent a little more time digging into this so-called Jack Smirnoff. While I suspected there was little or no chance Jack Smirnoff was the guy's real name—after all, what idiot would pull a stunt like this and give his victims his real name?—I figured the con artist must have gotten the name somewhere. Maybe from a coworker or neighbor or acquaintance. Hell, for all I knew, Jack Smirnoff could be the name of his childhood soccer coach or scout leader. Or maybe it was simply his favorite brand of vodka.

I searched online to find men named Jack Smirnoff. While several popped up, neither of the two who turned up in Colorado was the right age to be the suspect. One was seventy-six, the other a mere twenty-four. Despite the Colorado license plates on the Mercedes he drove, it was possible the suspect was actually a local man, so I searched in the North Texas area as well. I found three Jack Smirnoffs in the Dallas–Fort Worth metropolitan area, only one of whom was in the right age range. A quick look at his driver's license photo told me it wasn't the same guy. The Jack Smirnoff in the photo was black. "Nope," I told the screen. "You're not the man I'm looking for."

Next, I phoned the restaurants where the women had gone on their dates with the catfisher. While three had exterior cameras, none retained their footage for more than thirty days.

"If there's a problem," one of the managers told me, "we usually know about it pretty quick. You know, someone running out on their bill, or a fight in the parking lot, or maybe one customer backs into another's car. That kind of thing. I've worked here for years and you're the first person who's asked for older footage."

Darn. "Thanks for your time."

I contacted the Big D Dating Service next. "May I speak to the manager, please?"

"You got him." The manager, who identified himself only as J.B., refused to give me any information by phone. "I'll tell you this much," he said. "When a client makes a complaint, the Big D policy is to contact the person they've complained about and give that person a chance to refute the story. If the response isn't satisfactory, or if the person fails to respond within five business days, that person is removed from the site and banned from rejoining."

"Who at Big D makes this contact?"

"I do."

"So you communicated with Jack Smirnoff?" I said. "What was his response?"

"Hold up just a minute here," J.B. said. "You say a man on our site wasn't who he claimed to be. But how do I know that you really are who you say you are? How can I be sure that you actually work for the federal government? For all I know, you're this Smirnoff guy's wife or girl-friend and you're just trying to catch him stepping out on you."

Ugh. I'm going to have to go see this J.B. in person, aren't I? "I'll come to you, then. Prove I am who I say I am."

"But that means I'll have to put on pants."

Sheesh. "Would you rather I issue a summons for you to appear at our office?"

"No," he said. "That would require socks and shoes, too."

"So we're in agreement. I'm coming over. What's your address?"

He growled in protest but rattled off a number and a street in the Greenville area. "Unit Fifty-Six."

I plugged the address in my phone's GPS app. "I'll be there in twenty minutes."

"I'll start looking for some pants."

The address turned out to be a condominium complex, four modern three-story buildings of gray stucco with glass-enclosed balconies centered around a pool, hot tub, and small lawn area. Unit Fifty-Six was in the third building. *This is the home of Big D Dating Service?*

I rapped on the door and J.B. answered a moment later. The guy appeared to be in his late twenties, like me. He sported a slightly scraggly dark-blond beard and hair, a T-shirt, and hopelessly wrinkled cargo shorts. He was barefoot and held a bottle of hard cider in his hand.

He tipped the bottle toward me. "You the IRS investi-gator?"

"That's me." I flashed my badge before offering him a business card. "Special Agent Tara Holloway." I glanced into the unit. To the left was a kitchen and breakfast bar, to the right a living area with a couch, recliner, and big-screen television. A laptop computer sat open on the coffee table next to a large bag of potato chips. "This is the Big D Dating Service headquarters?"

"Sweet, isn't it? My morning commute is ten steps from my bedroom to my chair. Less if I fell asleep on the couch."

He stepped back in a manner that seemed to be an invitation for me to come inside, so I did.

He raised his bottle. "Want a beer?"

"Thanks, but I'm on the job."

"So am I."

"Yeah, but you're not going to fire yourself. My boss wouldn't look too kindly on me drinking while on duty."

He flopped down on the recliner and pulled the lever to raise the leg support.

I perched on his couch. "How long have you managed the Big D site?"

"Since I launched it three years ago. It started on a whim. I used to work as a programmer. Busted my ass for fifty hours a week in a cubicle in a windowless room. When my girlfriend and I broke up, I signed up on some of the national dating sites. I realized pretty quick that I could offer a locally focused site for a third the price the larger sites were charging and still break even. Nobody else had a site targeted for people in Dallas. I figured what the hell, you know? Nothing to lose. Now I'm pulling down six figures and I work only twenty, thirty hours a week tops, from home, in my underwear. Plus, I get first shot at the new girls who sign up."

"Sweet gig," I told him. "And thanks for putting on pants." Might as well show some appreciation, huh? "Like I said on the phone, one of your clients used the Big D Web site to prey on three women who have contacted the IRS for help. Your client took these women out on several dates, then asked each of them to cash a check for him. The women cashed the checks and turned the cash over to him but later learned the checks were fakes. Their banks recouped the losses from the women's accounts."

"I get complaints all the time," J.B. said, waving his cider. "*'She didn't look at all like her picture.' 'He's been sleeping on my couch for two months and won't leave.' 'She borrowed my car and disappeared with it.'* I'll tell you the same thing I tell them. That's not on me. My attorney made sure my ass is covered. The Big D client contract clearly states that the service merely provides an online venue to meet other people. We are up front about the fact that we don't run background checks and make no guarantees about anyone's behavior. Clients are warned to take precautions. They agree to hold us harmless for any losses. It's right there on page one of our contract in bold print."

"These women don't want to sue your company," I told the man. "They just want this guy to be stopped. I've run searches on the name Jack Smirnoff and nobody by that name matches your client's description. It's obviously an alias. You can help by providing me with all of the information you have on the guy and contact information for the women he was matched with."

"That contract I mentioned?" the guy said, taking a swig of his cider. "It's got a privacy clause in it. If I hand over information about the women he met through the site I'll be in violation of the terms. The clients could sue me."

"What about that 'hold harmless' clause?" I said, noting the provision he'd been so happy to hide behind only a moment ago. "Wouldn't that protect you?"

He mulled things over, his nose wriggling as he did so.

"I've got affidavits from the victims," I added, "signed under penalty of perjury. How about that?"

He sat up a bit, which I took as a good sign.

"See?" I whipped out copies of the affidavits and reached across the coffee table to hand them to him. "Official legal affidavits. They're notarized and everything."

I pointed to the notary seal. Many people thought that having paperwork notarized proved the veracity of the information contained therein. Actually, all it meant was that the notary had verified the identification of the person signing the document and thus prevented later legal challenges by signatories who might attempt to claim forgery. I wasn't sure whether J.B. knew any of this, but I had to use whatever means of persuasion were available to me.

He looked the affidavits over and let out a long, loud breath that let me know his resolve was dissipating. I could be fairly stubborn and insistent, but it was an effective way of wearing people down.

"Look," I pressed. "I understand you need to comply with your contract. But this kind of thing can give your site a bad name, even put you out of business. You don't want to end up back in that cubicle, do you? Having to put on pants every day?" *Oh, the tyranny of outer garments!*

He squirmed in his recliner, a sure sign his resolve was melting.

I continued to hammer at him. "The women who complained to the government are determined to have this guy tracked down and punished, and if I can't nip this case in the bud they might take things to the media." None of the three women I'd spoken with had threatened to do any such thing, but this guy didn't need to know that. Besides, it was possible they'd contact the newspapers or TV stations, right?

"I'm more concerned about a bad review on Yelp."

"Good point," I agreed. "And if I have to tell these women that you refused to help me, they might post a bad review of your service. So how about you tell me everything you know about Jack Smirnoff, since he's clearly not legit, and then you can contact the other women he met through your site and pass my name and phone number on to them? That way, you're not violating your contract's privacy clause. Besides, they'd surely appreciate you giving them a heads-up. You might save them from being ripped off, too. Heck, you'd be a hero!" Given his dislike of lower body garments, being a superhero would be a good job for this guy. Superheroes didn't wear pants, either.

He hesitated briefly but finally agreed. "All right. I suppose there's no harm in that." He picked his computer up from the coffee table, situated it on his lap, and tapped a few keys. "Here he is. Jack Smirnoff. His profile was taken down several weeks ago."

"After Nataya Lawan, Leslie Gleason, and Julia Valenzuela complained to you about him?"

"I suppose that cat's out of the bag," J.B. said, "so yes. My notes indicate that I tried to call the guy, but his phone had been disconnected. I sent him three e-mails, too, but he never responded. He listed a Denver address in his account information, but in his profile paragraph he says he's in the process of relocating to Dallas."

I asked him to read the Denver address, e-mail address, and phone number aloud and jotted them down as he recited them. The phone number was the same one Smirnoff had given to Leslie, Nataya, and Julia. They had reported the number being disconnected when they'd tried to call Jack Smironoff after learning the checks he'd given them were fraudulent.

"What about his credit card information?" I asked.

J.B. ran a finger over the mouse pad and clicked a few more keys. "He used a Visa."

Though I was fairly certain the Visa would prove to be one of those prepaid cards, I requested the number and wrote it down anyway. If I could determine where and when it was purchased, I might be able to nail the guy.

I looked over at J.B. "I realize you don't want to give me the names of the female clients he contacted, but can you at least tell me how many there were and when he got in touch with them?"

He played around on his laptop for a minute or so. "Other than the ones you know about, there were only two. One of them replied to his wink by saying she appreciated his interest, but she'd decided to get back with her old boyfriend. The other never responded to him. Guess she wasn't interested."

This news was both good and bad. While I was glad no other women seemed to have been duped by Smirnoff, without more victims I had less chance of getting a clue that would help me track the guy down. There was also less chance he'd receive a meaningful punishment. Still, I wasn't leaving here totally empty-handed. I had a phone number, address, and credit card information. Maybe that would get me somewhere.

I stood. "Thanks, J.B. I appreciate your help." I raised a palm. "I'll show myself out. Don't get up."

Not that he'd made any move to escort me to the door. But at least he sent me off with well wishes.

"Good luck catching the guy."

chapter six

$\mathcal{B}$ack in the Dating Game

On my return trip to the office, I drove through a taco stand and picked up a bean burrito for lunch. A special agent can't concentrate on an empty stomach. I ordered a couple extra for Nick. After all, the way to an *hombre*'s *corazón* is through his *estómago*.

While eating my burrito back at the office, I logged on to my computer, input the card number for the Visa the catfisher had used to pay for his Big D subscription, and confirmed it was an untraceable prepaid credit card. No surprise there. A call to the credit card company told me that the card had been purchased at a big box store in Dallas.

"It was loaded five months ago," the woman said.

"How much was put on the card?"

"Twenty-five hundred."

The same went for the phone. Also prepaid and untraceable. Also purchased at the big box store. To my chagrin, the store no longer had any security camera footage from that time.

"Ninety days is our limit," the store manager told me. "We don't keep footage any longer than that."

"All right." I sighed in resignation. "Thanks for your time."

As I hung up the phone, I wondered if there was any chance the martial arts lead could pan out. Of course I wasn't even sure the guy performed martial arts. Maybe the strap in his gym bag really was some type of workout equipment and the award in his glove compartment really did belong to his stepson. Then again, maybe not. Maybe I could visit the local martial arts studios with his picture and see if anyone recognized him.

I put my fingers to the keyboard, typed in "martial arts Dallas," and hit the "enter" key. Holy frijole! My search returned thousands of entries. I hadn't realized just how many different types of martial arts there were. Karate. Tae kwon do. Jiu-jitsu. Kung fu. Capoeira, which incorporated dance movement. Kenpo. Kickboxing. Tai chi. Judo. Aikido. Eskrima. Krav Maga. And that was only the ones I could pronounce. There were dozens more, originating in Asia, Israel, Germany, Brazil, and nearly every country in between. Some forms involved using only the body, especially the feet and hands, while others incorporated weapons, ranging from knives and maces to staffs and clubs. Who knew there were so many—*and such horrifying*—ways to engage in combat? And did Jack Smirnoff know how to handle a mace? Would this investigation end with my name on a death certificate along with *cause of death: blunt force trauma*?

As my intestines tangled themselves in anxiety, the words on a screen for a mixed martial arts studio caught my eye. *Free introductory lesson.* A single lesson wouldn't get me far, but it could give me a better understanding of exactly what I was up against. And, hey, *free.* Only a fool would pass up such a bargain. Besides, mixed martial arts, or MMA, would likely give me the best overview, right?

I logged into the site and signed myself up for a class

the following night. Nick, too. As a former linebacker on his high school football team and MVP of the Tax Maniacs, the IRS softball team that played in the federal interagency league, Nick was always up for sports. Besides, if I got scared at the lesson I could hide behind him. He wasn't just the love of my life; he was a potential human shield.

Of course my fears would be for naught if I couldn't track down Jack Smirnoff. Out of ideas for the moment, I sat back in my chair to think. If I was going to find this guy, I'd have to go about it a different way. *But how?*

As Leslie had pointed out, this suspect certainly didn't follow the typical catfishing pattern. Most of the people who engaged in a catfish scam never actually met their victims face-to-face. While they might schedule dates or meet-ups, they usually failed to show or bowed out at the last minute, claiming some type of emergency. It was unusual that Jack Smirnoff had actually shown up for multiple in-person encounters.

Like the guy who'd duped Nataya, Leslie, and Julia, many of the catfishers were after money. They'd prey on lonely people, developing a seemingly intimate relationship over time online. They'd share supposed secrets, engage in heart-to-heart discussions, and encourage their intended victims to do the same. Pure bullshit designed to develop a sense of closeness and trust. Once the catfishers thought they had their quarry on the hook, they'd ask for money to be wired to them, perhaps claim to be stranded somewhere after a mugging with no cash to get home. Still, most of these scam artists spent no money courting their victims. Jack Smirnoff had actually invested some money to further his illegal endeavors.

Of course some who engaged in catfishing simply seemed to get a thrill out of toying with people or living a fantasy existence online. After all, people could be anyone they wanted to be in cyberspace. A bored midwestern housewife with too much time on her hands after milking the cows could pose as a young lingerie model. A thirteen-year-old boy stinking of puberty hormones could pretend to be a successful architect in his mid-thirties and solicit dirty pics from young women he met online. A sixty-eight-year-old retired taxi driver from Sheboygan could become an all-star athlete turned aspiring feature film star and flirt with women young enough to be his granddaughters. Really, the Internet was one big masquerade ball.

Putting my meandering train of thought back on track, I pulled up the photos the women had e-mailed to me. I enlarged them to see Jack Smirnoff's face in more detail. He wore his eyeglasses in every snapshot. Attempting to make himself less readily identifiable without them, perhaps? In each picture, he had blue eyes and dark-brown hair. Nothing unusual immediately popped out at me.

I enlarged the pictures and zoomed in, looking the man over in minute detail. On closer inspection, I noted that he had a small freckle or mole on his jawline just under his left ear and that his roots were several shades lighter than his dark hair. It wasn't necessarily unusual for men in their forties to use hair color these days. After all, aging now seemed to be viewed more as an act of surrender than acceptance of a natural biological process. But I had to wonder if the dark hair was more of a disguise than an attempt to fight the forces of nature.

Hm-m . . .

My best bet for solving this case seemed to be posing as a potential victim for Jack Smirnoff on whatever dating site or sites he might be using now. Unfortunately, I had no idea how to track him down online. Though the Big D dating site had taken down his listing once the women registered complaints, he could be listed on other sites. He'd surely have used a different alias, though. Thanks to

Nataya, Leslie, and Julia, anyone who ran an Internet search for the name Jack Smirnoff would discover his shady history and steer clear of him.

I ran a simple search for "online dating sites." A multitude of general dating sites popped up, including Match.com, Chemistry.com, eHarmony, OkCupid, Zoosk, and Tinder. There were also niche dating sites. OurTime catered to the fifty and over crowd. Cougar Life matched women seeking younger men with men seeking older women. *Mommy issues, anyone?* VeggieDate catered to vegetarians, the only meat on its site coming in the form of beefcake. There was one called FarmersOnly.com for people interested in rural romance, a roll in the hay, perhaps. The Big and Beautiful site featured full-figured people. Sugardaddie.com matched successful men to the shallow women they deserved, while the Ashley Madison site connected married people looking to have affairs with unscrupulous people willing to indulge their adulterous desires. There were also sites for people looking not for lasting relationships but mere sexual hookups, no strings attached . . . unless, of course, one wanted to be tied to a bedpost. *Ick.* Just looking at the latter sites made me want to disinfect my laptop screen and keyboard.

There seemed to be as many dating sites as there were forms of martial arts. I supposed I shouldn't have been surprised by the number and variety of services. After all, online dating had become a multibillion-dollar industry. Love may be blind, patient, and kind, but it doesn't come cheap these days.

Clearly, trying to find Jack Smirnoff on the sites would be like looking for a needle in a cyber haystack. Short of signing up for memberships on the sites and paging through all of the listings one by one, which I didn't have time to do, I didn't know how to find the guy.

But while I didn't know a better way to go about cornering this guy on the Internet, I knew someone who might. Luckily for me, he sat right down the hall.

I picked up my phone and punched the three-digit code for the office of Josh Schmidt, my fellow special agent who was the office tech specialist. Maybe there was something he could do to help me keep this case moving along.

"You busy?" I asked when Josh answered.

"I could spare a minute."

"Great," I said. "I'll be right down."

I scurried down the hall to Josh's office, sliding my laptop onto his desk next to his state-of-the-art Alienware machine. Like me, Josh was on the short side, another "pipsqueak." He had pink cheeks, baby-blue eyes, and cherubic blond curls. But when it came to technology, the guy was a virtual cyborg. He made technology his bitch.

After explaining the situation and showing Josh the photos, I raised my palms. "I'm at a loss here. Since the three women I met with have gone public, I'd hazard a guess that if Smirnoff is still soliciting victims online he's changed the name and photo he's using for his profiles. I need to track this guy down, but I don't know how to do it. Do you have any ideas?"

"Of course I do." He nudged me out of the way to take control of my laptop.

While I had zero interest in technology, other than having it provide me with easy shoe shopping and the ability for my brothers to share cute photos of my nieces and nephews, I was curious to see what Josh might do to find the so-called Jack Smirnoff. I grabbed one of Josh's wing chairs, pulled it up next to his desk chair, and plunked myself down in it, peering over his shoulder as he began to type on the keyboard.

He turned my way and frowned. "Give a guy some space to work, will ya?"

"Oops. Sorry, buddy." I used my feet to scoot the chair back a foot or two.

Josh logged on to a site called TinEye and uploaded Jack Smirnoff's head shot photo. "TinEye has developed some good large-scale image search and recognition software."

Whuh? "Dumb it down for me."

Josh cast a look my way, obviously pitying my lack of technological savvy. "This site will find the image if it appears in other public places online."

Sure enough, a moment later the site gave a listing of two other places where the head shot had been posted. The first was on a site called Catfish Finder. Leslie Gleason had posted Jack's photo there, along with the words: *Does anyone know this a-hole? He ripped me off for two grand!* The picture also appeared in a blog about online scams. Nataya Lawan had posted Smirnoff's pic there and told women to *avoid this con artist at all costs!* Unfortunately, the listings didn't get me anywhere.

"What about private sites?" I asked Josh. "Can you search those?"

"I've got a similar program I can use to match photos on private sites," he said, "but you'll need the site owner's permission or a search warrant first."

Poop. I doubted the dating sites would willingly let us go on a fishing expedition through their clients' profiles. Too much personal information and too great a risk of backlash if their clients learned they'd turned over private data without a court mandate. I also knew there were dozens, if not hundreds, of dating sites. The chances of a judge issuing a broad warrant to cover even a small list of the most popular sites were slim to none. I'd probably be tossed out of court and told to prove a connection between the con artist and a specific site before making any such request again.

"What about these dating sites?" I asked. "Would they be able to run an internal search for the photo and see if he's listed on their site?" If so, maybe I wouldn't need a court order after all. Maybe I could get these sites to do the searches for me. After all, we had a mutual interest in stopping catfishers from preying on people online.

"It's possible," Josh said, "assuming their tech staff has the right programs and knows what they're doing. If I handled the search, there's less risk something will fall through the cracks."

"Got any other tricks up your sleeve?" I asked Josh.

"Abracadabra." Josh pretended to wave magic wands before pulling up another Web site and uploading the image a second time.

"What's this site for?"

"To assist people in locating stolen cameras."

"How's that going to help us?" I asked.

"Expensive cameras imbed their serial number and other data in the digital images," he explained. "People usually use this site to track down the person who stole their camera. But if we can find other images taken with the same camera used to take the catfisher's head shot we might be able to find out who he is or find other pictures of him posted in other public places online."

"Wow. The Internet is truly amazing."

Josh cast me a look. "It's only as amazing as the user."

"True," I said. "*You* are amazing, Josh." *Jeez.* Still, I supposed I couldn't fault the guy for having an ego in constant need of feeding. As small and nerdy as he was, he'd surely taken some crap back in high school. These were his glory days. Why not let him enjoy it?

A few seconds later, the site popped up with some information identifying the type of camera used—a Nikon D90—along with a seven-digit serial number. It also gave the date and time the image was recorded. Per the site, the head shot of Jack Smirnoff had been taken on January 14 at 2:33 in the afternoon. *Gotta love the World Wide Web!*

"Now," Josh said, "I'm going to input the camera model and serial number and see what other online images were taken with the same camera."

He typed in the information and hit "enter." A few seconds later, a seemingly endless list of links with thumbnail photos appeared. Josh enlarged several of the photos at the top of the list. All of them had the copyright symbol and the logo of a photography studio in the lower right-hand corner. © *GOODE PHOTOGRAPHIC ARTS.*

"A-ha! Now I know where the catfisher had his head shots done." Of course Smirnoff had been smart enough to crop the logo out of the photo before posting it. But not smart enough to realize the photo could still possibly be used to track him down. That gave me one clue as to his identity. He wasn't someone who worked in IT. "Thanks, Josh."

"Glad I could help." Josh handed my computer back to me. "The rest is on you."

I took my laptop, returned to my office, and looked up the phone number for the photography studio online. Fortunately, the photographer, Savannah Goode, was in between shoots and was able to speak with me when I called.

"What's this about?" Savannah asked, her tone tentative and suspicious. Who could blame her? I'd be a little hesitant, too, if someone in federal law enforcement phoned me out of the blue.

"You're not in any trouble," I told her. "I just have some questions about a photo that was taken at your studio." Or, more precisely, about the person in the photo.

"I'm pretty busy," she said. "Can I just answer your questions now by phone?"

In my experience, and as evidenced by my earlier trip to J.B.'s condo, in-person meetings yielded better results.

Witnesses felt less accountable to agents over the phone and didn't always put forth their best efforts to help. But in person they had a harder time refusing me. I'd like to think it was because of my charm, but more likely it was because of the gun holstered at my hip.

"I'll be as brief as possible," I told her, "and I'd be happy to work around your schedule. I can come in before or after your normal business hours if that would help."

"It would," she said. "I've got back-to-back bookings all day tomorrow. Why don't you come by at eight in the morning?"

"Great," I said though, to be honest, I was thinking, *ugggh*. I'm not much of a morning person. Besides, Dallas traffic at that time of day was a bitch. But it was a bitch I'd have to face. "See you then."

I put my phone aside and set about winnowing down the list of links Josh had found for me, the ones with photos that had also been taken by Goode Photographic Arts. Many of the links were to couples' wedding sites, which they'd made public either by mistake or because imposing a password proved problematic when trying to share with extended family and friends. The photos included bridal portraits, posed photographs of the wedding party and family, brides and grooms shoving cake into each other's mouths, and candid shots taken at the reception. My personal favorite was the one of a bridesmaid in a long pink brocade dress. She'd apparently enjoyed one too many glasses of champagne, fallen backward into a hotel fountain, and had a hell of a time pulling herself out with three yards of soaked brocade weighing her down. *Did that make it a night to remember, or a night to forget?* The next shot showed a laughing groomsman yanking her out by her arms. Such a gentleman. Unfortunately, neither the chivalrous groomsman nor anyone else at the wedding appeared to be Jack Smirnoff.

Dozens of professional head shots popped up on business sites, everything from a smiling dentist, to a serious-looking probate attorney, to a caterer in a white chef's coat and hat who was brandishing a wooden spoon. None of the head shots belonged to anyone who looked even remotely like Jack Smirnoff, however.

My gaze ran down the list, searching for listings on dating sites. *Bingo!* There was a link to a singles ad on Craigslist. I clicked on the link and took a peek. While the thumbnail appeared to be a sandy-haired man rather than a dark-haired one, it could still be Jack Smirnoff. After all, changing your hair color took only a trip to the pharmacy and a few measly bucks.

I couldn't tell from the thumbnail whether this guy had the telltale freckle or mole, so I clicked on the link to take a better look. *Nope. Definitely not our guy.* The man in the photo was too young, twenty-five or so, and had a black tattoo encircling his neck.

I backed out and returned to the list, clicking on the links and finding lots of nice shots, but none of Jack Smirnoff.

Looked like I'd hit a wall for the time being. But even if it took a battering ram, I'd get through that wall. I owed it to every lovelorn person who'd been duped in the name of romance.

chapter seven

*H*oles in Her Story

I decided to call some of the dating sites and see where that might get me.

After identifying myself to a female executive at one of the major sites, I explained the situation. "We'd like to search your database and see if this man has approached women through your site."

"What name did you say he was using?"

"Jack Smirnoff."

"Like the vodka?"

"Exactly."

"Hold on a moment. I'll see if we've got a listing for him."

So far, so good.

She paused for a moment as she apparently ran a search. "No. Nothing comes up under the last name Smirnoff. Could he be using a different name?"

"It's possible," I said, "maybe even probable. Unfortunately, I don't know what his other aliases might be. But we have his head shot. Our tech specialist has told me that if he has access to your site he can run a search for the pictures and see if they show up in one of your clients' profiles."

The woman exhaled sharply. "I can understand your

conundrum, and honestly I'd like to help. The problem is that our privacy statement assures our clients that their identities will be kept confidential. We don't put a client in touch with another client unless and until both parties express interest. Even then we provide only screen names and an internal messaging system that clients can use until they decide whether they want to share their true identities and contact information. They have to jump through a lot of hoops before they get any real information. These levels are put in place to give our clients a sense of safety and security. I don't see how we can willingly violate that trust without risking our reputation."

Ugh. "Isn't it just as risky to your reputation to let a predator use your site to troll for victims?"

"That's certainly a concern," she conceded, "though we take measures to warn our clients of the risks they assume by using any online service."

"So you won't let us access your database without a judge's order?"

"Sorry, but no."

"I figured as much." I decided to take a similar approach to the one I'd take with J.B. at Big D Dating Service. I'd much prefer to keep the investigation in the hands of the IRS, but a girl's gotta do what a girl's gotta do. Especially when her chances of getting a court order were minuscule. "What if I sent you the photograph we have of Jack Smirnoff? You could have someone on your tech team run a search and see if it matches any profile pics in your system. If that were the case, you could determine whether he'd contacted any women through your site, get in touch with them, and ask them to call me."

"That could work," the woman said. "I'll have to check with the tech department and see if they have the capability to search by picture. But assuming they do, this plan is a go."

"Wonderful! What e-mail address should I send the photo to?"

She gave me an address and within ten seconds of my ending the call Smirnoff's head shot was on its way to her. Over the next hour, I had the same discussion with staff at a dozen other dating sites. With any luck, one of them would soon be in touch to tell me that they'd found Smirnoff in their system and identified more victims.

I spent what remained of the afternoon listening to KCSH while working up some numbers in a tax evasion case against a window-washing service and discussing a potential plea bargain with Ross O'Donnell, an attorney at the Justice Department who handled many of the IRS cases.

Today, excluding the professionally produced commercials, Flo mentioned no fewer than twenty-nine local and regional businesses. She'd mentioned Doo-Wop Donuts at least three times. "Try a cruller and cappuccino," Flo said. "There's no better way to start your day."

On my drive home, I decided to make a detour by Doo-Wop Donuts. A cruller might be a good way to start a day, but it wasn't a bad way to end one, either.

The donut shop was housed in a fifties-style drive-in. The circular windows on the sides of the building appeared to be the holes in the sprinkled donuts painted on the walls around them. White Christmas lights were strung along the edges of the aluminum roof that overhung the parking spots, as well as along the poles that supported the menu boards and speaker systems. Two teenage girls wearing pink coveralls and roller skates carried bags and boxes of donuts out to the cars, making change from the money belts at their waists.

I pulled into an open bay next to a tired-looking young mother with three kids in a minivan. The kids were out of their car seats, high on sugar, screaming and hopping up and down and making the car bounce. "Stop that jump-ing!" the mother hollered. "You'll wear out the shocks!"

I climbed out of my car and walked to the building, ignoring the sign on the glass door that read: "EMPLOY-EES ONLY" and opening it to go inside.

Inside I found a blond woman wearing the same pink coveralls as the carhops but tennis shoes rather than skates. She glanced up from a table loaded with tray after tray of glazed donuts. "Bathrooms are around back."

"I don't need to use the bathroom," I said.

She held up the pastry bag she'd been using to apply chocolate frosting to the donuts and used it to point out-side. "You can order from your car. The girls will bring the donuts out to you."

"I'm not here to pick up donuts, either," I said. "I need to speak with the owner."

Her face clouding in concern, she set down the pastry bag, wiped her hands on a dishcloth, and stepped over to the counter, giving me a once-over. "I'm the owner. How can I help you?"

I handed her one of my business cards, which only made her face cloud over more. Yeah, people aren't so happy when an IRS agent shows up on their doorstep. We ranked right up there with magazine salesmen and purvey-ors of religions.

"Internal Revenue Service." She looked from the card to me. "Is there a problem?"

"No, not a problem," I assured her. "I just need some information. I noticed that you advertise on KCSH Radio. I'm wondering if you can tell me how much you pay the station for your ads. I believe you paid cash, correct?"

According to the financial records Flo had provided to the auditor, KCSH had received no payments from Doo-Wop Donuts. The business wasn't listed among the paid advertisers. Still, I'd bet dollars to these chocolate-frosted donuts that this shop had made some sort of under-the-table deal with Flo.

The woman was silent for a moment, her darting eyes telling me that a lot of thoughts were zinging through the brain behind them. "I don't know what you're talking about," she said finally, returning her gaze not to my face but to a spot over my shoulder. "We don't pay to advertise on the radio."

I moved my head slightly, forcing her to look me in the eye. "You don't?"

She swallowed hard. "No."

I call "bullshit." "I heard the radio announcer mention Doo-Wop Donuts no less than three times today. She even mentioned that you're running an early-bird buy-one-get-one-free promotion for customers who come in before seven in the morning this week. How would Flo Cash know about your special if she hadn't discussed it with you?"

The woman hesitated a moment, then gestured out the glass front doors. "Maybe she saw our sign."

I turned to look. Sure enough, the letters on the roadside marquee sign read: "EARLY BIRDS—BUY 1 GET 1 FREE B4 7 AM THIS WEEK ONLY." Still, the donut shop wasn't located between Flo's house and the station. If Flo wanted a donut, why would she drive out of her way to come here when surely there were plenty of other donut shops located conveniently along her route?

I eyed the woman intently. "You are familiar with Flo Cash, aren't you?"

As before, the woman hesitated. "I'm not sure. We get so many customers in here I don't remember them all."

There were as many holes in her story as there were in her donuts. But there didn't seem to be much use in pushing her, at least not at the moment. She might change her tune once she had time to think things over. Then again, I could be totally off base here. Maybe Flo was telling me the truth, that she simply liked the donuts and that's why she mentioned Doo-Wop on her show. This woman could seem hesitant simply because she was nervous. Having a federal law enforcement agent appear unexpectedly on your doorstep didn't exactly give people the warm fuzzies.

"All righty then," I said. "As long as I'm here, I might as well get a mixed dozen. Can you throw one together for me?"

The woman glanced out at my car and at the young girls in their coveralls milling about. It was clear she'd prefer I follow their normal ordering procedure, but I just as clearly didn't want spit in my donuts. I'd take them right here where I could keep an eye on things.

The woman seemed to sense that I wasn't going anywhere, and set about packing me a box of mixed donuts, even throwing in an extra blueberry. "I've made it a baker's dozen."

"Thanks." I wasn't sure if the extra donut was standard procedure or an attempt for her to get on my good side, but it would take more than flour and sugar and vanilla to ease my suspicions.

She set the box on the countertop. "That'll be nine dollars."

I handed her my debit card and she ran it through a machine. I typed in my four-digit PIN, took the receipt and box of donuts from her, and headed back toward the door. Just before exiting, I glanced back her way. "If you happen to remember anything," I said, "give me a call. It could be in your best interests." Unlike eating a thousand calories of pure sugar, carbs, and custard, which was definitely not in my thighs' best interests. Still, that fact didn't stop me from shoving a Boston cream into my mouth on the walk back to my car.

chapter eight

$\mathcal{R}$oad to Nowhere

KCSH kept me company as I slowly made my way through the Dallas morning rush-hour traffic on Thursday morning. My car's speedometer might as well have measured my progress in inches rather than miles. That they called the morning commute rush hour made no sense to me. Everybody might be in a hurry, but nobody was going anywhere fast. A more appropriate term would be "tush hour." After all, we were all sitting on our asses, cursing the cars ahead of us. At least I had a mug full of hot coffee and a couple of Doo-Wop donuts to enjoy on the way.

I crawled north on Central Expressway, exiting onto Lovers Lane and heading east. Finally, I arrived at Savannah Goode's photography studio, barely making my 8:00 appointment.

A black woman who appeared to be in her early thirties met me at the door, turning the lock with a *click*. Her hair hung long and straight, her big brown eyes rimmed with thick mascara. She wore a loose-fitting tunic belted at the waist and a pair of stylish leggings that would allow for easy movement as she moved around to take her camera shots. "Are you the lady from the IRS?" she asked.

I held out a hand. "I am. IRS Special Agent Tara Holloway."

We shook hands and I thanked her for agreeing to meet with me. She waved me in and led me to a small room containing an oblong wooden table with six chairs all angled to face the screen at the front of the room. A projector sat in the middle of the table. I surmised that this was the room where she and her clients reviewed the photographs she'd taken.

She pulled out one of the chairs for me, turning it back to face the table. "Have a seat."

"Thanks." I placed my briefcase on the table and dropped into the chair.

She took a seat next to me. "You said you had some questions about a photo?"

"About the person in the photo, actually," I replied. "He's one of your clients."

"A client?" She paused a moment. "I may not be able to tell you much. Most people come in, get their photos taken, look them over, and place an order. If they want digital images, I download them to a thumb drive before they leave. If they order prints, those are mailed to them later. Unless they're a wedding client, that's about the extent of things."

Unwilling to have my hopes dashed just yet, I snapped open the latches on my briefcase, removed the photos of Jack Smirnoff that I'd printed out, and handed them to her. "I'm trying to locate this man."

She glanced down at the photo. "Are you sure he had this head shot taken here? I don't see my copyright notice."

"I'm positive." I explained how Josh had been able to identify the source of the images online. "Any idea who the man in the picture is?"

She looked down at the photo once more and frowned. "He looks vaguely familiar, but I photograph so many people they tend to all run together after a while." She looked up. "Not that I'd ever tell my clients that."

Understandable. "The man in the photo has been going by the name Jack Smirnoff," I told her. "We suspect that's not his real name, though. He's wanted for questioning in connection with some financial crimes. Could you check your files and see if he gave you his real name? Maybe an address or phone number, too?"

"Give me just a minute." She stood and left the room, returning a moment later with a laptop. It took a few seconds to boot up, but once it did she put her fingers to the keyboard. "What was that last name again?"

"Smirnoff," I said.

"Like the vodka?" she asked.

"Exactly."

She typed the name in, hit the "enter" key, and leaned in to look at the screen. I leaned in with her.

She pointed to the display. "Looks like he provided that same name when he had his photos taken here."

Damn! So much for finding out his real identity.

She ran her finger down the screen, stopping an inch or two lower. "He provided an address on Royal Lane."

Royal Lane was a major east–west thoroughfare that ran just south of, and roughly perpendicular to, the northern stretch of the 635 freeway. I jotted the information down. 12705 Royal Lane, # 256, in Dallas. *Hm-m.* I made note of the phone number and e-mail addresses he'd provided, too, flipping back a few pages in my notes to compare them to the phone number and e-mail address he'd given Julia, Nataya, and Leslie. While the e-mail account was the same, the phone number didn't match. The phone number he'd given to Savannah Goode was a local number, while the one he'd given to the Big D Dating Service and the women he'd victimized began with 303, one of the area codes for Denver and surrounding communities.

I looked over at Savannah. "Do you know if this address and phone number are valid?"

She shrugged. "No idea. I only use the address for mailing printed photos. I don't recall any photos being returned for an incorrect address. I rarely need to call or e-mail a client other than for appointment reminders. I don't bother sending a reminder if the appointment was made within a day or two preceding the shoot since people usually remember to show up when they schedule so close in time."

In other words, even though the name he'd given was false, the contact information could be legit. My nerves began to buzz. The phone number he'd used with the three victims I'd met had since been disconnected, but maybe the local address and phone number would prove to be viable leads. After all, the guy seemed to think that cropping out the copyright that referenced Goode Photography was enough to cover his tracks. He probably wasn't aware that the photo could be digitally traced. I mentally crossed my fingers that the address or phone number would pan out.

I gestured to her laptop. "Can you tell me how he paid for the photos?"

She tapped the keyboard, pulling up his account records. "Cash. The account shows he paid for digital files only. He didn't order any print copies."

"Any chance he's had other photos taken here?"

Savannah tapped her keyboard, pulling up Smirnoff's image files. "Looks like he's done another shoot since the one that included the photo you showed me. I offer a twenty-five-percent discount for repeat customers."

Good marketing strategy. "When was the second shoot?"

"Early May."

So he was a repeat customer. That could work to my advantage.

Savannah cut her eyes my way. "Do you want to see the more recent shots?"

I fought the urge to hug her. So many people we agents talked to were uncooperative and fearful, but Savannah was willing to share information and evidence. She was making my job easy, God bless her. "That would be great."

She pulled up a screen full of thumbnails, enlarging the first one.

A-ha! Jack Smirnoff appeared on the screen, but in these photos his hair was longer, shaggier, and colored a lighter ginger brown rather than the dark brown he'd had in the photos his victims had provided to me. He wore a different pair of eyeglasses, ones with thin gray frames and boxy lenses, and his once-blue eyes were now chocolate brown. Whether blue, brown, or some other shade was his natural color was anyone's guess. The only constant was the telltale freckle or mole on his left jawbone, near his ear.

I raised hopeful brows at Savannah. "Any chance you can e-mail me copies of those photos?"

"Sure," she said. "What's your e-mail?"

I rattled off my IRS e-mail address and she set about sending the photos to me right then and there. *If only every witness we interviewed could be so helpful!*

When she finished, we rose from the table and I extended my hand for a good-bye shake. "I really appreciate your cooperation. Will you let me know if he makes an appointment to have more photos taken?"

"Of course."

With that, I gave her my business card, left the studio, and climbed into my car. The instant my butt hit the seat I whipped out my cell phone to dial the number Jack

Smirnoff had given when he'd had his portraits made. It was probably another burner phone, but due diligence required I try it. While I expected an annoying three-tone sound and a recorded voice informing me that the number was no longer in service, what I got instead was a recording for a Tom Thumb grocery store.

Huh?

The recording instructed me to press "1" for the store hours and location, "2" for the bakery, "3" for the deli, and so on. I jabbed the button on my phone to turn on my keypad and hit the "0" button to be transferred to customer service. When a man answered, I asked to speak to Jack Smirnoff.

"Like the rum?" the man asked.

"Vodka," I corrected, "but yes."

"Is he an employee?"

I had no idea, but said, "Yes," anyway. If he'd intentionally given this number, he must work there, right? But if he'd simply pulled the number out of the air—*or his ass*—then he'd have no traceable connection to the store and they'd be unable to help me.

"Just a moment," the man said, putting me on hold.

My knee bounced up and down in excitement. Would he soon connect me with the catfisher? If so, what would I say? I certainly didn't want to clue him in that the federal government was on his tail. He'd flee the store and disappear.

There was no time to figure things out before the man returned to the line. "Sorry, but there's nobody in the system by that name."

Darn it! "Maybe he used to work there," I speculated. "Would he still show up if he'd quit or been fired?"

"No," the man said. "I've only got the current list. But I'd be happy to transfer you to the management office if you'd like."

"Please do."

I was put on a brief hold; then a woman came on the line. I identified myself and explained my situation.

"Sorry," the woman said, "but I can't give out information on employees. Not without a subpoena or court order. I'd get fired for it."

Ugh. Everyone was so afraid of being sued, it's a wonder anyone got out of bed without a court order these days. I hated to pressure this woman, but I would also hate to waste my time getting a court order requiring her to provide me the information if she didn't actually have any information to give me. "If Jack Smirnoff's never been an employee," I said, "you wouldn't be breaking any rules by simply telling me he's never worked there, right?" *Slick move, huh?*

She hesitated a moment. "I suppose not. Just a second." There was the sound of keys being struck as she apparently ran a search of their employment records. "No," she said a few seconds later. "We've never had an employee by the name Jack Smirnoff."

"Thanks for checking. I really appreciate it."

We ended the call. *Rats.* Looked like Jack had pulled the random phone number out of his ass, after all.

I mulled things over for a moment. Royal Lane wasn't far from the photography studio, so why not check out the address he'd provided? It, too, could be a dead end, but then again, maybe it wasn't. It couldn't hurt to check things out.

I started my car and drove up Central Expressway to Royal Lane. Fifteen minutes later, I'd been up and down the road, passed Koreatown twice—once on my way west and a second time as I headed back east—and still hadn't found the address I was looking for. To make matters worse, my car was running on fumes.

I pulled into a gas station and, while the pump was

filling the tank, searched for the address online. Nothing came up. A visit to the Dallas Central Appraisal District Web site told me that the highest address on Royal Lane was 10805. Looked like Jack Smirnoff had pulled his supposed home address out of his ass, too. His colon was evidently filled with all kinds of fictitious information. I wonder if he had any truth up there, too. I'd like to give the jerk an enema and find out.

chapter nine

Misfortune Cookie

When I returned to my office, I had several voice mails and e-mails from the dating services. All of them said the same thing. The head shot Jack Smirnoff used in his Big D Dating Service profile had appeared on none of the other sites.

What did this mean? Had he only listed a profile on the Big D site? Or had he used different head shots on other sites? If he used different head shots, had he taken photos at another photography studio in addition to Savannah's? My lack of luck in the catfishing case was causing me no end of frustration.

I logged into my e-mail and sent copies of the new head shots to the dating sites, along with a message that read: *The catfisher had additional head shots taken. Please search your site for these new pics. Thank you!*

I also forwarded Smirnoff's new head shots to Josh and dialed his office from my desk phone. "Hey, buddy," I said when he picked up. "I just sent you some new photos." I asked if he could mine them for data like he'd done with the earlier pic and send me the resulting links.

"I'll get right on it."

The only way I knew to try to find the guy was to see if he'd posted the new head shots on a public dating site somewhere, dropping the bait for his next catfishing victim. I crossed my fingers something would turn up, though I doubted it would. The free, public sites didn't seem like places a con artist would look for financially stable victims. Anyone who couldn't afford a membership fee at a more reputable dating site probably wouldn't be able to successfully cash his bogus checks.

Nataya had sent me her credit card bill that showed the fraudulent charges made at The Galleria. Whoever had used her card clearly had good taste. He—or she, since it wasn't certain Jack was the culprit—had spent hefty sums at the Armani store, Michael Kors, and the St. Croix Shop. I decided to make a trip to The Galleria and see what Security could tell me.

Twenty minutes later, I entered the mall, window-shopping as I made my way to the administrative offices. Luckily for me, the security supervisor was in his office, his round, shiny forehead reflecting the fluorescent lights above like a miner's headlamp. Appropriate, since I was here to mine for information, hoping to hit the mother lode.

"Take a seat," he said, gesturing to a boxy vinyl chair in front of his desk.

I jumped right in. "I'm working a check fraud case," I told him. "One of the victims believes the man who passed the bad check also stole her credit card. It was used at a half-dozen stores here a few months ago."

I pulled out the copy of Nataya Lawan's MasterCard bill and laid it on his desk.

He looked it over, his eyes narrowing. "This name sounds familiar." He raised a finger. "Give me just a second." He logged on to his computer, tapped a few keys, and read over the screen before turning his focus back to me. "I've got a file on this." He gestured toward his screen. "It says she called Security several days after the card was used here and reported the thefts. One of my men spoke with the staff at the stores and checked the security camera footage. He was able to determine which customer used the card." He glanced at his screen again. "Says here it was a Caucasian male estimated to be around forty. Brown hair. No distinguishing characteristics of note. The outdoor feeds caught him exiting the mall but lost him at the edge of the parking lot."

Damn.

He shook his head. "I hate to tell you this, but this is pretty typical. These credit card thieves know they've got a limited window to use the stolen cards, and they rack up as many charges as they can before the card gets canceled. They also know to park off-site so they can't be identified by their license plates."

I, too, was all too familiar with this kind of fraud. I supposed it had been too much to hope the guy would have slipped up.

I stood to go. "I appreciate your help."

"Anytime," he said.

I returned to my car feeling frustrated. Sometimes it seemed that my work was futile, a vain attempt to put out financial fires. While I was busting my ass trying to nab one crook, ten new crooks cropped up to take his place, taking advantage of more victims. Would it never end?

Probably not, I told myself. *But that's no excuse to stop trying. Quit your whining.*

While I was out of the office, I figured I might as well follow up with some of the other businesses Flo Cash had mentioned on KCSH. The owner of Doo-Wop Donuts might have claimed she'd paid nothing in return for Flo promoting her business on the radio, but I wasn't buying that she hadn't bought the ads. It was doubtful Flo would take up valuable airtime extolling the virtues of a business

if she weren't being paid. Flo might not charge top advertising rates for the casual shout-outs she gave some of the
businesses, but surely she wasn't simply mentioning them
out of the goodness of her heart. Somewhere, somehow,
she was getting compensation. I was sure of it.

I pulled out the list of businesses Flo had mentioned
yesterday and looked for ones that were in the general
area of where I was now, north of downtown. I decided to
spend the rest of Thursday morning visiting two of the
businesses—a hair salon and a children's consignment
shop.

The salon, Hair to Dye For, sat on Walnut Hill Lane,
near the Dallas North Tollway, and appeared to cater to the
well-heeled clientele who lived in the upscale neighbor-
hoods nearby, including Preston Hollow, home to former
president George W. Bush. A string of silver bells hung
from the front door, announcing my entry with a *tinkle-
tinkle-tinkle*. The smells of fruit-scented shampoo and
styling products danced in my nose.

The receptionist sat on a stool behind an elevated
counter. "Good morning. Do you have an appointment?"

"No," I said. "No appointment."

She turned and called back over her shoulder at the four
stylists working on clients at their stations, "Can anyone
take a walk-in?"

I raised a palm. "I'm not in need of services."

She ran her gaze over my locks. "Are you sure about
that?"

Okay, so maybe I'd skimped on my usual morning routine to make sure I got to the portrait studio on time.
Sheesh. "I'm from the federal government," I said. "I need
to speak to the owner."

She looked just as incredulous that I could be a federal
agent as she was about my professed lack of need for styl-

ing services. Really, how many asses would I have to kick before people would start taking me seriously?

The woman stood from her seat. "Mitzi's the owner. Give me a second." She walked over to an attractive sixty-ish blonde who was putting the finishing touches on a raven-haired thirtysomething. The receptionist pulled the stylist aside to whisper in her ear.

Mitzi's gaze snapped from the floor to me, her posture stiffening. Once more I felt like the unwelcome magazine salesman. She said something to the receptionist, then stepped back to her client to apply a final coating of hair spray.

The receptionist returned to me. "Let me show you to the office."

"Thanks."

She led me to an open door at the end of a short hall-way at the back of the space and gestured to a leopard-print chair inside the room. "Have a seat. Mitzi will be back as soon as she's finished."

My butt had barely hit the chair when Mitzi entered the room, closing the door behind her. "How can I help you?" she asked as she circled the small antique desk to take a seat behind it.

I laid my business card on the desk and nudged it toward her. "I'm with the Internal Revenue Service. I'm investigating a company that your salon advertises with."

"*D Magazine*?" she asked, referencing a ritzy local rag.

"No."

"*The Dallas Morning News*?" she inquired. "We buy ads in their *FD* magazine insert."

The insert was a luxury lifestyle mag, a glossy supplement published ten times a year. Surely those ads cost a pretty penny.

"No," I replied. "Not that, either."

Parallel lines formed between her perfectly waxed brows as they drew inward. "The only other ads we run are discount coupons for first-time clients in the Dollar Deals mailers. Is that what you're referring to?"

The mailers arrived once a month in a thick envelope that included coupons for neighborhood businesses offering anything from carpet cleaning to shoe repair. I routinely used the coupons for my dry cleaning.

"I'm not referring to print ads," I told the woman.

"Print ads are all we do," Mitzi replied. "Commercials on television or the radio are too expensive and not well targeted. There's no point in paying for that type of advertising when our primary clientele are higher-income people who live within a two- or three-mile radius of the salon."

Hm-m. Not only did this woman know Brazilian blowouts; she also knew business.

"I'm talking about your ads on KCSH Radio."

"Like I said," Mitzi replied with a shrug, "we don't do radio ads."

I eyed her closely. "Flo Cash has mentioned your salon multiple times on the air."

"Ms. Cash is a client," Mitzi said. "If she's mentioned the salon on air it must mean she's happy with our services."

"So you're not paying her cash for the ads?"

"Absolutely not. I need tax deductions as well as the next business. If I were paying for ads I'd want a paper trail in case my business was audited. Surely you, as an IRS agent, can understand that."

I could. Was I off base here, or was this woman not giving me the full story? Either way, it seemed I'd get no further with her. She'd risen from her seat, clearly dismissing me.

"All right, then." I, too, stood to go. "Thank you for your time."

She reached over to a basket on her desk, fished out a sample of conditioner, and held it out to me. "Try this. It'll do wonders to fight your frizz."

Frizz? The nerve of this woman! "We can't accept anything from taxpayers." Other than insults, that is. Those were generously and frequently tossed our way.

As I walked back through the salon, one of the stylists shook her head at something her client had just said. "What was he thinking, talking to you like that?" She pointed her scissors at her client's reflection in the mirror. "Next time he says something so stupid, you send him my way. I'll take care of him." She made a *snip-snip* motion with her scissors, and she and her client shared a raucous laugh.

I returned to my car and headed to Hand-Me-Down Town, the children's resale shop. I found the store's owner wrangling a secondhand portable crib in the back corner.

"Hello," I said. "I'm Special Agent Tara Holloway with IRS Criminal Investigations." I held out my business card.

Rather than taking it, she continued to wrestle with the crib but lifted her chin to indicate a high chair nearby. "Put it on the tray."

I laid my card on the plastic tray attached to the chair. "I'd like to ask you about your advertising," I said. "Specifically about payments to KCSH for radio time."

She hardly bothered to look up as she snapped the legs into place. "I don't pay KCSH for ads."

Ugh-h-h-h. . . . "You must compensate the station somehow," I said. After all, this was America, land of capitalists. You don't get something for nothing here. "Airtime is valuable. They wouldn't give it away for free."

She put a hand on the upper rail of the crib and jiggled it to test its stability. Satisfied, she finally focused her attention on me. "Look. I already told you I don't pay KCSH. I'm not giving you any further financial information. How do I know you're not some scam artist trying to steal my bank account number? How do I even know you're from the IRS?"

I gestured to my card on the high chair and pulled out my badge, holding it out to her. "Does this convince you?"

"No," she scoffed. "I've got no idea what an IRS badge is supposed to look like. How do I know it's for real?"

This wasn't the first time my position would be questioned, and it probably wouldn't be the last. While Americans were accustomed to hearing about armed agents from the FBI, ATF, and DEA, most people didn't realize the Treasury Department also had a crew of criminal law enforcement agents.

"How about this?" I said, pushing back my jacket to reveal the GLOCK holstered at my waist. "Standard federal government weapon."

The woman gasped, sputtered, and pointed to the door. "Out! Now!" she shrieked. "I don't allow guns in my shop!"

As a federal agent, I was exempt from regulations that allowed private store owners to prohibit weapons on their premises. But there seemed no point in pressing the issue, at least not right now. The woman was agitated and continued to scream at me. "This is a family business! A children's shop! You have no right to endanger my customers!"

I looked around the empty shop. *What customers?* I was tempted to ask. Nonetheless, I chose to comply, backing toward the door. "Don't be surprised if you get a subpoena from me."

She ushered me outside and stepped back into the shop, turning the inside knob and locking me out with a *click*. She issued a final glare and muffled shriek through the glass. "Don't be surprised if you get a call from my congressman's office telling you to stop threatening innocent people!"

She stepped away from the door without bidding me good-bye. *Seriously, where are people's manners these days?*

With a deep sigh of resignation, I returned to my car. By this time, it was nearing noon and my stomach growled to remind me to fill it. But first, I decided to drive by KCSH. I didn't expect to learn anything from merely driving past a building, of course, but I felt an instinctive urge to do it, like a shark circling its prey. Besides, part of me hoped Flo might spot me passing by and feel a little heat.

As I approached the building, a silver Toyota with a car-top sign for Szechuan Express turned into the lot. I rolled to a stop at the curb and pulled my dad's oversized field glasses from my glove compartment. A twentyish Asian deliveryman exited the car and carried two large bags inside. Putting the binoculars to my eyes, I aimed them through the front glass door of the radio station. Through the lenses I saw the man hand the bags to the young woman I'd met when I'd come to the station before. Rather than waiting for payment or even a tip, he turned immediately around and left the building, returning to his car. Odd that he hadn't collected payment for the food. *Maybe they'd ordered online with a credit card?*

The man slid into his car, closed the door, and appeared to be typing his next delivery address into the GPS system mounted on his dash. I took advantage of the time to pull up the restaurant's Web site on my phone. While the site listed a phone number customers could call to place orders, there appeared to be no way to submit an order online. *Hm-m . . .*

The delivery driver backed out of the space. I followed the car as it turned out of the lot, stopping behind it at a red light a block down. I waved my hand behind my windshield, hoping to get the driver's attention in his rearview mirror so I could signal him to pull over. Not easy to do without a siren or flashing lights. He failed to notice my flailing arm.

The light turned green and traffic began moving. I tried a different tack, pulling up next to the delivery driver and unrolling my window, waving again to try to get his attention. I even hollered, "Law enforcement! Pull over!"

No such luck. A throbbing bass line loud enough to reverberate through his car had drowned me out.

As the light turned green and we moved on another time, I pulled ahead of him and cut in, slowing so I could signal him to pull to the side behind me. He didn't give me a chance. Before I could even attempt a hand gesture, he zipped around me like a NASCAR driver hell-bent on winning a race. This guy could give Jeff Gordon a run for his money.

As we approached the next intersection, the light ahead cycled to yellow. The delivery driver gunned his engine to make the light. *Vroooom!* I gunned mine, too—*vroom!*—sailing through it a couple seconds after it turned red.

Whoop-whoop! Lights flashed as a police cruiser pulled up on my tail.

"Dammit!" I slammed a palm against my steering wheel. I couldn't manage to pull the delivery driver over, but Dallas PD had no problem getting me to pull aside. I knew better than to exit my car, which could appear to be an aggressive, threatening move, but once I'd stopped on the shoulder I put my hand out the window and gestured to hurry the cop up.

Unfortunately, he wasn't about to be rushed. He climbed slowly from his squad car and sauntered up to my vehicle, taking his sweet time about it. Apparently he'd failed to notice my U.S. government license plates. A rookie, no doubt.

I stuck my head and badge out the window. "IRS agent on official government business!" I hollered.

He stopped in his tracks and took a couple of steps in reverse to check out my back bumper. "Sorry, ma'am!" he called, raising a conciliatory palm. "Be on your way."

I pulled back into traffic, my eyes scanning the road ahead and the side streets for any sign of the Toyota. The Szechuan Express delivery car was nowhere to be seen. *Phooey, phooey, chop suey.* Still, it couldn't hurt to go directly to the restaurant, right? It was lunchtime, after all. I could pick up an order of orange chicken while I was there and kill two birds with one stone. Then I could eat one of those birds with a side of rice.

At the next red light, I checked the Web site for the restaurant, which was still pulled up on my phone. It was only a mile from my current location. *Good. Mama needs an egg roll.*

A couple of minutes later, I walked into the restaurant. A Chinese woman in a pretty silk blouse waited at the hostess stand. "Just one today?" she said in perfect English.

"Actually, I need to speak to the owner or manager," I said.

"What about?" she asked, her face drawing in alarm and her English sounding a little less perfect now.

"I'm from the IRS. I have some questions about the restaurant's advertisements."

Her mastery of the English language evaporated like steam from a dumpling. "I owner," she said. "But English not good."

I fought the urge to roll my eyes. "All I need to know is why your deliveryman just dropped two bags of food at KCSH but collected no payment."

"No pay?" the woman said. "Food no free. Customer must pay bill."

"Even Flo Cash?" I asked. "Or does she get some type of special deal because your business runs commercials on her station?"

"Specials?" the woman said. "Today special Buddha's delight."

I lost the battle. I rolled my eyes. "So suddenly you're going to pretend not to understand me, huh? In that case, hand me a take-out menu." I might have gotten no answers, but I would get lunch.

I placed my order for the special. I hadn't managed to kill the first bird, so I might as well let the other live, too. Besides, it wouldn't kill me to eat more vegetables.

I took a seat on a padded bench next to a bamboo plant in the small foyer. While I waited for my food, I thought things over. Maybe the businesses that Flo promoted off the books weren't paying her in cash. Maybe they were paying her in donuts and haircuts and moo goo gai pan. If only one of them would fess up. So far, all they'd been was a moo goo gai pan in the ass.

When my food was ready, the woman handed me the bag. "Thirteen eighty-five," she said, the perfect English having returned.

After paying for my lunch, I carried the bag out to the parking lot. The Toyota I'd been following earlier pulled in. I scurried over and cornered the deliveryman as he climbed out of his car. The restaurant's owner had been tight-lipped, but maybe I could get a confession out of this guy.

"I'm with the IRS," I said, flashing my badge. "I need to know why you didn't collect payment for the food you delivered to KCSH Radio."

He scrunched his shoulders. "I do what my boss tells me and she says not to collect when I deliver there. That's all I know."

"So you take food to KCSH regularly, then?"

"At least once or twice a week."

"How long has this been going on?"

"As long as I can remember," the guy replied. "I started working here three years ago."

The door to the restaurant banged open and the woman I'd spoken with a moment earlier stepped outside and shooed me away. "No time for questions! He busy! Many delivery!"

I rolled my eyes. "Thanks," I told the young man, stepping back to let him return to his job.

As I walked back to my car, I performed some mental calculations. The deliveryman had taken two large bags into KCSH, probably enough food for Flo and her three employees. Even assuming they'd chosen some of the less expensive items on the menu, their bill would be at least forty dollars. Multiply that by an estimated six meals per month and Flo had received $240 in value per month. Multiply that monthly amount by twelve and she'd received nearly three grand in food per year for at least three years. That amount warranted a quick mention or two on the air, didn't it?

I drove back to the IRS building, parked, and carried my lunch inside.

As I returned to my office, Nick looked up from his desk. "Got enough to share?"

"Sure," I said, angling my head in invitation toward my office. "It's a date."

Several minutes later, the two of us were kicked back in my wing chairs, our feet propped on my desk, chowing down.

In between bites, I told Nick about my unsuccessful morning trying to get information from the businesses Flo touted on air. "Nobody will tell me anything," I lamented. "Even when I showed my badge and gun. Am I losing my edge?"

"Nah," Nick said. "People just play dumb. Of course some of them don't have to play too hard."

He had that right. I swallowed a bite of rice. "You think Flo's giving these businesses air time in return for services and food? That she's got some type of off-the-books quid pro quo going on?" Or, in the case of the hair salon, *curl pro quo*?

"It wouldn't surprise me." He gave me a pointed look. "Now all you have to do is prove it."

Easier said than done.

Having polished off my egg roll and my portion of the Buddha's delight, I tossed my trash into my wastebasket and pulled a fortune cookie from the bag, tossing the second cookie to Nick. Of course the softball MVP snatched it easily from the air, despite my off-aim throw. I removed the clear crinkly wrap and snapped my crunchy cookie in two, stuffing the empty half into my mouth. As I chewed— *crunch-crunch-crunch*—I pulled the white slip of paper from the other half of the cookie and read it.

The empty vessel makes the loudest sound.

Huh. I swallowed the cookie and read it aloud to Nick. "What do you think it means?"

"Heck if I know. It makes me picture some hillbilly blowing into a jug to make music."

I doubted a jug band was what the fortune cookie manufacturer had in mind, but I supposed these cryptic fortunes were subject to all kinds of interpretation. "What's yours say?"

He looked up from the slip in his fingers. *"And they lived happily ever after."*

"That's not a fortune," I said. "That's the ending to a fairy tale."

"Maybe," he said, a grin playing about his lips. "And maybe I'm your Prince Charming."

"I don't want a Prince Charming," I said. "He didn't earn his position; he was born into it. Anyone can do that. I'd rather have a man of action, one who'd earned his place in the world. You know, a knight in shining armor."

Nick gathered up his things and tossed them in the trash can, too.

"Back to work?" I asked.

"Nope," he said, his face bearing a full-on grin now. "Off to see a blacksmith for a metal suit."

Aw. Sweet, huh? "Forget the metal suit for now," I said. "Put on your workout gear and come with me to an MMA class tonight. I found a place that offers a free introductory class and signed us up."

Given my small stature, my targets often underestimated me and rarely gave up without a fight. Tonight's class could come in handy in case I tracked Jack Smirnoff down, history repeated itself, and the two of us ended up going head-to-head. While I was a sure shot with my gun, I knew I'd be up shit creek if I fired on an unarmed person, even if that unarmed person was a black belt. I'd faced one excessive force charge already, and I wasn't about to go through that ordeal again. Of course I knew one class wouldn't be sufficient for me to best a black belt. But maybe they'd at least teach some evasive maneuvers that could keep me from totally getting my ass kicked.

"Sounds fun." A grin played about Nick's lips. "I hope you and I get a chance to spar."

I narrowed my eyes at him. "I'd kick your butt."

He crossed his arms over his chest. "I'd like to see you try."

Lu flitted past in the hall, shaking a finger as she went. "I told you two no flirting on the job!"

chapter ten

Everybody Was Kung Fu Fighting

On my drive home from work, I swung by Flo Cash's house to check on things. The blue tent was still draped over her residence, the mass execution of termites purportedly happening inside. But, in addition to the dead or dying bugs, did the home also contain a safe full of cash as Flo had told me? Or was it a lie, intended to put me off, string me along, buy Flo some time while she came up with a strategy for avoiding a tax assessment? I supposed I'd find out tomorrow when I met Flo at her house at 6:00 PM.

I took a left at the end of Flo's street and continued on home. When I arrived at my town house, I found a small padded envelope addressed to Alicia in the mailbox, along with a larger one for me. Also a grocery store circular and a reminder that it was time to renew my salsa-of-the-month subscription. Next month's can't-miss flavor would be roasted corn and red pepper. *Yum!*

I tucked my package into my briefcase and hurried inside. Given that CPAs were enjoying a summer reprieve from tax-filing deadlines, Alicia had arrived home before me and was already lounging on the couch in a pair of yoga pants and a soft tee.

"Catch!" I called, tossing her package in the direction of the sofa.

She deftly caught the envelope and eyed the return address. "It's my garter!"

While I slung my purse and briefcase onto the couch and kicked off my loafers, she tore into the package, dropping the wrap to the coffee table next to the glass of sangria she'd poured for herself.

"It's perfect!" she squealed, holding the garter up, stretched between the thumb and index finger of each hand.

I stepped over to take a closer look. "It's even prettier than it looked online." I flopped down next to her and reached for her sangria to take a sip. Alicia and I had shared apartments, bills, and even some tears over the years. Sharing a few germs was nothing new, either.

She elbowed me gently in the ribs. "Maybe Nick will be the one to catch the garter. You two could be the next ones going down the aisle."

Nick and I certainly seemed to be moving in that direction. The office had a pool and he'd even placed a bet that he'd propose in September. But that was still over three months away. Was I ready yet? Nick and I had often shared a bed, but was I prepared to share my bathroom and my closet space with someone else for the rest of my life? To wake up every day to the same face on the pillow next to time? To find Nick's dirty socks on the floor? To accept that I'd never have another first date, another first kiss? To forsake all others?

I realized something big then.

I was.

Nick really was my knight in shining armor, though his typical "armor" consisted of a Western shirt, blue jeans, and a pair of scuffed cowboy boots.

I turned to my best friend. "You ready to be my maid of honor?"

"*Matron* of honor," she corrected. She gave me a smile. "All you have to do is ask."

"Well, Nick has a certain little question he'd need to pop first," I replied. "But if and when he does, it's nice to know you're on standby." I reached over, draped an arm over her shoulders, and pulled her to me for a sideways hug. "You're the best."

"Thanks, Tara. I feel the same way about you."

When I reached for her sangria this time, she playfully slapped my hand away. "Friendship has its limits. Get your own glass."

I stood, but rather than going to the kitchen for a glass of sangria I went upstairs. In my bedroom, I changed into a loose-fitting burnt-orange T-shirt with my college mascot, a longhorn steer, on the front. I exchanged my trousers for a pair of stretchy black yoga pants and my business loafers for sneakers. Strolling into the bathroom, I pulled my locks back into a high ponytail and rounded up a hand towel. Now properly attired and equipped for exercise, I went back downstairs, grabbed a bottle of water from the fridge, and bade good-bye to Alicia and my cats. "See you later!"

Returning to my car, I drove down the street to pick up Nick. As I headed up the front walk, Daffodil, his adorable Australian shepherd mix, pushed back the curtains in the front window, spotted me, and announced my arrival. *Woof! Woof-woof!* Or, in human terms, *Daddy! The woman who makes me fried baloney sandwiches is here! Yippee!* While I tended to be more of a cat person, I had to admit that canines had felines beat when it came to welcomes. My cats had never greeted me with such unfettered delight.

Nick opened the door and Daffy bounded onto the porch, running in three circles around me before slowing down enough that I could crouch down and ruffle her ears.

"Hey, girl! Good to see you, too!" Before I could stand she whipped out her tongue and licked me from chin to cheekbone. "Thanks for the kiss," I told her as I stood again.

Nick, too, gave me a kiss. When I stepped back, he offered a mock frown. "Aren't you going to thank me for my kiss, too?"

"Hers are more enthusiastic," I countered.

"I'll work on it."

Nick wore a pair of loose knee-length basketball shorts, a sleeveless Mavericks jersey, and running shoes. Like me, he'd brought a towel and a water bottle, geared up to tackle the MMA class. He rounded up his frisky pet, put her back in the house, and the two of us climbed into my car.

We sang along to the latest country hits as we drove to the martial arts studio, Nick doing his best falsetto to match Martina McBride's voice as she belted out her hit "My Baby Loves Me."

I sang along, too, adding commentary during the instrumental section: "I should have Alicia add this song to her wedding play list."

"Heck, yeah," Nick agreed.

We pulled into the lot of the strip center, took a space near the entrance to the studio, and gathered up our things to head inside. While I'd expected to find a group of people dressed in the standard white martial arts uniform, what I found instead was a bunch of beefcake in shorts, many of them shirtless, several sporting black boxing gloves. Only one woman stood among them, and she stood at least five foot eleven, her black hair shaved in a buzz cut a la Charlize Theron in *Mad Max: Fury Road*. The place reeked of sweat, the sound waves filled with grunts as men grappled on the mats and the *bap-bap-bap* of punches thrown against a heavy bag by a guy with six-pack abs and apparent anger issues.

"Yikes," I muttered under my breath.

The woman cut a glance my way. "Yeah?"

"We're here for the free introductory lesson," I said. "I signed us up online." *Is it too late to back out?*

A man with a shaved chest and head stepped up next to her and the two unabashedly looked Nick and me over. The guy snickered and tightened the wrist closure on his boxing glove. "You sure you're up to this?"

Nick stiffened next to me. He might be more than ready, but I wasn't. Still, after Flo Cash calling me a pipsqueak and her advertisers refusing to cooperate with me, I was tired of being bullied. No way was I backing down, even if they had to wheel me out of this studio on a gurney.

"We're federal law enforcement agents," I said with far more bravado than I felt. "We're up to it and then some."

The man and woman exchanged glances and smirks.

"Federal agents, huh?" The woman gestured to a shelf against the wall. "Grab some pads. We'll see what you're made of."

"Don't you need to teach us a few moves first?" I asked. "Maybe some blocking maneuvers? The proper fighting stance?" I'd picked up a bit of jargon while perusing the martial arts sites.

"We'll get to that," the woman said. "We need to get an idea of your agility and reaction speed first. See where you're starting from."

As Nick and I slid the pads onto our arms, I cut a look his way. "It was nice knowing you," I said under my breath so the others wouldn't hear. "Be sure to put some daisies on my grave once in a while."

"You can handle her," Nick whispered back. "I don't doubt you for a second."

"Are you crazy?" I angled my head to indicate the woman, who'd taken the brief respite while we put on the pads to engage in mortal combat with a man who stood six foot three and weighed 240 pounds if he weighed an ounce. "She's got nine inches and fifty pounds on me. She'll kill me."

"You're quick," Nick said. "Crafty, too."

I wish I had his confidence. At the moment all I had was an anxiety-induced urge to toss my cookies.

The shaved guy motioned for Nick to step over to the mat. "Let's go, James Bond."

Nick stepped over and positioned himself directly in front of the behemoth, instinctively offsetting his legs and bending his knees for more stability, no doubt muscle memory from his days going head-to-head with the opposing team on the football field. He'd barely raised his padded arm to his chest before the man erupted in a series of kicks, spins, and punches, landing them with such incredible force and frequency it was a wonder Nick managed to stay upright despite his linebacker experience. The guy landed a solid kick with his right foot. *Thwap!* Two rapid punches. *Bap-bap!* Another kick, this one preceded by a hop. *Thop!*

When the guy threw the next punch, he aimed not for the pad but for Nick's face. Surely that wasn't an acceptable move to make against an untrained novice. Wasn't there some sort of code of conduct for this sport? Fortunately, Nick's reflexes kicked in right away and he managed not only to raise the pad in time but also to deflect the punch to the side. *Ha! Take that, jerk.*

"Not bad," the guy said, raising his gloved fists to bump knuckles congenially with Nick. How men could be at each other's throats one minute and bros the next was beyond me.

"You're up, ponytail," the woman said, giving my hair a flick to set my ponytail swinging.

Once again my intestines tangled inside me. If she was going to kill me, I hoped she'd do it fast.

I raised the pad high in front of me, instinctively

protecting my head. A person could go on after suffering cracked ribs or a broken leg, but a head injury might mean the end of life as I knew it.

I peeked at the woman over the top edge of the pad. Her upper lip quirked in a sneer and a glint of determination flashed in her eyes. She threw a punch. *Bap!*

Good. I'd managed to get the pad up in time to protect myself from the blow. Still, there had been quite a bit of strength behind the hit. We might just be practicing here, but this woman wasn't holding back.

She spun and threw a kick in my direction. Again, I somehow managed to get the pad into place in time to protect myself, though the impact had me stumbling backward toward the wall. Before I could recover, *Pow!* She punched the pad so hard that my hand flew backward and I ended up hitting myself in the mouth. My lip split, blood trickling over my teeth and tongue, the copper taste and smell flooding my senses.

"Hey!" Nick called, stepping toward us. "Stop! Tara's bleeding."

But my wound only seemed to fuel this woman's bloodlust. Before Nick could reach her, she'd kicked at me again, the force slamming me back against the wall, my elbows taking the brunt of the impact, my head hitting the painted cinder blocks a split second later with with a brain-rattling *conk*. Pinpoints of light danced around the periphery of my vision like tiny fairies. The next thing I knew, she grabbed my wrists and pinned them to the wall next to my shoulders, using her legs and body to full immobilize me. I was stuck flat to the surface like a human pin-the-tail-on-the-donkey game.

She laughed, the sound as evil and nasty as they come. Her face was only inches from mine and coming closer. I could see the dark hairs like parentheses framing her upper lip and count the pores on her nose. *One. Two. Three.* She put her sweaty forehead to mine, pinning my skull against the wall, too. "Not so tough now, are you, Miss Federal Agent?"

The smart thing to do would have been to cry, *Uncle!* But my mental faculties had been not only shaken by the blow but also fully taken over at that point by my sense of survival. Having two older brothers who'd lived to torment me when we were young had taught me a few things, made me scrappy. Nick was right. I was indeed crafty.

The only thing I could move at that point was my mouth. Just as Daffodil had licked me earlier in the evening, I whipped out my tongue and swiped it over the woman's cheek, the copper taste of my blood now replaced by the salty taste of her sweat. Disgusting, no doubt, but effective. She cried out and backed away, wiping my bloody saliva from her cheek and giving me the opening I sought. With a primal cry, I pounced, catching her off guard, shoving her with all my might. Now it was she who was stumbling backward. And I'd give her no quarter.

I hooked a foot behind her ankle, angled my body, and rammed my shoulder into her chest. She lost her footing and fell back, her ass meeting the mat with an inglorious *fwump.* I teetered for an instant, momentum threatening to take me down with her, but windmilling my arms managed to keep me upright. When I regained my balance, I threw victorious fists in the air. "Yes-s-s!"

"Wow!" called the man who'd been working the heavy bag. "You took her down. Hell must've froze over." He gave me a respectful nod while the other men murmured in surprise. Looked like I was the first to put this brutal bitch in her place.

Hell might have frozen over, but a fiery fury raged in the woman's eyes. When she sprang from the mat to come after me, the hairless guy grabbed her and held her back. "That's enough."

"This is bullshit." Nick jerked his head to indicate the door. "Let's get out of here."

He wouldn't have to ask me twice. Casting the woman one last look that said, *You got what you deserved,* I ripped open the door and stormed out into the lot.

Once we were seated in my car, Nick turned to me. "I knew you'd show her up."

"But at what price?" I said, putting a finger to my throbbing, oozing lip. "Alicia's wedding is only a couple weeks away. A bridesmaid with a fat lip isn't going to look good in the pictures." I owed it to my friend not to look like a street brawler in her wedding photos.

I lowered my sun visor and examined my lip in the mirror. It wasn't a pretty sight, but I had to admit I was proud of myself. I'd bested an MMA instructor and had a red badge of courage to prove it. *Something must be seriously wrong with me to think such a thing, huh?*

"Jack Smirnoff can't be any tougher than that woman," Nick said. "He better watch out for Tara Holloway." Nick cast me that chipped-tooth grin of his, the one that made me feel soft and squishy and special. "Now let's get you to the doc so he can take a look at that lip."

chapter eleven

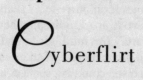

Cyberflirt

Twenty minutes later, I sat on a paper-covered examination table in a room at a minor emergency clinic. Dr. Ajay Maju had treated me for a variety of injuries over the years, including burns, accidental exposure to pepper spray, and a puncture wound inflicted during a cockfight. That's a story for another time. But suffice it to say that my job as a special agent had taken quite a toll on me physically.

What had begun as a doctor-patient relationship between me and Ajay quickly evolved into a more personal connection when I'd brought DEA Agent Christina Marquez with me to the clinic after inadvertently scorching my skin and hair. Christina and I had been working together to bust a drug-dealing ice-cream man. Ajay had taken one look at my partner and scheduled a personal appointment with her for dinner. The two had been dating ever since and, just recently, he'd put a ring on her finger. Yep, my friends were dropping like flies, saying *sayonara* to the single life. Pretty soon, I'd be the last one standing, a spinster. At least I'd be able to say *neener-neener* when my friends complained about their boring sex lives or their husbands leaving their dirty socks on the floor.

Ajay felt around the back of my skull and shined a small beam of intense light into my eyes. "Why were you hitting yourself?"

It was the same stupid question my brothers had asked when, as kids, they'd grab my arm and manipulate it so I'd end up repeatedly slapping myself in the face.

"I didn't hit myself on purpose," I snapped. "A woman at the mixed martial arts studio punched the pad I was holding really hard." *Too* hard, given that I was a novice. She'd been out to prove herself. If she was trying to prove what a nasty bitch she could be, she'd done a good job.

Ajay turned off the light and looked to Nick. "So Tara and this other woman were going at it?"

"Yep," Nick replied. "Major catfight."

"Was it as hot as it sounds?" Ajay asked.

"You know it."

Nick might be joking now, but I'd seen the look of concern in his eyes as we'd left the studio. He'd been worried.

Ajay slid the light into the pocket of his white lab coat and returned his attention to me. "Your pupils look normal, so I don't think the head injury caused any real damage. I can feel a lump coming up, though. I'll have the nurse get you an ice pack for it."

"What about her lip?" Nick asked. "I can't survive too long without a kiss." He shot me a wink.

Ajay put a gloved finger to my tender lip. "That's a pretty nasty split, but it's not jagged and it doesn't extend to the surrounding flesh. No need for stitches. Those types of injuries tend to heal up on their own. But ice can help ease the pain and swelling there, too."

He reached over to the intercom and buzzed the nurse. "Bring a couple of ice packs to exam room three, please."

Her voice came back over the speaker. "On my way."

While we waited for the ice packs, he instructed me to

open my mouth so he could check my teeth. "None of them feel loose."

Thank goodness. I was much too old for a visit from the tooth fairy.

There was a quick knock at the door and the nurse entered, carrying the ice packs. Ajay used medical tape to secure one in place on the back of my head, while I simply held the other to my lip.

When the doctor finished, he pronounced me, "Good to go." As I stood, the paper crinkling with my movements, he reached into his pocket and pulled out a pineapple Dum Dum. "A sucker for a sucker punch."

"Gee, thanks." I snatched the candy from his hand.

"See you at the wedding!" he called after me. "Save me a dance!"

Friday morning, I woke bruised and sore. The knot on the back of my head was now the size of a walnut and my lip, though no longer bleeding, continuing to throb. But the pain wouldn't slow me down. If anything, it solidified my resolve to nail Jack Smirnoff. It was his fault my head was misshapen and my lip was puffy. His fault my elbows were black-and-blue. *I'm going to get that jackass if it's the last thing I do.*

When I arrived at the office, I headed straight to Josh's office. "Got any news for me? Did you find Jack Smirnoff's new head shots online?"

He reached over to a paper on his desk and pushed it toward me. "His photo popped up on a site that's offering one of those free preview weeks."

I grabbed the page from the desk and flopped down in a chair to look it over. The document was a printout from the dating site PerfectCouple.com. Included in the profile was the more recent head shot taken at Goode Photographic Arts, as well as a teaser snippet of details from his profile, which identified him only by his alleged initials, M.W. The excerpt noted that he was "a health-care professional looking to make a fresh start." These limited details were intended to be enough to pique the interest of potential subscribers, without providing enough information for them to identify the guy and locate him elsewhere online for free. To get full details about him or anyone else listed at PerfectCouple.com, the Web site advised that a paid subscription would be necessary.

When I finished reading over the paperwork, I looked up at my coworker. "Thanks for tracking him down, Josh. You are a tech god."

"Feel free to leave sacrifices on my altar."

I fished through my purse until I found half a roll of fruit-flavored Life Savers and placed them on his desk. Not exactly a slaughtered lamb, but sufficient for my purposes. Besides, the coating of lint the candy had accumulated while in the bottom of my purse resembled wool.

I left Josh's digs and headed straight down the hall to the office of Hana Kim, a Korean-American agent who ranked second only to Nick when it came to batting averages on the Tax Maniacs. I put my knuckles to her door frame. *Rap-rap.*

Hana looked up from her desk, where she'd been transferring numbers from a stack of invoices to a spreadsheet. "Tara. Hey."

"Hey, yourself," I replied, stepping inside. "You busy?"

She cut her eyes to the stack of files towering on her desk. "Little bit."

I supposed it had been a dumb question. The IRS Criminal Investigations office ran lean and mean. Good thing we agents were hard workers. Still, as busy as each of us was, we tried to help one another out when we could. We knew the shoe could be on the other foot at any time. "Want to help me hook a catfisher?"

"A catfisher?" She leaned back in her chair and folded her hands on her well-toned stomach. "You've got my attention."

I perched on the edge of a wing chair and gave her a quick rundown. "This guy ripped off at least three women for a couple grand each. Found them on dating sites, took them out for dinner, and fed them a bunch of BS about a dead wife, a deadbeat stepson, and an estate tied up in probate court. He gave his victims bogus checks to cash. They all thought their banks wouldn't cash them if they weren't legitimate."

Hana sighed. "Another thug exploiting a common misconception. Someone should do a public service announcement."

Too bad Flo Cash and I weren't on good terms. Her financial show would be the perfect venue to inform the public about how to avoid theses types of scams.

"Josh helped me track him down," I continued. "The guy's got a new alias, but he's up to his old tricks. I figured if you and I both try to land dates with him, that could speed things up, maybe help us get more evidence." I handed her the printout. "This is him. What do you think?"

She ran her gaze over the page. "So this guy will take me out for a free dinner and I get to bust him afterward? Sounds fun. Sign me up."

"Great. Thanks, Hana." I took the printouts back from her. "Can you shoot me a photo of yourself? I'll need it to set up your online profile."

She pulled out her phone and thumbed through her photos. "What do you think of this one? It was taken at my cousin's baby shower."

She held out her phone and I eyed the screen. Hana appeared in a pale-blue blouse, her black hair tossed back, a broad smile on her face. She looked cute, approachable, and easygoing. Totally unlike the homicidal hellion who stepped up to bat at our softball games.

"It's perfect," I said. "Now I just need to know what name you'd like to go by and what job and interests you'd like your alter ego to have."

She looked up in thought before frowning. "I don't know. I can't imagine myself as anyone else. I'm not exactly creative."

Good thing. Creativity and an accounting degree could be a felonious combination. Just ask those guys from Enron.

She lifted a shoulder. "Surprise me."

"Okeydoke." I stood. "I'll let you know when I hear something back."

I returned to my office and set about entering a profile for myself on PerfectCouple.com. I resurrected an alias I'd used twice before, first when I'd gone undercover in a strip club and later to lure in a crook running a charity scam on Facebook. "Welcome back to the land of the living, Sara Galloway."

I scrolled through my phone, searching for a pic that would make me look naïve and trusting, someone the catfisher would immediately peg as an easy victim. *Bingo.* A recent candid photo Nick had taken of me with my cat Anne cradled in my arms would fit the bill perfectly.

Next, I filled in the boxes for my alter ego's personal information, making her three years older than I really was so that I'd fall into the acceptable age range for Morgan Walker, which he'd listed as thirty to fifty. I had to give the guy a little credit. At least he wasn't going after the barely legal crowd. Of course his tactic probably said less about his appreciation for mature women and more about the fact that women in their early twenties were less likely to be able to cash a check for two grand without raising eyebrows at their bank. He was probably trying to avoid scrutiny or the bank holding the funds until they were certain the check had cleared. A bank was more likely to give immediate credit to an older and financially proven long-term client.

My alias ran her own independent bookkeeping business to mild success. I noted this detail in the profile, as well as the fact that Sara Galloway, like me, was a big fan of sushi, cats, mystery novels, and romantic comedies.

Now that I'd paid my fee and input my profile, I had unfettered access to all the men on the site. But I was only after one.

M.W.

It took a few moments for me to read over the instructions and familiarize myself with the site's functions. It offered a variety of search options. I could peruse the listings by interests, age range, location, keywords, or a combination of these factors. *Okay. I think I've got it.*

First, I narrowed my search to men looking for women within Dallas and a thirty-mile radius of the city. I wasn't sure how far out M.W. might have expanded his search, but I figured thirty miles should cover it. I also narrowed the listings by my preferred date's age range, inputting forty to fifty for my target range, though I'd listed myself as thirty-three. I also limited my search to include the key words "health care."

I clicked the "search" button and waited for a moment until a list of photos and names popped up.

An Asian physical therapist. *Nope. Not the man I was looking for.*

A gray-haired hospital administrator. *Nope. Not him, either.*

A black-haired insurance salesman. *Nope.*

A-ha! There he was in his newer head shot, his thieving face smiling at me from the reaches of cyberspace. Per the profile, Jack Smirnoff was now going by the name Morgan Walker. *Odd.* Most criminals who used aliases tended to use ones that were somewhat similar. But "Morgan Walker" and "Jack Smirnoff" sounded nothing alike. *Where is he getting these names?*

Once again, he claimed to be relocating to the area, allegedly transitioning from Oklahoma City this time around. Rather than claiming to be a psychologist, he now touted himself as a substance abuse counselor for high-profile clients, another occupation that would require him to keep a low profile and would explain the lack of a well-developed online presence. I had to hand it to this guy. He was a smart cookie. Unfortunately for him, I liked to eat cookies.

Morgan had kept his list of interests broad and vague, probably on purpose so that he could appeal to a wide range of potential victims. According to his profile, he was a man *who enjoyed the variety entertainment options Dallas had to offer and loved to try new things.* I'd give him a new thing to try. My foot in his ass.

I ran a quick Internet search for obituaries that included the name Morgan Walker. Sure enough, there was one in the *Oklahoman* newspaper online edition dated a few months back for a Michelle Walker. Per the obituary, she was survived by her husband of nine years, Morgan Walker, and her son, Shane.

I grabbed my mouse and maneuvered it to an icon at the bottom of the page. "Prepare to meet your dating doom, Morgan Walker." Okay, so busting criminals made me a little melodramatic on occasion. 'Scuse me for that.

With a click of my mouse, Sara Galloway gave Morgan Walker a "wink," engaging in a little cyberforeplay. I added a note that said: *Hope to hear from you soon!* I crossed my fingers that Morgan would respond, and quick. I wanted this guy behind bars before he could rip off another unsuspecting, trusting woman.

Finished with myself, I moved on to set up an account

for Hana. Like me, she, too, needed a name enough like her own that she'd respond to it. Given that her last name, Kim, could also serve as a first name, I decided to go with Kimberly, or "Kim" for short. *Huang would be a good surname, right?* Sure. Thus, Hana Kim became Kim Huang.

Her make-believe profile took a little more thought. *What should Kim Huang do for a living?* It would have to be a type of job that Hana would know enough about that she could fake it. *Hm-m* . . . Hana had once mentioned in passing that she'd attended Texas State University in San Marcos on a full-ride softball scholarship. Good for her. Heck, I'd been lucky for the fifty bucks the PTA had tossed my way, and that was only because my mother had been the historian all four years I'd attended high school. That woman could crop the shit out of a scrapbook. But that was neither here nor there. Right now, I needed to give Hana a new occupation. *Why not make her an independent college softball scout?*

"Good thinking, Tara," I told myself as I entered the data into her profile. Sometimes you have to be your own cheerleader.

Choosing Kim Han's interests was easy. I chose ones Hana had in real life. Thriller novels and horror movies, the grislier the better. Microbrewed beers. And softball, of course. Just for kicks I tossed in the fictitious fact that she liked bluegrass music and collected vintage harmonicas. Hey, she'd said to surprise her.

When I finished, I searched under her profile for Morgan Walker. *There you are, freckle and all.* A few keystrokes later and Kim Huang had given him a wink, too. She'd also passed him a cybernote that read: *You're cute! Game for some fun?*

With that, I logged off the site. I'd check back later to see if my foreplay had gotten me anywhere. With any luck, I'd soon have a hot date with a hot-check writer.

chapter twelve

An Impromptu Picnic

At a few minutes after five, I logged off of my computer, gathered my things, and turned off the light in my office. Josh, Eddie, and William came up the hall, their brief-cases in hand, heading out for the day, smiles on their faces. Lucky them. Their workweek was over. I still had a matter to take care of.

That matter was Flo Cash.

I stepped to Nick's doorway. I'd asked him to accompany me tonight. I was a little uncomfortable going into Flo's house alone. For all I knew she'd try to push me down the stairs and claim I'd tripped. It couldn't hurt to bring a witness. Also backup in case I needed to arrest Flo and she put up a fight. I'd learned never to make assumptions about taxpayers. Some were all bark and no bite, and some were no bark but big bite. "Ready to go?" I asked.

Nick looked up from his computer. "Give me two sec-onds." He entered a few keystrokes before announcing his work "done." He shut down his computer, grabbed his briefcase, and followed me out to the parking lot.

"Let's take my ride." He angled his head to indicate his government-issued car, which was much newer than mine and retained all of its stereo knobs and a complete set of floor mats. *Luxury.*

I hopped into the passenger side, while he stowed his briefcase in the back and slid into the driver's seat.

"Which way, boss?" he asked.

"Lakewood Heights," I said.

Nick aimed his car for the neighborhood, which sat northeast of downtown. We crept along on the freeway, boxed in by commuters heading home from work. Many were talking or texting on their cell phones. At least at these slow speeds the worst thing that could happen would be a fender bender.

Nick cut a questioning glance my way. "How are Alicia's wedding plans coming along?"

"All done," I told him. "The last thing she had to do was buy a garter and we took care of that the other night."

"What's it look like?" Nick asked.

"Pale blue with a white satin ruffle."

"Sexy," he said. "Maybe I should buy you a couple of garters and some thigh-high stockings."

"Sure," I said. "They'd go great with my cowgirl boots."

A smile played across his lips. "Careful now or you'll turn me on."

He exited and turned into Flo's neighborhood. Shortly thereafter, we turned onto Flo's street and pulled up to the curb in front of her house. The termite van with its disco eyeballs on the roof sat in the driveway, the back doors hanging open as the two exterminators wrangled the large blue tent into the back bay.

With the tent removed, I could now see what Flo's house looked like. It was a beautiful two-story country French–style home, with a rounded tower on one end, hipped roofs, and multiple dormer windows. The façade was composed of a combination of brick and stone, with corner quoins in a lighter, contrasting color. A narrow balcony with an iron railing extended from the upper floor, shading the front walkway, which was flanked with fragrant gardenia bushes.

"Not too shabby," Nick said.

He and I climbed out of his car and made our way up the stone walkway to the front door. I rang the bell and waited. When there was no response after twenty seconds or so, I tried a second time, using my knuckle to jab the button twice in rapid succession. *Ding-ding-dong!* When that got me nowhere, I lifted the heavy iron knocker and sounded it three times. *Clack! Clack! Clack!*

The men had finished loading the tent back into their van and walked around to climb in.

"Hold up a second!" Nick called, raising a hand and stepping toward them. "Have y'all seen Ms. Cash around? We have an appointment with her."

"The only time we saw her," said the driver, "was the first day we came out here."

"So her car's not in the garage?" I asked, walking over to stand next to Nick.

"Not if she's driven it in the last three days," the man said. "We just uncovered the garage a half hour ago. No-body's taken a car in or out."

Nick and I exchanged glances before both of us checked our cell phones for the time. It was straight up 6:00 now. The time Flo had agreed to meet me here.

"Have a good weekend," I told the men as they climbed into the van. As they backed out, I turned to Nick, "You think we've been stood up? Or do you think she's just running late?"

"Hard to say," he said. "Dallas traffic can be a night-mare."

That was true. With so many freeways crisscrossing one another it seemed like there was always an accident somewhere causing residual slowdowns throughout the entire system. Residents knew to pad their commute times to account for the unpredictability.

We stood out front for fifteen minutes before I grew bored and plucked a gardenia bloom from the nearby bush. I plucked the petals, dropping them on the ground. "He loves me," I said, tossing the first petal aside. "He loves me not." The second petal hit the Bermuda grass. "He loves me"—pluck, toss—"he loves me not. He loves me. . . ." I continued on, a pile of petals forming around me, until I reached the last petal. "Damn." I dropped the petal. "He loves me not."

"Don't you worry your pretty head about it," Nick said, kicking the last petal aside and sliding me a soft smile. "I know for a fact that he loves you. A lot."

"We're talking about Chris Hemsworth, right?" I teased.

"Bite your tongue, woman."

We stood there another ten minutes before my stomach growled. "She better get her butt home soon. I'm hungry. Another ten minutes and I'm going to start eating her lawn."

Nick pulled out his cell phone. "Let's order some take-out. We can have them deliver it here."

"Good idea."

"What sounds good? Chinese?"

"We had Chinese for lunch earlier in the week, remember?" The fortune cookie strip was still sitting on my desk at work. *The empty vessel makes the loudest sound.*

"Oh, right. How about Italian?"

"Nah," I said. "Benedetta's Bistro is the best, but we're outside of her delivery range." Damn shame, too. I'd worked undercover in the restaurant and they made the best chocolate cannoli on earth. I could've really gone for one of the delicious desserts right now.

"Thai?" Nick suggested. "Sushi? Barbecue? Greek?"

I raised a finger. "We have a winner. I haven't done Greek in a while."

"Greek it is." He used his phone to find a Greek place in the area. Fortunately, they offered delivery service. We placed an order for grape leaves and falafel, along with drinks.

"What should we do while we wait?" I asked. Patience might be *a* virtue, but it wasn't one of *my* virtues.

Nick gestured toward his car. "We could get in the backseat and make out."

I scoffed. "Real professional."

"Says the woman who tossed flower petals all over the yard."

"Touché." I reached out and touched Nick's shoulder. "Tag. You're it!"

I took off running across the grass, but he caught up with me in three short strides. *Rats!*

"That was easy," he said.

"You have a distinct advantage," I said, gesturing to his long legs. "How about hide and seek?"

He chuckled. "I haven't played that since I was twelve."

I sighed. "I hardly remember what it was like to be twelve."

"I remember," Nick said. "One of my friends came across a girlie magazine his father had hidden in the garage. He brought it over to my parents' house and we invited all of our friends over to the barn to take a gander. We stashed it in the hayloft, but my mother must have found it, because the next time we went to the barn to peek at it all the naughty bits had been covered with black marker."

"Serves you right."

We stepped over the curb and took seats on it to wait for our food. As we waited, a couple of Flo's neighbors drove by, eyeing us suspiciously, clearly wondering what was going on. If our presence started a rumor Flo would have no one to blame but herself. If she'd been here at six like she'd agreed, this matter could have already been resolved.

I pulled out my cell phone and tried the phone number for KCSH. All I got was an automated system telling me that their business hours were 8:00 AM to 5:00 PM Monday through Friday and that I could either call back during business hours or leave a message at the beep. The message was followed by the foretold beep.

"Hello, Miss Cash," I said into my phone. "You agreed to meet me at your house at six o'clock. I've been waiting here since. Give me a call as soon as possible so I'll know when to expect you. Otherwise I'll have to take more serious measures." With that I hung up.

"*More serious measures*?" Nick said. "What's your plan?"

"If I can't get what I need from Flo," I told him, "I'll have to keep hammering away at her advertisers until one of them breaks." It wasn't an efficient process, but she was leaving me with no choice. One way or another, I had to get some evidence against her.

A car came slowly up the street, the driver craning his head to search for addresses.

"That's gotta be our food," Nick said, stepping into the street and waving his arms over his head to get the driver's attention.

When the man noticed Nick he sped up, coming to a stop behind Nick's car. He climbed out, retrieved a bag of food from a box in the backseat, and handed it to me. "Twenty-two fifty," he said.

Nick pulled out some cash and handed it to the man. "Keep the change."

"Thanks."

Nick and I climbed back into his car to eat, rolling down

the windows to enjoy the evening air, which was beginning to cool down. We ate our food while listening to KCSH on the radio. The morning's *Cash Flow Show* was being repeated, Flo suggesting that listeners would be wise to invest their funds in hotel companies that offered resort-style accommodations in the United States. "Thanks to all the terrorism and unrest, people with disposable income are staying closer to home these days," she said. "While they once might have toured Europe, they're choosing to visit Jackson Hole or Savannah or Bar Harbor. We're already seeing an uptick in reported profits for these businesses, and I think this trend will continue for the next few years. Remember, make your money make money for you, folks."

When we tired of listening to KCSH, we watched some recent episodes of television on my phone's Hulu app. The night continued to grow darker around us, the crickets chirping, the moisture in the air increasing as the temperature dropped, my hair absorbing the moisture and expanding like a sponge.

When ten o'clock arrived, but Flo still hadn't, I jotted: *Call me immediately!* on the back of one of my business cards, lifted her door knocker, and slid the corner of the card under it where the knocker would hold it in place. Though the card wasn't big, it would be hard to miss.

"You better call me, Flo," I muttered to her door, giving it a solid kick. "Or I'm going to cash you out."

chapter thirteen

$\mathcal{A}$ Fitting Way
to Spend the Day

Nick and I played a very lively and satisfying round of Uno at his place Friday night and another on Saturday morning before dragging our lazy butts out of bed. Daffodil padded down the stairs after us, more than ready for her morning potty break. While Nick let her out into the backyard and set about making coffee, I logged on to my laptop and checked my profile on the PerfectCouple.com site. Sure enough, Morgan Walker had winked back at me. He'd also left me a message: *Are you free Wednesday evening? Thought we could meet at an Olive Garden near you at 7:30*.

The coffee began to burble as I replied back to Morgan Walker: *Sounds great!* I suggested a location in Lewisville, one of the many smaller cities that surrounded Dallas. Lewisville was actually several miles from my real home and I didn't know anyone who lived there, so the location reduced the chance that I'd inadvertently run into someone I knew at the restaurant. *See you then!*

I sat back in my seat. Funny, I'd realized the other day that I was ready to settle down with Nick, yet here I was planning a first date with someone else. Ironic, huh? I stood and snagged a couple of mugs from Nick's cabinet. "Morgan Walker winked back at me. We've made a date for Wednesday night."

Nick cut a grin my way. "You really think you should be dating other guys after what we did this morning?"

"*And* last night."

"You realize you're only proving my point, right?"

I set the mugs on the counter and retrieved the hazelnut creamer from the fridge. "Uh-oh. Someone's getting jealous," I teased.

"I'm not jealous," Nick said. "This guy isn't after you. He's after your bank account."

"Gee, thanks." I scowled as I poured a dash of creamer into each of our mugs.

Nick stepped over and ruffled my hair, which was already still ruffled from the bed. I had a strict I-do-nothing-until-I-get-my-coffee policy, so my hair hadn't yet been brushed this morning. "Once this guy lays eyes on you," Nick said, "he'll probably fall in love and change his ways. A good woman can make a man do all sorts of things he'd never thought he'd do. You know, like let her sleep over and keep a toothbrush in his bathroom drawer and drink his coffee." He punctuated his words with a wink of his own and gave me a kiss on the cheek.

"You're saying I've changed you?"

"Hell, yeah. But all for the better."

Had Nick changed me, too? Had our relationship caused me to evolve in some way? I mulled that over for a moment as I waited for the coffee to finish brewing. *Hm-m . . .*

Yes, I was different now than I had been before Nick. My previous boyfriend, Brett, never quite understood why I'd take on such a dangerous, demanding job when I could have stayed at Martin and McGee and worked my way to a partnership and cushy corner office. Nick, on the other hand, knew how much I loved my work. He loved the job, too, and for the same reasons. It was a great feeling to be understood and accepted. On a more personal level, Nick made me feel attractive and feminine and sexy, despite the fact that I was in no way built like a Victoria's Secret model and he saw me most often dressed in boring, conservative clothing for work. Nick could have had his pick of more fashionable women who were built like centerfolds, but he'd chosen me instead. Yep, Nick loved me as-is, and that had made me infinitely more confident.

The instant the coffeemaker expelled its last burble and a final gasp of steam, I snatched the carafe and filled the mugs, handing one to Nick and keeping the other for myself. He let Daffodil back inside, fed her a can of dog food for breakfast, and joined me at his kitchen table.

"Keep a close eye on this catfish guy," Nick said. "If he realizes you're law enforcement there's no telling how he might react. He could grab a knife."

"True," I said. "Or maybe he'll beat me with a breadstick." Those things were delicious. There'd be much worse ways to go.

Nick skewered me with a pointed look.

"I'm only joking. I'll be careful."

"It would be better if you had some backup. I wish I hadn't promised my mother I'd come over for dinner that night. Maybe I should reschedule."

"You'll do no such thing," I said. "You know how much your mother enjoys your visits."

Nick enjoyed them, too. His mother was one heck of a cook. Besides, she was a widow. Nick's father had passed away years before, and Nick was an only child. It wouldn't be right for him to cancel.

"I'd be more comfortable if someone was there, keeping an eye on you."

As usual, the part of me that was bad-ass special agent

felt annoyed at the implication that I couldn't take care of
myself. I always carried my gun and was one of the best
shots in the IRS, if not the entire federal government. Another part of me, the girly part, felt warm and fuzzy and
appreciated Nick's protective instincts. Not only would I
have to compromise with Nick; I'd have to compromise
with myself, too. Besides, even the toughest federal agents
were smart to enlist backup.

"I'll see if Eddie can get a sitter for his girls." Eddie and
his wife, Sandra, lived in Plano, one of the northern sub-
urban cities not far from Lewisville. Between school and
soccer practice, their twin girls kept them running nonstop.
They probably hadn't had a date in months. Surely they
could use a night out.

Though it was clear he'd prefer to provide the backup
himself, Nick acquiesced. "All right. I know I can count
on Eddie."

I knew it, too. The guy had once saved me from an angry man with a box cutter who'd tried to slash me to bits.
Eddie had leaped onto the bastard's back and ridden him
like a rodeo bronc until I'd shot the blade out of the guy's
hand and taken him to the ground. *Fond memories.*

After a healthy swig of coffee, I made banana pecan
pancakes for me and Nick and a plain one for Daffodil.
After all, breakfast is the most important meal of the day.
Also the only one where you can get away with eating
something for your main course that virtually amounted
to dessert.

As Nick washed his last bite of syrup-drenched pancake
down with a swig of coffee, he eyed the clock on the micro-
wave. "I better get cleaned up. My appointment to get fitted for my tux is at eleven. Why don't you come with me
and help me pick one out?"

While I much preferred to undress Nick rather than
put more clothes on him, it couldn't hurt for me to tag

along and give him a woman's opinion. Otherwise he might end up in something powdered blue and ruffled. "Count me in."

An hour later we pulled up to the men's formal wear shop. The window featured contemporary faceless mannequins sporting a variety of tuxedos ranging from a classic black tux to a more modern style with a white jacket and black lapels. We went inside and checked in at the counter.

"I'm Nick Pratt," Nick told the older man behind the counter. "I'm here for my fitting."

The man looked from Nick to me and smiled. "You two getting married?"

"No," I said.

"Not yet, anyway," Nick added, cutting a glance in my direction.

Though my heart was performing a happy dance in my chest, I rolled my eyes casually at Nick and returned my attention to the man. "He hasn't proposed. And if he did, I'm not even sure I'd say yes."

What a lie. Of course I'd say yes! Nick knew it, too.

He turned back to the man as well. "I'd get a 'yes' out of her eventually. No matter how much begging and groveling it took."

"Smart man," the clerk said. "Never give up on the one you want. It took me two years to convince my wife to marry me, but we've been together thirty-nine years now. We've got three children and five grandchildren. Also arthritis and bunions and cataracts."

"How wonderful," I told him. "I mean, about the kids and grandkids. Not the health issues."

He raised a shoulder. "That's life, eh?"

Nick looked down at me. "If you get bunions I'll rub your feet."

"Good to know." I turned back to the man. "My best friend is getting married. It's a black-tie wedding."

"Gotcha." The man cocked his head and looked Nick up and down as if visually taking his measurements. "Forty-six long coat. Thirty-six long pant."

Nick dipped his head in acknowledgment. "You nailed it."

The man waved a dismissive hand. "You've been in this business as long as I have, you get good at sizing people up." He placed a binder on the counter and opened it. "Take a look at the options. Let me know what you like."

Nick flipped through the pages. They contained photographs of attractive men in a wide variety of tuxedos, everything from a classic gray tux with tails and a matching vest to a skinny-style tux trimmed with shiny satin. When he reached the end, he shrugged. "They all look pretty much the same to me."

Good thing I'd come along, huh? I turned to the clerk. "Let's try a classic tux with a red vest and bow tie."

"No cummerbund?" Nick asked. "Good. I can never remember whether the flaps are supposed to go up or down."

"Up," the man said. "Think of them as crumb catchers."

"Ah," Nick replied. "Good to know."

The clerk stepped out from behind the counter. "Your dress is red, too, I assume?"

"Yep."

He led us over to a rack loaded with vests and pulled out several in varying shades of red. "Is your dress an orange-red?" he asked, holding up one in a vibrant shade, "or candy-apple red?" He held up one in a darker shade of red bordering on burgundy.

"Somewhere in the middle," I said.

He returned the two vests he'd held up to the rack and together we went through the others until I found the right shade. "This is it."

After selecting a jacket, pants, a bow tie, and shoes for

Nick, the man took him back to the dressing room. I waited on a padded chair for a few minutes until Nick emerged.

"What do you think?" he asked.

What did I think? I rose reflexively from the chair. "Wow."

Nick looked gorgeous, somehow appearing refined and elegant while losing none of his masculinity and animal magnetism. While he was undoubtedly more at home in his boots, jeans, and Western shirts, Nick could pull off this look like a professional *GQ* model.

The man put his index finger in the air and twirled it, directing Nick to spin. Nick complied, turning to give me a view of all sides.

"It's perfect," I said.

"Good," Nick said. "Can I get out of it now?" He wriggled inside the tux like a little boy who'd been forced to wear an uncomfortable suit to church.

"Not yet," I said. "Can I get a pic?"

"Be my guest." The clerk stepped back to get out of the shot.

While I snapped a series of photographs, Nick hammed it up, performing a series of poses that included arms crossed over his chest, a casual hands-in-pockets stance, and looking up and off in the distance, as if pondering life's eternal questions. Finally, he turned back to face me. "Are we done yet?"

"Fine." I sighed and pointed into the dressing room. "Go."

My parents arrived at my place in the early afternoon.

As usual, Mom was all hugs and kisses and exclamations of how cute I looked in the sundress I'd thrown on. "I've missed you to pieces, Tara!"

I gave her a hug in return. "Right back at ya, Mom." I'd also missed her blueberry pie, peach cobbler, and pecan pralines. Fortunately, she had a large tin and two foil-covered pie plates in her hands. Looked like I wouldn't be missing them for long.

As I took the pies from my mother, Dad stuck his hand out to shake Nick's. "Good to see you, Nick."

Nick took it, simultaneously grabbing my father's shoulder with his other hand in an amiable yet manly welcome. "Good to see you, too. Ready to head out to the lake? We're burning daylight."

"It's June in Texas," my mother said. "The sun'll be up till nine o'clock."

Dad raised a hopeful brow. "Then you won't expect us back until ten?"

Mom pointed a finger in Dad's face. "I'll expect you back by suppertime, and I'll expect you to bring the supper with you."

My father raised his hands in surrender. "All righty then."

With that, Dad and Nick headed out to the driveway. Nick's bass boat was hitched to the truck, his fishing poles and tackle box in the bed of his pickup next to a cooler of ice-cold beer. The both waved good-bye as they backed out and headed off.

Mom watched them go. "Those two are peas in a pod."

I might be more disturbed by the thought that I'd picked a guy so much like my father if my dad weren't such a great guy. He and Nick were both hardworking, loyal, and down-to-earth. I could do much worse.

While a day on the lake could be enjoyable, Mom and I had more girlie things planned. We parked the pies and pralines on the kitchen counter and headed out to find my mother a pair of shoes to go with the dress she'd bought to wear to Alicia's wedding.

We returned to my town house at six, having scored a pair of cute open-toe pumps with satin trim. As Mom and

I dragged out the cutting boards, cornmeal, and pans to prepare the kitchen for a fish fry, the men returned.

"We've got dinner!" Dad called from the foyer.

Mom and I went to view the catch. Instead, we found Nick and Dad wearing sheepish grins and carrying take-out bags from the Italian place around the corner.

Mom shook her head. "How you two can spend an entire afternoon on a lake, not catch a single fish, and think it's fun is beyond me." She took the bag from my father's hand and carried it into the kitchen.

While I adored my mother, I had no idea how she could think spending hours in a kitchen could be fun, either. I much preferred to eat food that someone else had prepared.

A few minutes later, the four of us were seated around the table in my kitchen.

I passed the basket of garlic bread to Nick. "What do y'all do out there when the fish aren't biting? Sing seafaring songs? Swab the deck? Twiddle your thumbs?"

"We talk sports and politics," Nick said. "Among other things." He cut a glance at my father, a knowing look passing between them.

Hm-m. Just what were those "other things?"

My mother took a bite of her pesto fettuccine and moaned in delight. "I'd had my heart set on fried catfish," she said, "but this isn't bad at all."

We chatted as we ate, sometimes debating, sometimes laughing, but all the while enjoying one another's company. Nick was right at home among my family. He'd fit in from the first day they'd met.

When we'd finished dinner, Mom stood from the table. "Who wants pie and who wants cobbler?"

"You mean we've got to pick?" Nick lamented. "That's like asking a man to pick between his girl and his dog."

"Quit your bellyaching." I stepped over to the counter. "You can have both."

We topped off the Italian food with generous servings of desserts. After Nick helped me with the dishes, I saw him off with a kiss at the door.

Mom stepped up behind me. "You coming back for my biscuits and gravy in the morning?" she called after Nick.

"Heck, yeah!" he called back. "I'd be a fool not to."

As I shut the door behind him, I turned to my mother. "Sometimes I'm not sure whether Nick sticks around because of me or because of your biscuits."

"Either way," she said, "he's not going anywhere."

After a late breakfast Sunday morning, my parents headed back to Nacogdoches, my mother leaving a dozen biscuits and a pint of cream gravy in the fridge, God bless 'er.

Nick and I spent the rest of the morning at his place. We moved his coffee table aside, covered the floor of his living room in couch cushions and pillows, and pulled up martial arts how-to videos on YouTube, trying out the moves on each other.

Nick crouched and wiggled his fingers at me. "Come on, Tara. Show me what you've got. Don't hold back."

"You asked for it. Don't blame me when you end up in the ER." I got into position. "Hi-yah!" I shrieked, throwing a kick at him.

He grabbed my foot and held it up in the air, forcing me to hop around to keep from falling.

"No fair!" I cried.

"You think Morgan Walker is going to fight fair?" Nick asked. "Try again."

I went for a fake this time, pretending I was going for a kick but throwing a punch instead. His arm swung upward, easily deflecting my blow.

"Dammit!" I snapped.

I tried a third time, putting my back to him and attempting to elbow him in the gut.

He tackled me from behind, rendering the blow ineffective and taking me down to the pillows. He rolled me onto my back, pinned my arms to the ground, and straddled my thighs. He looked down at me. "I'd be really turned on right now if I wasn't so worried that Walker's going to hurt you."

Hell, I felt the same way. I might be a virtual sharpshooter, but I was no karate kid. If Walker was a black belt, he'd probably chop me in two before I could get to my gun. At the very least he'd break my arm. How was I going to aim if my radius and ulna were flapping around?

Seeing us on the floor, Daffodil yanked her leash off the hook in the kitchen and carried it over to us, insisting we get off our butts and take her for a walk. *Woof!*

Nick stood, ruffling her ears as he took the leash from her mouth and clipped it on to her collar. "Seems there's always some female bossing me around."

"Hush," I said, rising from the pillows.

"You're proving my point."

We took Daffodil for a long walk, allowing her to stop and sniff the thousands of mailboxes in the neighborhood, to exchange nasal to anal introductions with other dogs out for walks, and to give a squirrel a thorough tongue-lashing for daring to enter her domain.

Later that afternoon, Nick and I climbed into his pickup. There was the matter of Carl's chair and desk to attend to.

Nick aimed his truck for Carl's house and we arrived fifteen minutes later. Carl stood waiting on the porch of his gray wood-frame home, an eager smile on his face. He waved us down. *As if we could miss him in his royal-blue polyester slacks and shiny white shoes.*

"Hi, Carl!" I called as I hopped out of the truck in the driveway. "Ready for your big move?"

"Sure am!" He pushed an errant strand of his comb-over back up onto his head. "Y'all come on in."

We followed him into his house. Like Carl, everything in it was out-of-date but nonetheless functional and cheerful.

Carl stepped up behind an easy chair covered in threadbare navy velveteen. "This is the one."

The relic would be right at home at Lu's place.

He crouched down, risking both a hernia and the seams of his decades-old pants giving way. "I'll get the bottom if you can grab—"

"No worries." Nick easily scooped the chair up in his strong arms. "I got this."

Carl grabbed the matching ottoman and I followed them out to the truck. I stepped ahead of Nick to lower the tailgate, and he slid the chair into the open bed. He took the ottoman from Carl and set that in the bed as well.

The three of us returned to the house for the desk. It, too, came from another era, a once-contemporary model made of fake wood and chrome, modern having morphed into retro.

"Let's remove the drawers," Nick suggested. "We don't want them falling out on the drive over."

"Good idea."

While Carl pulled out the two drawers on the left, Nick removed the two on the right, discovering the December 1953 issue of *Playboy* hidden underneath the bottom one. Marilyn Monroe graced the cover. She wore an open-mouthed smile and a revealing black-and-white dress cut low in front, her left arm raised high over her head as if she were riding a wild steer in a rodeo. *Yippee kai yay!*

Nick held up the magazine. "Well, well, well. Looks like someone's been a naughty boy." He arched an accusing eyebrow at Carl.

Carl blushed, the skin under his comb-over turning bright pink.

"Give him a break," I said. "He was probably just a kid back then."

"I was born that month!" Carl cried in his own defense. "Besides, it's their inaugural issue. It's a collector's item. My father gave it to me when I turned eighteen."

Nick eyed the cover. "Can't blame you for keeping it. Marilyn was quite a looker."

I scoffed, "You realize you're ogling a woman who'd be old enough to be your grandmother if she were still alive? Maybe even your great-grandmother?"

Nick scowled. "Way to take the fun out of it." He handed the magazine to Carl. "Here you go, buddy."

While Carl and Nick each took one end of the desk to carry it out, I made two trips to carry the drawers, carefully situating them in the truck and cushioning them with a blanket to prevent them from being damaged in transit.

Carl returned to the front door, locked it, and stepped back into his yard, staring at the house. I stepped up on one side of him, Nick on the other.

"It's a little hard to say good-bye to the place," he said softly, his shoulders slumping with emotion. "My wife and I had a lot of good years here."

I put a supportive hand on his back and gave it a little pat. We stood in silence for a moment, as if paying tribute to the time Carl had spent here.

"Except 1982." He straightened, his resolve returning. "That year stunk."

He didn't elaborate, and we didn't question him. From my own dating life and from watching my parents' marriage evolve over the years I knew every relationship had its ups and downs, its happy years and its 1982s.

We returned to the truck, climbed in, and headed back onto the freeway to make our way to Lu's house. The Lobo's home featured green brick with lavender shutters and trim, a testament to both my boss's colorful personality and what can happen when a neighborhood lacks a homeowners association and its attendant rules and regulations.

The instant we pulled into the driveway, Lu was out the door to meet us. She must've been watching from the window.

She flounced down the walk in a bell-bottom pantsuit, giving Carl a quick smooch after he descended from the truck. "I've cleared a place in the living room for your chair," she said. "We'll put your desk in the study next to mine."

Nick circled around to the back of his truck and lowered the tailgate. Carl grabbed the ottoman while Nick wrangled the chair down from the bed and carried it over to Lu. "Lead the way."

I grabbed one of the desk drawers and followed them inside. The last time I'd been to Lu's house was shortly after she'd been diagnosed with cancer. I'd come to drive her to chemotherapy. She'd lost some of her hair and spunk during the ordeal, but luckily the treatments took and she'd been cancer-free and spunky since. With any luck, she and Carl would have lots of happy years together here.

Lu stopped and pointed to a spot next to her love seat. "Put it there."

Nick plunked the chair down on the shag carpet. "How's that?"

Lu waved her fingers. "Move it a couple inches to the right."

Nick did as he was told.

She waved her fingers the other way. "Couple inches to the left."

The chair was now back in the spot where Nick had first set it.

"Perfect," Lu said.

The chair now in place, Carl placed the ottoman in front of it.

I set the drawer on the couch and we returned to the truck for the desk and remaining drawers. A few minutes later we had the desk situated in Lu's study. It was a tight fit with all of the existing furniture in the room, but they could make it work.

Lu grabbed her purse. "Who's up for pizza and beer? That's standard compensation for moving services, isn't it?"

Nick and I had talked earlier about going to my favorite sushi bar, but a double date on our boss's dime sounded just as enticing.

"Let's do it," Nick said.

The four of us ended up at a neighborhood restaurant sharing an extra-large pizza, a pitcher of Lone Star, and a good time.

Carl slid a slice onto his plate. "I've been telling Luella that she should retire so we can spend more time together."

Lu had been planning to retire shortly after I joined the IRS last year but had later changed her mind and decided to stay on the job. Was she rethinking that decision? "You gonna do it, Lu? Call it quits?"

"I wasn't sure last year," she said. "But after the cancer scare and another year under my belt, I'm ready. Besides, if I don't get out of that position none of my senior agents can move up without relocating. It's time. Of course I'm not going out the door until I find a suitable replacement. I want to leave the department in good hands." She turned a pointed gaze on Nick. "On that note, would you be interested in the job, Nick?"

Nick froze, his beer at his lips. "Me? Director of Criminal Investigations?"

"It's either you or Eddie," she said. "You're the two most senior agents."

He set his glass down on the table. "Have you talked to Eddie about it?"

"I did," Lu said. "He's mulling it over."

I wasn't surprised. Eddie had filled in for Lu while she'd been out on medical leave and spent most of the time pulling his hair out. While handling her desk job was certainly much safer than working as an agent in the field, it came with an abundance of red tape and a fair share of headaches. Then again, it came with a nice bump in pay, too. Those extra dollars could more than cover the cost of the aspirin needed to deal with the headaches.

I cut a glance at Nick. He looked both flattered and wary.

"Can I mull it over, too?" he asked Lu.

"For a week or two," she said. "Then I need a solid answer. First one to call dibs gets it."

While I was excited that Nick had been given this opportunity, I found it nearly impossible to imagine the office without Lu in it. She'd be leaving some big shoes—or go-go boots—to fill.

After dinner, Nick and I left the two lovebirds in their new nest.

On the drive home, I asked Nick about the promotion. "Think you'll take it?"

"I don't know," he said. "There's a lot to consider. Field-work can be fun, but I'm not getting any younger and it might be nice to move up the chain. It would be less risky, and the hours would be more regular. That could be a plus for a family man."

"Like Eddie, you mean."

"Like any man who's a father." He eyed me intently. "You and I would make great babies, you know. They'd be strong and smart and tough."

"We would. Maybe I could find steel-toed baby booties for them to wear."

He continued to look my way, as if assessing me.

"Eyes on the road, bucko." After all, this was Dallas,

where people braked for no apparent reason and took an exit by crossing three lanes of traffic at the last second.

"I'm just trying to picture you at Lu's age. You know, with crow's-feet and extra neck skin."

"Why in the world would you want to do that?"

He fought a grin. "I have my reasons."

I cut him a sideways look back, trying to visualize his dark hair turned gray, laugh lines around his mouth. *Damn.* Geriatric Nick still looked good. And if his current prowess was any indication, he'd never have a need for those little blue pills.

Despite my admonishment to keep his eyes on the road, he glanced my way once more. "You think we'd make it through a 1982 if we got married?"

Nick and I had been through so much together already. He'd seen me through a major head trauma and hospitalization after a target took a baseball bat to my head. Nick and I had faced down armed criminals together on multiple occasions, gone undercover together in a sleazy strip club, and pursued members of a violent drug cartel and the Mob. We'd survived an embarrassing phase where I'd gone gaga over my celebrity crush, made Nick feel like a fool, and nearly botched the case because of it. I'd even seen Nick through the loss of his beloved pet. We'd endured tragedy and sorrow, pain and humiliation, love and loss, good times and bad. *But we'd endured.*

I met his gaze and gave him a smile. "We'd kick 1982's ass."

chapter fourteen

_H_oodwinked

Monday morning, Hana Kim—aka Kimberly Huang—poked her dark head into my office. "Morgan Walker nudged me back. We're meeting at Chili's in Addison on Thursday at six."

"Good. I'll see about getting you some backup."

A blond head poked itself in next to Hana's. _Josh._ "I can do backup."

While Josh was our go-to guy for tech support, with his small stature and tendency to nearly wet himself when facing danger he didn't exactly have a reputation for bravery. But if he wanted to prove himself, who was I to stand in his way? Especially since Hana gave me an almost imperceptible nod, letting me know she'd be okay with it. Like me, Hana was a woman who could take care of business.

"Thanks, Josh," I said. "That would be great."

"Can I bring Kira along?" he asked, referencing his Web designer girlfriend. "And charge the meal to your investigation?"

Sheesh. Maybe Josh wasn't looking so much for an opportunity to prove himself as a chance to snag a free meal on my expense account. The tight-asses in Internal Accounting might balk at reimbursing Kira's dinner, but if they did I'd cover it myself. I wanted to take Jack Smirnoff, or Morgan Walker, or whoever the hell he was to the mat. Not only for Julia, Nataya, and Leslie but for his other victims, too. It was bad enough to dupe people out of their money, but to take advantage of women who were merely looking for romance and companionship seemed especially cruel. I considered myself very lucky to have found Nick, and I hadn't yet forgotten all the slimy, wart-covered frogs I'd had to kiss to get here. I wasn't merely fighting for justice. I was fighting for love.

"Sure," I told Josh. "Bring Kira."

The matter settled, the three of us went back to work.

Later that morning, I drove to the KCSH studio, timing my arrival to coincide with the end of Flo Cash's *Cash Flow Show*. That woman owed me an explanation. And an apology. Eating takeout in her front yard wasn't exactly how Nick and I had planned to spend our Friday night. We'd planned to eat takeout at his place and fall asleep on his couch halfway though a movie on Netflix. Okay, maybe that doesn't sound much better, but we worked hard all week and when Friday finally came around we were tired.

As I pulled into the parking lot, Flo's voice came across the airwaves. "Gotta tell you folks. If you're looking for a luxury vehicle, I can't recommend Ledbetter Cadillac highly enough. Great cars, great service. Next time you're in the market for a new car, head on over to Ledbetter Cadillac and tell them Flo Cash sent you."

Oddly, though, Flo's blue Cadillac was nowhere to be seen. She was here at the station, wasn't she? She had to be, right? I mean, her show was on the air. Of course it could be a repeat of a previously recorded show, but it didn't seem to be. After all, she'd commented on the cloudy weather and today's skies were gray and overcast.

I parked and climbed out of my vehicle, striding to the

front door of KCSH in my cherry-red steel-toed Doc Martens. The shoes might be a little funny looking, but they were great for kicking ass, crunching nuts, and serving as door stops when a tax evader attempted to slam a door closed on me. The soles also provided perfect traction should a foot pursuit become necessary. The only way to improve upon them would be to add some sort of rocket boosters.

I pulled the door open and went inside, stepping up to the receptionist's desk. "I need to see Flo Cash as soon as possible."

The young woman gestured up to the speaker, which was spouting Flo's voice. "She's finishing up her show. But as soon as she's done I'll let her know you're here."

Good. The woman's words meant Flo was on the premises and not hiding out elsewhere again like a lying, cheating coward.

I took a seat and perused a financial magazine, though my attention was much more focused on the show coming out of the speakers than the words on the pages. As soon as Flo signed off with her signature line—*"Make your money make money for you!"*—I was on my feet and standing again at the receptionist's desk. "The show's over. Get Flo."

The young woman cast me a narrow-eyed look that said she clearly didn't like being bossed around by someone who wasn't her boss, but the fact that she stood and headed through the door that led to the sound booth told me she was smart enough to realize that pissing off an IRS agent wasn't a wise move.

A moment later, she returned. "Miss Cash can see you now."

"Thanks."

I walked the few steps back to Flo's booth and found her sitting inside, her feet propped up on the console. She was drinking fruit-flavored tea from her oversized *TUNE IN TO THE FLO CASH CASH FLOW SHOW!* mug. The scent of lemon hung in the air.

"Hello there," she said, setting her oversized mug down. "To what do I owe this pleasure?" She jabbed a sound-effect button and a speaker on her desk emitted a hearty, "Yee-ha!"

So she was going to play dumb, huh? "You were supposed to meet me at your house at six o'clock Friday evening."

"I was indeed," she replied, pushing the clock sound effect. *Tick-tock. Tick-tock.* "Unfortunately, my car had other plans." She pressed a series of buttons and the speaker spewed the *ahoogah* of an old-timey car horn followed by a *sque-e-e* of squealing of tires and a *crash*!

Flo was getting on my last nerve, but clearly that was precisely what she was trying to do. I wasn't about to give her the satisfaction of knowing she was getting to me, even if I'd like nothing more at the moment than to yank my GLOCK from the holster at my waist and put a few rounds in her sound board. *Bang-bang!* "What do you mean, your car 'had other plans'?"

"It futzed out on me on the freeway. Had to get it towed." She reached over, grabbed a piece of paper from a plastic bin, and held it out to me. "See for yourself."

I took the paper from her. It was a receipt from a towing service indicating that her car had been picked up at 6:42 Friday evening and towed to Ledbetter Cadillac. I handed the paper back to her. "That explains why you weren't at your house. But it doesn't explain why you didn't call me to tell me you'd be late."

"You never gave me your card."

Hadn't I? It felt like I passed the things out willy-nilly, but perhaps I had forgotten to give one to Flo. I couldn't be certain. "My contact information appears at the end of my e-mails. I sent you one several days ago to verify our initial appointment here."

She shrugged. "Didn't think to check my e-mails."

I pulled a stack of business cards from my wallet and placed them on the console. "Here you go. That's enough cards that you can put one in your purse, keep one here at the office, and take another home." Hell, there were enough she could wipe her ass with them if she wanted.

She reached out, picked up the cards, and set two on their sides at odd angles, building a house of business cards. It was an ironic gesture, one that told me she was playing with me, that this investigation was nothing but a game to her. Well, it was much more than a game to me, and I wasn't playing around.

"What time did you get home?" Presumably she had no idea how long Nick and I had waited at her house. Maybe I could catch her in a lie.

"Didn't," she said. "Not Friday night, anyway. I called a friend to pick me up and then I spent the night at her place."

"You could've had your friend drive you to your house."

"Didn't see the point. By the time she showed up it was well after seven. I figured you'd have been long gone by then. You government employees aren't exactly know for your hard work and dedication, you know."

She chuckled, her words and her laughter rankling me. Government employees were no lazier than employees in the private sector. Lu wouldn't tolerate any of her agents giving less than 100 percent, either.

"Besides," Flo continued, "my friend had Rangers tickets and it wouldn't have been right to make her miss the game." She jabbed another button, this one playing the organ refrain from the "Charge" song commonly played at baseball games.

"So you went to the game with her?"

"Had to. It was the only polite thing to do."

Polite, my ass.

"Weird thing, though," she continued, eyeing me intently. "When I got home on Saturday morning, there were gardenia petals all over my lawn. You wouldn't happen to know anything about that, would you?"

I ignored her question. Mostly because I wasn't sure if one of her neighbors had seen me playing "he loves me, he loves me not" with Flo's flowers, and didn't want to get caught in a lie myself. "You've been quite uncooperative, Miss Cash," I said, cutting to the chase. "You realize I can issue an assessment based on the average of income for a radio station like this and it would be up to you to prove the numbers wrong in court. You could lose this station, put an end to everything your family worked so hard to build. Is that what you want?"

She snorted. "No need for all this drama. You want to take a field trip to my house, let's do it right now."

I extended an arm toward her door. "After you."

The house she'd built with my business cards toppled over as she stood and left her booth. She stepped across the hall, opened the door to the glass-enclosed room where her two tech guys were sitting, and gestured for them to remove their headphones. Both slid one side off, leaving the other ear covered.

Once they could hear, Flo said, "I'm leaving the station for a bit. You two keep things up and running."

Both young men were apparently used to silently communicating with Flo so as not to be overheard on her show. Each of them gave a quiet thumbs-up in response.

I followed Flo out to the parking lot, where she climbed into a plain white Chevy Impala that, like her Cadillac, bore a license plate frame with the Ledbetter Cadillac motto. Apparently the Impala was the dealership's loaner car.

I followed Flo out of the lot and onto the surface streets.
Being the uncooperative pain in the ass that she was, she
took advantage of the drive to stop by a dry cleaner to drop
off a couple of blouses, fill her tank up with gas, and make
a run through a burger joint drive-thru to pick up lunch.
Finally, we turned onto her street. This time, rather than
parking at the curb, I pulled into her driveway. My G-ride
had a minor oil leak. *Why not repay Flo's hospitality by
leaving a greasy stain in her driveway?*

Carrying her soft drink and bag of food, Flo headed to
her front door. I followed on her heels as she unlocked the
door and stepped inside.

Whoa.

The outside of the house was grand, but the inside was
even more opulent. My eyes scanned the space, taking it
all in. A chandelier sporting more crystals than a meth
dealer hung in the foyer. A wide, circular staircase swept
upward to the second floor. Thick Persian rugs graced the
marble floors in the living and dining rooms flanking the
foyer, while oversized antique china cabinets and book-
cases soared toward the twelve-foot ceilings. Rather than
sporting the same color throughout the house, the walls
were painted in varying shades of red, ranging from a light
rose in the entryway to a deeper burgundy in the adjacent
rooms.

Flo carried her food with her, the scent of onions and
pickles and French fries trailing the woman as she led me
up the staircase. She opened a French door and entered a
nicely appointed study with hardwood floors, heavy cherry-
wood furniture, and walls the color of merlot. She dropped
her bag of food on an end table but carried her drink with
her. "Safe's in here," she said, walking over to a narrow
closet and pulling the slatted door open.

At the bottom of the space was a large black safe with
a combination lock. She crouched down and took a noisy

sip of her drink—*sluuuurp!*—while twirling the combination lock with the fingertips of her right hand. Flo stopped the lock and, with a *click,* it released. She swung the door open, stood, and stepped back, jerking the straw up and down inside the plastic lid. *Squeaky-squeak.* "Have at it, Miss Holiday. I'll just take a seat here and keep an eye on you, make sure you don't pocket any of my funds." With that, she flopped backward into an upholstered armchair, retrieved her bag of food from the table, and shoved her hand inside. *Crinkle-crinkle.*

Her insinuation that I might steal from her incensed me so bad it was a wonder my hair didn't explode in flame. *Keep cool, Tara. Don't let this bitch get to you.* I knelt down and peered into the safe. Inside sat stack after stack of bills held together by red rubber bands. Most of the bills appeared to be twenties, but there were also stacks of tens, fives, and ones.

It took several trips for me to carry the stacks over to the desk. Once I finished, I spent the next twenty minutes counting out the bills, attaching a sticky note to the top of each pile to denote the total. Flo continued to tug on her straw throughout my count. *Squeak-squeak. Squeak-squeak.* She also attempted to derail my mental counting by calling out random numbers. "Twenty-three!"

Eighteen, nineteen, twenty—

"Sixty-five!" she hollered with a laugh.

Twenty-one, twenty-two, twenty-three—

"Ninety-seven!"

Ninety-eight, ninety-nine—

Shit. I grabbed a tissue from the box on the desk, tore two strips from it, and shoved them in my ears to drown her out.

One, two, three . . .

Once the bills were sorted and counted, I pulled out my pocket calculator to add up the total and pulled the makeshift plugs from my ears. "Twelve thousand three hundred eighty-nine dollars."

"If you say so." She slurped the last of her drink. *Sluuuurp*. Obviously her mother hadn't sent her to Miss Cecily's Charm School like my mother had.

I jotted the amount down. "Where's the rest of your cash?"

"That's all of it."

I eyed the bills. While it was an impressive pile, twelve grand represented a paltry accumulation for someone like Flo, who'd earned a good living for many years before she'd reduced her salary to the pittance it now was. I returned my gaze to Flo. "You're telling me that this twelve thousand dollars—"

"Twelve thousand three hundred and eighty-nine dollars," she corrected with a smirk I was tempted to slap off her face.

I took a breath to calm myself. "This cash represents all of your assets other than your house, your car, and the radio station?"

"Yes," Flo replied. "That's what I'm telling you."

"So you spent all the savings you had from back when your father paid you a good salary?"

"Sure did," she said. "I like to travel and eat out and have a good time. You only live once. Might as well enjoy it."

"Everything, other than the cash on this desk, is gone, then?"

She released a long huff of air. "I can say the same thing fifty different ways if you like, but that's all of my cash holdings. I don't own any stock, any bonds, any mutual funds, any other real estate, any checking account, any savings account, or any offshore accounts. I've got one credit card I use for shopping, but I pay it off each month via money orders."

She seemed to have her story down pat. But I still didn't believe it.

I gestured to the stacks. "What are you going to do when this runs out?"

She shrugged. "I'll figure something out."

I stared the woman down for a long moment. "What aren't you telling me, Miss Cash?"

She returned the stare before responding. "Well, for starters," she said, "I'm not telling you what I think about the federal government invading my private home and sticking its fingers in my pockets. And I'm not telling you what I think about those shoes you're wearing." Her nose scrunched in distaste.

Frankly, I didn't give a rat's ass what this woman thought about the IRS or my shoes. Her failure to pay her fair share of taxes didn't only impact the government; it also affected everyone else who had to pick up the slack for deadbeats like her. I wondered what her neighbors would think if they realized Flo had left them to foot the bill for defense, highways, and national parks and willfully failed to pay her part. They might not be so eager to look out for her best interests and report the federal agent who'd tampered with her gardenias.

I cocked my head and gave Flo a pointed look. "What do you think your listeners and neighbors and staff would say if they knew you weren't paying your taxes? That the woman who claimed to be a financial expert was flouting her debts? Violating federal law?"

She sent me a pointed look right back. "They'd wonder why a federal agent had also violated the law by leaking confidential information about a taxpayer."

She had me there. *Still* . . . "You realize that if the IRS has to file a lawsuit against you the petition will be in the public record, don't you? Reporters routinely check the filings for potential news stories. When they see a local celebrity like you has been sued, they'll have a field day. Your name will be plastered all over the newspaper headlines. It could put an end to your career and your family's radio station." I let that sink in for a moment before giving her one last chance. Softly, I said, "Look, Miss Cash. It gives me no pleasure to ruin someone. But I have a job to do. If you come clean, give us the information we need, and pay up, you can avoid a scandal and jail time. If you don't, all bets are off. What do you say?"

She looked at me for a long moment, and somewhere, deep behind her eyes I saw the first sign that she was wavering. But a moment later her eyes gleamed with fresh resolve.

She leaned toward me. "I say, 'It's on,' Agent Holloway."

I fumed the entire drive back to my office. *Oh, it's on, all right! It's on like Donkey Kong!* Flo Cash had met her match; she just hadn't realized it yet. If she thought being obstinate and uncooperative would cause me to relent in frustration, she didn't know Tara Holloway.

Back at my desk, I stared at the wall and pondered how to proceed. *Hm-m*... It couldn't hurt to call Ledbetter Cadillac, right? To verify Flo's story? After all, for all I knew she'd faked the invoice from the towing company.

I looked up the phone number for Ledbetter Cadillac online and called their service department. Realizing that they weren't likely to give information to a third party and realizing I couldn't impersonate a taxpayer, I simply said, "Good afternoon. I'm calling to check on a car and wondering what all you've done and when it might be ready. The name in your paperwork will be Flo Cash."

Hey, it's all about plausible deniability. After all, I hadn't actually claimed to be Flo, right?

"Just a moment," the man said. He returned to the line

thirty seconds later. "We've finished the routine maintenance and oil change. The only thing left to do is rotate the tires. We'll have that done here shortly if you want to pick the car up today."

Routine maintenance? Oil change? Tire rotation? "What about the engine problem?"

The man paused for a second or two, probably scanning the work order. "I don't see anything here about an engine problem. Only that you requested the fifty-thousand-mile recommended maintenance, an oil change, and the tire rotation."

The bitch lied about having trouble under her hood. I've been hoodwinked! "How much will the work run me?"

"Says here that per the general manager there's to be no charge."

"Fantastic," I said. "Can't beat that price with a stick."

If I hadn't been sure before, I was now convinced more than ever that Flo was trading airtime for cars and food and services, including automobile maintenance.

Now I just had to prove it.

chapter fifteen

$\mathcal{G}$o with the Flow

Tuesday, I decided to try a new strategy and tail Flow after she picked up her car at Ledbetter Cadillac. Maybe she'd do something that would tip me off, lead me to an undisclosed stash of cash somewhere or to a client who'd actually admit to trading products or services for on-air advertising.

Given that Flo had seen my government-issued car yesterday and her neighbors had likely reported Nick's from the Friday before, I borrowed Josh's G-ride to tail Flo. As the office tech specialist, Josh sometimes moved equipment and had thus been issued an SUV, which had much more cargo space than a sedan. Luckily for me, the black Yukon also had darkly tinted windows that would make it harder for Flo to see inside. Nonetheless, I pulled my hair back into a ponytail, tucked it down the back of my shirt, and borrowed the white cowboy hat I'd bought for Nick months ago in order to disguise myself. Along with sunglasses and a fake mustache drawn on Scotch tape with a black marker and adhered to my upper lip, I'd appear to be a smallish man behind the wheel, compensating for my diminutive stature and a presumably undersized penis by driving an enormous gas guzzler.

I waited in the parking lot close to Ledbetter's service center. Sure enough, at a few minutes after two Flo pulled up to the bays in the loaner car. A mechanic waved her in, helped her out of the car, and took the keys, moving the loaner to an outdoor parking space while Flo went inside to retrieve the keys to her Cadillac. She came outside a minute later and headed for her car. As she backed out of the space, I started my engine and eased out after her.

She turned out of the dealership and made her way down an entrance ramp and onto the freeway. I trailed her, staying a lane to the right and back several car lengths where she'd be less likely to spot me. A few exits later, she left the freeway. I followed along, continuing past a chiropractic clinic when she turned into the lot. I pulled into a dentist office across the street and turned left to find a good vantage point that would allow me to spy. *A-ha!* That spot under the tree would be shady and give me additional cover.

I parked and watched as Flo went inside the clinic. As I waited, I opened my briefcase and removed the list I'd compiled of businesses Flo had mentioned on KCSH. Sure enough, the name of the clinic appeared on my list. I had no doubt Flo was lying on a table right now receiving a complimentary spinal adjustment. If I didn't have a bone to pick with this woman before, I sure as hell did now. A vertebra.

I waited ten minutes to give the staff time to call Flo to a treatment room. I removed the ridiculous fake mustache and cowboy hat but kept the sunglasses on. Leaving the Yukon in the lot, I walked across the street to the clinic. As I'd hoped, Flo was no longer in the waiting room. A thin, thirtyish man in blue scrubs manned the reception desk, and a middle-aged woman waited in a chair, thumbing through a magazine, but they were the only ones in the room.

I took a seat in the back corner and snatched a copy of *Woman's World* from the magazine rack nearby.

The man at the counter called over to me, "Do you have an appointment, ma'am?"

I shook my head. "Just waiting for a friend."

Friend, my ass. I wouldn't be friends with a woman like Flo Cash if she were the last person on earth.

I held the magazine at the ready near my chest. When the door to the back rooms opened, I held it up. *False alarm.* A man in nylon running pants and a fitted tee exited to the waiting area. He stepped over to the front desk and whipped out a credit card.

The man at the desk took the card and consulted his computer. "Looks like you've got a thirty-five-dollar co-pay." He ran the card through the skimmer and handed it back to the man, along with the printout and a ballpoint pen. He pointed to a spot on the slip. "Sign here, please."

The man signed the paper slip and handed it back to the receptionist. "Thanks."

The clerk wished him a good afternoon before picking up a phone call.

When the door to the back rooms opened twenty minutes later, I raised the magazine to cover my face, peering around the edge.

Flo emerged and stepped to the front desk. "Got me down for next week?"

"I sure do, Miss Cash," the man said. "See you then."

She left without making a payment.

Tossing the magazine aside, I stalked to the desk. "Hello," I said. "I'm Special Agent Tara Holloway from the IRS." I pulled out a card and positioned it facing him on the countertop. "I have some questions about Florence Cash."

The guy looked from me down to my business card and back up. He pointed a finger at the door. "Was she the friend you were waiting for? 'Cause she just left."

"I'm well aware of that," I said. "And I notice she made no payment. Could you tell me why?"

"Um-m-m . . ." He grimaced with reluctance. "I don't know if I can do that. Let me check with the doctor." He picked up his phone and dialed a two-digit number. "There's someone from the IRS at the front desk. She's asking about a patient's account." He listened for a moment before saying, "Okay," and returning the receiver to the cradle. "Dr. Keele will be right up."

"Thank you."

A moment later, a stocky man with short gray hair appeared behind the receptionist. He, too, wore scrubs. "I'm Dr. Keele. How can I help you?"

I put my index finger on my business card and pushed it closer. "I'm with the IRS. I need to know why Florence Cash is receiving free services here. Is it in return for advertising?"

The doctor opened his mouth as if to say something but then seemed to think better of it and closed his mouth. "I'm pretty sure the HIPAA laws prevent me from disclosing anything to you."

"I'm not asking about her health information," I said. "I'm asking about her bills. Whether she had any."

The man chewed his lip, appearing to vacillate. "I'm sorry," he said finally. "I'd like to help you out, but I can't risk a HIPAA violation. The board could take my license. But if you get Miss Cash's consent I'd be happy to provide the information to you."

Thanks for nothing. Of course I supposed I should have expected this type of response from a health-care provider. I should've thought this through first. Still, to ensure that the day wasn't a total loss the least I could do was put a little fear in the doctor, leave him shaking in his blue paper booties.

"Just so you know," I said, "if you're trading chiropractic care for advertising on KCSH, you need to reflect those transactions in your reports to the IRS."

Of course, even though reporting would be required, such swaps in a business context would result in no net taxable income so long as the services or products provided were equal in value to those received. The income would be offset by an equal deduction. But in a personal context, such as Flo Cash receiving a spinal adjustment in exchange for advertising, things were much more complicated. KCSH would have to report the value of the care as advertising income. KCSH could then take a deduction for its transfer of the care to Flo for her personal use. The value of the services transferred would be reported as compensation to Flo and would be subject to income and Social Security taxes, just like salary or wages paid in cash. Flo would be required to pay income tax on the in-kind income. Of course, given the financial records I'd seen, none of these transactions were being accounted for. Instead, Flo was engaging in some off-the-books bargaining.

"Obviously, you're on my radar now. I'd hate to see you end up in hot water, too. Cooperation is to your benefit." I left my card on the counter. "Talk to your accountant," I said as I backed out the door. "Unless you want to find yourself in the hot seat for misreporting."

The door swung closed behind me. Though I had yet to get any concrete evidence against Flo Cash, I felt a small sense of satisfaction knowing I'd put a little fear into at least one of her advertisers.

As I walked back to the Yukon, I decided it couldn't hurt to pay a visit to Ledbetter Cadillac and speak with the general manager. Maybe he'd give me some rock-solid evidence to nail Flo. Had he given her the blue Cadillac in return for ads? Or maybe given her a substantial discount off the price in exchange? Or had their deal only involved free servicing for her car? If this case went to court, it wouldn't be enough for me to show that Flo had made some trades on behalf of herself and KCSH. The judge would want some proof as to the value of the trades. Without that proof, the court would rely on industry statistics. Given that KCSH had earned far more than the average radio station back when her father was in charge, I had a feeling Flo's trades, too, generated much more income than the industry standard. She'd probably be thrilled if the assessment was based on average data.

I parked at the dealership, this time taking a spot near the front. My feet had just hit the pavement when three salesmen were on me like white on rice.

"Hi, there! In the market for a Cadillac?" asked the first.

The second eyed the Yukon. "Looking for an upscale SUV? The Escalade is pure luxury."

The third merely scowled at the other two, turned around, and headed off to await the next potential customer.

"Sorry, guys," I said, pressing the button on the key fob to lock the doors. *Bleep.* "I'm only here to speak to your general manager. Can one of you show me to his office?"

The men who'd been so eager to assist me only a moment before were suddenly too busy to help.

The first backed away. "I need to check on something. Steve can help you."

The other, who had to be Steve, hurled eye daggers at his coworker. "This way," he barked grudgingly, jerking his head toward the showroom.

I followed him into the space, which was glass on three sides and housed several top-of-the-line Cadillacs, one of each model.

He stopped just inside the door and pointed toward the

back of the room. "The GM's office is the middle one over there."

"Great. Thanks."

I headed across the room toward an office with a wide window built into the door to allow the manager to keep an eye on the goings-on. Though the door was closed, the mini-blinds mounted over the window were raised, offering a clear view into the space. A large man with faded rusty hair sat behind a desk talking with someone on his phone. The nameplate on his door told me he was Vince Conover. The squint of his eyes and the tightness in his jaw told me that either the caller or the topic of discussion didn't sit well with him. He looked up as I approached, said some final words into the receiver, and hung up.

I rapped on the window. *Rap-rap.*

He stood and came to the door but opened it only a few inches, clearly not intending to invite me in. "Can I help you with something?"

I introduced myself and handed him my business card through the narrow opening. "I'd like to speak with you about Flo Cash and the free services your dealership has provided to her."

He tucked the card into his breast pocket. "She told me the IRS has been tracking her whereabouts and harassing the people she does business with."

"That was her on the phone? When I walked up?"

"Yes, it was."

I didn't like what this guy was telling me, but at least he was being up-front. It looked like Dr. Keele must have called Flo after I left his chiropractic clinic. *Snitch.* She must've realized I'd followed her to the clinic and wondered if I'd trailed her here to the car dealership earlier.

"What Miss Cash told you is not exactly true," I said. I had tracked Flo, but I hadn't harassed anyone. At least *I* didn't consider it harassment. I considered it doing my job.

Of course, Dr. Keele and the owners of Doo-Wop Donuts and the consignment shop would probably be inclined to agree with Flo's take on things, but that's only because they were engaging in shady financial shenanigans and didn't like being called on the carpet about it. "I'm only trying to gather information," I assured the man, "to ensure that proper tax reporting and payment is taking place."

"Well, you won't be gathering any information from me," Conover said. "Not without going through the dealership's attorney and not without a court order. Even then I can't guarantee we won't fight it."

Ugh. I really wasn't in the mood to waste two or three hours traipsing over to the Department of Justice, rounding up an attorney, and waiting in court until we could find an available judge to sign an order. But push was clearly coming to shove, and I had no choice but to shove back. "Looks like I'll need to speak with your attorney, then. Who is it?"

The man stepped over to his desk, fished a business card from a drawer, and returned to the door to hand it to me. I glanced down at the card. The firm listed there was one of Dallas' largest and most prestigious. In other words, they'd make things as hard on me as possible. Still, I had the law on my side. If third parties wouldn't voluntarily give me information in a case, I could contact an attorney at the Department of Justice who could issue subpoenas and take depositions and get court orders requiring the third parties to provide the requested data and documentation. Unfortunately, these things took time and patience and I had little of both.

I slid the card into the pocket of my blazer. "You'll be hearing from me again, Mr. Conover."

I could feel his cold gaze like a frozen laser on my back as I turned and headed out of the showroom.

When I was seated in the SUV, I closed my eyes and

mulled things over. The fact that Flo now knew I was contacting the advertisers would make things even harder on
me. Catching one of them by surprise was no longer an
option. They would be on notice that I was coming. No
doubt she'd advise them all that they could find themselves
in trouble for misreporting, and would suggest they keep
mum. She had to know the IRS had limited resources and
couldn't run down every rabbit hole. *Damn!*

I opened my eyes and glanced at the clock on the dashboard. It was half past four. Ross O'Donnell, an assistant
U.S. attorney who regularly represented the IRS, would
likely still be in his office. I started the car and drove to the
DOJ offices.

Minutes later, I stood in Ross' doorway. Ross had the
pale skin that came with long hours in an office and the
receding hairline of a man who'd been around the block a
time or two. But despite his high-stress job, Ross somehow managed to always keep his cool. He must do yoga or
meditate. His shirtsleeves were rolled up, his tie hanging
loosely from his neck, his suit jacket draped over the back
of his chair. His desk, like mine, was piled high with files.
A male paralegal scurried about the room, sorting through
and organizing documents. *And people think government
employees are shirkers. Sheesh.*

"Hey, Ross," I said by way of greeting. "Can you make
some time for your favorite special agent?"

"Always," he said. "Come on in and join the fun."

I glanced around the room. Box after cardboard box sat
on his floor, while stacks of documents and accordion files
stuffed full of exhibits covered his credenza. Next to them
towered a stack of DVDs of children's shows. One of the
shows was playing on a laptop, an animated butterfly fluttering through a garden, stopping to have a conversation
with a ladybug. "Watching cartoons?" I asked.

"It's evidence," he said. "I'm working a huge DVD piracy case."

I gestured toward the laptop. "My nieces love that show."

"Lots of kids do," Ross replied. "Unfortunately, bootleggers violated the production company's copyright and stole over six million in sales."

Crooks were everywhere, huh? Even in butterfly gardens.

I plunked myself down in one of his wing chairs. "My latest investigation involves Florence Cash. She hosts a radio show on KCSH."

"Flo Cash's *Cash Flow Show*?" he said. "I listen to that program on my drive to work sometimes. 'Make your money make money for you,' right?"

"Right," I said. "Only she doesn't take her own advice. She's got no investment accounts, not even a checking or savings account that I can find. She inherited the house she lives in, as well as the radio station and the building it broadcasts from. She's got around twelve thousand dollars in cash in a safe, but she claims that's everything she owns. She pays herself minimum wage but is somehow managing to keep herself afloat. She says she's been living off cash she accumulated before her father passed away and left the station to her. The station's financial records indicate that advertising revenue has decreased significantly since she took over, but the station is somehow staying afloat, too. It's not adding up."

Ross sat back in his chair. "Any theories?"

"Yep. I think she's trading on-air advertising for products and services. Taken things off the books."

His head bobbed as he appeared to weigh the idea and find it possible. "Got any proof of that?"

"I followed her to a chiropractic appointment today and

she made no co-pay when she left. She also got her car serviced for no charge at Ledbetter Cadillac. She's promoted both the chiropractic clinic and the car dealership on air, though neither of them would admit to making a trade with her. I stopped by some of the other businesses she's mentioned, too, but nobody would tell me anything. They're all playing innocent, like they have no idea what I'm talking about."

"Typical."

"Can you get some kind of court order for me? You know, something that forces these businesses to disclose any transactions they might have had with Flo Cash?"

"I can," he said, "but only if you get some proof first to support it. You'd need witnesses from the businesses to testify that they'd made deals with her to do in-kind swaps. Two or three should be sufficient to show a pattern of behavior on Flo's part."

Two or three? I groaned. I hadn't been able to get a single one to come clean so far. Though the clerk at the dealership had admitted they hadn't charged Flo for the maintenance and the delivery boy for the Chinese restaurant had told me he'd never collected a cent for the food he'd brought to the station, neither of them had said outright that charges had been waived in return for on-air promotion. "So I have to somehow gather evidence in order to get a court order that will allow me to gather more evidence?"

Ross offered an empathetic groan. "Ironic, huh?"

Ironic and frustrating. "Flo's on to me. She's been contacting the businesses and warning them I'm running an investigation. They're starting to clam up and lawyer up. Getting even one of them to cooperate will probably be difficult."

Ross offered me a soft smile. "Has your job ever been easy, Tara?"

Since I'd joined the IRS, I'd been shot at, knocked unconscious, tackled to the ground, and very nearly blown to smithereens by explosives placed under my car. I could reply with an unequivocal and emphatic, "No. Never."

"Your job being difficult has never stopped you before," Ross said. "So get on out there and keep doing what you do."

As much as I'd hoped he would offer me a quick and easy solution rather than a pep talk, I knew he was right. This wasn't my first rodeo, and I'd learned—the hard way—that there were no shortcuts when it came to enforcing tax law. I stood. "Thanks for the encouragement. And the legal advice."

"Anytime," he said. "Come back when you've got something."

"Will do." Of course I wondered if his "when" should be an "if." *Will I ever be able to prove that Flo Cash is up to no good?*

chapter sixteen

$\mathcal{T}$he Lost
Art of Conversation

I hit the ground running on Wednesday, hoping that by the end of the day I'd have two or three advertisers willing to spill the beans. Surely some of them would cooperate, see the value in being on the side of the government. Right?

My first stop was at Jitter Juice, a small neighborhood coffee shop that also served smoothies with a caffeine additive. Their paper cups featured their slogan—*Jitter Juice Gets You Going*—in a lime-green font with lines next to the *J*s to give the illusion that they were shaking.

A blond female barista met my eye over the pastry display case. "What can I get you?"

"Your boss," I said, holding up my badge. "I'm with the IRS."

The young woman took a look at my badge, walked to a door in the back wall, and knocked. When a male voice called, "Come in!" she stuck her head through. "There's a lady from the IRS here to see you."

I couldn't see the man speaking, but I could hear him clear enough. "Tell her I'm out."

Sheesh.

The barista turned back to me and cringed. "Um . . . he's out?"

I didn't fault the young woman. She was between a rock and a hard place here.

Better take matters into my own hands. "I heard you back there!" I called to the owner. "I know you're there."

"Then I'm busy!" he shouted back.

"I'll come back another time, then!" I hollered. "When are you free?"

There were a few seconds of total silence as the man apparently tried to come up with a response. "I left my calendar at home! Leave your card and I'll call you!"

I sighed and met the barista's eyes over the display case. "He's not going to call, is he?"

She cringed again, lifting her shoulders. I slipped her my card. These people might not have spilled any beans, but they could at least grind some for me. "Give me a large toffee latte to go."

I sipped my coffee on the way to my next stop, a high-end paint store. As I walked inside, a weathered man in his late forties approached me. If his skin was a shade of paint, it would be called Southern Sunburn. He must not only sell the stuff but also perform some of the outside painting work as well.

"You looking for interior or exterior paint?" he asked.

"Actually," I said, "I'm looking for the owner of the store."

The man dipped his head. "You've got him."

I handed him my card.

He read it over and frowned, but he didn't seem surprised.

"I need to ask you a few questions about KCSH and the promotions they've run for your store."

"Can't help you there," he said, holding out my card as if to return it to me.

I didn't take it back. "Why not?"

"I have no control about what some person says or doesn't say on the radio. You'll have to talk to the people at the station about that." He jabbed the card at me, as if he could wash his hands of things by ridding himself of it.

I narrowed my eyes at him. "You traded some paint to Florence Cash in exchange for advertising, didn't you? Sent a crew out to her house? I've seen it. It's beautiful. Your guys did a good job."

When he failed to respond, I stepped over to the color display, running my eyes over the selections until I found one with a color family that matched the walls in Flo's home. "These are the colors you used," I said, pointing to each in turn. "Beautiful Burgundy in her living and dining rooms. Magnificent Merlot in her study. Rustic Rosé in her foyer."

The man turned reddish now, too. A color I'd called Pissed-Off Purple.

"Like I said," he growled. "You'll need to speak with Flo."

My brows rose. "So you two are on a first-name basis."

"I'm only repeating what you said."

"I referred to her as 'Florence.'"

He sputtered for a moment before coming up with an excuse. "Everyone in Dallas knows who Flo Cash is. You'd have to live under a rock not to have heard of her. That's the name she goes by. Flo."

Ugh. Didn't seem I'd get anywhere with this guy, and the tinkling bells on the door told me that he had customers on their way in. "Keep my card," I said, "and think things over. You're not the only business I'm talking to. The first two or three to come clean will be in a much better position to get any penalties waived." I raised my palms. "I'm just sayin'." With that, I turned and left.

My third stop was a wine store. This time, I was stared down by both a husband and wife, who owned and ran the place together.

"You want information," the man spat, "go through the proper channels."

Damn, these people were chapping my ass! "There's nothing improper with me coming to your place of business to speak with you. Not every conversation I have with taxpayers requires legal representation or a court order."

"Any conversation you have with us does." The woman tapped the corkscrew in her hand against the palm of the other.

Is she threatening me? Two could play that game. I put a hand on my hip, easing my blazer back to casually reveal the gun holstered at my waist. *Neener-neener. A Glock trumps a corkscrew.* "If you change your mind, you know how to reach me."

As I pulled to the curb in front of a gourmet cheese shop twenty minutes later, the lights went off inside and the blinds came down. Whoever was inside must have identified my car as a government vehicle. I climbed out and headed to the door, only to hear a *click* as it was locked. A hand reached from behind the closed blinds to turn the sign on the door from "OPEN" to "CLOSED."

I banged a frustrated fist on the glass. *Bam! Bam! Bam!* "I know you're in there!" *Wuss.* "You're only making things worse for yourself!"

Alas, my words failed to prove persuasive. Five minutes and fifty *bam*s later, I gave up.

My luck was no better at the day spa or the gift store. No doubt Flo had been a busy little beaver, placing calls to all of her under-the-table advertisers, telling them not to cooperate, that as long as they stuck together they could defeat the government. Given that Flo was known as a financial guru, she enjoyed a certain amount of respect and authority. People listened to her. *Damn them.*

Having gotten nowhere, I decided to return to my office, where I spent the rest of Wednesday on the phone, placing calls to the businesses Flo had promoted on KCSH. Though I realized I might have better luck going to the businesses in person, there simply wasn't time for me to go traipsing all over the city and surrounding suburbs. I'd only be able to hit a few businesses during a workday if I went door to door, but by phone I could contact dozens of them. Unfortunately, all I got in return for my efforts was vague answers and outright refusals to speak without an attorney present, all of them reading from Flo's uniform script. I told them all what I'd told the guy at the paint store, that it could be to their advantage to be among the first to come clean. Unfortunately, it seemed they trusted Flo Cash more than they trusted me.

When the end of the day came, I actually found myself looking forward to my date with Morgan Walker that evening, and not just because it would take me one step closer to nailing him but because today had been a total waste of effort and I could really use a night out and a glass of wine.

Nick sat on the patchwork quilt that covered my bed as I went through my closet, looking for something to wear.

I found a cute sundress and stepped out of the closet, holding it up in front of me. "What do you think of this?"

"Bare shoulders and leg?" He frowned. "I don't like it. Don't you have an old feed sack and rubber boots you can wear? Maybe cover it all with a plastic rain poncho?"

I scoffed, "C'mon. You know I have to make an effort or the guy will realize I'm not legit."

"All right," Nick acquiesced. "Just no heels, no mini-skirts, and no lace panties."

I ventured back into my closet and found a lightweight white cardigan. Not only would it make Nick happier and keep me warm in the restaurant; it also would hide my bruised elbows. "What if I put this over the sundress?"

"Better," he said, though he still didn't look thrilled.

Once I was dressed, I went to the bathroom to freshen my makeup and hair. I gave myself a quick spritz with lavender body spray and reached for my lip gloss.

Nick leaned against the door frame, watching me, his arms crossed over his chest. "Absolutely not."

"Why?"

" 'Cause I don't want this bastard looking at your lips. In fact, if he tries to kiss you good night you should knee him in the groin."

"You know I can't make any promises," I told Nick. "I'll offer a cheek if he tries to kiss me, but I'm going to have to play this by ear."

"Order a meal with lots of garlic and onion," Nick said. "Then he won't want to kiss you. Maybe get some spinach in your teeth."

"Ew." Finished, I stepped over to Nick and reached up to put my arms on his shoulders. "You know you're the only man for me."

He pulled me to him for what I expected would be a hug, but instead he rubbed himself against me.

I pushed him back. "What the heck are you doing?"

"Marking you with my scent. Maybe he'll pick up on it subliminally."

Men. Sheesh. "I'm not your property, Nick."

"Ouch!" He slapped a hand over his heart. "Way to hurt a guy."

"You don't think you're my property, do you?"

"Hell, yeah, I do!" He bent down and nuzzled my neck. "I'm all yours," he whispered in my ear. "Do with me what you will."

"That'll have to wait." I squeezed past him and headed toward my stairs. "I'll call you when it's over."

"Better yet," he said, "come over. I'll mark you head to toe."

"Go home and take a cold shower," I suggested, descending the steps.

He followed after me. "Have a terrible time."

I grabbed my purse from the table in the foyer. "Thanks. I'll do that."

chapter seventeen

$\mathcal{M}$y Last First Date

I arrived at the restaurant ten minutes early, unsure whether to go on inside or wait in the car I'd borrowed from the undercover fleet. I decided to check in with Eddie. I pulled out my phone and sent him a quick text: *You here yet?* While I was trying my best to be brave, my nerves were nonetheless on edge. I was dealing with a possible black belt here. One swing of his bladed hand and he could break my neck. It was more than a little disconcerting.

Eddie's reply came a few seconds later: *We're heading in.*

I sent him a second text: *Decide on the director job yet? Still thinking it over.*

If it were up to Eddie's wife, he'd take the job. She'd fallen to pieces when he'd been shot in one of our earlier cases and lived in constant fear he'd be hurt again. I wondered if he'd even told her about the job offer: *Does Sandra know?*

His only reply was *Sh-h-h.*

So he hadn't told her. *Yet.* I knew he would eventually. Eddie was a good man and wouldn't hide something like this from his wife forever. He was probably just waiting to tell her until after he'd sorted through his feelings on the subject. As for my feelings? I was still conflicted, too. Eddie had been my first partner, the only agent who'd agree to take on the scrawny rookie everyone else had seen as a liability. He'd become my trainer, mentor, and friend. I enjoyed working cases with him, too, and would miss his companionship and smart-ass commentary. Not that I thought those things would end if he became director. But it would be on different terms.

I pulled down my visor, performed a final makeup check in the mirror, and fluffed my hair. Unnecessary, probably. After all, this guy wouldn't really care whether I was attractive. He was only after my bank account, not me. Still, it wouldn't hurt anything if he thought I was cute, right? And after my hitting wall after wall today in the Flo Cash investigation, my ego was bruised. Was it so wrong of me to seek a little boost, even if from a criminal?

Another text came in from Eddie: *He's waiting in the bar.*

This catfisher might be a crook, but at least he was punctual.

I climbed out of the car and walked to the doors, waiting as a family with three young children entered the restaurant. I stepped inside behind them. As they made their way to the hostess stand, I scanned the foyer and bar area.

My eyes met those of Morgan Walker as he spotted me across the way. He sat in the bar, a cocktail glass in front of him. When he realized I matched the photo of Sara Galloway on the dating site, his mouth spread in a broad smile and he stood. I raised a hand to wave and headed toward the bar.

"Sara, right?" he said, extending a hand.

"Yep. That's me." *Nope.*

"It's great to meet you."

It's great to be one step closer to busting you. I gave his hand a shake. "You, too, Morgan." *Who are you, really?*

Morgan wore a stylish brown dress shirt with contrasting black lapels and epaulets, black pants, and shiny black loafers, a look that managed to be both sophisticated yet fun at the same time. His hair was the same ginger color as in his second round of head shots, his eyes chocolate brown behind the eyeglasses. I looked for the telltale edges of a colored contact lens, but his glasses and the dim lighting in the bar made it impossible for me to tell if he was wearing them. The freckle on his jawline near his left ear was unmistakable, though, marking him as the man who'd presented himself as Jack Smirnoff to Leslie Gleason, Julia Valenzuela, and Nataya Lawan. Despite the fact that he was a con artist, I had to admit that the guy was attractive.

His gaze flickered to my lips. At first, I took it as a sign that he found me attractive and was already scouting the real estate for a potential kiss later on. But when his gaze lingered a bit too long and his nose crinkled slightly, I realized he was staring at the split on my lip, which had yet to fully heal. He seemed a little disgusted by it. Unfair, really, since I wouldn't have the damn injury if it weren't for him. I debated telling him not to worry, that it wasn't a cold sore or a sign of disease, but then I figured what the hell, let him think I had herpes. I didn't want the guy trying to kiss me anyway, and he'd be far more interested in my bank balance than my health history anyway.

He finished off the small amount of amber liquid in his cocktail glass and held out a hand to indicate the hostess stand. I found myself analyzing his movements. *Is that hand a lethal weapon?*

"Shall we?" he asked.

"Sure."

We proceeded to the hostess stand, where Morgan requested a table for two. A moment later, a woman approached us with menus in her hand. "Right this way."

She led us past Eddie and Sandra, who sat at a table in the center of the room, and stopped at a table in a quiet back corner.

"This is perfect," Morgan told her with a winning smile. "Thank you."

Nice to the waitstaff, huh? That was a plus. Over the years, I'd dated one or two guys who'd been condescending to our servers. Of course I'd only gone out with those guys the one time. Excessive ego was such a turnoff. Besides, one could never be sure whether an irritated waiter had spit in their dinner.

When Morgan circled around behind me, I found myself instinctively turning to keep him in my sights. When I realized he only intended to push in my chair, not grab me by the throat, I turned forward and took a seat, hoping my paranoia hadn't been obvious. I hoped, that if anything, he would only think me awkward.

He made his way to the other side of the table. After taking his seat, he unwrapped his silverware from the cloth napkin and placed the napkin in his lap. Someone had taught this man good manners. I wondered if he, too, had attended something like Miss Cecily's Charm School.

He sat up straight and looked across the table at me. "How has your day been going so far, Sara?"

I'd put some thought into my character on the way over. I realized that staying as close to the truth as possible would make it easier for me to keep my story straight. "Honestly?" I said to this dishonest man. "People seemed bound and determined to drive me nuts today. I asked several of them for the information I need to get my work done, but they all put me off."

He eyed me intently. "So they aren't respectful of your time and schedule, and that causes you to feel frustrated."

Wow. This guy gets it. "Exactly!"

"Why don't we get some wine?" he asked with a grin. "I find a glass or two is a good cure for frustration."

I offered him a smile in return. "I like the way you think, Morgan."

This guy certainly had charisma. If I hadn't been fore-warned about him, I could easily succumb to his charms, just like the other women had.

The waitress came over and Morgan and I placed orders for wine. I chose a light white, while Morgan went for a red. Normally, drinking on duty would be frowned upon, but I had an undercover persona to maintain here. Sara Galloway was no teetotaler. *Bottoms up!*

Once the server left, we reviewed our menus.

"Everything looks good," I said. "I'm going to have a hard time deciding."

"I'm partial to the mushroom ravioli," he said. "I think I'll get that." Having decided on his dinner, Morgan put his menu down on the table, and, as before, his gaze locked on mine. "So today wasn't great for you," he said, "but there must be things you like about running a bookkeep-ing business or you wouldn't have done it for so many years."

Though he hadn't phrased his comment as a question, it was clear he was attempting to engage me in conversa-tion. I quickly tried to put myself in the place of my alter ego. If I were actually Sara Galloway, bookkeeper extraor-dinaire, what would I like about my work?

"I like being my own boss and setting my own hours," I told Morgan. "The flexibility is fantastic. And, of course, there are no office politics, though I sometimes get into an argument with my printer when it jams."

He responded with a light chuckle.

"On the flip side," I added, "working by myself from home can leave me feeling a little lonely and isolated at times. I'm not learning many new things, either. I'm doing the same type of work now that I did when I started the business years ago."

"You'd like to grow professionally?"

He'd offered me the perfect opportunity here to plant my seed of feigned innocence. "I would. I mean, I'm proud that I earned an associate's degree, and bookkeeping is a good profession. There's always work and I've been fortunate to make a good living at it. But sometimes my clients ask me questions about complex financial matters and I don't know enough to answer them. It's made me realize that much of what I do is organizing data. I know where the numbers go in the bookkeeping programs and I'm really good about finding discrepancies and reconciling errors, but that's it. I'd like to learn more about how finances work so that I can help my clients with business decisions and tax planning."

He tilted his head. "Are you thinking of going back to school?"

I nodded. "Since my schedule is flexible, it wouldn't be hard for me to go back to college and get an accounting degree, maybe pursue a CPA license."

"Sounds like a smart plan, Sara."

The waitress arrived with our wine. Morgan thanked her and, once she'd gone, raised his glass to me. "To you and your ambition."

I clinked my glass against his and took a sip. "What about you? What do you like and dislike about your job?"

He leaned toward me across the table, lowering his voice. "Substance abuse isn't pretty. People use drugs or alcohol to escape their problems, but they only end up making them worse."

It seemed an ironic thing for him to say, given that only minutes before he'd suggested wine as a cure for frustration.

"When a client who's had some success suffers a relapse," he continued, "it can be heartbreaking. But when a client finally kicks the habit and gets his or her life back on track, it's a great feeling to know I helped them get there."

Liar. He wasn't helping anyone get their lives back on track. All he was doing was helping unsuspecting women empty their bank accounts. I fought the urge to toss my glass of wine in his face. Instead, I said, "What a noble profession."

Counseling was indeed noble, for those who actually did it. But it crossed my mind at that point that maybe he actually provided therapy services for a living. He'd claimed to be a psychologist earlier, and now he professed to be a substance abuse counselor. The women who came to my office all claimed he was a good listener, and so far I had to agree. He appeared to hang on my every word and asked good follow-up questions. *Hm-m . . .*

There was a flurry of activity to my right as the waitress brought a large bowl of salad and a basket of breadsticks to Eddie and Sandra's table. Though I cast a glance his way, Eddie didn't make eye contact, keeping our connection discreet.

The waitress came to our table next, likewise bringing us a salad and breadsticks, along with plates. Once she'd situated everything on the table, she pulled a pad and pen from her apron. "Are you two ready to order?"

I smiled up at her. "I have it on good authority that the mushroom ravioli is delicious. I'll try that."

Morgan cut a grin my way before handing his menu to the waitress. "I'll have the same."

The waitress left to turn in our order and my date returned his attention to me. "Your profile mentioned you like cats. The one in your profile pic was adorable."

"Thanks. I have two cats, but the other one refuses to be photographed with me."

"Tell me about them."

"Really?" I picked up the tongs and served myself some salad. "Are you sure you want to get me started? My cats are my babies. I could go on for hours."

He smiled. "I happen to like cats, too."

I returned the tongs to the bowl and turned it to give him access. "The cat you saw in my profile picture is Anastasia," I told him. *Hey, if I had an alias, my pets should, too, right?* "But I sometimes call her Annie, or Anna Banana. She's skittish, but very sweet. Sleeps next to me every night. I adopted her at a shelter a few years ago along with a male Maine coon. His name is Hank." I'd come up with that name quick, probably because a Hank Williams Jr. song had been playing on the radio on my drive to the restaurant. I took a sip of my wine. "Hank is arrogant. He thinks I exist solely to serve him."

Morgan laughed. "I bet you love him anyway."

"With all my heart." It was true. And pathetic. That furry little jackass had me wrapped around his paw. I pulled out my phone and swiped through my pics until I found one of Henry—*Hank*—lying on my bed pillow, shedding. "This is him." I held the phone up to show Morgan.

"He may be arrogant," Morgan said, "but he's handsome, too."

"I spend more time brushing his hair than I do my own."

As I stashed my phone back in my purse, Morgan said, "You showed me yours. Now I have to show you mine."

I cut him a grin. "We are still talking about cats, here, right?" Okay, so I was flirting a little. But that was all part of this charade, right?

Morgan pulled his phone from his pocket and showed me a photograph of a fluffy orange tabby. "Her name is Marmalade. She was my wife's cat."

He paused a moment, as if waiting for me to respond to the fact that he'd mentioned a wife. *He certainly has his shtick down.*

"Wife?" I said, purposefully stiffening like I presumably would have had I not expected to hear this. "You have a wife?"

"I did." His voice and expression became solemn now. "She passed away a few months ago from an inoperable brain tumor."

"Oh, Morgan! I'm so sorry to hear it." I reached across the table to give his hand a squeeze, already looking forward to the time when I'd get to slap cuffs on it—assuming, of course, that he didn't karate chop me in half before I got the chance.

He returned his phone to his pocket. "It was a horrible loss, but I know she'd want me to move on and find happiness. I'm trying to do that."

Yeah, right. All you're trying to find is a trusting woman to take advantage of. "Good for you."

He served himself some salad and tore a bit off a breadstick. "Relocating to Dallas is part of my plan to get a fresh start. Oklahoma City has too many memories."

"That's understandable," I said, selecting a breadstick for myself. I tore off a bite and put it to my mouth. *Ow!* The garlic coating burned my injured lip. *Great.* I opened my mouth wider and popped the bread inside, avoiding my lips altogether this time. "How long were you married?"

"Just a few years," he said. "We didn't have any children of our own, but she had an adult son from a previous marriage."

"Are you close to her son?" I asked, knowing full well the answer would be—

"No."

Yep. Just what I'd expected him to say. Ten points for Tara!

Morgan looked down, as if with regret. "I treated Shane as if he was my own, but no matter how good I was to him he would never warm up to me. He'd hoped his parents would get back together. I guess some kids never move past that, even when they grow up. Shane saw me as an obstacle. Never mind the fact that neither of his parents wanted to reconcile. But enough about that." He looked back up and waved a dismissive hand, as if wanting to clear the air of the ugly topic, despite the fact that he'd raised the topic himself, on purpose. "Your profile mentioned that you like mystery novels and romantic comedies. What are some of your favorites?"

We spent the next few minutes eating salad and breadsticks and discussing our favorite authors and actors until our entrées arrived. We discovered that we both liked Carl Hiaasen's books and Armie Hammer's movies.

"Looks like we've got some things in common," Morgan said.

I offered him a coy smile. "We do." *We also both like taking money from other people, though I do it to serve justice and you do it to serve yourself.*

As we dug into our ravioli, I eyed him across the table. Was he a kung fu master? A karate chop king? A jiu-jitsu genius? I debated hurling the saltshaker at him to see if he could successfully deflect it. Instead, I asked about his local accommodations. "Where are you staying while you're in Dallas?"

"At the Omni hotel downtown," he said. "The central location makes it very convenient."

Also, mentioning the name of the exclusive hotel was sure to impress his dates. Not me, though. I knew the odds of him actually being a guest at the Omni were about as good as my odds of winning an Oscar for my acting performance tonight.

I moved on to a related topic, asking about his plans to move to the area. "Are you looking to buy a house or condo?" I asked. "Or are you going to rent something?"

"I'm definitely planning to buy," he said. "With my income, I need all the tax deductions I can get."

Though I forced a smile, my ire rose. After the way he'd tricked those women out of their hard-earned money, this cheat didn't deserve any deductions. Of course I also realized his comment was a subtle way of implying that he earned good money. I decided to let him think I'd taken the bait. "Is there good money in drug counseling?"

He acted sheepish. "When celebrities are involved, there is. I work at a private rehabilitation center outside the city. It's known for both luxury and discretion, so we get a lot of high-profile patients who will pay top dollar to maintain their privacy."

"Have you found a new job here yet?"

"I've put out some feelers and gotten quite a few nibbles," he said. "I'll be able to make a quick and easy transition once I get things sorted out in Oklahoma."

"What's left to sort out?" I asked. *Might as well help him along, huh?*

He frowned. "My stepson is challenging my wife's will. Everything's tied up in probate court. Our house, our investments, our bank accounts. But I'm hoping it will all be resolved in a month or two so I can get on with my life."

He changed back to lighter topics, probably realizing if he hammered too hard on the alleged probate problems it could send up a red flag or turn me off.

As we ate and chatted, I cast another casual glance at Eddie and Sandra. While they'd eaten slowly to give me and my date a chance to catch up, the waitress was now handing Eddie the bill and taking their plates. I didn't like losing my backup. Morgan hadn't given off a violent vibe, but I knew from experience that even the most seemingly calm and harmless person could snap under pressure. It never hurt to be careful. And I still wasn't sure whether my date was merely a catfisher or also some type of judo master. It's not like I could throw a punch at him and see how he reacted.

"Dessert?" the waitress asked as she stepped up to our table.

"None for me," I said, putting a hand on my tummy. "I'm stuffed."

"Me, too," Morgan said. "Just the check please."

chapter eighteen

$\mathscr{D}$econstructed

Morgan paid the bill in cash, probably dirty money he'd stolen from one of his victims. This guy was smart. If he'd paid with a credit card the waitress might have referenced his last name and given me a clue as to his true identity. I eyed him over the table as he handed the payment to the waitress. *Who are you, you rat bastard?*

Our date over, Morgan walked me outside, stopping on the front walk. I briefly toyed with the idea of trying to pick his pocket. Surely he carried his real driver's license in his wallet in case he got pulled over, right? I decided against it, though. The only pickpocket experience I had was watching *Oliver*, and the movie implied that the crime could best be committed while singing and dancing. I didn't have the skill set necessary to pull it off.

Though I couldn't see Eddie, I knew he still lurked somewhere nearby, keeping an eye on things, watching my back.

"I had a nice time, Sara," Morgan said.

"Me, too."

He cocked his head and gave me a hopeful smile. "Want to do it again?"

"Sure. When?"

"How about seven next Tuesday?"

Tuesday? Really? My face flamed at the insult. Everyone knows a weekday date is for someone you aren't truly interested in. It was one thing for Morgan to take me out on a weeknight for our first date. After all, Fridays and Saturdays were special and not to be wasted with someone you weren't sure you'd enjoy spending time with. But for him to relegate me to weekday status for a second date was an obvious insult.

He eyed me intently. "I would've suggested the weekend, but unfortunately I've got to be back in Oklahoma City. I'm on the schedule at the center."

He must've read my mind. My face flamed once more, this time with embarrassment. *Sheesh.* I hoped I could do a better job of hiding my true identity than I did hiding my feelings. Besides, it was ridiculous for me to be insulted by this guy when I had a man like Nick in my life and no intentions of pursuing a romantic relationship with this con artist.

I forced a smile. "Tuesday's great."

"Your profile mentioned that you like sushi, right?"

"I do! How sweet of you to remember." Especially when he surely had several other profiles to remember, too. This guy must have a good memory.

"Why don't you name the place?"

My mind reeled. I had several favorite sushi places, but all were near my town house or downtown, near the entertainment venues. Given that I didn't actually live here in Lewisville, I didn't know the area well and had no idea where a sushi restaurant might be. "Sure," I said, deciding to evade the question for now. "I'll e-mail you with the name and address of the restaurant."

"Great." He pulled his keys from his pant pocket, then patted his shirt pocket. "Looks like I'm out of business cards." He gestured toward the right side of the building. "I've got more in my car. I'd like you to have one so you can get in touch with me if you'd like."

"Okay."

He led me around to the back of the building, heading out to where the restaurant's parking lot merged with that of the adjacent shopping center. This part of the lot was too far out to be reached by security cameras on any of the surrounding buildings.

In my peripheral vision, I spotted Eddie's car easing around the other side of the restaurant where he could keep an eye on us.

Morgan pushed the button on the fob. The lights flashed and doors unlocked on a Mercedes parked nearby. However, unlike the car he'd driven on his dates with his three victims, this one was not a convertible. It also had Oklahoma plates rather than Colorado plates. I made a mental note of the license plate number, repeating it in my head three times to commit it to memory.

"Why are you parked way out here?" I asked.

"Don't want to risk the car getting damaged. I bought it for my wife for her birthday last year. She insisted it was too much, but she'd never had nice things. She grew up poor and her first husband hadn't been in a position to provide well for her. I only wanted her to have the things she deserved."

A clever response. It made him sound both responsible and generous. "Why are you driving her car instead of your own?"

He frowned. "Her son snatched the keys to my Porsche and took off with it."

"Did you report it stolen? Maybe the cops could get it back for you."

He let out a soft breath. "As difficult as Shane is being right now, I don't have the heart to have him arrested. He might be in his twenties, but in so many ways he's still a child. He's having a hard time dealing with his mother's passing. Besides, my attorneys have advised me to let things play out through probate court. I'm sure it will all be resolved soon."

He opened the door to the Mercedes, reached inside, and grabbed a business card from a slot on the dash. He handed it to me. I took a quick look. It was a basic gray card with black printing.

Morgan Walker, Therapist
Specializing in Substance Abuse and Addiction

The card also included an e-mail address and phone number that began with a 405 area code.

He rested his left arm on top of the open door and cocked his head. "Do you have a card, Sara? I'd love to be able to contact you directly rather than having to go through the Perfect Couple site. That is, if you're comfortable giving me your information." He raised his palms. "No pressure."

I reached into my purse and fished out one of the business cards I'd had made for Sara Galloway months before. "Here you go," I said, holding it out to him.

"Where are you parked?" he asked.

I gestured to the far side of the building. "Around that way."

"Can I give you a lift?"

"No thanks. It's not far."

The thought of climbing into this criminal's car frightened me, even if Eddie had me in his sights. Nonetheless, I wanted to see if there was anything in the car that might give me a clue as to who this man really was. "Mind if I take a look inside your car? It's so nice."

"Sure."

While he extolled the interior features—surround sound, over half a dozen speakers, leather seats, blah, blah, blah—I stuck my head in the driver's door snuck a peek into the backseat and at the floorboards, inspecting every cupholder. I saw nothing. No martial arts uniform. No gym bag. Not even an errant nickel or rock-hard French fry. *Damn.*

I stood back up. "If I wasn't looking at tuition, I'd be tempted to use my savings to put a down payment on a car like this." *Did you get that, Morgan? I've got savings.* Yep, might as well dangle that carrot.

"Get that degree," he replied, "and you'll be able to buy ten of these."

I offered him a final smile. "True."

He leaned down and for a split second I feared he might try to kiss me. Instead, however, he gave me a loose one-armed hug that involved no body contact other than his hand on my shoulder blade. He might be a con artist, but he wasn't a letch. I had to give him that.

He stepped back. "Good night, Sara."

"Good night, Morgan."

As he climbed into his car, I made my way around the side of the building. Eddie cruised past me on his way to follow Morgan's Mercedes. I gave Eddie a subtle thumbs-up as he passed.

I climbed into my car, buckled the belt, and immediately called Eddie's cell phone.

Sandra answered. "Hi, Tara. I'll put you on speaker."

I did the same, jabbing the speaker button and dropping the phone into the ashtray to free my hands for driving.

Eddie's voice came over the airwaves a moment later. "I'm on him. Looks like he's heading toward the on-ramp for the interstate."

I started my engine. "I'm heading after you."

Morgan hadn't seen my car, and besides, it was dark

now. All he'd see in his rearview mirror was headlights. Still, I'd hang back just to be safe. I was dying to know whether he actually lived in the Dallas area or was truly from out of town somewhere and staying in a hotel.

I caught up with Eddie at a light on the frontage road. "I'm right behind you, buddy."

"Walker is two cars ahead of me," he said. "How'd the date go?"

"It was good," I said. "He asked me to meet him for dinner again next Tuesday."

"Tuesday?" Eddie snickered. "If he planned a second date on a Tuesday it did *not* go well."

My face blazed for a third time. Much more of this and I'd suffer heatstroke. "It wasn't even a real date, you know! Not for either one of us."

"That's a good thing," Eddie said, "because he's clearly not into you."

I was tempted to shove the gas pedal to the floor and ram Eddie's back bumper. Luckily for him, the light turned green before I could do it. We proceeded straight through the intersection and onto the entrance ramp for Interstate 35 north.

"He told me he was staying at the Omni downtown," I said. Downtown was south of our current location.

"Either he's got a bad sense of direction," Eddie replied, "or he fed you a line of bull."

My money was on bull. *Is anything the guy told me true? Does he even* have *a cat named Marmalade?*

Eddie followed the Mercedes and I followed Eddie. We continued on for several miles before a solid wall of red brake lights appeared before us.

"There's road construction ahead," Eddie said.

I groaned. Seemed like the interstates in North Texas were always under construction. Our tax dollars, ironically slowing us down in the name of progress. As I pressed the brake, the acrid smell of asphalt infiltrated my car, causing my nose to twitch. Looked like the road crew was repaving the lanes.

We crept along for several minutes, everyone merging to the right lane and making little headway. Eddie's brake lights flashed bright, his car rolled to a complete stop, and his voice came through the speaker; "Dammit!"

I eased my car to the side and looked past Eddie's hood. A construction worker in a bright orange safety vest stood in front of Eddie's car, holding up a red sign that read: "STOP." Morgan's Mercedes continued on, the last car to make it through before a steamroller backed into the lane.

"Hurry up!" I shouted. "Go!"

Eddie's voice came back, his tone tight. "What do you expect me to do? I can't go anywhere, Tara."

"Sorry!" I called. "I wasn't talking to you. I was talking to the steamroller."

"He can't hear you."

"I know, but yelling makes me feel better." Blasting off a few rounds at the firing range always calmed my nerves, too. But I couldn't very well pull out my gun here on the highway.

A couple minutes later, after the steamroller had smoothed out the new asphalt in the blocked lanes, the worker turned his sign around. The other side was yellow and read: "SLOW." Eddie and I eased past the construction zone, then sped up once we were out of the work area, zooming past the other cars in an attempt to get back on Morgan Walker's trail.

"See the Mercedes anywhere?" I asked Eddie.

"Nope!" he called back.

"I'll keep an eye on the frontage road," Sandra offered.

We continued on, putting the pedal to the medal, hoping to catch Walker. But when we'd gone ten miles and hadn't caught up with him it seemed clear that the pursuit was pointless. We weren't sure whether he was still on the highway or had taken an exit. We weren't getting anywhere other than farther from our homes. I banged a hand on the steering wheel in irritation.

"Let's try again on Thursday after his date with Hana," I told Eddie.

"All right," he replied resignedly.

"Thanks for your help."

"Anytime," he said.

"Thanks for dinner!" Sandra called back.

chapter nineteen

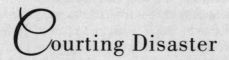

Courting Disaster

As Nick had requested, I went to his place after attempting to trail Morgan Walker. And, as promised, Nick marked me head to toe. The intimate interlude allowed me to work off some of my frustrations as well as calories. Four breadsticks was two too many, wasn't it?

Nick turned his head on his pillow and looked over at me. "You haven't told me how your date went."

"We're meeting for dinner again on Tuesday."

A snicker escaped him. *"Tuesday?"*

I sat up, grabbed my pillow, and whomped him with it. "Would you rather he'd fallen head over heels in love with me?" *Whomp!* "That he'd decided I was too wonderful to steal from and wanted to pursue a real relationship?" *Whomp!* I ended by throwing my pillow over Nick's face. Maybe that would shut him up.

He made no attempt to remove it. "I didn't mean to offend you," he said, his voice muffled by the pillow. "You're a unique and challenging woman, Tara. Not every man can handle you."

I pulled the pillow off his head. "I wasn't even being myself, anyway. It's not me he found unattractive and boring. It's Sara Galloway. If you've got a problem, take it up with her."

He reached for me. "Hi, Sara. How about you give me a peek at your general ledger?"

I slapped his hands away. "If we're going to engage in role play, I want to be Catwoman, not a bookkeeper."

Nick grinned. "I'll keep that in mind."

I snatched my clothes from the floor and dressed. Nick slid back into his boxer briefs and a pair of lounge pants.

We went downstairs to his living room, Daffodil trotting down the steps behind us. While Nick got down on all fours and wrestled playfully with Daffodil on the rug, I took a seat on the couch, logged into my laptop, and pulled up the Oklahoma motor vehicle department Web site to run a search on the Mercedes' license plate.

"A-ha!" I said when the site spit up the data. "The car Morgan Walker was driving is a rental. The records show it's owned by Hertz."

Nick looked up from the floor. "They rent fancy cars like that?"

"They must." I logged on to the Hertz site and took a look. "Yep. They've got something they call the Prestige line. They offer Infinitis and Lincolns for rent, too."

To Daffodil's disappointment, Nick pushed himself up from the floor and came over to flop down next to me on the couch. Though much too big to be a lapdog, Daffodil nonetheless leaped onto Nick, settling her front paws over his legs and giving him a loving lick under the chin.

Nick ran a hand down his dog's back. "So this catfisher is spending money, to look like he's got money, so that the women he plans to steal from won't think he needs money?"

"That pretty much sums it up."

"Seems like a lot of work. Why not just rob a liquor store like everyone else?"

"Maybe he doesn't own a ski mask." I searched online for the Omni hotel's phone number and dialed it on my cell. "Morgan Walker's room, please," I said when the receptionist answered.

A few seconds of silence ensued as the woman apparently attempted to pull up the guest account. "Could you repeat that name?"

"Morgan Walker," I said slowly, enunciating as clearly as I could.

"Hm-m, I don't see a guest by the name Morgan Walker. Could the reservation be under another name?"

"Try 'Jack Smirnoff,'" I said, spelling the last name for her. "*S-m-i-r-n-o-f-f.* Like the vodka."

"No," she said. "I'm sorry. There's no guest listed under that name, either."

"All right," I told her. "Thanks for checking."

"No luck?" Nick asked when I ended the call.

"No luck."

A few minutes later, he walked me out to my car. He leaned in to kiss me but pulled back at the last second. "That bastard didn't kiss you good night, did he?"

I sighed. "Don't worry. You won't catch his cooties. He planned our next date for a Tuesday, remember?"

"Oh, yeah," Nick said. "We're good to go, then."

He leaned in and gave me a long, warm kiss, making it clear he found me irresistible even if Morgan Walker didn't. And that was all I needed to know.

Thursday started off as a total bust.

When I looked into the cell phone number listed on Morgan's business card, I discovered it was another untraceable prepaid phone, another dead end.

My e-mail in-box was filled with messages from the dating sites. While I was flattered so many men had expressed interest in me, I was frustrated that none of the men had a client profile pic that matched Morgan Walker's new head shot. I banged a closed fist on my desk. "Damn!"

If I couldn't track down more victims, the guy would get off easy. There were more victims, weren't there? Surely there had to be, right? If not, he'd gone to an awful lot of trouble and expense to make a few bucks.

It took me fifteen minutes and three transfers to reach the proper person in the legal department at the car rental company. Except I didn't actually get the person. I got his voice mail.

"Your call is very important to me," his disembodied voice told me over the airwaves. "Please leave a detailed message and I will return your call."

I left a message explaining that I needed to know who had rented the Mercedes. "He's been involved in criminal activity. Please get back to me as soon as possible."

I spent the rest of the morning phoning thirty-six businesses Flo had mentioned on air but had no luck there, either.

Some played dumb. "KCSH? Never heard of it." "Flo who?"

Others proclaimed their innocence while at the same time covering their asses in case they were later proved to have lied. "I can't recall ever making payment to Flo Cash or agreeing to any kind of exchange. Of course we're so busy here everything's a blur."

One even feigned outrage. "How dare you imply I'd involve myself in unethical behavior!"

Some played the same old, tired card. "We'd be happy to comply with a court order." *Happy, my ass.*

None of them gave me anything to go on. Problem was, I couldn't get a court to issue an order until I convinced some of these people to testify that Flo had made trades with them. It was a vicious circle, a hamster wheel, and I was nothing more than a tiny, ineffective rodent running with all my might yet getting nowhere. The least someone could do was toss me a piece of cheese.

I was just about to head out to lunch when my phone rang. It was the paralegal from Hertz.

"I'd be happy to provide the information," the paralegal told me.

"Great!"

"Of course we'll need a court order first. Without that, I can't release anything."

My Lord, it was like everyone had become pull-string dolls, fitted with the same pre-recorded message: *No court order, no cooperation.* I'd like to yank out their strings and choke the puppets with them.

"I'll get you an order," I said on a sigh, putting a hand to my eyes. *This is not my day, is it?*

I realized I probably should call Ross O'Donnell first, but frankly, if I spent one more second with my phone to my ear my brain was likely to explode. I traipsed over to the Department of Justice armed with the women's affidavits and the computer printout showing the new dating profile for Jack Smirnoff, aka Morgan Walker, aka King of the Doo-Doo Heads. Unfortunately, Ross O'Donnell was nowhere to be found. He wasn't in his office, the library, the break room, or the file room.

I stopped at the desk of a harried administrative assistant. She consulted a log. "Ross signed out twenty minutes ago. Looks like he's in Judge Trumbull's court."

Should've called first, huh? At least with him already at the courthouse maybe he'd be able to slip my matter in between calling witnesses.

I hurried over to the courthouse, made my way through security and up to Judge Trumbull's courtroom. As quietly as possible, I slipped through the door and took a seat in the front row behind the prosecution table.

I glanced up at the bench. Judge Trumbull was a tough old broad, with a round physique under her billowy black robe and the saggy jowls of a bulldog. Still, despite being tough, she was undeniably fair. Nobody could complain that she always sided with the government, nor could they complain that she always sided against the government. She kept an open mind, and she made sure everyone did the job they were supposed to do.

The judge looked down at me and raised her brows in question. All I had to do was hold up my stack of paperwork for her to realize I had a quick matter that needed her attention as soon as there was a break in the current case over which she was presiding.

Judging from the stack of DVDs on Ross' counsel table, he was trying the video piracy case today. On the witness stand was a production expert, who described the telltale differences between an authentic copy of the children's cartoons and the pirated copy. "The pirated DVD," he said, holding up the fake, "is printed on a gold disc, as you can see. The authentic product is printed on a silver disc." He held up the silver disc to compare. "The packaging is also inconsistent with the authentic product. The version offered by the defendants came with no security seal and lacked the clear wrap." He held up two new DVD cases to show the difference.

Ross continued his questions for a couple more minutes before turning the witness over to defense counsel.

"Tell you what," Judge Trumbull said, cutting her eyes to her clock. "Let's hold the cross-examination for this afternoon and break for lunch now." She advised everyone to be back in their places by one o'clock. Using her gavel, she gestured to me. "Mr. O'Donnell, I believe Special Agent Holloway has a matter for us."

Ross turned around at his table. "Oh. Hey, Tara. What do you have?"

I stood and met him at his table, giving him a ten-second version. *Catfisher. Rental car. Desperate for information about Smirnoff/Walker.*

"All right," he said softly. "Let's give it a go."

With that, we stepped up to the bench and the waiting judge.

Ross addressed her first. "Agent Holloway would like an order requiring a rental car company to provide the name, contact information, and credit card number of a customer who is under investigation for criminal fraud and tax evasion."

Judge Trumbull waggled her fingers. "Give me details and give them quick. Mama's hungry for lunch and today's special is chimichangas."

I handed her the documentation and, as quickly as possible, ran through the events of the last few days. My meeting with the three women who'd filed complaints. My later meeting with J.B., the owner of Big D Dating Service. "The man known as Jack Smirnoff failed to respond to the service's e-mails," I told the judge. "The phone number he'd provided to the women and the dating service had been disconnected, too."

"Sure sounds like he was trying to hide," Judge Trumbull said, flipping through the pages in her hand. "Go on."

I told her how Josh had been able to search for the photograph online and identify the photographer and how a visit to Savannah Goode had led me to finding the new listing on PerfectCouple.com. "The photographer provided digital files of the catfisher's more recent head shots, and Special Agent Schmidt ran a search on them. They turned up on a dating site that was running a free trial period. I made up a profile for myself, contacted the target to express interest in meeting him, and went on a date with him last night."

"A date?" She tilted her head, her jowls jiggling with the movement. "How'd it go?"

"Good," I told her. "He asked me out again for Tuesday."

"*Tuesday?*" she scoffed. "Unless things have changed since my dating years, being asked out for a weeknight isn't a good sign, especially for a second date."

"Objection," I said. "That's irrelevant."

She tossed me a look of pity. "You can't object to something a judge says, and you can't object if you're not an attorney."

"Noted," I said through gritted teeth. "Anyway, Special Agent Bardin and I tried to follow the guy, but we lost him in a construction zone. I phoned the hotel where he'd claimed he was staying, but they told me they had no guest under the name Morgan Walker."

Trumbull's brows drew together. "Why didn't you just arrest this creep last night and be done with it?"

In hindsight, maybe that would have been the smarter move. "Because all we've got on him at this point is six grand in thefts. That'll get him a slap on the wrist at best. But if I can catch him trying to pass more bad checks, that'll raise the odds of him getting some real time. I suspect he's also ripped off women he's met on other dating sites, but since we don't know the guy's real name or what other aliases or profile pictures he's been using, there's no way to shut him down. If I can get some information from the car rental company, though, it could take me right to him."

"All right. You've convinced me." She signed the order with a flourish and handed it to me. "Got get 'im. Hopefully before Tuesday."

"Thanks, Your Honor." *And gr-r-r.*

When I returned to the IRS office, things began to look up even more. Morgan had sent a message to Sara Galloway's e-mail address: *Had a great time last night. You seem like a very accomplished and intelligent woman, and I'm looking forward to getting to know you better. Maybe someday we can even introduce Marmalade to Anastasia and Hank. Did you decide on a sushi place?*

I ran a search for sushi restaurants in Lewisville, chose the one that had the highest reviews, and included the name and address in my response: *I had a nice time, too. Looking forward to Tuesday.* [Jackass.] *See you there!*

I scanned the court order and e-mailed a copy to the car rental company. Until I heard back from Hertz, the case was at a standstill, so I returned to the list of KCSH advertisers. Next in line was Mister Sandman's Mattresses and More.

I dialed the number. "May I speak to Mr. Sandman?"

"He's busy bringing sweet dreams to another customer," the male voice on the phone said. "Can I help you?"

"I hope so. I'm Special Agent Tara Holloway with the Internal Revenue Service. I need to talk to the person in charge."

"You already are," he said. "Is this about KCSH? Flo Cash?"

Obviously, he'd been expecting my call. "I take it she's been in touch with you."

"She called a few days ago. Said the IRS was on a witch hunt and that the smartest thing I could do was keep my mouth shut. She said you'd eventually back off if I didn't cooperate."

Flo Cash had clearly underestimated me. If anything, her attempts to thwart me only fueled my determination to bring the woman down.

"Yeah, she's a peach!" I snapped. "So are you telling me that you won't talk?"

"Let me ask you something first," he said. "Has anyone else agreed to speak with you?"

I wasn't sure whether I should admit to this man that I was having a hell of a time getting anyone to confess anything. But something told me that he wasn't merely fishing for information. He was negotiating. After all, he'd been very upfront about getting the call from Flo.

"You'd be the first to come clean," I said. "That could work to your advantage."

"Ah," he said. "You see where I'm going with this."

"Do you want to get your CPA or attorney on the phone with us?"

"I've been in business twenty years and have yet to hire an attorney for anything."

That made him either very smart or very stupid. I wasn't sure which. Maybe both.

"What can you tell me?" I asked.

"Lots," he said, "but I want something in writing first that says I won't be prosecuted and if I end up owing any taxes the IRS will waive all penalties."

It was a small price to pay. "Consider it done."

"All right. You bring a waiver to my store tomorrow afternoon and we'll talk."

"Can we do it sooner?" I wanted to move this case along. *Now.*

"No can do," he said. "I've got a truck due to arrive with a big delivery any minute and tomorrow morning I'm getting a root canal."

"Ouch."

"Between the dentist and the IRS, it's shaping up to be fun day."

"It could be worse," I told him. "You could be getting a colonoscopy."

"Now that's thinking positive," he said. "See you tomorrow."

chapter twenty

The Other Woman

Thursday evening, Nick and I camped out in a parking lot across the street from the Addison Chili's a half hour before Morgan Walker and Hana Kim, posing as Kim Huang, were to have their date. While we were far enough away that nobody could have easily identified me from the restaurant, I'd nonetheless tucked my hair up under a Texas Rangers baseball cap and donned dark sunglasses to disguise myself. An agent could never be too careful. The last thing I wanted to do was blow this case after all the work I'd put into it over the past few days.

As we waited, we listened to KCSH. As usual, prerecorded messages by Flo Cash played in the commercial breaks built into the syndicated show now playing.

"Are you in the mood for some delicioso Mexican food?" Flo asked over the airwaves. "Be sure to try the Guadalajara Grill in Garland. Children under ten eat free on Thursdays. Bring the entire family! Guadalajara Grill is conveniently located on Forest Lane near Shiloh Road."

I cast a glance at Nick. "If that's not a commercial, I'll eat my hat."

He cut a look back at me. "I just might eat your hat regardless. It's dinnertime and I'm starved."

"I thought you might say that." I reached into the bag I'd brought with me, pulled out a plastic container, and handed it to him.

He pulled off the lid. "Fried-baloney sandwiches? I knew there was a reason I loved you."

"If that's the reason, I feel obligated to tell you that any woman with a frying pan could do the same."

"Maybe." He took an enormous bite of one of the sandwiches. "But I'd only want to eat yours."

Flo continued to promote businesses on KCSH: "Folks, the heat of the summer will be here before you know it. Why not make sure your air conditioner gives a peak performance by having it serviced? Call Milligan's Heating and Air today to schedule a maintenance appointment." She followed her words with their phone number.

"You still thinking over Lu's offer?" I asked. "You gonna take her job?"

"What do you think I should do?"

Admittedly, I had mixed feelings about it myself. If Nick become the director of Criminal Investigations, he and I couldn't work cases together anymore. I'd miss that. On the other hand, as he'd pointed out previously, the director job would have more regular hours. That could be a big plus if the two of us settled down and had children, which was a real possibility. I raised my shoulders. "Honestly? I don't know. Maybe talk to Eddie about it. Find out where he stands. That might help you make up your mind."

"Good idea. I will."

A dark car pulled into the Chili's parking lot. I raised my field glasses to my eyes to take a closer look. Sure enough, it was the rental Mercedes with Morgan Walker behind the wheel. "The catfisher has arrived."

The car made an immediate left turn and skirted the

perimeter of the lot before stopping in a remote spot at the back of the lot. A few seconds later, Morgan Walker climbed out of the vehicle. He wore the same clothing he'd worn on our date.

Nick wiped his hands on a napkin, then reached for the binoculars. "I want to take a look." He took the glasses from me and held them to his face. "Meh. He doesn't look like anything special to me."

"It's not so much his looks that draw women in," I told Nick. "It's his personality. He's a good listener and has impeccable manners. He's gentlemanly and charming."

Nick grunted.

"You're charming, too," I said, stroking his bruised ego. "Just in a totally different way." I squinted, watching Walker, well, *walk*. "What do you think?" I asked Nick. "Does he have the confident swagger of a black belt?"

Nick turned a dial, adjusting the binoculars. "Hard to say. He's just putting one foot in front of the other like everyone else."

As we watched, Josh and Kira arrived, too. Josh would be providing on-site backup should anything go terribly awry. He'd also likely be busting my budget on this investigation, but if the tight-asses in Internal Accounting wouldn't cover the cost, I'd take the hit. Josh had saved my ass with his tech skills on more than on occasion and had helped a lot in this case. Surely I'd need him in the future, too. A dinner bill was a small price to pay for the IT support.

Just after Josh and Kira headed into the restaurant, Hana's undercover vehicle pulled into the lot.

I pointed, keeping my hand below dash level where it couldn't be seen outside the car. "Elvis is in the parking lot."

She took a spot much closer to the doors than Walker had.

Nick and I took turns watching through the binoculars as the two met in the foyer, exchanged pleasant smiles and handshakes, and approached the hostess stand. The young woman seated them at a booth along the front window where we could easily keep an eye on them. *Good.*

Over the next half hour, the two smiled and laughed and chatted. Heck, they even shared a dessert.

"Looks like they're having a good time," Nick noted, peering through the binoculars.

Oddly, I found myself feeling jealous that their date seemed to have gone better than mine. *The jokes's on Morgan,* I told myself. *Hana isn't interested in men.*

"Wait," Nick said. "He just gave her something. What is that?"

I took the glasses from Nick and spied through them. "A vintage harmonica."

Nick's brow furrowed in confusion. "Why in the world would he give her that?"

"Hana let me draft her profile," I replied. "She said to surprise her, so I did."

"If I ever ask you to surprise me," Nick said, "forget the harmonica. Surprise me with sexy lingerie. Or a rib eye. Or Cowboys tickets."

Inside the restaurant, Hana nodded and grinned and appeared to express sincere appreciation for what I'm sure she considered the most ridiculous gift ever.

Josh and Kira finished their meal first and returned to his car in the parking lot. I sent him a text. *Nick and I are across the street. We'll follow Walker when he leaves.*

A few seconds later, a reply came back. *Good luck.* Josh started his car and he and Kira drove off.

When Morgan and Hana exited the building a minute or two later, Morgan gestured in the direction of the Mercedes. I grabbed the field glasses from Nick and watched as Morgan led Hana over to the car, reached inside, and, as he'd done with me the night before, handed her a business card. The task completed, he walked her back to her car.

"Think he'll try to kiss her?" Nick asked, leaning in next to me and squinting.

"No, but if he did she'd break his nose."

I was wrong on both counts. Morgan did kiss Hana, though it was a modest peck on her cheek, and Hana did not break his nose. *Why did he kiss her cheek and not mine?* Maybe I'd lost whatever touch I used to have with men. Maybe I'd used it all up on Nick.

As Morgan headed back to his car, Nick started the engine, preparing to follow him. Once the Mercedes pulled out of the lot, we eased onto the road behind it. Given that Hana's date tonight started an hour earlier than mine had the night before, the night was still light and our car clearly identifiable.

"You better hang back," I told Nick. "We don't want him to realize he's being tailed."

Nick took his foot off the gas and slowed down a little, letting a few cars pass us as we headed east on Belt Line Road.

When he reached I-35, Morgan turned to the north like he had before, heading away from Dallas rather than toward the city.

"This is the same way he went last night," I said.

"You think he's driving all the way to Oklahoma?"

"It's possible. Or he could be headed to Colorado." Though if the latter was true, at some point he'd need to veer farther west. "Of course he could be going somewhere else entirely."

Without knowing the guy's true identity, I had no way of knowing where he actually lived. With any luck, I'd soon hear back from Hertz and learn the real name of Jack Smirnoff/Morgan Walker.

We followed him for several miles. As we left the Lewis-ville city limits and drove over the lake, traffic thinned considerably. We'd reached the outer suburbs and would soon be in Denton, a much smaller neighboring city with a unique personality. Denton was home to the University of North Texas, which was known for its music program and had produced such greats as Roy Orbison, Don Henley, and, more recently, Norah Jones. The city served as the northern point of what some called the Golden Triangle, a region that was also defined by Fort Worth and Dallas.

"Uh-oh," Nick said. "He moved into the left lane and he's slowing, for no apparent reason."

"You think he realized we're following him?"

"Hell if I know."

If Morgan had become suspicious and Nick slowed, too, it would only confirm that we were trailing him. Nick had no choice but to maintain his speed. As we came up on the Mercedes I pulled my cell phone from my purse and held it up to my ear to further obscure my face from view. With the hat, sunglasses, and phone, surely he wouldn't be able to identify me as Sara Galloway, right?

Nick gave the car a little more gas so we'd pass at a good clip. "Shit," he hissed through barely open lips. "He's speeding up now. I think he's trying to get a better look into our car."

Dammit! Had he recognized me? "Take the exit!" I cried. "Now!"

Nick veered off just as Morgan pulled up next to our car. With any luck, Morgan would assume we'd left the highway to get gas or because we lived out here in the country. If we'd blown this case, I'd never forgive myself for letting Leslie, Nataya, and Julia down.

The Mercedes continued up the freeway as we slowed on the frontage road. Nick hooked a turn under the inter-state and headed back to Dallas.

I looked back over my shoulder, but the Mercedes had driven out of sight. Childish as it might be, I crossed my fingers and hoped Morgan Walker hadn't realized it was me in the truck.

I pondered our next move. "Maybe Hertz has a tracking system in the car. You know, LoJack or OnStar or some type of gizmo like that." It would make sense for rental cars to come pre-equipped with such a system, especially upmarket cars like a Mercedes. The rental company stood to lose big if one of their expensive luxury cars was stolen. "Think I should ask their legal department when they call back? See if they'll tell me where the car is?"

"Not much point in that. They'll make you jump through flaming hoops before they'll give you the information."

He was probably right. Besides, such a request would be beyond the terms of the court order.

"Borrow a tracker from Josh," Nick suggested. "I can put in on the Mercedes Tuesday night while you're on your date."

Nick and I had used a GPS tracking device in an earlier case, putting it on a target's car so we could determine his whereabouts. It had led to us discovering some very damning information.

"Good idea," I told him.

He reached over and toyed with a lock of my hair, running a finger up and down my neck as he slid me a sexy smile. "I'm full of good ideas. Want to hear another one?"

chapter twenty-one

*L*icensed to Party

Friday morning, Hana stormed into my office. She tossed a small harmonica case onto my desk. It featured a dark-haired woman with red flowers in her hair playing the instrument. The name "CARMEN" appeared next to her, along with the name of the manufacturer, "KOCH," and place of production, "MADE IN GERMANY."

"Vintage harmonicas?" Hana cried, throwing her hands in the air. "Are you freaking kidding me?"

"You said to surprise you."

"Surprise, not *blindside*. I know nothing about harmonicas, vintage or otherwise. When Morgan gave me the harmonica last night I had to make up some bullshit about my grandfather playing songs for me when I was a kid."

"Aw, that's sweet."

"That's the worst part," she said. "I had to be sweet! Uck!"

As she flopped backward into one of my wing chairs, I opened the case, removed the harmonica, and held it in front of my mouth. I wasn't about to put my lips on it. For all I knew the Führer's vintage saliva could have coated the thing. I puckered my lips and blew at it, moving it back and forth. *Twoo-twee-twoo-tweeeeee!*

Hana cringed. "Don't quit your day job."

"Wasn't planning on it." I returned the harmonica to the case and held it out to her.

She raised a palm. "Keep it as a souvenir."

"Really? Thanks." I slid the harmonica into my desk drawer and sat back in my chair. "From what Nick and I could see last night, it looked like you and Walker hit it off."

Hana raised her shoulders. "I must've done something right. He asked me out for Friday of next week."

"*Friday?*" I said. "He asked you out for a weekend?"

A snicker erupted from Nick's office across the hall. A "shut up!" erupted in return from mine.

"Yeah," Hana said, her brows drawn in question. "Why is that an issue?"

"It's not," I said. "It's just that he planned our second date for Tuesday."

"*Tuesday?*" She snorted. "Looks like he's only after one thing where you're concerned. Cash."

I ignored both the snort and the comment. "What did you think of him? Get any clues as to who he might really be?"

"Mm-hm." She cocked her head. "It was kind of weird, though. My gaydar was *bloop*ing all over the place. I mean, what straight man would go to an antique store to buy a vintage harmonica? He ordered a salad for dinner, too. *Bloop, bloop.*"

"*Bloop?* I thought gaydar *ping*ed."

She rolled her eyes. "We must have different models. But I'm guessing mine is better calibrated." At that, she arched a brow.

"Point taken." I mulled this news over for a moment.

Unfortunately, it didn't help me figure out who the guy was. "Did he ask for your phone number and e-mail?"

"Yeah."

"Be sure to check your e-mail regularly," I said. "He sent me a message after our date and he'll probably e-mail you, too. Make sure you respond so he thinks you're forging a connection."

"Got it."

"Did he mention martial arts? Say anything about earning a black belt?"

"Nope. He only mentioned liking Sonny Boy Williamson. I had to pretend to know who that was."

Putting my fingers to my keyboard, I performed a quick Internet search. "He was a blues harmonica player in the early 1900s." Walker had done his homework, probably hoping to impress Hana.

Hana stood to go. "We done here?"

My phone rang before we could finish our conversation. The readout indicated the call came from the Hertz legal department.

I raised a finger to stop Hana. "Wait just a minute. It's Hertz."

She flopped back into my wing chair as I raised my receiver and issued a greeting. "Good morning. Special Agent Tara Holloway."

"I'm calling from Hertz," the paralegal said. "I have the name, address, and driver's license number of the man who rented the Mercedes."

"Great." I grabbed a pen. "I'm ready." I wrote the information down as he read it off.

"His name is Kevin Michael Andersen," he said, spelling the last name for me.

He proceeded to read off an address on Farm to Market Road 407 in Argyle, Texas, a small town that sat about thirty miles north of Fort Worth and eight miles south of

Denton. My body began to hum in excitement. The address was consistent with the route Morgan Walker had taken after both dates, though he'd bypassed the exit for FM 407 last night. Of course, if he'd thought he was being followed maybe he'd driven past the road to throw us off his trail.

"What about his phone number and credit card number?" I asked.

The card number the paralegal provided matched the one Smirnoff/Walker had used to sign up on the Big D Dating Service site, so I knew that information was a dead end, unfortunately. The phone number was the same one he'd given to Leslie, Nataya, and Julia, the one that had been disconnected. Dead end there, too.

"Where did he pick up the Mercedes?" I asked.

"At our location in the Oklahoma City airport."

I tapped the pen against my cheek. "Does the rental agreement say when he's planning to return the car?"

"A week from this coming Tuesday."

A-ha! Looked like he planned to make his move on me and Hana before then.

"Thanks," I told the man. "I appreciate your help."

As soon as we ended the call, I logged into the Texas DMV records and ran a search for Kevin Michael Andersen.

Hana leaned forward in her seat. "What're you doing?"

"Looking up his driver's license photo." When his record popped up, I clicked on the link. "Huh?"

"What?" Hana asked.

I waved for her to come around my desk and take a look.

The photograph on Andersen's driver's license looked nothing like Smirnoff/Walker. Or at least I didn't think it did. It was nearly impossible to tell with the bushy beard and hair. It's not that they were unkempt; they were just thick and full of volume, the kind of hair featured in shampoo and electric razor commercials. His hair was listed as brown, as were his eyes. His physical details noted that he was five feet, ten inches tall, and weighed 170 pounds.

Hana pointed to the description. "Sounds about right. Doesn't look a thing like Morgan Walker, though."

"What if he didn't have the beard and all that thick hair?"

Hana leaned in, squinted at the photo, and shook her head. "I don't know. Hard to say."

I squinted at the screen, too. *Could this man be the catfisher?* I supposed it was possible. After all, he looked remarkably different in the two sets of head shots he'd had taken at Savannah Goode's studio and all he'd done was modify his hair and eye color and glasses. I knew from experience that facial hair drastically changed a man's appearance. Nick had grown a goatee once to go undercover and he'd looked very different. When the men on the *Today* show participated in the No-Shave November event, their appearances changed quite a bit, too. And with the beard covering his jawline, there was no way for me to tell if Kevin Andersen had the distinguishing freckle near his left ear.

Hm-m . . .

"Let's see what we can find about Kevin Andersen online," I suggested.

Besides his driver's license, the DMV records showed that he drove a Dodge Ram pickup. The Denton County Appraisal District property tax rolls indicated that Andersen owned sixty acres at the address listed on his license.

"See if he's on Facebook," Hana said.

I logged on to the site and searched for his name. Sure enough, he had a page. His profile picture looked nearly identical to his driver's license photo. A pair of eyes and the tip of a nose surrounded by a mass of brown hair.

My gaze ran down the page. While Andersen had posted a couple photos of cotton fields covered in puffy white plants, most of the posts had been made by his friends. A group of men roasting hot dogs around a bonfire. A group of men posed on and around a green John Deere tractor. A group of men drinking beer on a porch. Andersen seemed to be a guy's guy.

Hana pointed to a gray animal standing among the men. "That has to be the ugliest dog I've ever seen."

"It's not a dog," I said. "It's a miniature donkey."

"Well, if he were a dog," Hana said, refusing to back down, "he'd be an ugly one."

I clicked on the "photos" tab. "There don't appear to be any pictures of him in a martial arts uniform." I tried the About link to find out Andersen's romantic status. "Says here he's in a relationship."

"I'm not surprised," she said. "What woman could resist an ape-man with a tractor and a miniature donkey?"

I exited the site but found little else about Andersen on the Net. I turned to Hana. "Want to drive up to Argyle? Spy on him and see if we can learn anything?"

"Why not? Beats adding up invoices."

As I gathered my things, Nick strolled over from his office, stopping in my doorway. "Headed out?"

"We're going to pay a visit to Kevin Andersen," I said. "He's the one who rented the Mercedes from Hertz. He lives on a sixty-acre spread in Argyle."

"Want some company?" Nick offered. "If he lives out in the country he's likely to have guns. It can't hurt to have another agent along."

Nick had a point, though I suspected part of the reason he wanted to come along was merely to get out of the office. None of us agents were the types who could be happy being cooped up inside sitting at a desk all day. Fieldwork was much more fun, even if that field was a cotton field.

"The more, the merrier," I said.

The three of us headed out to my G-ride. Hana climbed into the backseat, while Nick rode shotgun. We drove up I-35 through Carrollton and Lewisville before taking the exit for FM 407 and heading west. In just under an hour, we pulled up on the grass shoulder of the road next to a rusty metal gate. A modern-day log-style house sat back a hundred yards or so from the road, a gravel road leading from the gate to the side of the house. The Dodge pickup sat in the drive, but there was no sign of the Mercedes. Around the house spanned an expansive field of green. It would be another couple of months before the cotton bolls would open, turning the land snowy white.

Nick removed my field glasses from my glove compartment and aimed them at the house.

Hana stuck her head between ours. "See anything?"

"Just a pair of really ugly dogs."

Oh, for Pete's sake. "They're miniature donkeys."

Nick adjusted the dial on the binoculars to better focus them. "You're right. They're a couple of little asses." He cut a grin my way. "Not nearly as cute as your little ass."

"Where's Andersen?" Hana asked. "I thought farmers were always out working in their fields."

"They are," Nick replied, "at planting and harvesttime. They've also got to fertilize and irrigate and check for bugs." Nick would know. He'd grown up on his parents' farm outside of Houston. "But there are days when you get to just kick back and watch things grow."

Hana scoffed. "Sounds boring."

"I don't know about that," Nick said wistfully. "Farm life can be quiet and peaceful, but I never found it boring."

As much as Nick enjoyed his job at the IRS and the things a big city like Dallas had to offer, I knew a part of him yearned to be back in the country.

He lowered the binoculars. "One of these days I'll have

to get myself a weekend spread somewhere. Ten acres or so ought to do me." He cast a glance my way. "It'd be a fun place for kids to play."

Was he referring to *our* kids? He certainly seemed to be. I had to admit I liked the idea of a weekend home out in the sticks. Nick could teach our children how to grow things and how to catch fish in the stock pond, and I could put a target on a hay bale and teach them how to shoot. Of course I was getting ahead of myself, as usual. There'd be no children until there was a wedding, and there'd be no wedding until there was a proposal and a ring. And, so far, there'd been no proposal and no ring, only some vague talking around the subject.

Movement at the door caught our attention and we all watched as a hirsute man stepped onto the porch. He wore boots, jeans, and a T-shirt, the same basic clothing Andersen had worn in his Facebook photos.

Hana snatched the binoculars and raised them to her face. "That's him. That's Andersen."

"He can't be Morgan Walker, too, then," I replied.

"No," Hana agreed. "There's no way he could regrow a beard that quickly. Besides, this guy just spit in the dirt."

"Ew." Morgan Walker had been courteous and classy. I couldn't imagine him spitting in the dirt, either.

She handed the field glasses to me and I peered through them as Andersen trotted down his steps and headed to a wooden barn, the donkeys following him. The donkeys waited outside the door while Andersen disappeared inside the barn, emerging a moment later with a bucket of feed that he poured into a small outdoor trough.

I lowered the glasses. "So, what now?"

"We hang around here much longer," Nick said, "he'll spot us and wonder what the hell we're doing. Let's go get some lunch and figure this out."

I started the car and we made our way down the road

until we found a small country café with a sign boasting the best corn bread in three counties. *Can't beat that, huh*?

Over lunch, we three agents debated our options.

"Assuming Andersen rented the Mercedes for Walker," Hana said, "we can't speak to Andersen without risking him tipping off Walker."

Nick took a long swig of iced tea. "It would be a shame to drive all the way out here and not learn anything, though."

"Maybe we should just confront him," I said. "Morgan Walker's head shots didn't show up on any of the other dating sites. It's possible that the three women who I met with are his only victims. Maybe we're only prolonging the inevitable and wasting our time by going out with the guy and hoping we'll catch him in the act. Maybe we should just ask Andersen where we can find Walker, arrest the guy, and proceed on the evidence we have."

"I'm all for that plan," Hana said. "I've got better things to do next Friday night than go out with a con artist, and Tara's probably got something better to do *Tuesday* night, too."

A grin played about Nick's lips. He tried, unsuccessfully, to hide it behind his glass of iced tea.

I palmed the handle of the gun at my waist. "Next person who says the word 'Tuesday' is getting a bullet in the butt." That wiped the smile off his face.

By the time we finished eating, we were all in agreement. We'd confront Andersen and deal with this matter head-on. I'd like to say our reasons were entirely because we were tenacious and forthright, but admittedly part of it was because we were impatient. Type A personalities, all of us, at least when it came to our work.

We paid the bill, complimented the waitress on what was, indeed, the best corn bread in three counties, and drove back out to Andersen's place. Nick climbed out to open the gate, and I drove on through, waiting on the gravel drive while he closed the gate behind us and returned to the car. As we approached the house, Andersen stepped out of his barn and walked toward us. The expression on the small part of his face that was visible said he didn't take too kindly to strangers trespassing on his private property.

I raised a hand in greeting and forced a smile as the car rolled to a stop. Nick, Hana, and I climbed out of the car and met Andersen on the drive.

"Hello." I extended my hand. "I'm Special Agent Tara Holloway from the Internal Revenue Service. These are my coworkers, Senior Special Agent Nick Pratt and Special Agent Hana Kim."

Though Andersen shook our hands, his tone was wary. "What brings you out here?"

"The Mercedes you rented at the Oklahoma City airport."

"Mercedes?" His head pulled back reflexively, his forehead becoming corrugated with confusion. "Run that by me again?"

"I was informed by Hertz that you rented a car from their location at the Oklahoma City airport. Can you tell me who's driving that car and where I might find him?"

"I can't tell you any of that," he said, "because I have absolutely no idea what you're talking about."

I eyed him closely. "Are you saying you didn't rent a car recently?"

"Why should I?" He gestured toward the Dodge. "I've got a perfectly good truck right there. Just put new tires on 'er. Spark plugs, too."

"How would Hertz have your name, address, and driver's license number if you hadn't rented the car?"

"I've got no clue," the man said, reaching into the back pocket of his jeans and pulling out his wallet. "I've got my driver's license right here." He held it up to show us.

"So you haven't misplaced your license, then," I said, thinking out loud.

"Not this one, anyway," he replied. "I went out bar hopping with some buddies late last summer and managed to lose my whole wallet. Had a few too many, I suppose. I called the bars later to see if anyone had turned it in but had no luck. I had to cancel all my credit cards and get replacements. Same for my debit card. I went down to the DMV a couple days later and got this new license."

Had his previous driver's license somehow made its way into the hands of Jack Smirnoff/Morgan Walker? It seemed likely. Heck, maybe the catfisher had pulled an Oliver Twist and picked Andersen's pocket. Maybe he'd taken one look at Andersen's hair and beard, realized that nobody could tell what the man might look like clean-shaven, and figured it would be easy to pass the license off as his own. Really, it was an ingenious idea.

"Are you sure you lost your wallet?" I asked. "Maybe someone picked your pocket."

He ducked his head in agreement. "That's a real possibility. I would've been an easy target that night. I was shit-faced."

"What bars had you gone to?" I asked.

He looked up in thought. "The Hidden Door in Dallas," he said. "JR's. We ended the night at Mable Peabody's up in Denton. I'm sure there were several more in there, but it's been a while and, like I said, I'd had a few." As if afraid he'd said too much, he quickly added, "I wasn't the designated driver that night, in case you were wondering."

I exchanged glances with Nick and Hana. Neither seemed to have any more questions for the guy.

I extended my hand. "Thanks for your time."

He gave it another shake. "If you find out who's using my license, you'll try to get it back, right? I don't want him wrecking that fancy car and sticking me with the bill."

"We'll do our best," I promised.

After we climbed back into the car, I said, "I'm not familiar with the bars he mentioned."

"Me, neither," Nick said.

"That's 'cause they're gay bars," Hana said.

Nick turned around in his seat. "You mean to tell me that when that bearded cotton farmer sows his wild oats—"

"He sows them with other men," Hana said. "Yes. That's exactly what I'm saying."

"Was your gaydar *bloop*ing?" I asked. Mine hadn't given off a single *ping*.

"Not at all," Hana said. "I wouldn't have known if he hadn't mentioned the bars."

I started the car. "Maybe it needs a tune-up."

chapter twenty-two

You Made Your Bed; Now Lie in It

When we returned to the IRS office, I bade good-bye to Nick and Hana, printed out the immunity deal Ross O'Donnell had e-mailed to me, and headed right back out to my car. This time, I aimed for Mister Sandman's Mattresses and More.

As I drove, I pondered the Sandman folklore. According to legend, he visited people in their sleep, sprinkling magical sand in their eyes to give them sweet dreams. In my experience, having good dreams only to wake to the reality of grainy, crusty, itchy eyes didn't seem like a very good trade-off. If I were going to have a nocturnal visit from a fantasy figure, I'd much rather it be the dollar-doling Tooth Fairy, thank you very much. Still, the Sandman was preferable to his scary cousin, the Boogeyman.

The mattress store was located in a shopping center on the frontage road for Central Expressway, just north of the 635 loop. It was a large shop, one of those places that moved significant quantities of merchandise for reasonable prices. The front windows bore colorful paint and bold promises. "Nobody beats Mister Sandman's prices!"

I stepped inside and glanced around the space. Two

small, squealing children jumped on a king-sized bed at the back, testing its springs much to the chagrin of the salesman who was speaking to their mother. To my right, an elderly couple were also trying out the mattresses, though they merely lay down on one after another rather than jumping on them. A saleswoman addressed a middle-aged man in the center of the store before lying down on a bed and spreading her arms and legs as if making a snow angel to show how wide it was. I supposed when you worked at a mattress store lying down on the job was encouraged rather than frowned upon.

Figuring my best bet for finding the Sandman was at the checkout counter in the back, I weaved my way among the beds in that direction.

"Hi," I said as I stepped up to the counter. "I'm looking for—" I realized then that I hadn't asked the man on the phone what his real name was. I went with, "The boss."

Before the clerk at the counter could respond, a black man in a dress shirt and tie stepped to the open door of an office behind her. "Are you the woman I spoke with yesterday on the phone?"

"Yep," I said. "That's me."

He waved me over. "Come on back."

I circled around the counter and walked back to his office.

He closed the door behind me, then held out a hand. "Max Brady."

I gave his hand a shake. "I appreciate your cooperation, Mr. Brady."

"You don't have it yet." He slid into his seat and gestured for me to sit in one of the padded lounge chairs that faced his desk. "Not until I see that immunity agreement."

He wasn't being rude or pushy, just no-nonsense. I could appreciate that. I'd pick a straightforward person over a bullshitter any day. I pulled the document from my brief-case and handed it to him. As he perused it, he took a sip from his coffee mug. Light-brown liquid ran down his chin and onto his shirt.

"Darn Novocain!" he snapped, grabbing a tissue from a box on his desk and dabbing at his shirt. "It's been three hours since my root canal and my face is still numb." He slapped his cheek as if to prove his point. "I can't feel a thing."

The coffee crisis dealt with, he returned his attention to the immunity agreement. Apparently satisfied, he pulled a pen from a cup on his desk and signed it. Turning to a desktop copier on the credenza behind him, he slapped the paper down on the glass to make himself a copy. He closed the lid, jabbed the button, and waited until the moving beam of light had traveled from one end of the machine to the other. His copy ready, he stashed it in his desk and handed the original back to me. The paper bore a few brown drips of coffee but was nonetheless enforceable.

"Thanks." I slid the agreement back into my briefcase and got down to business. "As we discussed on the phone, I'm trying to establish that KCSH has been offering on-air advertising in return for products and services. Can you tell me what arrangements you have with the station and how they came about?"

He sat back in his chair, elbows on the armrests. "Flo came into my store about a year ago looking for a queen-sized bed. She wanted a pillow-top model. Even with our discounted prices, those don't come cheap. She said if I'd give her the bed she'd promote the store on the station three times a day every weekday for the next two years. She'd brought in a price sheet with her, one that showed the rates KCSH charged for airtime, so we could compare. My cost for the bed she wanted was twelve hundred. We sold it for two grand. The amount of airtime she was offering would have cost me over three thousand dollars if I'd paid cash for it. Seemed like a good deal, so I took it. At the end of the day, I'd essentially made eighteen hundred dollars."

"I can certainly understand the attraction," I said. Bartering basically allowed people to obtain retail products and services for wholesale prices. "Did you get anything in writing to substantiate the agreement?"

"Sure did," he said. "I wasn't born yesterday."

He reached into a desk drawer, pulled out a sales agreement, and handed it to me. The pricing column showed the retail price of $2,000 for the pillow-top bed, along with sales tax of $165 and a delivery fee of $75, for a total of $2,240. Along the bottom was a handwritten note:

In exchange for the above products and services, KCSH Radio Corporation agrees to promote Mister Sandman Mattresses and More in three spots of no less than fifteen seconds each between the hours of 6:00 AM and 10:00 PM each weekday for two years from the date of this sales agreement. Signed: Flo Cash, CEO.

"Can you make me a copy of this?" I asked.

"Sure can." He turned back to the copier and ran the paper through. Seconds later, he handed me the copy of the document, all nice and warm.

"Thanks." I slid the copy into my briefcase, pulled out my laptop, and typed up an affidavit to attach to the sales agreement. After asking for his e-mail address, I sent him the affidavit. "Print that out and sign it," I instructed him. "I'll need it for court."

As he set about the tasks, I thanked him for agreeing to speak with me. "Your cooperation will help me get this case moving along."

He raised a nonchalant shoulder. "I don't want to find

myself in hot water. Not like I did with that shoddy plumber Flo sent over."

What? Flo sent a plumber over? "Excuse me?"

"The guy was young, had no idea what he was doing. He was supposed to fix a small leak in the water heater in our storeroom, but next thing I know we've got hot water an inch deep all over the floor. Steam, too. It was like a sauna in here. Ruined three mattresses before I was able to stanch the flow with a blanket."

"You said Flo sent the plumber over? I'm not sure I understand."

"I didn't mean it literally," Brady replied. "Only that I'd found him on her barter site."

"Her *what*?" My voice went up an octave into chipmunk range and I reflexively rose a few inches from my seat. *Did he say Flo ran a bartering Web site? Holy guacamole, this case could be even bigger than I'd thought!*

He rolled and clicked his computer mouse, reached over to the keyboard for his desktop computer, and tapped a few keys. Finished, he turned his flat-screen monitor so that I could see it. "That's the site."

Pulled up on the screen was a Web site called Trading-Post.com, the image at the top of an old-timey Western storefront. The verbiage on the home page stated that the site was intended to help individuals and businesses exchange products or services cash-free. A direct, two-party exchange was not required. Rather, to facilitate transactions members would earn "Barter Bucks" in the market value of the products or services they provided to another member. The Barter Bucks could be redeemed for products or services of equal value from any member of Trading Post. Thus, the Barter Bucks functioned as a type of currency.

The site had four clickable tabs along the side of the page. The first was designated with "LIST YOUR PRODUCT/

SERVICE," the second read: "SEARCH FOR PRODUCT/ SERVICE," the third read: "ACCOUNT INFORMATION," and the last read: "ABOUT BARTERING."

"Flo owns this site?" I said. "You're sure about that?"

"She told me about it when we made the trade. She suggested I sign up."

I pointed at the bottom tab. "Can you log in and show me your account data?"

"I suppose there's no harm in that. In for a penny, in for a pound."

Or a Barter Buck.

Brady did some keyboarding and maneuvering and up popped his account details. His balance showed he had an 8,750BB credit to spend on the barter exchange.

I gestured toward the screen. "You've got a credit balance. Who'd you give beds to?"

"I can show you the details if you'd like."

"That would be great."

He clicked on a drop-down menu to delve into his transaction history. The page listed a dozen transactions. Mister Sandman had traded beds to various small, local businesses, including a janitorial service, a jewelry store, and a company that provided freelance tech support. No doubt the owners of those businesses had taken the beds home with them, just like Flo Cash had done. Commingling corporate and personal finances like this was a big no-no.

"What's that?" I asked, pointing to a line that read: "TRANSACTION FEE." The number next to it was also designated in Barter Bucks.

"That's the part that goes to Flo Cash," he said. "She takes a three percent cut on every transaction."

And then spends those Barter Bucks on things for herself, no doubt.

I asked Brady to print out his transaction history, then requested he click on the "ABOUT BARTER" tab. The page discussed the history of barter, noting that early settlers had traded chickens and goats and eggs for things like medical care and fabric and tools. The site went on to say that cash had been invented as a way to make multiparty trades easier. Of course that wasn't the only reason. Cash wasn't perishable like eggs, nor did it crap all over your yard like a goat or chicken. Also, cash could be saved in a bank, where it would be safe and earn interest. She neglected to mention these facts, however.

But what grabbed my attention most was the statement at the bottom of the page: *"Off-the-books bartering is a great way to increase your wealth in cash-free, tax-free transactions."*

The statement was overly broad and misleading. Barter among individuals for personal purposes, such as two mothers trading babysitting services, was indeed nonreportable and nontaxable. But when trades were made in a business context, the situation was different.

Those running a commercial barter exchange, such as TradingPost.com, were required to report all transactions arranged via the service. Earned Barter Bucks were considered income to the member, just as if the member had sold the products or services for cash. In cases where the amount "earned" by a business in a given year equaled the value of that "spent," no net taxable income would result. But where the amounts earned exceeded the amount spent in a given year the business would have net income and owe tax.

What's more, when personal and business lines were crossed an individual could owe tax even where the things traded were of equal value. In Flo Cash's case, for instance, she had traded airtime owned by KCSH Radio Corporation not for something that would benefit the station but rather for a bed that she planned to use personally in her home. In cases like that, KCSH would have reportable income equal to the value of the bed received in return for the advertising service. The transfer of the bed to Flo would be treated as compensation paid by KCSH to her. KCSH could take a deduction for the in-kind "payment" to Flo, but it would be required to report the value to Flo on a W-2 along with her salary. Income, Social Security, and Medicare taxes would also apply to the in-kind payment.

Of course federal taxes weren't the only taxes at issue here. Just as barter transactions were treated the same as cash transactions by Uncle Sam, they were treated the same for state tax purposes. The Texas Tax Code imposed sales tax on these transactions. The Texas Comptroller of Public Accounts would surely be interested in this barter site.

"Can you print out this page, too?" I asked Brady.

He clicked his mouse and the printer fired up.

Curious how extensive the site was, I pointed to the "SEARCH FOR PRODUCT/SERVICE" tab. "Let's go there."

"You don't really need me for that, do you?" Brady stood and held out a hand, inviting me to take his chair. "I've got customers to tend to. How about I let you play around on the site while I go sell some beds?"

"Good idea." I went around his desk and dropped into his chair. As he stepped to his door, I stopped him. "Just one thing, Mr. Brady. You're going to have some state sales tax issues, too."

He looked up and groaned. "I hadn't thought of that."

"I might be able to help you there," I said. "I've worked with people in the comptroller's office on other cases. I can't guarantee anything, but I'd be happy to put in a good word for you, suggest they give you an immunity deal and waive penalties, too."

"I'd appreciate that." He shook his head. "I should've known this barter stuff was too good to be true. But Flo

Cash is a financial expert. I thought she knew what she was talking about. I trusted her."

No doubt the others involved in TradingPost.com did, too. They had no idea they were actually dealing with a modern-day snake oil salesman.

As he left the office to return to the sales floor, I clicked on the tab. *What product or service should I search for? Hm-m . . . How about exterminators?* I typed in "exterminator" in the search box. Sure enough, Cowtown Critter Control, the service that had provided the termite treatment at Flo's house, popped up as one of the options. Next I tried "chiropractor." Yep, Dr. Keele had listed his services on the site, too. I even found a listing for Szechuan Express, the Chinese restaurant that had delivered to the radio station. My mind flickered back to the fortune cookie. *The empty vessel makes the loudest sound.* Seriously, what does that mean?

I spent several minutes reviewing the offerings. They were extensive and varied, including everything from acupuncture to medical supplies to Zen gardens. Heck, virtually anything a person might need on any given day was listed on the site. No wonder Flo had been able to survive on such a small salary. With a barter network like this, who needed cash?

When I'd finished looking over the listings, I opened another search tab to verify that Flo Cash owned the Web site. Unfortunately, she'd paid extra for the privacy option. The domain was listed only in the name of the company from which she'd purchased it.

I painstakingly perused the site, page by page, printing them out for evidence. All kinds of people and businesses had listed things on the site, some noting as well the specific things they were looking to trade for. A dentist offered to exchange dental cleanings for maid service at his home. A tree-trimming service offered to keep power lines clear of limbs and branches. A mechanic agreed to trade oil changes and engine work for a date to his high school reunion. And, of course, an unnamed local radio station offered on-air promotion.

When I finished, I gathered the tall stack of printouts from the tray and stashed them in my briefcase.

You made your bed, Flo Cash. Now you're going to lie in it.

chapter twenty-three

$\mathcal{B}$achelorette Bash

I was wakened around ten Saturday morning when a *ting* sounded from my bedside table, where three cell phones lay charging. My personal cell. My government-issued phone. And the burner phone that belonged to my alter ego, Sara Galloway.

I rubbed my eyes, sat up, and looked at the table to determine which phone was active. A text had come in on Sara Galloway's cell.

Hi, Sara. It's Morgan. Hope you are doing well! I've been thinking a lot about you. I admire you for running your own business. You've got me thinking that maybe I should open an independent counseling practice when I move to Dallas. What do you think makes you so successful?

Clearly, he was trying to both flatter me and get me to open up. I had to give him credit that he'd picked up on the importance of Sara Galloway's career to her. That was something Sara and I had in common. But I wished he'd have let Sara sleep in. Another thing Sara and I had in common was that we liked to sleep late on the weekends. So did Sara's cat Anastasia/my cat Anne. She yawned, stretched out a paw, and turned over, curling into a ball and covering her eyes to shut out the sunlight. I felt like doing the same. But instead I wrote a reply, revising it several times before sending it.

It's simple, really. I think success in business requires really listening to your client's needs. You already know how to do that. :) It also requires some marketing savvy. And honesty. Deliver what you promise.

Yeah. Like don't try to pass yourself off as a straight man seeking a real relationship with a woman when you're actually a gay con artist only looking for victims. I sent the text. A reply came only minutes later.

I believe in honesty, too. And as long as I'm being honest, I should tell you that you looked very pretty the other night.

He'd probably have called me pretty even if I'd worn the rubber boots, feed sack, and rain poncho Nick had suggested.

That's sweet of you to say. How's Marmalade?

He came back with: *She's as spoiled as ever.*

Another smart ploy on his part. A cat lover like me would be impressed by a guy who treated his cat well. I'd bet dollars to donuts—make that Barter Bucks to Doo-Wop Donuts—that his furry feline was fictitious. *Are you on a break from work?* I wrote back.

Patient running late, he texted back. *Oh, she's here now. Talk later?*

I had a busy day planned, getting ready for the evening's festivities. *How about tomorrow evening? 8:00ish?*

He ended our exchange with: *Sounds good. I'll call then.*

All day long, Alicia pestered me for details about the bachelorette party. "Where are we going? What are we doing? How are we getting there?"

I gave her no answers, only a coy smile. "You'll see, bride-to-be."

Tonight, Alicia would enjoy a final night of debauchery before she tied the knot two weeks from tomorrow. Alicia had extended family coming in a week early for the wedding and didn't want to risk looking green and hung over in her wedding photos, so we'd scheduled the party early when we could celebrate with no worries.

Around six, the doorbell began to ring with friends arriving for the bachelorette party, gift bags and boxes in tow. Coworkers from Martin & McGee. A couple old friends from college who worked in other industries in the Dallas area. Alicia's snooty cousin Melody, a constant complainer but someone I'd been forced to invite as a courtesy. Also along for the fun tonight was Christina Marquez, the Latina bombshell and DEA agent I'd worked with on several cases, the one who was engaged to Dr. Ajay. Christina and I had become good friends and, through me, she and Alicia had become friends, too.

The usual pleasantries were exchanged.

"Welcome!"

"Cute shoes!"

"Your hair looks great!"

In return, everyone was handed a glass of peach sangria to start off the night.

As soon as everyone had arrived, I reached into a bag from the party store and pulled out a white sash trimmed in silver glitter. The sash read: "BRIDE-TO-BE." I draped it over Alicia's shoulders. I reached into the bag and pulled out a tiara with a long train of white netting attached. "Your crown, m'lady." Christina helped me situate it on Alicia's head.

"Now that you're properly attired," I said, "it's time for some *improper* attire."

"Uh-oh!" Alicia said. "That sounds naughty!"

I directed Alicia to her bridal "throne," a chair in my living room, over which soared a half-dozen white and silver balloons. "Here you go!" I called, patting the seat. "Your special spot."

Once she was seated, I handed her my bag first and took a seat on the couch next to Christina.

Alicia pulled the bag up onto her lap and looked down at it. "I'm afraid!"

"You should be!" Christina cried, laughing and chugging back her sangria.

Alicia pulled out the paper and tossed it to the floor, where Anne promptly pounced on it. Alicia reached into the bag and pulled out a black crotch-less see-through teddy, a whip, and a pair of handcuffs. "Daniel's going to love this!"

While the rest of us whooped it up, snooty Melody, who sat on the other side of Christina, turned up her nose. "I guess that's okay, if you want to look cheap."

Every party needs a pooper, right?

Christina gave Melody a not-so-soft nudge with her elbow. "Lighten up, Mel! It's a party!"

While Melody scowled, the rest of us raised our glasses in solidarity and whooped again.

Alicia moved on to the next gift, which contained an assortment of scented massage oils. Sandalwood. Musk. Brown sugar vanilla. "Fun!"

Christina's gift was next. "Ajay helped me pick it out."

Alicia tore the paper off the rectangular gift. "*The Kama Sutra!*"

Christina grinned. "I've dog-eared some of the pages for you."

Melody picked up an oversized box from the coffee table and thrust it at her cousin. "Open mine next."

Alicia set the book aside, took the box from her cousin, and tore off the wrap. She lifted the lid to find a white ankle-length robe and a pair of long-sleeved, high-necked pajamas in a pale-yellow hue. *Could sleepwear be any more boring?*

Christina leaned my way and whispered, "Is frigidity contagious?"

By the time Alicia had finished opening her gifts, she'd accumulated five pairs of sexy thong panties, three nighties, a pair of high-heeled satin slippers, the massage oil, some kind of sex toy that none of us really knew what to do with, and my teddy, whip, and handcuffs.

"Thanks, everyone!" Alicia cried. "Y'all are the best!"

A *knock-knock-knock* sounded from my front door. I went to the door and opened it. A handsome man in a black suit and hat stood on my porch.

Alicia took one look and squealed. "Is he a stripper?"

The guy chuckled. "Sorry to disappoint you, but I'm just the limo driver."

Alicia squealed a second time. "We've got a limo?"

I sent a smile her way. "Only the best for my bestie!" I knew Alicia would enjoy being chauffeured around the city in a shiny stretch limo. Even so, part of my reason for hiring a limo was admittedly selfish. No way did I want to be a designated driver tonight.

Once we'd all settled into the white limo and I'd poured everyone a glass of pink champagne from the car's mini-fridge, I reached into my purse and pulled out the padded envelope full of the sexy lace garters. "Party favors!" I called, retrieving one from the envelope and twirling it on my index finger.

Alicia grabbed it from me. "That's the sexy garter we saw online!"

"Yep. I've got one for everybody."

"I love it!" Alicia said, sliding hers up her leg and letting it show just below the hem of her miniskirt.

I passed them around and soon all of us were wearing garters, guzzling champagne, and dancing in our seats as the speakers blared Katy Perry's latest party tune.

Our first stop was Alicia's favorite restaurant downtown, where we stuffed ourselves silly and polished off five bottles of chardonnay. Next, we spent a couple of hours at a noisy, crowded dance club. As Christina and I waited at the bar for drinks, my gaze ran over the display of bottles behind the bar. There was the usual Tanqueray gin. Bacardi rum. Grey Goose and Smirnoff vodkas. Captain Morgan rum. Jack Daniel's Tennessee Whiskey. Johnnie Walker Black Label. *Wait a second—*

Naturally, the name Smirnoff had brought vodka to mind. But Jack, Morgan, and Walker were more common names used in liquors, too. *Had the catfisher devised all of his aliases from brands of spirits?* Right in front of me was eighty-proof proof. But did it mean anything? Maybe he worked in a liquor store.

I had no time to finish pondering the question before the bartender handed me three sugar-rimmed lemon drop martinis. One for Christina, one for me, and one for the bride-to-be. "Thanks!" I hollered over the music.

An hour later, when we'd danced enough to build up a sweat and drunk enough to build up our nerve, we headed back out to the limo.

"Where now?" asked the driver.

I threw a fist in the air. "LaBare!"

My proclamation was followed by hoots and hollers from the gaggle of girls around me. Even Melody had taken Christina's advice to lighten up and sent up a, "Woot-woot!"

We piled back into the car for the short drive. Minutes later, the limo pulled up in front of LaBare and filled with the giggles and shrieks of half-drunk women. The driver came around to open the doors, a smile on his face as we paraded past him on our way out of the car. "You ladies have fun."

"We will!" Alicia cried, giving the guy a high five.

Inside, the club was dark with flashing lights and loud music with a throbbing bass line. A male dancer with a waxed chest and a white lab coat moved around the stage, swinging a blood pressure device. He might not have a real medical license, but he definitely knew how to operate and he had our blood pressure rocketing to near stroke levels.

Alicia glanced up at the stage and turned back to me, wobbling a little in her heels. "I think I need a checkup!"

We found an empty table alongside the stage. I reached into my purse, this time pulling out a big stack of assorted bills and holding them up. "Table dances on me!"

As far as what took place the rest of the night, I plead the Fifth. Suffice it to say it involved many glasses of liquor, a leather G-string, and a dancer named Fiero. *I wonder if I could convince Nick to get flames tattooed up his arm. . . .*

We closed the place down at 2:00 AM, and the limo driver dropped us off at my place shortly thereafter. As the last of us exited the vehicle, he gave the group a knowing look and smile. "You ladies sure know how to have fun. But don't worry. I'll keep your secrets."

I gave him a huge tip. "Thanks for putting up with us all night."

"No problem." He slid the cash into the inside pocket of his jacket. "Y'all were well behaved compared to some of the bachelorette parties I've seen. None of you puked, cried, or got into a catfight."

"Does that happen a lot?"

He gave me another knowing look, this time without the smile. "You'd be surprised."

Our night out over, all of us changed into our pajamas for a good old-fashioned sleepover. Or should I call it a *sleep-it-off*-er? I dragged out every pillow and blanket I owned for my guests, and they found places to crash in my living room and on the floors of my bedroom and guest room.

The next morning, as I snuck downstairs to make coffee, Christina sat up from her spot on the floor and stuck her tongue out. "Hair of the dog." She plucked a piece of fur from her mouth and glared at Henry, who lay perched on top of the TV cabinet. "Or hair of the cat."

He merely continued to lick his paw and swipe it over his head, his morning grooming more important than Alicia's disgust.

Once everyone was up, we went out for breakfast at a nearby Mexican restaurant. Not ready for the party to be over yet, Alicia wore her sash and veil.

When our waiter stepped up to our table, I circled my finger to indicate the entire group. "Mimosas and huevos rancheros all around." Nothing cures a hangover like spicy food and more liquor.

When we'd finished our meal, we returned to my town house so everyone could gather up their things.

"Bye!" Alicia and I called, distributing hugs as everyone left.

Once everyone had gone, Alicia and I spent half an hour colleting the bedding and cleaning up before flopping down side by side on the couch.

She turned to me. "Best bachelorette party ever. How can I thank you?"

I shrugged. "I'm sure you'll find a way."

She rested her head on my shoulder. "I'll throw you a great party when you get married, too."

"Take me back to see Fiero," I told her. I certainly wouldn't mind seeing him dance some more. Besides, I wanted to ask him about my garter. Last time I'd seen it he'd been wearing it on his biceps.

* * *

Nick and I were watching television with Daffodil napping between us when Morgan Walker called promptly at 8:00 Sunday night.

Daffodil woke and raised her furry head as I stood from the couch. "I need to take this call. It's Morgan."

Nick grabbed my wrist and pulled me back down to the sofa. "Take it here. Put him on speaker so I can listen in."

I gave him a stern look. "You'll have to be quiet."

"I will."

I accepted the call and tapped the speaker button. "Hi, Morgan."

"Hello, Sara," he said. "How was your weekend?"

Filled with half-naked men and drunken debauchery. You? "Quiet," I lied. "Maybe *too* quiet."

Nick rolled his eyes.

"I know what you mean," Morgan replied. "My place seems too quiet, too. I really miss having someone else around."

In other words, he was hoping to find someone to get serious about—or at least pretending to feel that way. "You're still in Oklahoma then?" I asked.

"Yes. Finishing up some insurance paperwork. I'm planning to drive down to Dallas Tuesday afternoon so I'll be there in plenty of time for our date."

Sure you will. You're already somewhere around here, aren't you? "Great. I'm looking forward to it. I haven't had sushi in a while."

"Me, neither. It'll be fun." He went on to tell me that he'd attended a book signing the evening before at a local bookstore. "I had the author sign one for you."

Nick rolled his eyes again, looked to the phone, and whispered, "I'd like to shove that book up your—"

I put my free hand over his mouth to silence him. "Wow,

Morgan," I said. "You're so thoughtful." *Too bad it was all a ruse to rip me off.*

Through the window, I saw a squirrel run along the top of Nick's back fence. Unfortunately, Daffodil saw it, too. She leaped from the couch and ran to the window, barking up a storm. *Woof-woof-woof! Woof-woof!*

"Is that a dog?" Morgan asked.

How should I explain this? Think fast, Tara! "I'm pet sitting for a friend."

Nick pushed my hand from his mouth, cut a glance my way, and muttered, "Friend, my ass."

I covered the mouthpiece and whispered, "What part of 'quiet' did you not understand?"

"How nice of you," Morgan said. "What do Anastasia and Hank think about having a dog around?"

Who? Oh, yeah. Anastasia and Hank were my cats' aliases. Keeping up with all these details was difficult! Good thing this masquerade would be over soon. "They're a little jealous," I said, shooting Nick a pointed look. "Even though the dog won't be around long, they want me all to themselves."

"Can't say that I blame them," Morgan replied.

Nick scoffed, drained his bottle of beer, and got up to get another from the fridge.

Morgan and I chatted a few more minutes, but the conversation felt a little awkward and strange. At least it did to me. It was as if I'd forgotten how to flirt. I used to be good at it, too, back in the day. Finally, we ended the call. After I hung up, I turned to Nick. "You've ruined me for other men."

He grinned around the bottle of beer at his lips. "Darlin', that's been my plan from the first time I laid eyes on you."

chapter twenty-four

$\mathcal{M}$ass Mailing

The first thing I did Monday morning was drive through a coffee shop and pick up a vanilla latte for myself and a hot chocolate for Josh. Once I arrived at work, I took his drink straight to his office.

I stopped in his doorway and held up the cup. "More offerings for the geek god."

"Beats fuzzy Life Savers," he said.

I handed him the cup. "Any chance you'd have time this morning to whip me up a Web page for a fake restaurant?"

He glanced at his watch. "I've got a call scheduled for ten, but I think we could crank something out before then."

The two of us set about creating a fake Web page for Grand Palace Grill, an alleged Thai restaurant in the general vicinity of KCSH. Given that Flo had ordered Chinese food the time I'd trailed her delivery guy, I figured she must like Asian cuisine.

Josh and I devised a menu by consulting other Thai restaurant sites and choosing the most common offerings. I had him add the photo Hana had used for her PerfectCouple.com profile and dubbed her the alleged owner, Pang Tidarat. According to my Internet search, Pang was a common woman's name in Thailand. It also sounded like "hunger pang," which seemed appropriate for someone in the food service business.

Twenty minutes later, we had built a rather rudimentary site, but it looked like something a mom-and-pop operation would have and was sufficient for my purposes, which were to catch Flo Cash red-handed.

Hana passed by Josh's office and glanced inside, stopping and backtracking when she saw me sitting there, too. She frowned. "I spent an entire hour on the phone this weekend with Morgan Walker. He says he finds my conversation 'positive and uplifting.'" She made angry air quotes with her fingers.

"Sorry," I told her. "But thanks." I waved her into Josh's office. "Look. You own a restaurant now." I gestured to the screen where her picture and bio were displayed. According to the site, she'd grown up in Bangkok and had worked as a chef at restaurants there before immigrating to the United States.

"I'm not Thai," Hana said, frowning again. "I'm Korean. All Asians aren't the same, you know."

"I realize that," I said. "But I'm over budget on this investigation and can't afford a stock photo. You're the closest thing we've got."

"You owe me," she said as she left.

I thanked Josh for his help and went to my office. I promptly went about setting up an account for Grand Palace Grill on the TradingPost.com Web site. I listed Pang Tidarat as the contact person. I set up a Gmail account for Pang and provided the e-mail address and my Sara Galloway burner phone number in the contact information section. I'd set the phone to issue the automated general greeting rather than a personal greeting, so the phone could be used for both purposes without giving me away.

The restaurant set up now, I clicked on the tab to search

for services and typed "radio advertising" in the box. The search provided a single link to the as yet unidentified radio station. No phone number was provided, but there was an e-mail address. I sent a message that read: *I just opened a Thai restaurant and would be interested in exchanging meals for radio commercials. Please contact me.* I included a link to the Web site Josh and I had just created. With any luck, Flo would respond soon.

I spent the rest of the morning preparing letters to go out to the rest of the businesses that were either promoted on KCSH or listed on the TradingPost.com site. Of course the representatives of some of them had already claimed they wouldn't talk without an attorney and/or court order, but there was no point in wasting the judge's time when I had both the authority and administrative requirement to issue letters first demanding the information and documentation. Besides, until the recipients refused in writing to provide the information or missed the response deadline set forth in my correspondence, it would be premature to take the matter to court.

By the time I finished, my entire desk was piled high with letters demanding that the recipient provide details of any and all exchanges they'd made with Flo Cash or KCSH Radio Corporation. I picked up my phone and dialed the mail room. "Hi. This is Agent Holloway. Can you send someone up here with a mail cart? I've got a mass mailing to go out."

A few minutes later, a young male mail clerk pushed the cart into my room. "Whoa. I haven't seen this much mail on your desk since you went after that preacher and got all that hate mail."

My earlier investigation of Noah Fischer, a televangelist who ran a church called the Ark, had caused a virtual holy war. I'd been called all sorts of nasty names, assured I'd spend my afterlife in hell, and even received death threats. *Fun times.* "Lucky for me," I said, "this mail is going *out* instead of coming *in*."

"Yeah," he said, grabbing the stacks and putting them in his cart. "Lucky for *you*."

"Smart-ass."

He chuckled good-naturedly.

When I spotted the notice addressed to Doo-Wop Donuts on the top of a pile, I snatched it from him. "I'll deliver this one in person." I'd planned to do the same with the notices to Flo Cash and KCSH Radio Corporation.

"Suit yourself," the clerk said. When he finished filling his cart, he rolled it toward the door. "See you next delivery."

"Thanks!"

Nick popped his head into my office. "I'm ordering lunch in. You want anything?"

"Yeah," I said. "Pad thai noodles." Working on that menu this morning had given me a hankering.

"Thai it is," Nick replied.

My phone rang as he returned to his office to place our lunch order. It was Savannah Goode on the line.

"That guy, Jack Smirnoff?" she said. "He was just here getting new head shots. I would've called you sooner except he didn't make an appointment in advance. He just popped by to see if I could squeeze him in."

"Any chance he's still around?"

"No, he left already."

Darn. No chance of following him, then. "Did he pay cash again this time?"

"Yes."

"I appreciate the call," I told her. "Can you e-mail me his new head shots?"

"Sure."

The pictures came through a few minutes later. In these photos, he sported a light goatee. Given that he'd had dinner

with Hana on Thursday and today was Monday, he'd had
only four days to grow it, so the sparseness wasn't surprising. Still, the goatee, along with the leather jacket and
hoop earring he wore, changed his look significantly.

As soon as I'd looked the photos over, I shot them off to
my contacts at the dating sites: *Catfish alert! Please
have your tech team search for these new photos. Thank
you!*

Our food arrived a few minutes later and Nick brought
it to my office. I ate at my desk while he kicked back in
one of my wing chairs, his boots propped on the armrest
of the other.

"You know," he said, pointing an accusing plastic fork
at me, "you never did tell me about the bachelorette party."

Alicia's fiancée, Daniel, had also held his bachelor party
on Saturday night. Nick had been among the participants.

"I'll tell you all about it," I replied, shooting him a
pointed look, "right after you tell me about the bachelor
party."

Nick's only response was to whistle a tune and look ran-
domly around the room to avoid my eyes.

"Yeah," I said. "That's what I thought."

When we finished our lunch, Nick tossed his trash in
my bin and headed back to his office. I cleaned off my desk
and figured that, as long as my computer was logged into
Gmail I might as well check to see if Flo Cash had responded to Pang Tidarat's barter proposal.

Flo had. My heart began to tap-dance in my chest. Progress!

*I'm willing to do one fifteen-second on-air promo for
each meal provided. Please send suggested copy for the
promo.*

I mulled things over for a moment before responding.

*I'd like the promo to say "Grand Palace Grill serves
the best Thai food in Dallas. Dine-in, takeout, and deliv-*

ery are available. They've got low prices, too. Grand Palace Grill gives more bang for your buck than you'd get in Bangkok."

That last part was an intentional tongue twister. Might as well make Flo Cash work for it, right?

I sent the e-mail off. Not a minute later my phone rang. The caller ID readout indicated the call was coming from KCSH Radio.

"Hello?" I said in my best Thai accent which, admittedly, was pretty pathetic.

"Pang Tidarat, please," Flo said.

"Speaking."

"Send four orders of pad thai over to KCSH and I can get you on the air today."

"Okay," I said. "Half hour for delivery."

As soon as we ended our call, I phoned the same Thai place Nick had ordered from and requested four more orders of pad thai to be delivered. Fortunately, they used cheap, generic containers and bags with no logo on them. Next, I phoned the mail room. The male clerk who'd been in my office earlier answered the phone.

"Want to do me a favor?" I asked. "There's twenty bucks in it for you."

"This doesn't involve anything sexual, does it?"

"No," I replied. "But there will be wet noodles involved."

Half an hour later, the mail clerk and I were on our way to KCSH with four orders of pad thai noodles in a plastic bag. The radio was tuned to the station. A block away, I pulled over and climbed into the backseat. He took over the wheel while I hunkered down out of sight.

"So all I do is carry this inside?" he said.

"Right," I told him. "Tell them it's a delivery from Grand Palace Grill."

"Grand Palace," he repeated. "I've got it."

He drove the rest of the way to the station building, climbed out of the car, and carried the food into the reception area. Seconds later, he returned to the car and drove down the street, stopping in the parking lot of a strip center so we could switch places.

I'd just taken the wheel when Flo's voice came over the airwaves during a commercial break: "Grand Palace Grill serves the best Thai food in Dallas. Dine-in, takeout, and delivery are available. They've got low prices, too. Grand Palace Grill gives more bang for your buck than you'd get in Bangkok!"

Flo hadn't been tripped up at all by the last sentence, but I suppose years of talking on the radio had given her a nimble tongue. Still, my trick had worked. She'd promoted my fictional restaurant on the air. *Ha! No one outsmarts Tara Holloway.*

The mail clerk held out his hand. "You owe me twenty bucks."

My cell phone rang several times Monday afternoon with people wanting to place orders for Thai food. Flo's on-air promotions seemed to work wonders.

"Sorry," I told them, "we had to close. Plumbing problem. Hot water all over the floor." Thanks to Max Brady, I had that excuse locked and loaded.

Late that afternoon, I received a call from an executive at one of the dating sites.

"Those new head shots were just posted on our site," she said. "It's a new profile."

"What name is he using?"

"Bailey Chambord."

Irish Cream and black raspberry liqueur. What a combination.

"Do you want me to shut his account down?" she asked.

I didn't want the guy to rip off any more victims, but at

the same time I didn't want him to know he'd been caught. After all, we still didn't know who the guy was. If he was inadvertently tipped off, he might not show up for the dates he'd scheduled with me and Hana this week. We might never find the guy.

"Can you make it look as if his profile is active," I asked, "and allow him to reach out to others but block anyone from contacting him?" That would protect anyone else from falling into his trap.

"We can do that," she said.

"Great." Bailey Chambord was about to find himself a very unpopular guy. "Can you send me the profile he set up? I might need it for evidence later."

"Sure," she said.

I thanked her for contacting me and awaited her e-mail. It arrived a few minutes later. I printed the profile out and perused it. Sure enough, it contained the photo of the cat-fisher with the goatee. This time around, he'd claimed to be a counselor who worked with troubled youth. Once again, he'd declared himself to be a man with open-ended interests. He'd also offered his standard assertion that he lived out of state but had plans to relocate to Dallas. But this time, rather than targeting women, he'd requested to be matched with men. *Hm-m.* Looked like he was an equal-opportunity catfisher. Unfortunately for him, I was an equal-opportunity ass-kicker.

chapter twenty-five

*C*oyote Radio Host

On Tuesday morning, I got up an hour earlier than usual. I had a busy morning planned.

The first thing I did was swing by Doo-Wop Donuts to pick up a couple dozen for the office. As I'd done the time before, I bypassed the roller-skating carhops and went inside to speak directly with the owner.

The woman looked up at me and froze, her fist reflexively tightening on the pastry bag in her hand, causing it to expel a long string of pink frosting that curled itself into a pile on top of the donut she'd been frosting.

"That looks yummy." I gestured to the gooey mess she'd made. "I'll take that one."

She looked down. "Oh. Goodness." She set the pastry bag aside and wiped her hands on her coveralls.

"I need three dozen mixed," I told her, "and I need to know whether you want to come clean voluntarily or whether I should stick it to you with a bunch of penalties." I held the letter out to her.

She took it from me, opened the envelope, and read it over before looking back up. "Bartering isn't illegal."

"You're right," I said. "Bartering is perfectly legal. But

what's not legal is hiding it from the IRS and failing to pay taxes on any resulting net income."

Desperation clouded her face. "But I was assured that noncash transactions aren't taxable!"

"Assured by whom?"

She said nothing.

"An attorney?" I said. "A CPA?"

No lawyer or accountant worth their salt would have advised a client to hide barter transactions from the IRS. Obviously, Flo Cash had encouraged those she exchanged with to refrain from reporting so that she wouldn't be discovered.

When the woman still said nothing, I said, "It was Flo Cash who told you that bartering was nontaxable. I know it and you know it."

She stood in silence for another moment, apparently thinking things over. "I'll get your donuts," she finally said, resignation in her voice. "And I'll talk to my CPA."

"Good," I said. "You'll be doing us both a favor."

Three dozen donuts in hand, I made another quick stop before heading into the office.

The Flo Cash *Cash Flow Show* was playing over the speakers as I entered the radio station with one of the boxes of donuts. The young woman at the desk looked up. The glower on her face said she wasn't excited to see me, but the gleam in her eyes as she spotted the box in my hands said she was happy to see the donuts.

"I need to speak with Flo," I said.

"She's in the middle of her show."

I whipped out a pen and, using the donut box as an improvised writing surface, scribbled a note on the back of the notice I'd brought with me:

Nice doing business with you! Hope you enjoyed the pad thai.

XO,
Special Agent Holloway, aka Pang Tidarat

I handed the letter to the young woman, along with the box of donuts. "Enjoy them. It could be the last free donuts you ever get."

My work there done—*my work being to give Flo Cash a big neener-neener*—I returned to my car. I listened to her show as I drove. Within minutes it was clear she'd read both my handwritten note and official demand for information and documentation. She began to rant on the radio.

"The IRS has attempted to entrap me," she said, "by posing as a regular citizen online." Her words were followed by a sound effect of a crowd expressing displeasure. *Boooo!*

I visualized Flo in her glass booth, dunking one of the donuts I'd left into her mug of tea and ripping a bite from it.

The rant continued. "Special Agent Holloway is like one of those catfish types who make up a false identity and prey on people on the Internet."

I was nothing like a catfisher. I was a government employee doing her job. And doing it well, I judged, given the rage my visit had sent Flo into.

"Government entrapment should be illegal!" Flo cried.

"Bite me," I said back to my radio. "Better yet, if you feel trapped, chew your leg off, Flo."

I drove back to the IRS and carried the boxes up to our floor. Bringing two dozen donuts to the kitchen made me the office hero for the day. Government employees have limited perks. It's not like we worked for Google and got free coffee and pastries and scooters to transport ourselves around the office. Heck, we collected contributions for coffee in an old can on the kitchen counter.

Back in my digs, I checked my voice mails, logged on

to my computer, and dealt with my e-mails, including one from Morgan Walker.

Can't wait to see you tonight!

I was looking more forward to the sushi than I was the company. Nonetheless, I replied: *Me, too!*

As long as I was on my computer, I figured I might as well take down the Grand Palace Grill Web site and remove the listing from TradingPost.com. No sense disappointing more people who were craving Thai food.

I dialed Josh, because when I said *I* might as well take down the site I really meant *him*. I had no idea how to do it. "Can you take down the Grand Palace site for me?"

"Mission accomplished?" he asked.

"Yep."

I hung up the phone and entered "TradingPost.com" in my browser. Nothing came up. I squinted at the screen to check my spelling. I had it right. *Hm-m . . .*

I sat back in my chair. Looked like Flo had taken down her bartering site, too. She might have thought that by taking it down she could hide the evidence. Not so. I'd already printed out every page.

Broadcast that, Flo Cash.

chapter twenty-six

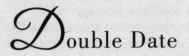

Double Date

Given that Morgan Walker had continued to contact me, we were fairly certain he harbored no continuing suspicions that he'd been followed when he left Chili's after his date with Hana. Nick thus insisted on being my backup inside the restaurant tonight. Like the catfishing Casanova, Nick took pains to disguise himself. He wore the white felt cowboy hat I'd bought for him. It would go a long way to keeping his face in shadow. He'd also pulled the collar of his Western shirt up around his face.

By the time I arrived at the restaurant, Nick had been siting at the sushi bar for twenty minutes. Being raised on a farm and fed meat and potatoes his entire life, Nick had only recently tried sushi for the first time. I'd been the one to introduce him. He'd been surprised to learn how much he liked the stuff.

I found Morgan in the lobby, dressed, as usual, in stylish designer clothes. The goatee he'd sported in his new head shots was gone, his face now clean-shaven, not even a five o'clock shadow to be seen. Not that I was surprised. He seemed to try a new identity with each set of victims. A smart move on his part. There was less chance of anyone recognizing him if he constantly changed his appearance. He was both a catfish and a chameleon. Either way, slimy and scaly.

"Hi, Morgan." *Or should I say* Bailey? I forced a broad smile to my mouth and opened my eyes wider, hoping they'd catch the light and sparkle. After all, I needed to make this guy think I was smitten with him. Of course I'd much rather smite him.

He ran his eyes over me. "You look gorgeous."

I'd dressed to impress tonight, Nick be damned. After all, I had to look like I was making a serious effort with this guy or he might realize I was a decoy. I'd worn a pair of stilettos, along with skinny jeans and a sheer, sexy blouse that provided a peek at the red bra I wore under it. Not that Morgan would care about the bra, assuming, of course, that Hana's gaydar was correct. But still, I had to look like I was trying to entice the guy.

"Here," he said, holding out the book he'd had signed for me. "This is for you."

"Oh, Morgan!" I gushed. "You're so sweet!" I took the book and opened it to the inscription. *To Sara, Enjoy life's mysteries.* The inscription was followed by a crazy squiggle that looked like the author had suffered a stroke while signing his name. Really, what was it with signatures? Shouldn't they be as legible as other handwriting?

Morgan and I stepped up to the hostess stand. "Would you like to sit at the sushi bar or do you prefer a table?"

"A table," Morgan said without hesitation. He turned to me and smiled. "I want to be able to look at you."

"Aw." I gave him a playful jab on the shoulder. "You're going to make me blush." Blush, nothing. It was more likely he was going to make me puke.

The hostess led us to a table for two in the center of the room. Being more accustomed to the flat shoes I wore to work each day, I wobbled a little on my heels. I took the seat on the side of the table facing the sushi bar so Morgan's back would be to Nick.

Over Morgan's shoulder, I saw Nick pick up a pair of wooden chopsticks and make a show of breaking them apart. If he had his druthers, he'd be snapping Morgan's neck in the same manner. Nick's possessiveness could be a little much at times, but I had to admit it was reassuring to know how much he wanted me for his own.

Morgan opened his menu to take a look. "What's good here?"

Hell if I knew. I'd never been to this particular restaurant before. But every sushi place served an avocado roll, right?

"They make a good avocado roll." I opened my menu, too, glad to see they also served a sweet potato tempura roll. That was less standard fare, but one of my favorites when I could get it. "Let's get a sweet potato roll, too."

The waitress came by to take our drink orders.

"Plum wine for me," I said.

Morgan looked up at her. "I'll have the same."

"No sake for you?" I asked.

He grimaced. "Ugh, no. That stuff burns."

I laughed. I'd never acquired a taste for the stuff, either. It was like drinking hot nail polish remover.

As we waited for our drinks, I asked about his stepson. "Did you see Shane when you went home last weekend?" *Might as well feign some concern, right? And pretend to believe that Morgan had been back home in Oklahoma?*

"He came by the house," Morgan said. "He asked if he could have some of the furniture and the big-screen television." He sighed. "I let him take it. I want to be fair to the kid. And at least I know he'll use the furniture and TV. It's cash I don't trust him with. He'd spend it on weed."

"He uses drugs?"

"Yes," Morgan replied. "Ironic, given my line of work,

isn't it? Problem is, he doesn't want to quit. No amount of therapy can help a person who isn't interested in kicking their habit. But maybe he'll outgrow it."

"Some people do," I said.

He lifted a shoulder. "And others use marijuana as a gateway to harder drugs."

"True. I hope he'll be the former case."

Morgan gave a soft smile. "You and me both, Sara."

The waitress arrived with our wine and took our food order.

As she left the table, Morgan raised his glass. "To new relationships."

I was much more inclined to poke a chopstick in his eye, but instead I smiled, raised my glass, and tapped it against his. *Clink.* As I took a sip of the wine, Nick looked over and made a stabbing motion with his chopsticks. *Great minds think alike.* An involuntary laugh burbled up and I choked on my wine.

"Are you okay?" Morgan asked, beginning to stand.

I motioned for him to sit back down. "I'm fine," I croaked out. "The wine just went down the wrong pipe."

We chatted more as we waited for our food. I gestured to the chefs behind the sushi bar. "Ever notice how their chef suits look like karate uniforms? Other than the hats, I mean." I watched Morgan closely, gauging his reaction to my reference to karate.

He merely shrugged, giving nothing away. "I guess they're both based on traditional Japanese clothing."

Ugh. Nothing in his response or demeanor told me whether the guy was a black belt. But the safest assumption was that he was. I couldn't be certain how much of a threat he posed, but I would be wise to be prepared.

"I'm not sure whether this is a fair question to ask," he said, changing the subject, "but I have to admit I'm curious. Did you get a lot of winks on the dating site?"

He'd been the only one. The site offered an option to put things on hold if something serious seemed to be developing with a member. After all, there was no sense wasting the other members' time or getting their hopes up if a person was essentially off the market. I'd taken advantage of that capability and put my profile on hold. Still, Morgan didn't need to know that, and even if he could somehow tell my listing was on hold now he had no way of knowing how many winks I might have gotten before doing so.

I decided to play it coy. "You tell me first. How many winks have you gotten?"

He played it coyer. "Gosh, it must have been hundreds."

I was going for coyest now. "Only hundreds? Why, I must have had several thousand winks. Millions, even."

He chuckled. "It's really about quality over quantity."

"Good point."

"And on that point"—he lowered his voice and leaned toward me over the table—"I have to say that you are by far the most enchanting woman I've met."

Enchanting? What did he think this was, some kind of fairy tale? Did I look like some type of damsel in distress waiting to be rescued by a handsome prince? *Screw that.* I took a sip of my wine. "Is that so?"

"I guess what I'm saying here is that I hope you'll give me a real chance and let me know where I stand." He stared at me intently. "I'm not sure I can take another heartbreak."

So he was playing the widower card now, going for pity, huh? Such pure bullshit. Even so, I knew I had to play the game, tell him what he wanted to hear. "I'll be honest with you, Morgan," I said. "I've gotten a few winks, but after e-mails and phone calls I could tell most of the men weren't even worth a first date. There's one other guy I'm keeping on the back burner, but at this point you are the definite front-runner, by far."

His mouth spread in a wide smile and he clenched a victorious fist. "That's exactly what I wanted to hear."

And that's exactly why I'd said it.

The sushi was delicious. I almost didn't mind that I was sharing it with a con artist.

Nick kept an eye on our table during our meal, timing his departure just before I snatched the last piece of avocado roll from the platter. I knew he'd be heading out to the parking lot to plant the GPS tracker on the Mercedes. Morgan wouldn't be able to ditch us now. Ha!

When we were done eating, Morgan paid the bill and walked me out to my car. The Mercedes was likely parked far away from the building, as usual. Little did he know I'd already traced it. Never mind the security cameras.

When we reached my car, I decided to take the bull by the horns. I didn't want this guy kissing me, even under a mutual pretense. Nick would likely run him over. And I knew this guy wasn't truly interested in kissing me. I stepped toward him and gave him a hug, brushing my cheek against his in a light, yet seemingly affectionate, embrace. The kiss thus avoided, I bleeped my door locks open and slipped quickly into the driver's seat. "Thanks for dinner!" I called back through the open door.

"Wait!" As I reached for the interior door handle, he grabbed the frame and held it open. "I have to go back to Oklahoma later in the week, but how about lunch next Monday?"

It would be our third date, and it would be during the day, when banks were open. This guy was following his typical MO. It would be his last time.

"Lunch sounds great," I said.

He smiled. "I'll be in touch so we can decide on the time and place."

"Okeydoke. Have a safe trip back home."

He closed my door and, once he'd stepped away, I backed out of my space. He stood in the lot, hand raised to wave good-bye, pretending that he was so taken with me he wanted to watch me ride off into the sunset. *Sheesh.*

I was half a mile down the road when my phone rang. It was Nick. I put him on speaker.

"Enjoy your date?" he growled.

"Only the food," I said, "not the company. Where's Morgan headed?"

"North on I-Thirty-Five. Same as before."

Clearly, his home had to be somewhere in that direction. The only question was, how far? Did he really live in Oklahoma? Or did he live in one of the towns between Dallas and the Oklahoma border?

We'd find out tonight.

chapter twenty-seven

The Buck Stops Here

I pulled into the lot of a nearby grocery store to wait for Nick to swing by to get me. After I'd climbed into his G-ride and buckled my seat belt, he handed me a tablet. On the screen was the site that linked to the tracker.

"He's still heading north on the interstate," I told Nick.

"And so are we," Nick said, driving out of the lot.

Fortunately, now that we had the tracker on our side we could hang back far enough that Morgan wouldn't know we were on his tail. We trailed him a dozen miles before the red dot on the screen stopped moving for several minutes straight.

"Looks like he's parked somewhere." I mentally crossed my fingers that wherever he'd stopped would tell us something about his identity.

We followed the path he'd taken, ending up at a bar in Denton. We circled through the parking lot, looking for the Mercedes.

I pointed when I spotted it. "There's his car. Look, someone wrote: 'Wash me, asshole' in the dust on the driver's door."

Nick raised his index finger into the air. "Not someone. *Me.* I couldn't resist."

I couldn't much blame him. I was guilty of these types of juvenile acts on occasion, too. The more frustration a target caused us, the more we needed to vent our emotions somehow.

We drove across the street and parked in the lot of a barbershop that was closed for the night. It gave us a good vantage point for keeping an eye on the Mercedes but made it less likely Morgan would spot us spying on him when he emerged from the bar.

We sat, watching the activity in the lot. Guy after guy went into the building, not a single woman among them. Evidently this was a gay bar. A busy one, too, given the two-for-one Tuesday night special advertised on the digital sign out front. The place appeared to be packed to the rafters.

My eyes began to droop. "I need a latte if we're going to be out here much longer."

"I could use some coffee, too." Nick started the engine and we drove down the road a ways, picking up drinks at a coffeehouse drive-through.

We returned to the barbershop to resume our surveillance, biding our time by watching sitcoms on my phone's Hulu app. Finally, it was closing time. Patrons swarmed out to the lot. Engines revved. Headlights illuminated. Cars drove every which way, some exiting onto the main road in front of us, others circling behind the nightclub to exit the lot via a side street. In the mad shuffle of people and vehicles we lost sight of the Mercedes. But when things settled down it was no longer in the lot.

"He's gone," I said on a yawn, the effects of the latte wearing off. I booted the tablet back up. "I'll see where he's at."

According to the screen, the tracking device was now a couple miles away. Once again it was stationary. "It's not moving. Looks like he's parked again." Did Morgan Walker live here in Denton? Dare I hope the car be parked in front of his residence, where we'd be able to use the address to determine his true identity?

As I navigated, Nick drove to the tracker's new location. It was one of those twenty-four-hour gas station/mini-mart places with a dozen pumps, an extensive fountain drink array, and a high-pressure car wash. Despite the late hour, there were two cars at the pumps, three more parked in the spots fronting the store. None were the Mercedes.

I eyed the tablet again to make sure we were at the right place. "I don't get it. The GPS says the tracker is here."

Nick raised his hands from the wheel. "So where's the car?"

I scanned the lot, my eyes stopping on the car wash, where a stream of sudsy water flowed out, draining through a grate built into the asphalt. While no car was in the wash now, it was clear a vehicle had recently driven through. "I think the asshole washed the car."

"Aw, hell!" Nick shoved the gearshift into park, ripped off his seat belt, and bolted from the car, walking into the car wash despite the big red warning sign that read: "SAFETY HAZARD—VEHICLES ONLY." He emerged a moment later with a scowl on his face and the small black device in his hand.

Stupid undercarriage spray.

On Wednesday, I received a call from Max Brady.

"The Trading Post site is down," he said. "You know anything about that?"

"I didn't take it down, if that's what you're asking. But I did let Flo Cash know I'd learned about it. She must've taken it down herself."

"Darn it!" he snapped. "I had quite a few Barter Bucks accumulated. How am I supposed to recoup that money?"

"You could sue Flo." She claimed that the twelve grand in her safe was all she had to her name, but I still wasn't buying it. She'd proved herself untrustworthy. Nothing she said could be taken at face value. "For what it's worth," I told Brady, "I'm sorry that happened. That's not fair to you or anyone else who had a credit balance."

"I'll chalk this up to a hard lesson learned," he said. "From now on I do business the old-fashioned way. With cash or credit only."

As I discovered over the course of the day, Max Brady wasn't alone in his discontent. Many of those who'd participated in exchanges on the Trading Post site were furious that their Barter Bucks had been rendered worthless. Flo Cash wasn't honest with them, either. In fact, she told them I'd forced her to close the site down and gave them my number to call. My phone rang all week with irate people wanting to tear me a new one.

"I was owed five grand!" screamed a caterer. "How am I going to collect that now?"

"You'll have to speak to Flo Cash," I told the woman. "She's the one who made the decision to take down the site. Not the IRS."

"That's not what she says."

"She's a bald-faced liar." I wasn't about to pussyfoot around the issue anymore. "Ask your accountant. They'll tell you. Everything Flo told you about bartering being nonreportable and nontaxable was wrong."

As soon as I ended the call with the caterer, an auto mechanic called.

"You've cost me over two thousand dollars! I'm taking that off my tax bill."

"That's not how this works," I told the man. "You need to speak with Flo Cash about the Trading Post. She alone made the decision to take down the site."

While I was able to convince some of them of the truth, others didn't want to buy it. I did the best I could and, frankly, if the others wanted to believe Flo Cash over a licensed CPA/IRS agent, well, they could kiss my little round ass.

Despite the flack I was getting from some of those with credit balances, I was nonetheless beginning to receive responses from members of the Trading Post network and others who had done exchanges with Flo for promotions outside the Web site. The notices I'd mailed had put the fear of God—or the fear of Uncle Sam—in some of them, and they were beginning to cooperate. *Woo-hoo!*

The mail clerk rolled his heavily laden cart into my office. "More mail for you. You must be working on something big."

"I am," I said. "It's that case you helped me with."

"When I delivered the pad thai?"

"Yep."

He cocked his head. "So, do I get a cut of what's collected?"

I snorted. "No. I don't, either. But I'll put a good word in for you with your supervisor. Maybe you'll get a big raise this year."

He dumped a pile of envelopes, some manila, some business sized, on my desk. "Have fun with this."

"I always do."

By the end of the workday on Friday, I'd amassed quite a collection of data. According to the documentation I'd received, a window-cleaning service had provided four hundred dollars in services at Flo's home. An electronics store had given her a state-of-the-art curved television and surround sound system for her media room, all to the tune of ten grand. A flooring company had installed hardwoods in several rooms of Flo's house. The value of the flooring and labor was nearly six thousand dollars. A multitude of restaurants had provided thousands of dollars—and thousands of calories—in meals to Flo. The woman probably hadn't had to cook in years.

As the information rolled in, I input the data into a spreadsheet. The amounts were really beginning to add up, and I'd barely scratched the surface. In virtually every instance, Flo had received personal items and services yet paid for them via KCSH Radio Corporation ads. None of the amounts appeared in KCSH's financial records or on their corporate tax returns, and none of the income appeared on Flo's individual income tax returns, either. As a financial expert, she knew these kinds of shenanigans weren't kosher. I supposed she'd thought she was flying under the radar. *Surprise!* My radar begins at ground level and doesn't stop until it reaches the stratosphere.

Friday evening marked Hana's second date with Morgan. He'd taken her to a seafood restaurant. It seemed fitting a catfisher would want to eat there. After all, bigger fish often eat smaller fish.

Tonight, Nick and I were driving a different car from the government fleet. We needed to mix things up a bit if we didn't want to be spotted.

I pulled up next to Morgan's Mercedes, which sat at the back of the lot out of view of both the security cameras and the windows. His attempts to keep the car from being picked up on video had made our task of planting the device easier. Ironic, huh?

Tonight, Special Agent Will Dorsey had agreed to back Hana up inside the restaurant. While he was married, his wife and kids were out of town for the weekend visiting her folks. The Lobo herself had agreed to accompany Will to the seafood restaurant. If we needed agents to observe

Hana and Morgan without attracting notice I wasn't sure a conservatively dressed thirtysomething black man going to dinner with a sixtysomething white woman sporting a polka-dot dress, go-go boots, and a strawberry-blonde beehive was the best way to go. But hey, maybe it's just me.

Nick and I drove across the street and parked behind a crepe myrtle tree, where we'd be partially hidden. I squinted at the building through the specs but could see nothing. The setting sun had set the sky ablaze and the restaurant staff had pulled down the shades over the windows. It was impossible to see inside. I tossed the field glasses aside. "I can't see anything."

Nick picked them up and held them to his eyes. "Me, neither."

A Luke Bryan song came on the radio, and Nick turned it up, singing along. When a song by Brazos Rivers followed, Nick jabbed the button to turn the radio off. "I'm not gonna sit here and listen to that jackass and his caterwauling."

I fought down a laugh. Brazos Rivers had at one time been my celebrity crush. He'd also at one time been the subject of an IRS investigation for tax evasion led by yours truly. Long story short, Nick had been jealous then, too.

"You want some good music?" I reached into my purse and retrieved the Carmen harmonica. I'd taken the thing apart and given it a thorough cleaning with a toothbrush, vinegar, and lemon juice. "Listen to this." I put the harmonica to my mouth and blew. *Twee-twoh-twoo-twee!*

That last high-pitched note made Nick's eye twitch. "That is *not* good music."

I harrumphed. "I bet they'd love me in Appalachia."

The doors to the restaurant opened, and Lu and Will stepped out, looking like some kind of sugar mama and her boy toy.

"We've got movement," I said, dropping the harmonica back into my purse and pointing to the restaurant.

We watched as Will and Lu returned to Will's car and drove out of the parking lot. A minute later, we received a text from Will: *Sitch normal. Nothing to report.*

I texted back: *Thanks for the backup.*

His reply came a moment later: *Thank YOU for the lobster.*

Lobster? My budget was soooo busted on this case.

A few minutes later, Hana and Morgan emerged. Hana carried a take-out box in her hand. At least her meal had been on Morgan, not my account. I put the field glasses back to my eyes and spied as Morgan walked her to her car. They stood next to the car, talking for another moment. "I bet he's asking her for a lunch date on Monday."

Finally, he bent down and gave her a quick peck on the lips. I snorted when both of them stiffened. "This date was no good for anybody."

Nick started the car and eased into position to follow Morgan. "Lead us home, you conniving bastard."

Unfortunately, Morgan did not lead us home. Instead, he led us on a forty-five-minute road trip back to the gay bar in Denton. I tracked him on the tablet. Several times the red dot indicating Morgan's car disappeared, but it always popped back up a second or two later. Probably had something to do with the satellites or the tablet's data provider network.

Nick groaned as Morgan turned into the nightclub's parking lot. "Been here, done this."

"Well, it looks like we're going to be here and do this all over again."

Nick drove across the street and parked in the lot of a convenience store that sat next to the barbershop, taking a place along the side of the building where it was darker and we'd be less obvious hanging out for hours on end.

I gestured toward the building. "Should we go inside? Give the clerk a heads-up that we're out here?"

Nick mulled it over for a moment. "I think we're better off just lying low. We don't know who knows who around here. As close as the bar is to the store, I'd hazard a guess that the employees and patrons of the bar stop in here on occasion. It's probably better not to notify the store clerks and risk them giving the wrong person a heads-up."

I had to concur. There seemed to be more risks to giving notice than not.

My phone rang with an incoming call. The caller ID readout indicated it was Hana.

I jabbed the button to take the call. "Hey, Hana. How'd it go?"

"He asked me to meet him for a late lunch on Monday at a sandwich shop in Addison."

"What time?"

"One thirty."

No doubt he'd ask me for an earlier date when he got back to me.

"Thanks," I told her. "We'll have this catfish on the line before we know it." Then we'd fillet him and fry him up.

"We better," Hana said. "I'm not sure how much more of this I had can take. I've got much better things to do on a Friday night than be a beard for a thief."

We ended the call and I resumed watch on the bar. Nick and I had been sitting about an hour when dusk kicked in. Footsteps to our left caught our attention. A store employee carried a black garbage bag out to the Dumpster behind the store, lifted the hard plastic cover, and tossed the bag into the bin. When he turned around, he spotted us. He also spotted us spotting him. Nick and I immediately began to fiddle with things in the car, attempting to look nonchalant. *Yep, nothing unusual here. Nothing at all. Just, uh, twiddling this dial here for no apparent reason.*

We sat there for another hour when movement to the right caught our eye. The same clerk carried a package of folded paper towels out to refill the dispenser mounted at the gas pumps. He cast another glance our way, alarm flickering across his face, but made no attempt to confront us.

The night was completely dark by then. We could hear the faint notes of dance music drift across the road when patrons ventured in and out of the nightclub. Nick rolled up the windows to keep the hungry mosquitos from flying in to feast on us.

My eyes began to droop and my face felt heavy. It had been a long, busy week. I sat up straighter, hoping the movement would revive me, but within seconds my head flopped forward. I jerked awake only to repeat the head flop a few seconds later.

"Don't fight it," Nick said, reaching over me to pull the lever to recline my seat. "I'll keep watch."

In a lying position now, I said, "Are you sure?" But my mind didn't wait for his answer before drifting into oblivion.

RAP-RAP-RAP!

"What the—?" I sat bolt upright to see a Denton Police offer standing outside our car, tapping his flashlight on Nick's window.

Nick, however, continued to snore away. He'd somehow managed to fall asleep sitting up, his head bent back at an odd angle. No doubt he'd have a nasty crick in the morning.

I reached over and shook him. "Nick! There's a cop at the window!"

"Whuh—?" Nick scrubbed a hand over his face and looked from me to the police officer shining the light through his window. "Oh, crap. I must've fallen asleep."

He raised his right hand to keep it in the officer's sight while lowering the window with his left.

The cop shined his beam over Nick before blinding me

with it. "The store clerk told me you two have been out here for hours."

"We have," I admitted. *So much for lying low, huh?* "We're federal law enforcement."

"Feds, huh?" he said. "Which department?"

"IRS," Nick replied.

"IRS?" The cop's brow furrowed. "What is the IRS doing out here at this time of night?"

"We're working an undercover case," I said.

The cop scoffed, "You were both asleep."

"*Deep* undercover," I said, as if that somehow explained anything.

The cop shook his head.

I gestured to my purse, which sat on the floor at my feet. "Okay if I reach in there and show you my badge?"

He looked wary. "You got a gun in that purse?"

"No," I said. "My Glock's here on my hip." I raised my hands in the air and shifted in my seat to show him.

"What about you?" he asked, shining the flashlight beam on Nick once more.

"Same." Nick, too, put his hands in the air so the guy would know we weren't reaching for our weapons. He cocked his head to indicate the gun holster on his belt.

"All right," the officer said, "show me some ID."

As I went for my purse, my eyes spotted the time on the dashboard clock. *3:08.*

"Is that the right time?" My gaze moved across the street to the parking lot of the nightclub. It was dark. And it was empty. No Mercedes in sight. "Dammit!"

Nick let out a frustrated huff. "I'm sorry, Tara. I was supposed to stay awake. I let you down."

"You didn't mean to," I said as I dug for my wallet. "Besides, we're both tired from being out here late earlier in the week. I'm the lead investigator on the case. I'm the one who should've stayed awake." Besides, the GPS tracker would tell us where Morgan had gone to now.

I found my wallet and showed the officer my driver's license and badge. Nick did the same.

Satisfied, the officer let us go. "Next time you go undercover at night," he said as he stepped back from the car, "you might want to take a nap first."

chapter twenty-eight

Cashing Out

Once the police officer had gone, I grabbed the tablet and logged into the GPS tracker app. There was no red dot to indicate the location of Morgan's car. Instead, a message popped up that read: "SIGNAL NOT FOUND."

"Dammit!" I showed the screen to Nick. "What do you think that means?"

"Hell if I know. The device was sitting in a puddle of water inside the car wash when I picked it up. I dried it off on my pants, but maybe some of the water had seeped inside. Maybe it's shorted out."

Just my luck. It seemed the closer I tried to get to the catfisher, the more he kept slipping past me. I just hoped I wouldn't end up like the proverbial fisherman, with no catch and only a story of the one that got away.

An e-mail from Morgan arrived in my in-box on Saturday: *I've got an interview Monday afternoon, but there's time for us to have lunch beforehand. How about 11:00?*

He suggested a deli in Lewisville. A quick consult with my GPS app told me the deli was in an area near several major branch banks. It was a safe bet that Sara Galloway would bank at one of them.

I responded with: *Sounds great, Morgan! See you then!*

Immediately after sending the e-mail I contacted Hana and gave her the details. "You want to be part of the bust, right?"

"Are you kidding me?" she said. "After having to let that guy kiss me and pretending to love the harmonica? Of course I do!"

We spoke for several minutes, devising our plan. When we finished, I contacted Nataya, Leslie, and Julia and gave them the scoop. "You want in?"

They responded with a unanimous, *"Yes!"*

Early Monday morning, the mail clerk brought me another load of responses from members of Flo Cash's bartering network. "Here you go," he said, setting the stack on my desk.

"Thanks."

"You close to busting her?" he asked.

"Closer every minute."

I was even closer to busting Morgan Walker. My nerves were already abuzz with excitement. I barely had time to get through three of the responses before it was time for me and Hana to head up to Addison. I gathered up my purse, slid my blazer on to hide the gun holstered at my hip, and all but cartwheeled down the hall to Hana's office. Busting crooks is good for one's disposition.

I stopped in her doorway. "You ready?"

She slid her gun into her holster and covered it with a jacket, too. "I am now. Let's go."

As we passed Nick's office, he called out, "Give 'im hell, girls!"

He'd wanted to come along but had a pre-arranged deposition he had to attend early this afternoon that got in the way. To be honest, though I'd appreciated his help getting us to this point, I kind of liked the idea of Jack/Morgan's dates taking him down on their own. Of course Hana and I would take the lead. We couldn't put innocent civilians at risk. But at least they'd get a chance to see things go down.

Hana and I walked outside to the parking lot, hopped into our G-rides, and caravanned up to Lewisville. While I parked at the sandwich shop, Hana got into place at the bank.

I found Morgan sitting at a Formica booth inside the shop, cleaning his eyeglasses with a napkin.

He put his glasses back on, gave me a warm smile, and stood to give me a hug. "It's good to see you, Sara."

"You, too." *Prepare to go down, jerkface.*

We made our way to the counter, where we ordered sandwiches and drinks. When they were ready, we carried them back to the booth.

I took a sip from my straw. "How was your weekend?"

"Honestly?" He dropped his gaze. "Not so good."

"Why's that?"

"Shane's causing more problems. He found his mother's debit card and used it to wipe out our entire checking account. The card was in a drawer in the bedroom. I hadn't thought to cut it up."

"I'm sorry to hear it." *I wasn't sorry at all. I had the fictional Shane to thank for allowing me to bust his sorry-ass stepfather today.*

Morgan changed topics, mentioning the rain they'd had in Oklahoma City Friday night. *As if he'd know.* He'd been shaking his tush at the nightclub. Or at least I assumed he'd been shaking his tush. For all I knew he was a wallflower.

"That new Armie Hammer movie opens this weekend," he said. "I'd love to take you. How's your Saturday night look?"

Saturday night I'd be helping Alicia take care of last-minute details for her Sunday wedding. But this guy didn't need to know that. I knew he had no intention of taking me out on Saturday. He was only mentioning the future to make it seem as if we'd have one, to put me off my guard, give me hope.

"Saturday?" I said. "Sure, I'm free. You won't have to be in Oklahoma?"

"Not this weekend, luckily," he said.

I continued to eat my sandwich, having a hard time getting the food down with all the excited butterflies fluttering around in my stomach. Only a few more minutes and this guy would be going down. I could hardly wait!

Finally, we finished our lunch and tossed our trash in the bin. He walked me out to my car.

As we stopped next to it, he pulled out his wallet. "Sara, I have a big favor to ask you. If it's an imposition, feel free to say no. I haven't had a chance to open a new bank account since Shane emptied mine over the weekend. I also want to talk to my attorney first, and see what he suggests. Unfortunately, this leaves me without access to my cash or anywhere to cash my paycheck. If I sign this check over to you, would you mind cashing it for me?"

He held out the check to show it to me. It was a standard blue business check with the name "TRANQUILITY TREATMENT CENTER, INC." printed across the top, along with an address in Oklahoma City. It was made payable to Morgan Walker in the amount of $2,000.00.

I looked up at him. "Shane's really put you in a bind, huh?"

"He has."

"I'd be happy to cash it for you." I gestured across the street. "In fact, there's a branch of my bank right over there."

"Thanks so much, Sara." He smiled broadly. "You're a lifesaver."

Oh, Morgan, you poor idiot. You'll have such a different opinion of me ten minutes from now.

"Let's just walk over," I suggested. "No sense moving our cars, since the bank's so close."

"Okay," he said, though I sensed he was a little nervous not having his getaway vehicle nearby.

We walked across the street. In my peripheral vision I saw Hana's G-ride parked in the employee area at the back of the bank lot. She'd put up a window screen to hide the fact that she was in the car, but I knew she was nonetheless watching me and Morgan approach.

We were halfway up the main drive when Morgan said, "Uh-oh. My phone's vibrating. I think I'm getting a call."

Yeah, right.

He pulled his phone from his pocket and pretended to consult the readout. "It's the center. I'm going to have to take this. But I don't want to waste more of your time than necessary. Why don't you go on inside and cash the check and I can meet you back out here?"

He didn't give me a chance to object before putting the phone to his ear and saying, "Hello?" The turd even had the nerve to make a shooing motion with his hand, telling me to go on into the bank.

Stupid dumbass.

I went inside the bank and waited in line for a teller, offering a discreet wave to Leslie, Nataya, and Julia, who were seated in an area at the side of the lobby. When it was my turn, I approached the woman at the counter. "Hi," I said. "Do you have any brochures on mortgages?"

"We sure do," the woman said, reaching under the counter and pulling out a pamphlet. "This will tell you all about the various options."

"Thanks." I took the brochure from her. "Any chance I could get one of your cash envelopes? I've got a bunch of loose change in my car and I need something to put it in."

Loose change was a lame reason for needing an envelope, but it was as good as any other, I supposed. And it got the job done. The woman handed a white cash envelope over the counter to me.

"Much appreciated," I said. Just for grins, I grabbed a red lollipop from the basket on the counter, too.

As I headed back toward the front door, I folded the mortgage brochure, stuffed it inside the cash envelope to make the envelope appear full, and licked the seal to close it. Without turning my head, I winked at the security guard stationed in the lobby. I'd spoken with the branch manager and Security by phone this morning and warned them there was likely to be one hell of a scuffle in their parking lot around noon. They'd seemed excited by the idea. I supposed banking could be a fairly routine, uneventful business. It might be fun to shake things up a little.

I headed out the door and looked around, putting a hand over my eyes to shield them from the sun. *Where did Morgan go?* I didn't see him, but I did catch a glimpse of Hana darting between cars, her gun drawn.

Oh, there he is. Morgan had walked even farther away from the bank, standing almost back at the street we'd crossed. He was still pretending to talk on his phone. *Such a chatty Cathy.*

I held up the cash envelope. *Come and get it, sucka!*

He smiled, nodded, and ended the call that had never actually even started. As I walked toward him, he took a few small steps in my direction, just enough to allow Hana to circle around on foot behind him. She crouched at the front fender of a bright yellow Mustang, ready to pounce.

I stopped a few paces short and held out the envelope. "Here you go."

He stepped forward and took it from me, putting a finger under the seal to release it. I eased back to put some distance between us as he reached into the envelope and pulled out the mortgage brochure. Every molecule of his charm instantly dissipated. He glared up at me. "What the hell is this?"

"Today you've got a date with justice." Okay, so it was a corny thing to say. But it felt good to say it, anyway. My gun was out and pointed at his face in an instant. "IRS! Put your hands up! Now!"

He turned as if to run but changed his mind when he spotted Hana standing in his path, her legs spread for balance, her gun at the ready. Between me, Hana, and the cars, he was pretty much blocked in all directions.

"Are both of you with the IRS?" His face was equal parts rage and befuddlement as he raised his hands and looked from one of us to the other. "What is this?"

"You're busted," I said, punctuating my words with a scoff. "I'd think that would be obvious."

"Busted?" he cried, his glasses glinting in the sun. "For what?"

Playing innocent this late in the game? Please. "On your knees!"

"But these pants are Armani!"

"What do you care?" I spat. "You didn't pay for them. Not with your own money, anyway."

"It's June!" he shrieked. "In Texas! The asphalt's going to burn me!"

I motioned downward with my gun. "Ask me if I care."

He didn't ask. And I didn't care.

Still he didn't obey. Instead, his eyes went wild, his head snapping back and forth between me and Hana as if he was trying to determine which of us would go down easier. He chose me, storming in my direction.

Instinctively I backed toward the line of cars.

"Hi-yah!" Morgan whipped around like a top, his right leg kicking out.

Yep. The guy's a black belt, all right.

I jerked back, his foot missing my head by mere inches. *Uh-oh.* I'd known this guy could be good at martial arts, but I hadn't realized he'd be able to move this fast.

He spun again, the force causing his eyeglasses to fly from his face, his leg a blur as it swung at my face. I fell to a crouch a split second before his leg whipped over my head, barely missing me.

My thoughts rocketed through my brain at warp speed. *Should I shoot the guy?* It was tempting. After all, if he managed to land one of those kicks I could end up with a serious head injury. He might knock me out and get my gun, killing me or Hana or both. Maybe even innocent bystanders, too. But I also knew that shooting him would be risky. Any use of potentially lethal force would be scrutinized under a microscope. If I were found to have used excessive force, I could lose my job or end up in prison. This guy hadn't physically hurt anyone. He'd only taken their money. He'd been a nonviolent offender, up until now.

I hadn't fully processed my thoughts and was still in a crouch when he came at me again. I did the only thing I could at that point. I curled into a ball and rolled backward between two parked cars. His kick missed me by inches, instead hitting the back fender of a black SUV with enough force to cause a loud *kadunk* and a dent. The car's alarm system activated: *Eert-eert-eert!*

I was still on the ground when he stepped back to the opening between the cars and threw a punch, his fist coming at me like a piston. I drew my head back and he ended up punching the SUV's tire. *Thump!*

"Hey!" Hana hollered, coming up at Morgan from behind.

Eert-eert-eert!

He turned to go after her now, giving me a chance to recover. Grabbing a door handle, I pulled myself to a stand between the cars.

Eert-eert-eert!

Morgan hurtled toward my partner. Hana raised her gun as if to shoot. In a millisecond her face went through a range of emotions. No doubt she was having the same thoughts I'd had. *Would shooting this crazed ninja prove to be a bad decision?*

Eert-eert-eert!

At the last possible instant she dove sideways between a sedan and a pickup. Momentum carried Morgan forward and he impacted the tailgate of a pickup, his knee smashing against the trailer hitch that extended from under the back bumper. He might be a martial arts expert, but without his glasses his vision had clearly gone screwy. All those slick moves were of no use if you couldn't get a good bead on your target.

As the truck's alarm erupted in a *whoop-whoop-whoop*, Morgan fell to the ground, clutching his knee, screaming in agony.

Eert-eert-eert! Whoop-whoop-whoop! *"Aaaagh!"*

The cacophony was deafening.

Eert-eert-eert! Whoop-whoop-whoop! *"Aaaagh!"*

I shoved my gun back into my holster, reaching instead for my pepper spray. With his knee injured, he probably wasn't going anywhere, but I wanted to be ready just in case.

As I held my pepper spray aimed at him, Hana returned her gun to her holster, stepped behind him, and pulled his hands down into position to be cuffed.

"I don't understand!" He looked over his shoulder at Hana before returning his eyes to me, grimacing in pain. "Why are you doing this?"

I rolled my eyes and addressed Hana. "Why do people play dumb?"

Seriously, did they think playing innocent was somehow going to fool us? That we hadn't gathered substantial evidence before arriving at this point? *Sheesh. Give us some credit.*

Eert-eert-eert! Whoop-whoop-whoop!

The guy was not to be deterred. "I have a right to an explanation!" As footsteps sounded to my rear, his gaze traveled from my face to a spot behind me. He squinted, trying to make things out but having a little trouble without his glasses. "Oh, shit!"

Leslie, Nataya, and Julia stepped up next to me.

"Are *we* enough explanation for you?" Nataya asked.

Eert-eert-eert! Whoop-whoop-whoop!

"Bastard!" Julia cried.

"I want a lawyer!" Morgan yelled up at me, a look of terror on his face. "Now!"

I'd heard about as much as I wanted to hear from this guy. I pulled out the lollipop, ripped the wrap from it, and shoved it in his mouth. "You have the right to remain silent," I told him. "Anything you say or do—"

Before I realized what was happening Leslie had stepped forward and kicked Jack/Morgan/Bailey where the sun doesn't shine, just as she'd said she wanted to do. He coughed out the lollipop and lolled to the side. With his hands cuffed behind him, he fell onto the hot asphalt, his cheek smacking with the impact.

Eert-eert-eert! Whoop-whoop-whoop!

As he writhed in agony, I bent down to his level, put my face in his, and finished reading his rights. Well, more like I hollered his rights. It was hard to be heard over the car alarms. When I was done, I pulled the harmonica out of my pocket. "Seems like an appropriate time for some blues." *Twee-twoh-twoh-twoo-twoo.*

He curled into a fetal position and glared up at me.
Eert-eert-eert! Whoop-whoop-whoop!

Returning the instrument to my pocket, I grabbed his hands and yanked him to his feet. "Okay, Jack Smirnoff, Morgan Walker, or Bailey Chambord, let's go."

chapter twenty-nine

Getting to Know You, Getting to Know All About You

Hana and I spent the rest of Monday getting the catfishing Casanova processed. Though he'd been excessively verbal in the bank parking lot, he became very tight-lipped once he'd been placed in the U.S. Marshal's squad car.

"What's your real name?" I asked through the open window.

No response.

"What dating sites have you posted profiles on?"

Still no response.

I stuck my head through the window, got in his face, and hissed, "Why would you think a woman like me is only worth a *Tuesday*?"

He didn't respond to that question, either, though I couldn't much blame him. Anything he said could earn him a bullet between the eyes.

Hana retrieved his keys and wallet from his pockets. While Kevin Andersen's license was found in the locked glove box of the Mercedes, according to the con artist's real driver's license his name was Dustin Haverkamp. His home address was listed in Denton.

Once the marshal had hauled Haverkamp off to jail, Hana and I bade Nataya, Leslie, and Julia good-bye.

"Y'all take care now," I said.

"Thanks for everything!" Julia called, Leslie and Nataya murmuring in agreement.

I tossed Haverkamp's broken glasses into a trash bin, and Hana and I returned to the IRS office. We gathered around my computer, where I ran a quick search of the W-2 filings for the previous year. According to the records, Dustin had worked at a tavern in Fort Worth.

"That explains his aliases," I said. "He got them right off the bottles at work."

"It also explains his good listening skills," Hana said. "Sympathetic bartenders get bigger tips."

Hana and I obtained a search warrant for his home and drove up to Denton. I had to give the guy credit. He'd been clever to stay in the Dallas area for his dates. Though his hometown of Denton wasn't too far up the road, those who lived in Dallas had little reason to go to the smaller city unless they were University of North Texas alums attending a football game. His chances of running into one of his victims in his hometown were slim.

Armed with the warrant and his keys, we drove to his address. He lived in a contemporary condo with a modern, spare decor.

"Nice place," Hana said as we came in the door and took a glance around.

I sniffed the air. There was no telltale odor of a litter box, no fur on the couch or chairs, and no food or water bowls in the kitchen. Looked like Marmalade was even more fictitious than Morgan Walker. He'd probably found the photo of the orange tabby online somewhere. After all, there were 987 million cats on the Internet to choose from.

The place had two bedrooms, one of which had a closet full of designer clothing and one of which was set up as a home office. On the desk next to his laptop I found a loose-leaf binder. I flipped it open to look inside. *Whoa! Talk about smoking guns.* "Hana, come look at this."

She wandered in from the living room to take a peek.

The binder was the holy grail of evidence. Inside, Haverkamp's multiple identities were separated by labeled tabs. Not only had he purported to be Jack Smirnoff, Morgan Walker, and Bailey Chambord; he'd also posed as Jim Cuervo, Remy Cointreau, Gordon DeKuyper, and, my personal favorite, Glenn Fiddich.

Behind each tab was the head shot he'd used for each persona. Most of the photographs had been taken at chain portrait studios in Forth Worth, though three had been shot at Savannah's studio and one had been shot at a JCPenney store. After each head shot was a printout of the profile he'd posted on the dating sites, a cheat sheet of sorts.

I shook my head. "I guess he needed this notebook to keep his alter egos straight."

"It is a lot to remember," Hana agreed. "It was hard enough for me just pretending to be Kim Huang."

Behind each of his profiles were the listings his victims had posted on the dating sites, along with handwritten notes he'd made as he'd come to know his victims over the course of their short relationships.

Has a Yorkie named Pippa.

Favorite band is the Eagles.

Broke her pinky toe salsa dancing.

In addition to these factoids, he'd written some scathing opinions.

Talks too much.

Most annoying laugh ever!

An abundance of ear wax. Q-tip, anyone?

"Let's see what he wrote about us." Hana flipped to the tab marked "MORGAN WALKER."

On her profile page he'd written: *Gaydar pinging all over the place. Come out of the closet, girlfriend!*

Hana laughed. "He nailed that, didn't he?"

"Especially the *ping*. I told you gaydar doesn't *bloop*."

She flipped to my page. Underneath my profile pic he'd written: *2 cats—Anastasia and Hank. Thinking of going back to school for accounting degree. Eats more than her fair share of sushi. Can't walk in heels.*

"What do you know," Hana said. "He nailed you, too."

Okay, admittedly he had a point about the sushi. I had been known to snatch an extra piece or two when my table-mates weren't looking. *But the heels comment?* I could manage heels. Well enough, anyway. What's a little wobble?

Hana and I looked around for cash, peeking under the mattress, in the toilet tank, and in the freezer. All we found were a couple hundred dollars in his top dresser drawer, and most of that was singles. Probably tips from his bartending job.

"I suppose he planned to refresh his stash today," I said. Of course things hadn't gone as he'd hoped. Instead of coming back here with a cool two grand, he'd been shuffled off to the klink with blurry vision, a busted knee, and a sore crotch.

We found no bank statements to show where he might have deposited stolen funds, but that wasn't a big surprise. Many people had gone paperless and kept everything online these days.

I tried to log into his laptop, but it was password protected. "What do you think his password might be?"

" 'Bacardi'?" Hana suggested.

I tried that. "Nope."

" 'Tanqueray'?"

I tried that, too.

"Nope."

"Try 'Zac Efron.' "

Ten taps of the keyboard and I was in. "How'd you know that?"

"It's a trade secret."

I played around on his computer for a bit. When I checked his browser history, I could see that he'd recently logged on to the Bank of America site. Unfortunately, even if his password for banking purposes was also 'Zac Efron,' I didn't know his username. But with his tech skills Josh could hack into the computer and get it for me in seconds.

Once we'd accumulated all of the evidence we could, Hana and I loaded it into my car and drove back to the office in Dallas. By then it was early evening and everyone had gone home for the day. Everyone, that is, but Nick. When I'd texted him earlier to tell him the good news about the bust, he said he'd wait at the office until we returned. It was nice of him to keep the home fires burning, so to speak.

He stepped to the door of my office and leaned against the door jamb. "Congratulations, you two. There's one less bastard out there trying to make an easy buck now."

"I don't know how easy it was," I replied. "Take a look at all this homework." I handed him the notebook.

He flipped through the pages. "Heck, he's done your work for you. No need to organize the evidence."

"I wish every crook would be so kind."

Hana begged off. "I'm starving. Gonna head home and get some grub. See y'all tomorrow."

Nick eyed me. "It is about that time. Why don't we grab some sushi?"

I grabbed my purse and flipped off the light switch. "Sounds yummy."

He draped an arm over my shoulders and leaned in to whisper in my ear, "I won't even mind if you eat more than your fair share."

chapter thirty

$\mathcal{R}$adio Silenced

By the end of the week, everything had come together.

Eddie and Nick had discussed the director position, realized they both had some interest and some reservations, and spoken to Lu about whether the job's duties could be divided so that they could serve as codirectors, still doing fieldwork on occasion. Lu liked the idea and had floated it up the chain but was still waiting to hear from the higher-ups to see if it would fly.

Thanks to Dustin Haverkamp's notebook, I was able to discern which dating sites he'd used and identify his other victims. If he decided to plead not guilty to the fraud and tax evasion charges, I had forty women and three men more than willing to testify against him. With eighty grand stolen, most of it spent, and none of it reported on his tax return, he'd no longer get a mere slap on the wrist. He'd serve some jail time and spend several years having his life overseen by a parole officer.

Neener-neener.

Documentation and information continued to roll in from those involved in Flo Cash's bartering site, as well as those with whom she'd traded advertising independent of the the site. But I had enough irrefutable evidence now that she'd enjoyed hundreds of thousands of dollars in tax-free services and products in exchange for radio promotions and reported none of it as compensation.

Armed with this documentation and with Ross O'Donnell by my side, I returned to Judge Trumbull's courtroom early Friday morning to request an order requiring the domain registry to turn over the name of the owner of TradingPost.com.

As I stepped up to the bench with my stack of documentation, Judge Trumbull looked down at the papers and sighed. "It's Friday and it's been a long week. Please tell me I don't have to read all of that."

"You don't." I pulled my spreadsheet off the top. "I've made a summary."

"Thank God. If I had to go through all of that documentation I'd knock myself in the head with my gavel."

I handed her the spreadsheet. "This page lists the value of barter transactions that were conducted with Florence Cash, who owns and manages KCSH Radio Corporation. She traded the radio corporation's advertising services for personal items for her own use. Meals, car maintenance, even a mattress set."

The judge ran her eyes over the page. "She owes over two hundred grand in taxes?"

I nodded. "She's been doing these exchanges for years. Things have really added up."

"Okay," Trumbull replied. "I'm with you so far."

Good. I handed her a second page. "Max Brady, the owner of Mister Sandman Mattresses and More, signed this affidavit testifying that Flo Cash suggested he sign up on a Web site called TradingPost.com, which operated an extensive barter exchange network. Trading Post never filed the required tax reports for the exchanges it facili-

tated, and even falsely stated on its site that barter transactions are tax-free and not subject to reporting."

The judge raised a finger to silence me as she read the
affidavit. When she finished, she looked up. "Go on."

"Flo Cash signed up for a private Web site," I told the
judge. "That means I need an order requiring the domain
registry to reveal her as the owner of the bartering site."

"All right," Trumbull said, picking up her pen. "You've
convinced me." She signed the order with a flourish and
handed it to me along with the affidavit.

"Thanks, Your Honor. Have a good weekend."

I thanked Ross for his assistance, too, and returned to
my office. There I tuned my radio to KCSH, phoned the
domain registry, and asked to speak to their legal department. Once I had an attorney on the line, I said, "I've got a
court order to send you. I need to find out who owns a domain. Any chance you might be able to get to it this
morning?"

"Sure," the woman said. "It doesn't take long. If you
e-mail the order to me I can take a look while you've got
me on the phone."

"Wow. I hadn't expected such a fast turnaround. But I
appreciate it very much."

"Forget about it," she said. "I used to work for the state
attorney general's office. I know how frustrating it can be
to get information out of people."

She gave me an e-mail address and I sent the order over
via attachment.

"I see it," she said a few seconds later. She mumbled into
her mouthpiece as she apparently read it over. "Okay. Let's
take a look." I heard the tapping of fingers on a keyboard.
"According to our records, the owner of TradingPost.com
is someone named Florence Cash."

Yes! "That's what I'd hoped to hear. What address did
she provide?"

The attorney rattled it off. Flo had given the radio station's address.

"Can you send me a copy of your registration records?" I asked.

"I'd be happy to."

I thanked the woman and, a minute later, the domain registry popped up in my e-mail in-box. I printed it out and added it to my stack of evidence against Flo Cash.

I carried the documentation down to the copy room and ran the stack of papers through the machine, making a copy of everything for Flo. She and I were due for a come-to-Jesus meeting.

Lu walked in for a coffee refill as the papers were *swish-swish-swish*ing through the copy machine.

"Good job on the catfisher case," she said as she filled her cup. "Where do things stand with Flo Cash?"

"I'm on my way to see her." I motioned to the machine. "Just as soon as the copies are ready."

"Good," Lu said. "I've got a backlog I need to assign. Since you seem to be wrapping up your biggest investigations, I'll send some of the new cases your way."

No such thing as downtime on this job.

The papers stopped swishing, the copies complete. Before leaving the room, I snatched an empty copy paper box from the recycle bin to carry the paperwork in.

It was a few minutes before eleven when I pulled into the parking lot of KCSH. The Flo Cash *Cash Flow Show* was beginning to wrap up.

I carried the copy paper box to the door. Though the young woman at the desk inside looked up and made eye contact with me through the glass, she made no move to come open the door for me. Looked like those donuts I'd brought to the station hadn't bought me any goodwill. Not even the one with three inches of pink frosting on top.

"Buzz me in!" I called. I placed the box on the ground,

pulled the door open when I heard the lock release, and held the door open with my butt as I picked the box back up and stepped inside. "Good morning. I need to speak with Flo."

The young woman pointed up at the speaker, over which Flo's voice could be heard. "She's still on the air."

"I'll wait." I put the box on one of the chairs and sat down in another.

A minute later, Flo issued her standard sign-off. "Make your money make money for you!"

I eyed the receptionist, cocked my head, and pointed to the speaker, which was now broadcasting the introductory theme music for a syndicated show.

Exhaling a long breath, she stood and went through the door behind her to speak with Flo. A moment later she returned. "Go on back."

"Thanks." I grabbed the box and managed to catch the door with my foot before it swung closed. I carried the box down the short hallway to Flo's booth. The door was closed, but since it and the upper part of her booth were glass, there was no need for me to knock to announce my presence. She could see me through the window.

Flo's eyes went from my face to the box in my hand and back. Like her receptionist, Flo made no move to get out of her cushy chair and open the door for me. She merely stared me down while sipping steaming tea from her oversized mug. Obviously, her mother hadn't sent her to Miss Cecily's Charm School.

"Oh, for Christ's sake," I muttered to myself. I repeated the same process I'd done at the main door, setting the box on the floor and holding the door open with my butt to carry it into the booth. As I eased through, the two tech guys in the room across the hall eyed me through the glass before turning back to their work.

Flo's door swung shut behind me.

"You've got a lot of nerve coming here," she spat, "after everything you've cost me."

I dropped the box at her feet. "I'm about to cost you a lot more."

She looked down at the box but made no move to open it or peruse the contents. Rather, she tugged on the string to the tea bag in her mug, steam rising from the surface as she repeatedly and aggressively dunked the bag.

I gestured to the box. "That's the documentation your advertisers and the Trading Post participants have provided to me so far." I pulled the lid off the box, retrieved the copy of the spreadsheet, and held it out to her. "You owe two hundred and thirty-six thousand dollars in taxes, interest, and penalties so far. Of course, that number is going to go up as more evidence comes in, and that doesn't include what you'll owe in sales tax. The state comptroller's office will be in touch with you about that."

She made no move to take the spreadsheet from my hand.

"Look," I said, "the less you cooperate, the worse it's going to be for you. I came here as a courtesy to let you know where things stand."

"A *courtesy*?" She stopped tugging the string and smirked. "You call this a courtesy?"

"Actually, yes. I could've come to arrest you, but instead I'd hoped maybe you'd come to your senses and we could work something out."

"Senses?" Flo stood, her fingers wrapped around the dollar-sign handle of the mug, its bottom cradled in her other hand. As she stared at me, something dark and evil flashed in her eyes. "Here's some senses for you!"

Before my mind could process her movements, she flung the contents of the mug at my face. Piping-hot tea washed over my skin, scalding my face, the tea bag sticking momentarily to my forehead before falling to the floor with a soft, soggy *thup*.

Flo smirked at me, her expression self-righteous and smug. Or at least it was until my blood began to boil as hot as my face and I pounced on her. Then her expression was sheer terror.

Having suffered full-body impact from a human projectile—*me*—Flo fell backward over her console, her ass hitting the control panel. *Click*. The "ON AIR" light illuminated over the booth. *We'd gone live*. Ironic, really, because at the moment the two of us wanted nothing more than to kill each other.

With a primal roar Flo pushed herself off the console, inadvertently pressing several of the sound-effect buttons. *Kaboom! Bzzz! Aoogah!* Wielding her now-empty mug over her head like a weapon, she rushed at me with the force and fury of a Cowboys offensive lineman.

I threw myself to the side while raising my forearm to block her. It was an effective maneuver. While she'd managed to push me back a foot or two, I'd managed to block her attempts to impose blunt-force trauma to my already-blistered face.

She spun around to come at me again. She hurled the mug at me but missed. The mug landed on the console but remained intact, rolling across three of the sound-effect buttons. The clock. *Tick-tock*. The laugh track. "*Ha-ha-ha!*" The scream. "*Aaaaah!*"

The mug having proven ineffective, Flo hurled herself at me now. "You bitch!"

She knocked me back over the sound panel. *Arf! Arf-arf!* The effect was an appropriate follow-up to the insult she'd slung.

"I'm going to kill you!" she shrieked.

With thousands of listeners tuned in, I knew better than

to respond out loud. But inside my mind I yelled back at her, *Not if I kill you first!*

We struggled for several seconds—*Quack-quack! Kaboom!*—as Flo tried to pin me to the control panel. Knobs and buttons and switches poked me in the ass, thighs, and back as I squirmed. *Screech! Ding-dong! Flushhh! Boing!*

Though I fought as hard as I could, Flo had a forty-pound advantage on me. Normally my weapon skills would compensate, but with her on top of me I couldn't get to my gun or pepper spray.

I rolled to my right, apparently activating the barnyard sound section of the keyboard. *Cluck-cluck! Baaa! Oink-oink! Moooo!*

I rolled to my left, across the superhero series. *Crash! Bang! Pow! Bam!*

By this point, Flo's entire three-person staff had come to the hallway and stood at the glass watching us brawl, their expressions dumbfounded, their mouths gaping. None of them made a move to get involved. At this point, they probably weren't sure whose side to be on.

When I slapped at Flo's face she grabbed my wrists and forced my arms up over my head. If she thought that would disable me, she'd thought wrong. I might look scrawny, but I was scrappy.

Ding-dong! Tick-tock! Kaboom!

Pulling my knees up, I put my Doc Martens to her belly and used my legs to shove her back with every bit of might I could muster. The force sent her sailing in reverse across the room. She tripped over the leg of her rolling chair and sprawled to the floor, landing flat on her ass. *Fwump!*

"That's enough!" I hollered, pushing myself off the console and onto my feet. *Oink-oink! Chirp-chirp! Boing!* "This is over!"

Flo glared up at me from the floor, her eyes ablaze. "I'll tell you when it's over!"

Before I could free my gun from its holster she launched from the floor as if she had rocket boosters on her butt. I did the only thing I could at that point. Grab her mug from the console and swing it at her head.

THUNK!!!

Looked like the fortune cookie was right. An empty vessel does make the loudest sound.

Flo hovered in front of me for a moment, as if in suspended animation. Then her eyes rolled back, her knees buckled, and she flopped in a heap to the floor.

Knowing the staff standing frozen in the hall could hear the broadcast, I grabbed the microphone. "Can someone call an ambulance?"

The guys just stood there with their mouths hanging open, but the receptionist scurried back through the door to make the call at her desk.

Exhausted, I dropped into Flo's chair and looked down at her. *What a shame.* She'd inherited a profitable business and turned it to shit. With any luck, someone else would buy KCSH, polish the turd, and turn the station back into the aboveboard, valuable enterprise it had once been.

After checking to make sure Flo was still breathing and had a pulse—*check and check*—I glanced over at the console. As long as I was here, I might as well jump on the microphone and give the world that public service announcement it needed.

I pulled the device toward me and spoke into it. "Hello, everyone out there in radioland. Yo-yo-yo! Special Agent Tara Holloway is in the house!" I jabbed the "applause" button. *Clap-clap-clap!*

I continued my broadcast, though I ditched the hip-hop DJ voice. "You might be wondering why the Internal

Revenue Service is here at KCSH. Well, I'll explain it to you. Flo Cash has been engaging in something called barter. Barter is where two parties exchange goods or services rather than paying cash for them." I hit the cash register sound-effect button. *Cha-ching!*

"There's nothing illegal about barter," I said, "but the thing to remember is that all business transactions are subject to reporting and tax. And when a person receives an in-kind payment in exchange for work, that payment is taxable compensation. So be sure you report and pay tax on any exchanges you make, okay?"

Hey, this radio thing is kind of fun!

"While I'm here, let me give you a little what-what about online scams, help you protect yourself. Just yesterday I arrested a catfishing Casanova who'd found women and men on dating sites, gained their trust, and asked them to cash checks for him. He gave some sob story about a stepson who'd drained his bank account. Don't fall for these scams, folks! If someone tells you that a bank can tell immediately whether a check is legit or bogus, they are lying to you. It takes several days for your bank to run a check through the network and discover that the account either is empty or doesn't exist. Protect yourselves, people!"

The three-line phone lit up, all lines flashing with incoming calls. I pushed the first button. "Hello, caller. You're on the air."

"Hi," came a man's voice. "I was wondering whether my teenage daughter needs to report her babysitting earnings on a tax return."

I hit the sound-effect button labeled: *Coo.* I got lucky. It was the coo of a baby, not a dove. *Goo-goo-ga-ga.*

"Good question, sir," I replied. "If and how your daughter reports depends on whether her babysitting activities are regular enough to constitute a trade or business and how much she earns."

"She only watches kids on occasion," he said. "She bring in about two or three hundred dollars a year."

"Does she have any other income?"

"Just allowance."

"Then no need to report. She's below the filing threshold." I thanked him for his call and pushed the second button. "Hello, caller. What's your question?"

It was a woman this time. "I'm a stay-at-home mom," she said. "Somebody said I could open an IRA to save for retirement, but I thought you could only have an IRA if you earned money at a job."

"Whoever that somebody was is right. A nonworking spouse can qualify to contribute to an IRA. For more details, check out the IRS Web site."

I pushed the third button. "Hello, caller. What's your question?"

Lu's voice came over the airwaves. "My question is *what the hell is going on over there?*"

"Hello, Lu!" I called. "Listeners, this caller is my boss, Lu. She's one hell of a woman and a cancer survivor." I hit the "applause" button. *Clap-clap-clap!* "As for what's going on over here, I bested Flo Cash and now I'm dropping some knowledge on the good folks of Dallas."

"Once the medics arrive," Lu said, "get back to the office."

"Will do. Thanks for your call."

I answered a couple more questions, one about treasury bonds and another about tax-preferred ways to fund college education expenses, before the EMTs showed up. Two loaded a groaning Flo onto a stretcher and wheeled her out the door while another dabbed ointment on my blistered face.

"That ought to do ya'," he said, screwing the cap back on the tube.

Once the medics were gone, I picked up the microphone

and stood. "This has been fun, y'all! Remember to file on time and file accurately. Special Agent Tara Holloway out!"

I lifted the mic over my head and dropped it, cool-style. Unfortunately, I wasn't as cool as I'd thought. The mic hit the steel toe of my Doc Martens and gave the listeners an earsplitting *KUNK* before softly thudding to the floor. *Oops*.

chapter thirty-one

$\mathcal{T}$he Big Day

Alicia's big day had finally arrived. I woke Sunday morning to the sound of her thundering footsteps as she ran from my guest room across the hall and jumped onto my bed, scattering my cats and nearly bouncing me off in her excitement.

She jumped up and down like a kid in a bounce house. "I'm getting married today!"

"Not if you bash your head on my ceiling and break your neck!" Before she could suffer such a fate I grabbed her arm and yanked her down onto the bed. The number-one duty of a maid of honor was to make sure the bride arrived at the wedding alive.

She flopped onto her back next to me. "Can you believe it? Sometimes I thought this day would never come."

Daniel hadn't exactly been in a rush to seal the deal, but once he'd come around and proposed he hadn't once looked back. He'd be a good husband and, with any luck, would get a chance to be a good father one day, too.

"I'm so happy for you, Alicia."

"I'm happy for me, too." She sat up and looked at me.

"Thanks for letting me stay here these past few months. It's been fun."

"It has. I've gotten used to having you around, too. It's going to be awfully quiet without you here."

Anne jumped back onto the bed and strode across the patchwork quilt, settling beside me.

Alicia reached over and scratched her under the chin. "You could always get another cat to replace me."

"There's a thought." I glanced at the clock. "I suppose we should get moving. It's going to be a busy day."

We ate a light breakfast and showered before packing our shoes, jewelry, makeup, and hair products in my car. When Alicia's mother arrived, we carefully carried Alicia's dress out to the driveway and hung it draped across the backseat.

"Be good, you two." I gave Henry and Anne good-bye kisses on the top of their heads and headed out to the wedding chapel.

The afternoon was a whirlwind of activity as we prepared for the event. The ceremony would begin at four, with dinner and dancing to follow in the ballroom. We bridesmaids flitted about the dressing room, fixing our hair and applying our makeup. I had to dab on extra concealer to cover the pink, tea bag–shaped burn mark on my forehead but managed to cover it well enough. Hair and faces ready, we slipped into our shoes and dresses. I paired mine with a beautiful pair of ruby drop earrings that Nick had given me months before.

"The flowers are here!" Alicia's mother called.

The florist entered the room carrying a gorgeous bouquet of red and white roses for Alicia, lilies for us bridesmaids.

Once the flowers had been distributed, the photographer, who'd captured some candid shots inside, ordered us outside for formal group shots. "This way, ladies!"

She posed us on the stone steps, issuing a variety of orders: "Chins up! Tummies in! Smile!"

Between shots, we fanned ourselves with the wedding service bulletins, trying not to sweat in the June Texas heat.

Nick came up the steps on his way into the chapel. Hell if he didn't look even more handsome today in the black tux and red vest than he had when he'd tried them on. "Hey, gorgeous," he said.

I sent him a wink. "Right back at ya."

He gave me a peck on the cheek. "Your parents here yet?"

"They're on their way," I told him. They'd texted me a couple minutes earlier to let me know they'd be arriving shortly.

"I'll wait for them here so we can sit together."

We bridesmaids greeted guests as they arrived and took seats inside the chapel. My parents, who'd driven in from my hometown of Nacogdoches in East Texas, arrived just a few minutes after Nick. I gave them both a hug.

My mother put a hand on each of my shoulders and stepped back to look at me. "Aren't you a beautiful sight?"

"Thanks, Mom. You look great, too."

She turned side to side, her lips spread in a smile. "I do, don't I?"

Dad stuck out his hand to shake Nick's. "Good to see you, Nick. We've got some baseball and basketball scores to discuss."

Nick jerked his head toward the door. "Let's get in there and get down to it."

With that, my parents and Nick headed into the chapel.

At five minutes before four, we bridesmaids returned to the bridal suite to prepare for our procession.

Alicia appeared radiant in her dress, beaming with happiness. No nervous bride here. Her mother, on the other hand, couldn't stop weeping, both of her hands clutching fistfuls of tissue as dark mascara ran down her cheeks.

"Here, Mom." Alicia thrust a cardboard box of tissue at her mother. "You better take the whole box with you."

Her mother tossed her old tissues in a wastebasket, grabbed the box from Alicia, and dabbed her eyes with a fresh tissue. "I keep thinking back to when you were a little girl and you'd play wedding. You wore a white pillowcase for a veil, remember? You forced that boy next door to marry you at least a dozen times."

"You should look him up," I teased. "He probably owes you alimony."

Alicia pulled my pearl bracelet out of the box and held it up. "Help me with this, Tara?"

"Of course." I stepped over, laid my bouquet on the dressing table, and fastened the clasp around her wrist. Noting the garter lying on the tabletop, I picked it up. "Don't forget this."

"Oh, my gosh! I almost forgot my something blue!" Alicia slid her foot out of her shoe, slipped the garter over her foot, and slid it up to a spot a few inches above her knee.

A moment later, we made our way out into the now-empty foyer and met up with the groomsmen. We formed a line along the wall where we'd be out of sight of the guests until each of us stepped into the doorway to enter the chapel.

The flower girl and ring bearer, Daniel's niece and nephew, fidgeted with impatience and excitement. The ring bearer decided a pillow fight might be a fun way to pass the time while we waited, and hit his sister on the shoulder with his miniature pillow.

"Hey! No hitting!" Having no pillow of her own put the flower girl at a distinct disadvantage, forcing her to make do with the only weapon she had, her basket of red rose petals. She swung it at her brother, sending up a shower of red petals, covering the ring bearer and the floor. This looked like a job for the maid of honor, huh?

"Settle down, you two!" I called softly, giving them a smile to let them know they weren't in trouble. It was hard to expect too much from a four- and five-year-old, after all. "Let's get those petals back in the basket."

We scooped the petals up from the floor, though the boy tossed them into the air several times before getting them into the basket, giggling all the while. *Little goofball.*

When the time came, the groomsmen took their spots at the front of the chapel. Flanked by his parents, Daniel made his way to the front as well. Beautiful harp music beckoned, and the bridesmaids floated down the aisle accompanied by the soft, sweet sound of the strings. Finally, it was time for the maid of honor to make her entrance.

My heart pitter-pattered in my chest when I stepped into the chapel. So many faces turned my way, so many eyes on me. I began the walk down the aisle, smiling at those I passed. As I approached my mother she grinned up at me, virtually glowing with pride. If she was this excited about me being a maid of honor, I could only imagine how thrilled she'd be when I finally got married. My father gave me a stoic nod, already looking bored and probably counting the minutes until the reception and dinner. Nick shot me a wink. I shot him one in return and proceeded to my place beside the chuppah, where Daniel waited for his bride. Daniel and I exchanged smiles. Though today was his and Alicia's day, as her closest friend I was so glad to be a part of it.

Everyone stood as Alicia came up the aisle, escorted by both her mother and father. She looked absolutely radiant, as if she'd stepped right off the cover of a bridal magazine. Her parents left her next to Daniel under the wedding tent, took their seats on the front row, and the ceremony began.

Admittedly, while the bride and groom went through

the rituals my mind and emotions ventured in a million different directions. They went first to my best friend, who was moving into a new phase of life. I was happy for her, yet couldn't help but engage in some melancholy reverie, thinking back to our crazy days in college, our first jobs together at Martin & McGee. My gaze moved to the chuppah, draped with a prayer shawl that had been in Daniel's family for generations, and my mind considered the cycle of life, the continuity of family and love. Last, my eyes and thoughts went to Nick, watching me intently from his seat. What was *he* thinking about? Probably the prime rib being readied in the reception hall. The smell had wafted over, mingling with the scent of the flowers.

I had little time to ponder the last question before Alicia and Daniel broke the glass and the guests sent up good wishes in unison. "Mazel tov!"

Grinning ear to ear, Alicia and Daniel returned down the aisle. The best man stepped over and offered me his arm. I took it and we followed in the bride's and groom's footsteps, heading out of the chapel and over to the reception hall.

While Alicia, Daniel, and their parents formed a receiving line, I waited for Nick and my parents at their table, waving them over when they entered. I gestured to three of the chairs. "These are your seats."

"Thanks, hon," Mom said, dropping into her chair. "These shoes may be pretty, but they are hurting my feet like all get-out."

"Wine?" Nick asked her, angling his head to indicate the bar.

"White, please."

He turned to me. "And a red with a cherry for you."

"You know it."

He pulled out a chair for my dad. "Have a seat, Harlan. I'll get you a beer."

Dad sat and tossed me a glance as Nick headed to the bar. "That one's a keeper."

"He is, isn't he?"

A moment later Nick returned with our drinks. By then the hall had filled and it was time for me to take my place at the main table nearby with the rest of the wedding party. Christina and Ajay joined Nick and my parents at their table, along with a couple of assorted cousins and Daniel's uncle Joe, who, as Alicia had promised, regaled those at his table with tales of his gallbladder surgery.

"Want to see my scar?" he asked.

Though all the others declined, Ajay said, "Sure."

Uncle Joe pulled out his waistband and Ajay took a peek down the man's pants. "That's some good work. Hardly left a mark."

Once the dinner was served, the toasts began. Each time a toast was made, I clinked glasses with those at my table, then raised my glass in Nick's direction. He did the same.

Finally, it was the maid of honor's turn to make a toast. I stood, holding my glass of champagne before me. "Alicia and I met back in our first accounting class at the University of Texas in Austin," I told the crowd. "We bonded over general ledgers, balance sheets, and profit and loss statements." I put a hand to my heart. "I was the debit to her credit."

A smattering of chuckles ensued, mostly from the accountants in the audience.

"The two of us moved to Dallas," I continued, "leased an apartment together, and took jobs at the same accounting firm. It was there that Alicia and Daniel met, when his law firm hired Martin and McGee for a consulting project. Being the smart CPA she is, Alicia realized that Daniel came with some impressive assets. Meanwhile, Daniel had his eye on Alicia's bottom line."

More laughter filled the room. Even the nonfinancial types got that joke.

"Now," I said, smiling down at the couple, "they've officially entered into a joint venture." I raised my glass over my head. "To Alicia and Daniel. May your love always earn a one hundred percent return on investment."

There was a clinking of many glasses and cries of, "Hear! Hear!"

I touched glasses with those at my table, sat, and tossed back a slug of champagne. Alicia's parents had sprung for the good stuff. I wouldn't mind if these toasts went on all night.

When the meal was finished, the DJ cued the music. While the rest of us gathered around the dance floor, Alicia and Daniel had their first dance as husband and wife, swaying to a sappy but appropriate Michael Bublé song. Once they'd finished, the DJ announced a father-daughter dance. Alicia's father stepped onto the dance floor and began leading her in a classic waltz. When they twirled past me and my dad, Alicia called, "Come on, Tara! Grab your dad and join us!"

I took my father's hand and led him onto the dance floor.

"I'm a bit rusty," he said with a chuckle, "but I'll try not to step on your toes."

A few other men and their daughters joined us, the flower girl standing atop her father's feet as they made their way around the space.

"Cute, huh?" I said as we stepped past them.

"Sure is," my father said. "You know who else would make a cute flower girl? Jesse."

"She would, wouldn't she?" Jesse was my favorite niece, a girl after my own heart what with her pink cowgirl boots and sure-shot aim. Of course she had only a BB gun rather than a Glock and fired only at empty root beer cans. But it wouldn't surprise me a bit if she followed in my footsteps and pursued a career in law enforcement.

The song ended, a classic disco number cued up, and the dance floor was opened to all wedding guests. Nick ditched his tuxedo jacket, grabbed my mother's hand, and pulled her onto the floor next to me and my father, holding her hand above her head and spinning her in a circle.

"Oh, Lord!" she cried, laughing all the while. "I'm getting dizzy!"

"She's all yours now!" Nick turned my topsy-turvy mother over to my dad for handling and stepped into place in front of me. When a slow song came on, Nick pulled me up against him. "This just feels right, doesn't it?" he whispered in my ear.

I looked up at him. "Yeah. It does."

He gave me a soft, warm kiss.

After several songs, the cake was cut and served. Although Alicia made a show of shoving Daniel's piece into his mouth, the stern look she gave him when he held her bite to her mouth told him he'd better think twice about messing up her makeup.

Alicia's cousin Melody was back in party-pooper mode. She took one bite of her cake and gasped. "It's so dry! Ugh!" She slid her plate onto a discard tray and headed to the bar for more champagne.

Christina took a big bite of the cake and moaned in bliss. "Alicia's bitchy cousin has no idea what she's talking about. This cake is delicious!"

It was. And plenty moist, too. There's just no pleasing some people.

After cake there was more dancing; then it was time for the bride to throw the bouquet.

"Go get 'em, tiger!" Nick gave me a grin and a pat on the ass to send me on my way.

Christina was already engaged to Ajay, so she stayed

back with him and Nick. I found myself standing on the dance floor in the center of a group of women, many of whom were a few years younger than me but at least three of whom were significantly older, perhaps single for the second time in their lives.

Alicia stepped into place, taking a quick glance over her shoulder to spot me and offer me a grin before turning back to face away from us.

"One!" the gathered groomsmen called out. "Two! Three!"

On "Three!" Alicia sent the bouquet sailing into the air. I rushed forward, nearly tripping on my heels. The bouquet spun in the air, blooms over stems, as it soared toward the ceiling. It seemed to hover in the air over the throng of women for a moment before descending toward us. I took three elbows to the ribs—*Umph! Oomph! Ow!*—before the bouquet dropped perfectly into my hands. It was as if it knew it belonged there.

"I got it!" I cried. When I looked around me, my gaze met several angry faces. Some relieved ones, too, of young women who weren't ready to take the plunge yet. Hey, I'd been there once. Not too long ago, either. Finding the right person really changes your perspective.

Nick stepped over to me. "Nice job, there."

"Those single women are vicious!" I rubbed my side. "My ribs are bruised."

"Don't worry." He leaned in and whispered, "I'll kiss them later and make them feel better."

I hid my smile behind the bouquet as I pretended to sniff it. "I'm going to hold you to that."

Daniel placed a chair on the dance floor and Alicia took a seat in it. She kicked off her shoe, pulled the hem of her dress up, and lifted her leg to expose the satin garter. Catcalls erupted from around the room. One of them came from me. *You can dress me up, but you can't take me anywhere.*

Daniel slid the garter off his bride's leg and stood, waving it in the air. "C'mon up, guys!"

The other single men filed toward the dance floor, but Nick made no move to join them. I gave him a hip check. "You better get on up there."

"Ugh. Do I have to?"

I cut him a look.

"All right, then," he muttered, casting me a grin to let me know he was teasing.

By that time, a thick crowd had formed and Nick was stuck at the back of it. Though he was tall, his chances of catching the garter were slim. It would have to make it past two dozen grabbing hands for him to even have a chance. *Oh, well.*

We bridesmaids gathered around Daniel and Alicia to do the countdown.

"One!" we called out. "Two! Three!"

As Daniel threw the garter, the sea of single men in front of Nick lowered their arms and dropped to their knees, leaving only him standing tall.

What the . . . ?

Nick snatched the garter out of air and held it up in one hand, throwing the other fist up in victory. "Woo hoo!"

The other single men stood back up and exchanged high fives with Nick. When they'd finished, his eyes sought mine. I raised a palm in question but got only a mischievous grin in reply.

I marched over to him. "What was that?"

"I have no idea what you're talking about." Nick raised his shoulders in an exaggerated shrug. "I just got lucky."

One of the groomsmen walked past and whispered, "Lucky, my ass. He paid us each twenty bucks and promised to prepare all of our tax returns next year."

chapter thirty-two

$\mathcal{W}$ith This Ring

Nick proudly wore the garter around his upper arm the rest of the night. We danced some more, drank some more, celebrated some more. Finally, it was time to send the bride and groom off.

The wedding guests formed two lines on either side of the flagstone path outside. A limo waited at the end of the path to whisk the two off to the wedding suite at the Magnolia Hotel downtown. We tossed red rose petals at Alicia and Daniel as they made their way down the row, smiling and laughing and bidding good-bye to their guests.

Before climbing into the limo, Alicia stopped to give me a tight, warm hug. "Thanks for everything, Tara."

I hugged her back. "Have fun tonight, Mrs. Blowitz."

"We will," she whispered. "I packed the handcuffs."

They slipped into the back of the car and the chauffeur closed the door. We waved good-bye as the car pulled away.

My mother and father stepped up next to me and Nick.

"That sure was fun," my mother said. She gave me a peck on the cheek. My father did the same.

"Are y'all sure you don't want to stay the night at my place?" I asked.

My mother waved a hand. "After all this excitement, you need to get some sleep. We'll be fine in a hotel."

"All right then."

My mother turned and gave Nick a hug.

My father shook his hand. "Always good to see you, son."

"You, too," Nick said.

I returned to the dressing room and gathered up my things, adding them to my bridesmaid's bouquet and the bridal bouquet I'd caught earlier.

Nick helped me carry the stuff to my car. Once everything was safely packed in my trunk, he reached out and toyed with a lock of my hair, running a thumb along my cheek. "Stay at my place tonight," he suggested softly.

Knowing the wedding would run late tonight, we'd both taken the day off from work tomorrow so that we could sleep in.

I leaned into his warm, strong hand, savoring the sensation. "Okay."

"Stop by your place first and pick up some of those leftover biscuits. Gravy, too."

"Forget it." I pushed his hand away and treated him to a scowl.

"Aw, come on," he pleaded. "I've got your favorite coffee creamer in my fridge."

I raised my brows in question. "You'll get up and start the pot?"

"For your mother's biscuits and gravy? Hell, yeah, I will."

"All right then." Did this guy know how to play me or what? Of course, I knew how to play him, too.

I drove back to my place, stepping inside to grab the biscuits and gravy and check on my cats. They were both asleep. Annie opened her eyes to peek at me, yawned, and promptly returned to her slumber. Henry didn't move a muscle.

"Where do you want all of this?" Nick asked as he came in the door, his arms loaded with the things from my trunk.

I pointed upstairs. "My bedroom."

When he returned, we climbed into his truck and drove down the street to his place. As we stepped inside his town house, Daffodil danced around in the hallway, happy to have her daddy home. Rather than turn on the light in the living room, Nick lit a candle that sat on the coffee table. Looked like this romantic night wasn't over yet.

Still wearing the garter around his arm, Nick took the dog out back for a few minutes while I flopped down on the couch. I supposed I'd have to get out of this pretty red dress at some point, but I wasn't quite ready yet. The suits and blazers I wore for work made me feel strong and capable, but this dress made me feel flirty and feminine. After making two busts this week, both of them involving violence, it felt good to indulge this softer side of myself.

The back door opened and Daffodil darted in, the garter now around her neck. She bounded over to me, her fluffy tail whipping back and forth, creating a stir of air that set the candle's flame flickering.

I ruffled the fur around her neck. "You silly girl. That garter is supposed to go on your leg."

Nick leaned against the door frame that led from the kitchen to the living room, a smile playing about his lips. The top two buttons of his tuxedo shirt were undone, the sleeves pushed up, the bow tie hanging loose. He looked sexy and classy at the same time. His eyes went from me, to Daffodil, and back to yours truly.

"What?" I looked down at the dog. At first all I saw was fur and fangs and a pink tongue intent on licking me to death. But then I noticed something else. Tied to a thin ribbon on the garter around her neck was a ruby ring in a platinum setting.

Oh, my God.

Though I'd known Nick and I were likely headed in this direction, I hadn't known that he'd planned to propose tonight, that he'd already chosen a ring for me. *And what a beautiful, perfect ring it was. . . .*

"Nick," I said on a breath.

"Your father gave me his blessing when we were out on my boat. Of course I threatened to throw him overboard in the middle of Lake Ray Hubbard if he refused."

"But you've got money in the office pool!" I squeaked, choked with emotion. "You bet you'd propose in September."

"What's another twenty bucks?" He chuckled. "Besides, I don't want to wait anymore." His face grew more serious. "I *can't* wait anymore."

My heart soared as he stepped toward me, untying the ring from the ribbon and dropping to a knee next to Daffodil. He took my left hand in his, holding up the ring. The ruby glimmered in the candlelight. Nick's amber eyes looked into mine as he put the ring to my fingertip. "I think you and I should get hitched. What do you say, Tara?"

Tears of joy sprang to my eyes. *What do I say?* I said, "Yes!"

A fresh grin graced his lips. "That's just what I'd hoped to hear." He slid the ring onto my finger, sealing the deal, and pressed his mouth to mine.